"Oh, my God," Theresa moaned as she wrapped her arms around Zeke and nuzzled the crook of his neck. "You're a *dragon slayer.*"

"Ex-slayer." He staggered as she ran her fingers through his hair and showered frantic kisses on his throat.

"This explains a lot," she mumbled as she tried to unbutton his shirt. She got his shirt open and pressed her face to his chest, inhaling deeply. "You smell so amazing. You're going to kill me, aren't you? Ooh . . ."

"No." He made it to the couch and set her down. Her eyes were closed, her body arching toward him. Old instincts swirled to the surface, and he had to look away from her exposed throat. "I'm an ex-slayer. Ex."

"You can't be an *ex*-slayer." She tried to hit him, but she missed and nearly fell off the couch in a sluggish mound of female curves.

"Come on, T." He pulled her back up. "Help me out here."

"Help you? Help you kill me?"

"No." He stepped back, clutching his fists against the instincts pushing at him to do what he was born to do. "Help me resist."

———

"Rowe is a paranormal star!"

—J. R. Ward on *Date Me, Baby, One More Time*

Turn the page for more raves! And don't forget to turn to the back of this book for a preview of Stephanie Rowe's next novel, *He Loves Me, He Loves Me Hot*.

Also by Stephanie Rowe

Must Love Dragons
Date Me, Baby, One More Time
He Loves Me, He Loves Me Hot
Sex & the Immortal Bad Boy

MUST LOVE DRAGONS

STEPHANIE ROWE

FOREVER

NEW YORK   BOSTON

Forever is an imprint of Grand Central Publishing. The Forever name and logo is a trademark of Hachette Book Group USA, Inc.

Cover design by Diane Luger
Book design by Stratford Publishing Services, Inc.

Forever
Hachette Book Group USA
237 Park Avenue
New York, NY 10017
Visit our Web site at www.HachetteBookGroupUSA.com

Printed in the United States of America

First Printing: November 2006

11 10 9 8 7 6 5 4 3 2

For Debby Zimmerman, Judi Luallin, and the Bignell family, my dear friends who came to my rescue when I needed it most.

Acknowledgments

As always, I would be nothing without the fantastic guidance of my brilliant and tireless editor, Melanie Murray, who brings my writing to new levels with each book I write. And to my agent, Michelle Grajkowski, for everything, but especially her support, her laughter, her faith in me, her advice, and her friendship. My deepest thanks also to all the great folks at Warner who worked so hard on this book: Diane Luger, Claire Brown, Tanisha Christie, and Marcy Haggag. And thank you also to my mom, for keeping my life in balance during revisions. And to Josh and Ariana, who are my world.

One

Theresa Nichols was going to starve to death and no one cared.

She didn't know which was ticking her off more, the fact that she hadn't had her no-carb pretzel fix in a week, or the fact that Quincy LaValle had apparently forgotten her yet again, like everyone else in her life.

Her stomach growled and a sharp pain ground through her gut.

Who needs to eat?

Certainly not an eleven-foot winged dragon under house arrest, hidden away because people in New York City would freak out at the sight of a real dragon. No need to be spotted by someone who could start the next world war with shrieks of invasions, Martians, and other such panic-inducing nonsense.

Because of the close-mindedness of humans, she'd been stuck behind closed doors for two hundred years, and quite frankly, it was getting old. Especially when she was withering away, alone and forgotten and starving to death.

Since she'd been put under Quincy's neglectful care, she'd lost 161 pounds. Completely unacceptable! She was a dragon, dammit, and dragons had needs! Food, violence, destruction, incineration. None of which she was allowed to indulge in Quincy's house. Heaven forbid she burn anything up or turn his neighbors into crispy critters.

Being deprived of food was making it that much harder to resist all her other dragon desires. She groaned and leaned her head against the fridge, willing away her insatiable craving to blow up his kitchen. *Keep it together, Theresa. You can handle this.*

She let out a deep breath that was a little too smoky for comfort, then marched over to the phone and punched the speed dial. Again. And again, his answering machine came on. "Quincy! It's Theresa. I haven't eaten in two days and I'm starving. I know you don't care about me or the Goblet, but your brother's now the Assistant Guardian, in case you forgot. He'll kick your butt if he comes home from his honeymoon to find that Mona has been stolen because you let the Interim Guardian die of starvation while you were obsessing about some stupid math equation that no one but you cares about. And the Council will skewer you if you screw up Guardianship. Literally." She paused to take a breath, forcing herself not to shudder at the thought of the Council, the ruthless governing body in charge of the Guardians and the Goblet. Guardians who screwed up were seriously toast, even Interim Guardians. "And if you don't get home with food in thirty minutes, I'm burning down your house and moving in with Becca." She slammed down the phone and glared at the Goblet of Eternal Youth, which was currently masquerading as an espresso machine. "Mona! This is all your fault."

The espresso machine said nothing.

Of course it wouldn't. In two hundred years, Mona had

never so much as hinted at being sorry for turning Theresa permanently into dragon form. Yeah, yeah, so Theresa was the one who'd actually drunk from the Goblet of Eternal Youth, but wasn't it the Goblet's duty to warn her that a sip while in dragon form would keep her that way forever?

Apparently not.

Theresa yanked open the freezer and stared at the contents. Empty. She supposed she could eat some more ice cubes. She'd at least be hydrated when she died of starvation. Bonus.

Or maybe she could eat some chairs. Nothing wrong with fiber, right?

Now that Justine, her best friend, roomie, and personal servant for the last two hundred years, was off on her honeymoon, it was all too apparent what kind of a life Theresa had: none.

No job.

No social life.

No friends.

And most important, no way to get food.

She slammed the door shut as her stomach rumbled again and a burning sensation clawed at her belly. She'd bet a box of Vic's Pretzels that her body was beginning to eat itself. Wouldn't that be a fun way to die?

No! A dragon should die a violent and fiery death! Dying of starvation was completely unacceptable.

Dammit! She slammed her tail against the fridge, too hungry to bother checking to see if she'd left a dent. She wasn't even allowed to order delivery because she was guarding Mona, and it was a big no-no to have strangers parading up to the door when the Goblet of Eternal Youth was hiding out. You never knew if the skinny little delivery boy might be packing a sword in his stay-hot pizza bag. Plus, how was she supposed to explain her appearance when she answered the door? *No, you're not really seeing an emaciated eleven-foot dragon with gold eyes. It's the scent from the pizza causing your hallucinations.*

Yeah, right.

She stalked over to the window of Quincy's house and stared at the darkened suburb. If she were in her own condo, she could probably get Xavier the doorman to get her some food, but no, their condo was still a shambles after Justine and Derek had gotten a little trigger happy with Becca's machine guns.

Becca.

For a moment, she considered calling Becca, Satan's favorite Rivka and right-hand badass, but finally dismissed it. The Rivka had more important things to do than bring carryout to a dragon, and Theresa had too much pride to beg.

She closed her eyes and dug her claws into the windowsill. *You are not hungry. You are not lonely. You are a goddess.* The shattering of the wood jerked her back to the present, and she jerked her claws away from the window. Even the house wasn't built for helping a dragon through the throes of misery.

There was only one thing that would help her now. One man. If Zeke wasn't online, heaven help her and the neighborhood she was hiding out in.

She grabbed her computer and IM'd Zeke, the only man she'd had cybersex with in the last six months. Six months of monogamy for Theresa Nichols, former Queen of the Sluts. Astounding, wasn't it? Just proved how good a cyberlover Zeke was. For him to satisfy a dragon who was completely deprived of all other outlets was quite the feat. Thank God for Zeke.

"Zeke? You there?" she typed.

His reply was instant. "Yep. You?"

Tension eased from her body at his immediate response and she smiled, imagining what his voice must sound like. Deep. Manly. He probably had thick whiskers that would make a woman tremble with longing. Zeke was definitely a badass. She could sense the undercurrent of violence in him. She loved bad boys. What dragon wouldn't? Whoever she dated had to be able to deal with a girl who liked to burn things up and ate six pizzas for an afternoon snack. "I bought a new piece of lingerie off the Internet yesterday. Want me to describe it?"

Silence.

She frowned at his hesitation, and an anxiety spark shot out of her nose and sizzled on the keyboard. "Zeke? Don't leave me hanging. Not tonight."

He finally typed an answer. "Listen, I think we should meet."

She jerked upright in Quincy's microfiber recliner, slamming the footrest back to the floor with an ominous thud. "I can't meet you!" She scowled as a wave of longing washed over her, smashing her claws onto the keyboard as she typed her response. "I'm still in isolation at the FBI containment center, remember? They haven't figured out how to keep my contagious disease from infecting everyone who comes within ten feet of me." She felt a little guilty about the lie, but it wasn't as if she could tell him she was a dragon. Besides, being locked up in an FBI containment facility was sort of dramatic and cool, and way better than her real life.

"I think you're avoiding me."

She grinned at his perceptiveness, imagining his brows furrowed in aggravation as he typed. "Tell that to the dude with the machine gun guarding my door."

"Give me his number and I'll call him up."

Some of her amusement trickled away at his continued pressure. "He won't get close enough to talk to me. Afraid I'll infect him."

"Isn't that convenient?"

Her tail switched at his thinly veiled sarcasm and she accidentally dropped a puff of ash onto Quincy's hand-woven carpet from India. She'd been fending off Zeke's requests to meet for months, but something felt different tonight. Or maybe her perception of reality was being distorted by the fact that her stomach was beginning to eat her brain. "No, it's not convenient. I'd love to meet you in person and engage in some real flesh-to-flesh activities." Understatement of the year. Cybersex was better than nothing, but it was no substitute for having a man wrapped around her. She'd even had Justine buy her some of the aftershave Zeke said he wore, and she sprayed it around whenever they had cybersex. The woodsy, masculine scent was nearly enough to give her an orgasm on its own, let alone when Zeke was working his magic with the keyboard.

And when she couldn't sleep, she sprayed it on her pillow and pretended he was there, hugging her pillow to her chest. Not that she'd admit that to anyone. Dragons didn't need nighttime comfort, and she was no exception. She was just sexually deprived and she loved to bask in the scent of the man of her fantasies. And if she liked it when he talked about his favorite movies and places he'd like to take her on their first date, it was only because she was so desperately lonely for any kind of a real life, even if it was vicariously through Zeke. Not because she *liked* him or anything. Because that would be incredibly stupid, given her permanently scaly state.

"Seriously, T, I don't care about your infectious disease. I can buy a biohazard suit anywhere. We need to meet."

Theresa's heart started to pound and her hind claws curled into the floor. Zeke was her one contact with the outside world. He was the one person who would notice if she died. Their wild and daring cybersex and late-night gossip sessions were the only outlet that kept her sane, since violence, gorging on food, and incineration weren't options. She took a deep breath and tried to focus. She had to reel him in before he ruined everything, before he demanded what she couldn't give. "What's the point in meeting if you're wearing a biohazard suit? We wouldn't be able to have sex."

His reply was quick, as if he'd anticipated her answer. "I want to know what you look like."

She scowled. She was an eleven-foot winged dragon with bluish-green scales and golden eyes. Would that do it for him? Doubted it. "Sorry. No pictures, remember?" It had been so long since she'd been in human form, she wasn't sure she'd even recognize herself.

Silence.

At his hesitation, Theresa shoved the computer off her lap and jumped to her feet, pacing past the beautiful ash color coffee table that Quincy had specifically forbidden her to burn up. Heat roiled through her, struggled to escape.

A spark slipped out of her nose and landed on the hardwood floor. Crap! She stomped it out, then spun back to face her computer when she heard it beep. She was afraid to read Zeke's reply.

After a moment she lifted her chin, straightened her tail, and marched back over to read what he'd written.

"I think maybe it's time to change the rules."

She growled at the screen. There could be no rule-changing! Face-to-face meetings were not happening!

"T? You still there? I'm serious. Things need to change. I can't keep this up."

How dare he ruin the only decent thing in her life by demanding something she couldn't give, no matter how much she might want to? She wouldn't let him. Not tonight. "The scientists are here to run more tests on me. Gotta run." She hesitated, then added her usual sign-off. "Love your body."

Then she disconnected before he could reply.

She slammed the lid closed on her laptop and stomped across the room, ignoring the pictures rattling on the walls. Well, wouldn't that be fine and dandy? Not only was she starving to death, but she would die alone and sexually frustrated because Zeke was about to bail on her.

Forget it. Things had gone too far. A girl had her limits.

She smashed her hip into the kitchen door and shoved it open, ignoring the trickle of sparks that dropped on the tile. Quincy would just have to get over a few burn marks. He'd be lucky if she didn't burn down his house by accident. She narrowed her eyes at the espresso machine. "I have to eat, which means it's time for a highly illegal field trip. And you're coming with me, since I can't leave you behind unprotected." She picked up the espresso machine and tried to tuck it under her arm. Not comfortable, especially for a dragon who wasn't exactly in top flying shape. "I don't suppose you could turn into something smaller and easier to carry?"

The espresso machine didn't so much as flicker.

"What if I take you on a flying tour of the New York City skyline so you can see this city that you've been living in for the last five years?"

Mona immediately changed into an ankle bracelet.

Theresa grinned, all too familiar with the desperation Mona would be feeling at being locked in her inanimate cell for so long. "That's my girl. Maybe we can be friends after all." At least there was something in this world that was more desperate than she was.

Forty-five minutes later, Theresa was perched on the roof of the Vic's Pretzels that was down the street from the condo she used to live in. She was wearing her favorite come-hither outfit: a leather miniskirt, a black lace bra under a transparent white top, the topaz earrings she'd bought during their brief stay in the Amazon (so what if dragons don't have ears? The scales located on the side of her head worked just fine), a new diamond stud in the piercing at the end of her tail, and, of course, her new ankle bracelet.

She might not have any breasts or even a waist to do the outfit justice, and her blue scales weren't exactly sexy, but one should never underestimate the effect that sexy clothes can have on a woman's mood. Or a dragon's.

She took a deep breath and inhaled the amazing scent of fresh dough rising, letting it soak into her lungs. Vic's

No-Carb Pretzels were her reason for living, definitely worth taking a forbidden trip out into the night air.

The sounds of the humans working the ovens drifted up to her, and she took a moment to sort out their scents. There were at least three of them, two male and one female. Probably one person manning the kitchens and two customers getting their late-night pretzel fix. Unfortunately, incinerating all of them was out. Someone would notice three piles of human ash.

She growled, realizing that food would have to suffice to appease her needs. If she could get the people outside for a few minutes . . .

She eyed the roof and found what she was looking for. Didn't anyone have the foresight to protect their vents from dragons anymore? She glided over to the vent (yes, she might weigh several tons, but that didn't mean she had to stop practicing the double-jointed-hips walk that had brought men to their knees two hundred years ago) and pressed her face up to it. "Hope you all are wearing your gas masks."

Wasn't this going to be fun? She hadn't tortured humans in forever.

She grinned, rolled some smoke around in her chest for a moment, then expelled a huge black cloud into the vent.

Then, for kicks, she did it again.

The sound of coughing and the scent of human alarm drifted up to her, and Theresa flopped down on her belly and let the sensations wash over her. It wasn't actual destruction, but it soaked into her pores and eased the desperation off her needs.

It took less than three minutes for the humans to vacate the premises. Once they were hacking away out front, she sat up, shook off the soothing effects of the assault, and coasted down to the back door. She tugged on it, found it locked, then grinned with delight and yanked it free, along with the doorframe. She tossed the still-locked unit into the alley and scooted inside the kitchen of Vic's Pretzels.

Three feet inside the door, she was hit by the intense aroma of baking dough and melted butter and fell flat on her face. *Holy mother of pearl.* She groaned and rolled onto her back, drinking in the heavenly odors. Cinnamon. Fresh bread. Melted frosting for the dessert pretzels. Her claws curved against her chest and she closed her eyes, inhaling deeply as euphoria slackened her muscles, slowed her heart rate. She would never move again. Just lie here forever.

A distant clang caught her attention, and she shook her head, trying to clear it. This wasn't a safe environment. She shouldn't be sprawled on the floor. She tried to uncurl her claws, but she was too relaxed, too overcome by lassitude.

Come on, Theresa. Block your olfactory receptors. Now she remembered. That's what she was supposed to do. Basic dragon survival technique. God, but how? She couldn't recall, and it felt so good. The freshly cooked bread smelled so divine. She didn't want to block it out. She just wanted to lie here and suck it in.

No. She had to get up. *Get up.*

She held her breath, then rolled over, landing with a thud on her belly. Progress. Good.

Somehow, she managed to stagger to her feet. *Starting to suffocate. Need to inhale.* She closed her eyes and concentrated on shutting down her scent receptors, taking a careful breath through her mouth. She got a whiff of hot pretzel and almost went down again.

She slapped her claws to her face, pinching her nostrils shut. Two hundred years of being locked away with no threats to worry about had obviously eroded all her dragon defenses, not that she'd ever been a model dragon, even as a kid when she'd still been living among dragons. She'd gotten sloppy, and if there'd been real danger, she'd be dead now.

Her head began to clear, and she surveyed her surroundings. She was in the kitchen. Tile floors, racks and racks of pretzel ingredients, huge metal ovens, trays of cooling pretzels, pretzel-shaped pot holders hanging on neat little hooks shaped like more pretzels.

Her stomach rumbled, and her mouth began to water.

Having food in her belly would help her control her nose, wouldn't it?

She lurched toward the racks of cooling pretzels, took a deep inhalation through her mouth, then released her nose to grab a tray of pretzels. She dumped a rack of no-carb delights down her throat. Then another. Then another. No time to savor. She needed to eat and run before she collapsed again.

She started to feel dizzy, so she grabbed a couple of pot holders and wedged them in her nostrils. Better. She turned back to the pretzels and tossed six more down her throat, the intense ache in her belly barely beginning to ease.

It occurred to her that this was what the Dragon Cleansing of 1788 must have been like, when the dragon slayers wiped out the dragon population. In a normal attack, a slayer would disorient a dragon with his incredibly powerful scent and then come charging in to gain the advantage before the dragon could recover. During the Dragon Cleansing, all the slayers had joined together and attacked at once. She shuddered at the thought of being hit with all that olfactory stimulation.

Any halfway decent dragon learned how to shut down her scent receptors before she was two years old. It was the first line of defense against the slayers.

Well, guess what? She wasn't a halfway decent dragon, apparently. She'd almost been knocked out by pretzel dough. Imagine what a single dragon slayer's scent would do to her. She was too pathetic.

"Holy Jesus! What the fuck is that?"

Theresa dropped the tray she was holding and spun around. A guy in a chef's hat stared at her from the doorway, his mouth hanging open and his eyes wide.

She immediately bowed low, kneeling before him. "You must be the pretzel chef. I adore your pretzels, and I am honored to meet you."

He made a strangled sound and began backing around the corner. Theresa snapped her head up and narrowed her eyes at him. "Hey! Where are you going?" She couldn't allow him to report a dragon sighting.

He yelped and dove out of sight.

She sighed and stood back up. She was going to have to kill him, wasn't she? Then she smiled and her tail flicked. How fun! An added bonus for the evening. She always slept well for at least a week after she got to incinerate someone.

Then her tail sagged. But who would make the pretzels if she killed him?

Crud. What was she supposed to do? Protect herself or the pretzels?

Dammit. Exposing herself meant exposing Mona. She *had* to kill him. She stomped toward the door he'd vanished through. How unfair that she finally got to kill someone and it was a pretzel chef. The remorse was going to gnaw at her for weeks.

She followed his trail, taking a moment to peek around the corner into the front of the store, noting the two customers had apparently decided to head home.

Lucky for them.

Satisfied they were alone, she stepped into what looked like a supply room and saw the chef hunched behind a stack of boxes to her right. She whacked the boxes aside with her tail, and he jerked to his feet. His face was stark white and terror was cascading off him.

"I'm really sorry I have to do this," she said. "But I promise to visit you in the Afterlife with pretzels, okay?" She closed her eyes so she didn't have to watch, then opened her mouth, but before she could expel even a trickle of ash, she heard a loud explosion and a searing pain ripped through her left shoulder. "Hey!" She snapped her eyes open just in time to see the bastard aim his gun at her face.

Theresa threw her arm across her face as he shot again, and the bullet ripped through her right front claw, sending pain spiraling up her shoulder.

"Get out of here, you freak!" he screamed. "I'll kill you before I'll let an ugly monster take me alive!" He shot again, and the bullet tore through her tail, nearly taking out her new tail ring.

"*Ugly monster?* Are you serious?" How dare he insult

her like that. She was wearing her sexiest outfit! Was even that not enough to overcome the scales and lack of breasts? She was already sensitive enough about her appearance without having some idiot scream insults at her.

"Your mother won't have to look at your disgusting face again after I get through with you!" the chef shouted.

Her mother? Now, that was going too far. She lunged for him, and he shot her in the neck as he dove over a box of yeast and crawled behind an ice machine. She jerked in pain as blood gushed down her neck, and rage roared through her. She kicked the ice machine out of the way, reared back, and exploded fire at him.

But all that came out was a hack and a small puff of white smoke.

He yelped and scooted across the floor as she frowned and tried again. Nothing but a harmless wisp. What the hell?

She flung a metal storage rack out of her way and slammed her tail into the chef's gut, pinning him against the wall as a faint memory trickled into her mind. Wasn't there something in the annals about how dragons should always protect their necks in battle?

Maybe she should have gone to class more often instead of running around her home village causing trouble with the other delinquent dragons. Had she realized she was going to be orphaned and thrust into nondragon society so soon with no dragon mentors to teach her, she would definitely have paid more attention to the lessons she was supposed to be learning.

The chef whimpered and tried to get his gun free of her tail, to no avail. She pressed harder, and her frustration eased. She could still kick his heinie with her superior dragon strength. She smiled and leaned her face up against his. "Insult my mama, will you? We are going to have some fun tonight . . ."

Something twitched around her ankle and an espresso machine dropped to the floor in front of her.

Oh, no! She'd forgotten about Mona! The ultimate failure in Guardianship would be to let something happen to the Goblet of Eternal Youth. Each moment she stayed endangered Mona and put her closer to being at the brutal mercy of the Council.

She might be a failure as a woman and as a dragon, but God help her, she would *not* fail at being a Guardian. She flung the chef aside, grabbed Mona, and spun around, bolting for the door. She lurched into wobbly flight as soon as her wings were clear.

It took her less than a minute to realize she was too injured to make it all the way home. Didn't that figure? She couldn't even rescue Mona competently.

Two

Theresa closed her eyes just before she crashed through the window of Becca Gibbs's tenth-floor apartment. She landed just in time to get a face full of fireball. "Hey! It's me!"

The fire retreated to reveal Becca standing in the living room doorway wearing a black leather outfit more fitting for a biker prostitute than the executive VP of Vic's Pretzels and Satan's favorite Rivka. "I knew it was you, Dragon."

Theresa sneezed at the flames still flickering in her nose. "Then why'd you fireball me? And my name's Theresa."

"I know your name, and you broke into my apartment in the middle of the night." Becca was tossing a fireball back and forth between her hands, no doubt contemplating whether to shoot it at her. "You know I hate visitors."

"Didn't you notice I was bleeding?" Theresa cradled Mona against her chest, her blood dripping on the pale blue carpet.

"I noticed."

"I come to you for aid, and you still flame me?" She took a quick scan of the room. Antiques, floral patterns, and lots of pastels. Not what she would have expected from Becca-the-badass-bitch-from-hell.

"I didn't want to encourage any invasions of my privacy. Besides, you're a dragon. It's not like a low-level fireball's going to hurt you. Much."

And to think Becca was the only person Theresa had in her life to go to in an emergency. Sort of summed up her life nicely. "Sometimes you're kind of hostile."

Becca shrugged. "I'm Satan's right hand. Do you really expect me to be a sweetheart?"

"Got me there." Theresa sighed. Justine would never let her starve or try to burn her up. Then again, Justine would never let her out of the apartment, either. Getting shot hadn't been fun, but being outside . . . it had almost been worth it. "Just so you know, the only reason I tolerate your attitude is that you do such a good job running Vic's. If you didn't, I'd fry you right back to hell."

"You have no chance against me, Dragon." The glimmer of a real smile curved Becca's mouth. "But if you're going to say such nice things about my work, I suppose I could let you come in." She extinguished the fireball in her fist. "You can put Mona in the kitchen. She'll blend in."

Theresa stepped around an Oriental rug that looked way too nice to bleed on, even if it did belong to Becca. "Thanks." She followed the Rivka into a surprisingly bright and cheerful kitchen. White laminate cabinets, yellow walls, a bouquet of flowers on a very cool old table. "Got any food?"

"Plenty. Help yourself." Becca leaned against the counter and folded her arms over her chest, the action making her leather-clad breasts even more prominent.

Theresa tried not to think of the breasts she'd had before she became a full-time dragon.

Becca moved to the freezer and pulled out a two-pound hunk of hamburger meat. "Want this?"

Theresa's stomach growled before she could answer, and Becca gave a brisk nod before tossing it in the microwave.

Then . . . awkward silence.

Um, hmm. Two centuries of total isolation except for one friend didn't do a lot for maintaining small-talk skills. Theresa covered the silence by searching through Becca's cabinets.

Becca cleared her throat. "So, did you get shot?"

"Yep." She found a mixing bowl and dumped an entire box of cereal into it. "I broke into the Vic's near my old condo and got some dinner. I'll pay you back for all the pretzels I ate."

Becca lifted a brow. "You got shot robbing a Vic's?"

"Yep. The chef was packing heat."

"Excellent. I'll have to get him a raise. I'll check the schedule and see who was on duty tonight at that store and—"

"Hey! Where's the sympathy? Where's the love? I got shot!" She scowled at the Rivka.

"You're immortal," Becca said dryly.

"Well, he also insulted me repeatedly. And my poor, dead mama."

Becca grinned. "You were robbing the place."

"I know, but he still hurt my feelings. Not that I care, of course. I'm a dragon and I don't need the accolades of others." She shook off the self-pity and held up a gallon of milk. "Is this skim?"

"Always."

"Good." She poured the whole container of milk into the bowl, then grabbed a ladle from above the stove and scooped up some cereal.

"You're bleeding into your food."

"Am I?" She looked down at her right hand, then wailed in dismay. "He blew up my human fingernail!"

Becca raised her brow. "You had a human fingernail? Since when?"

"This is so unfair! I spent two hundred years trying different spells and I finally got a fingernail back and he shot it off!" She threw the spoon down and stared at the tip of her claw where her French manicure used to be. "It was my only sign of humanity and now it's gone!" She shoved her chair back, flames spewing ungracefully out of her nose. "I'm going to go back there and cut off his most precious part and see how he likes it and—" She suddenly realized her claws were stuck to the table. She bared her teeth at Becca. "Let me go before I toast you."

Becca rolled her eyes at the threat, making Theresa want to fry her just to prove she could. "I can't let you murder one of my chefs. If it was the competition, no problem. Hell, if it was anyone else, I'd go along with you and cap his soul for Satan after you finished the job, but all the rules change when you mess with my day job."

"But he destroyed my fingernail!" Theresa yanked on the table to try to free her front claws and the wood cracked.

"Hey!" Becca leaped across the kitchen and slammed her hands down on the tabletop. "I had to harvest a law school professor's soul before Satan would give me that table! Don't break it!"

Black smoke curled out of Theresa's nose. "Then let me go!"

"You really want to murder a Vic's chef? What about the pretzels?"

She glared at Becca. "My humanity is more important than pretzels."

"Really?" Becca looked surprised.

"Of course, really! To those of us with a soul, humanity matters." She blinked hard, growling at the lump that suddenly appeared in her throat. "Of course, you're nothing but an extension of Satan, with no personality or life force of your own. You could never understand."

Becca's eyes darkened and her fingers curved into the wood, her knuckles turning white. "Is that so?"

Theresa jerked back as the Rivka's eyes turned red and began to glow. "Are you going to turn into something scary?" Theresa tugged at the table, trying to get her hands free. "Because if you are, I'm outta here."

"No, I'm not." Becca closed her eyes for a moment and took a breath. When she opened them again, her eyes were back to their regular green color.

The table released Theresa, and she yanked her hands back into her lap. She sagged with relief, and her tail thudded to the floor. "You are one scary chick sometimes, you know that? No wonder you don't have any friends."

Something flashed in Becca's eyes. "It's my choice to be alone."

"Well, then you're an idiot, because being alone sucks."

"That's a matter of opinion." Becca turned away and yanked open a drawer and began rifling through utensils. "You want me to pull the bullets out, or what?" She retrieved a pair of needle-nose pliers from the drawer. "Derek would be disappointed if I let you heal with the bullets under your scales."

Theresa stiffened. Derek. Of course. How silly of her to actually hope that the gesture might have been an indication of some sort of concern on Becca's part. She gave a bored sniff and picked up her ladle again. "Suit yourself. Extract away."

They didn't exchange another word until Becca was pulling out the third bullet, the one that had taken out her human fingernail. Becca eyed the mangled claw. "You really had a human fingernail?"

Theresa sighed. "It was beautiful. Feminine. I loved it." She tried not to wince as Becca dug around in her claw for the bullet. "It was the one indication I had that there was still a chance I could change my life. Now I'm back to where I was. Completely stuck in this stupid dragon form."

Becca made a noise of sympathy, then leaned back and studied Theresa, chewing her lower lip. "You know, if you promise not to go after my chef, I might be able to get you another fingernail."

Theresa stopped breathing for a full minute. "How?"

"Satan."

"Oh, no." She shook her head vehemently. "I'm not giving him my soul. No way."

"He wouldn't expect an entire soul for a single fingernail. If it gives you hope for your future, it might be worth his price."

Becca's voice was suspiciously empathetic, and Theresa cocked her head to look at her. But the Rivka dropped the bullet on the table with a clang and shoved the forceps into Theresa's neck.

A stab of pain blistered through Theresa's neck and slammed into her head. "Ow!"

"Sorry." Becca held up the last bullet. "Got it."

The sharp pain faded to a throbbing ache, and Theresa rubbed her neck. "Did you get some of my vertebrae while you were in there?"

"No, but I could give it another go if you like." Becca looked far too cheerful as she gathered the bullets off the table. "How long will you have bullet holes?"

"A few hours at most."

Becca shot her a curious glance as she stepped on the foot pedal to lift the lid of a smoothly polished stainless-steel trash can. She dropped the bullets in with a thunk. "Does it hurt?"

"Yup. But a dragon is never bothered by pain, of course." Sounded good, at least.

"Of course." Becca washed her hands then grabbed her keys. "I don't suppose you're strong enough to fly home tonight?"

"Nope." Theresa sighed with satisfaction as she leaned back in the chair that was too small for her dragon-sized butt. "I can't possibly go home to my lonely existence. I'm stuck here with you. You're not exactly warm and fuzzy, but you have a full kitchen and you acknowledge I'm alive, so that's something at least." At Becca's scowl, Theresa added, "There's no food at Quin's. I'll starve if I go back."

Becca grabbed a smooth leather wallet out of a drawer, removed a credit card, and slipped it into her bra. "I'll take care of that while I'm out."

Theresa frowned. "Where are you going?" Becca might be Satan's right hand, but at least she was someone to talk to. She'd had kind of a crappy night, and the thought of being alone was almost too much to take. "Maybe you could stay here. We could get drunk and rent movies with hot guys and complain about our lives. Justine and I used to do that a lot. It's kind of fun."

Becca gave her an odd look as she shoved the utensil drawer closed with her hip.

"What? You don't know how to do the girl bonding thing?" Theresa hopped up and yanked open the freezer. "My God, girl. You've got sixteen different kinds of ice cream in here. This is perfect for a bitch session." Her belly rumbled as she picked up the nearest pint. "Chocolate fudge brownie? And cookie dough? I love this stuff!" She glanced at Becca. "I didn't know Rivkas needed comfort food."

Becca yanked the ice cream out of Theresa's claws, put it back inside, then slammed the freezer shut. "I can't stay. I have to get some souls. Satan's running low." She flashed Theresa a glimpse at a very skimpy ensemble under the black leather coat. "Trolling the alleys in this outfit at this hour makes it easy to find souls who deserve hell."

"You have awesome breasts." Theresa sighed with envy. "I wish I had boobs men could gawk at."

Becca managed a half-smile. "You're one warped dragon."

The Rivka's smile made Theresa feel better, and she sat back down at the table. "Well, you're one psychotic Rivka. Bring me breakfast when you come back?"

"As long as you promise not to go eat my chef."

Theresa took a bite of her cereal and pretended to contemplate the request. "Mmm . . . I won't eat him until after you get back. How's that?"

Becca lifted one eyebrow. "Funny dragon."

Theresa grinned. "You know you love me."

All she got in return was a snort and a visual of Becca turning into an inky black puddle and disappearing through the floor. Cool. But certainly not cool enough to tempt her to deal with Satan.

She looked at her mangled claw and sighed. A human fingernail, though . . . maybe.

No. She would not succumb.

She wasn't that desperate . . . was she?

Heaven help her if she was.

It was just before midnight and Zeke Siccardi was in his sparsely decorated office, nursing too-old coffee while negotiating a bribe . . . er, payment . . . for some confidential information. His contact was just about where he wanted him when Zeke sensed someone approaching his office. "Hang on a sec, please." He hit the phone's hold button and closed his eyes, letting his senses explore.

Two human males. One was angry. Tense. Carrying a freshly oiled gun. He smelled like money. The other . . . nervous. Not armed. The scent of desperate sweat rolled off him. He also carried the odor of cash.

And the energy pulses of both men were directed toward Zeke.

He connected to his call again. "I don't like the price you're setting. I'll have to think about it." Then he hung up.

Oh, sure, he would have paid the price they'd negotiated to, but since he had to get off the phone anyway, he might as well use the interruption to his advantage. The information wasn't going anywhere.

He leaned back in his favorite chair, a well-worn black leather chair that had soothed him for years. He turned up the jazz emanating from his CD player, laced his fingers behind his head, and watched the door.

His visitors didn't disappoint.

The door flew open to reveal a huge man with a shaved skull and a neck that blended into his head. He looked twitchy and was wearing an expensive suit, probably custom to fit those steroid-induced shoulders. "You Siccardi?"

"Yep." Zeke tapped his foot in time to the jazz, trying to stay focused on the trumpet, and not on the violence rolling off his visitor.

Twitchy Guy did a quick scan of the room. "Anyone else here?"

"Nope."

"Don't move."

"Wouldn't dream of it." Involuntarily, Zeke's gaze flicked to the locked gun drawer by his left shin. It had been decades since he'd unlocked it, but the urge was strong. He closed his eyes for a moment and let the music wash over him.

Twitchy Guy went back into the hall and returned a minute later with a tall, bony man who was also wearing an expensive suit. Zeke would lay odds that the new addition was the negotiator.

Zeke checked the clock radio on his desk. He'd give them three minutes and then send them on their way.

Bony Guy sat down in Zeke's guest chair while Twitchy set up guard at the door. "Nice office."

"Thanks." He kept one eye on Twitchy, but so far his hands were by his side and not near his gun. "What can I do for you?"

"I hear you find people."

"That I do."

"I hear you're the best."

"I am."

Bony Guy nodded his approval, then slid a photo across the desk. A name was scrawled across the bottom. "Find him."

Zeke didn't even glance at the photo. "Why?"

Bony Guy gave him a grin. "Because his dad misses him. Wants to bring him home for the family reunion." Then he winked.

Zeke didn't buy the story for a second. The only way they wanted to bring this missing person anywhere was in a body bag, which wasn't his gig anymore. "Sorry, but I can't help you."

Bony Guy set an envelope on the table. "Full cash payment up front. We know you're good for it. You have a reputation."

"And Twitchy will kill me if I stiff you."

"Who?"

"Never mind." Zeke finally took his hands from behind his head and leaned forward, folding his hands on his desk. "I'm sorry you wasted your time, but I no longer take cases like yours."

Bony Guy frowned. "What does that mean?"

"No violence. No men with guns. No dirty cash." He spread his hands. "I'm clean and I run a clean shop here." The scars all over his hands told another story. Maybe he should get them lasered off. Bite wounds didn't exactly enhance his clean image. Hell, while he was at it, he should get a manicure.

Then he grinned. Some things were just never going to happen.

Bony Guy cleared his throat. "There's two million dollars in that envelope."

"Find someone else." Zeke had never been driven by money, even back in the day. Women? Maybe. A good battle, definitely. Money? Not so much.

Bony didn't look happy. "Listen, I did my research. I know what you can do. You don't have morals or a conscience and you're lethal, but you've never been caught. You're the man I need."

Zeke felt the familiar twitch at the back of his neck. No matter how long he went without, the allure of that lifestyle would never go away. No worry. He was stronger than the temptation. "You're working with dated information." Like a century or two old. "I find people for the right reasons. And yours won't qualify."

Bony grinned. "The man I want you to find is a dragon."

The twitch immediately flared up into a full-fledged roar and Zeke had to close his eyes for a moment to imagine his field of dandelions. Chirping birds. His happy place. *A real live dragon?* A cat sprang up out of the dandelions and munched a bird. *Damn.*

He growled as the urge crept down his arms, making them itch. He tried to imagine Labrador puppies. Snuggly little black Labs. Puppy kisses. *No way could he take a case about a dragon.* The mother of the puppies suddenly appeared in his fantasy, saliva dripping from her chin, her eyes narrowed with the fury that only a mother could feel. She lunged for him and he felt the teeth sink into his arm, sending his adrenaline spiking.

Crap. He shook his head hard and tried again. Theresa Nichols. In her lingerie. Licking a path down the inside of his thigh. Her hair would be silky, scented of vanilla. Her skin smooth, with a tattoo over her left collarbone, described so vividly by her that he could picture it exactly. There was no baggage between them. No deep emotions that could destroy them. Just fun and great sex. Ah. Better. He opened his eyes again, stillness settling over his limbs. "No. I will not find the dragon for you."

Bony chuckled and tossed a business card on the table. "When you change your mind, call me. You know you can't resist."

Still tingling with thoughts of Theresa and her soft lips, Zeke picked up the card and photo, walked over to the shredder, and sent them both through. "Don't underestimate me."

He always enjoyed it when people underestimated him, though now he was too civilized to make them pay for it, unfortunately. His life might be clean, but sometimes it was as boring as hell. Or rather, as boring as heaven. Hell would probably prove pretty interesting. Not that it mattered. He'd walked away from his violent lifestyle, and he'd likely live at least another five hundred years or so before having to worry about the Afterlife. It was almost an embarrassment he was going to live this long. Most slayers died by the time they were a couple of hundred years old, their life sucked away by the munch of a dragon.

"Oh, I know all about you, Mr. Siccardi." Bony stood up. "Don't you want to at least find the man and warn him that we're after him?" He set a replacement photo on the table. "Either way, you know you'll track him down. If you work for us, at least you'll be paid for your efforts." He set another business card on top of the picture. "Think about it. Have a nice day."

Zeke watched them leave and wished for a moment that he'd met them a couple of hundred years ago.

His phone rang and he picked it up automatically, figuring it was probably Bony trying to up the offer. "Siccardi here."

"Mr. Siccardi, it's Ralph Greene, attorney-at-law. On behalf of my client, I am following up to see if you have had any success in locating Theresa Nichols."

He settled back in his chair and kicked his feet up on his desk. "I may have a lead, but I need to confirm she's the right Theresa Nichols." If the elusive woman would simply meet with him, he'd be able to compare her to the sketch he was working from, and he'd know whether she was the right woman.

And, well, once he met her and this whole client thing was over . . . well . . . who knew? He grinned to himself. He had plenty of time to waste on a woman, especially Theresa Nichols. At least he wouldn't have to lie about his day job anymore. Either one of them.

"Mr. Siccardi, the situation has changed. It is simply of the utmost urgency that we locate Ms. Nichols by the end of this week. If you are unable to find her, I have been instructed to assume she is dead and take appropriate action."

Zeke's feet thudded to the floor and he sat up. "Mr.

Greene, I have never failed a client, and I won't be starting with you. You'll have your answer by Friday."

"Excellent. I'll be expecting a call. Until then."

Zeke hung up the phone then leaned back in his chair,
tapping his fingers thoughtfully on his desk. It was time.
He grabbed his laptop and pulled it toward him. He hesitated for a moment, then gritted his teeth and typed: "T?
You there?"

Three

Theresa nearly fell off Becca's red velvet antique couch when Zeke's message popped up on her computer screen. She'd just logged on to Becca's laptop less than a minute ago. She grinned and typed, "I think we're psychically connected."

There was a brief pause before the reply came. "You know we are."

Theresa tensed, and her tail twitched in alarm at his hesitation. "What's wrong?"

"Ah, T, you're too perceptive."

"Yeah, I'm a goddess. We've already confirmed that." She stopped typing suddenly. What if he was about to break up with her? Her breath caught, and she had to close her eyes for a moment to regroup before she could keep typing. "I had a bad night. I tried to break out of my holding cell to come see you and got shot five times. No, four. Four times. Dr. Gibbs operated on me and saved my life. I'm quite traumatized and could use some cybersex. What say you?"

She nodded with satisfaction. Only a heartless scum would break up with her now. Not that you could break up with someone you weren't dating. Cut her off would be the better term. Cut her off from the greatest cybersex on the planet. Not to mention the personal connection. Trading funny stories with him provided her only moments of salvation from those bouts of insurmountable loneliness.

"I love your imagination," he typed. "Shot four times, huh? Good one, T."

Her nostrils flared and she typed faster, her claws clicking on the keys. "No, I swear it's true. Once in the shoulder, then the tail, and—" She stared at what she'd written, then cursed and slammed her tail into the end table. It shattered with a crack and she winced.

"Tail?"

She pressed her claws to her head and tried to think of an explanation for her slip. Drugs? Temporary insanity? Brain freeze from being fireballed by a Rivka?

"T?"

"That's how a lady refers to her derriere." She let out a deep breath of relief at her quick thinking.

"You were shot in the ass?"

She could almost hear him laughing and she grinned. Zeke never got all sappy on her, and she loved that. He was bad boy all the way, and it was perfect. "Yep. I have a war wound. Want to see?"

"You know I do."

She gave herself a high five. She had him right back where she wanted him. What man could resist the allure of a woman's naked butt?

"Listen, T. I met a girl."

A girl? She sat back with a frown, picking at the silky tassels on one of the throw pillows while she considered his statement. "You want to do a threesome with her?" she finally typed. She shoved the pillow away and growled.

Two guys and one girl, maybe. Sharing Zeke with another woman? Unacceptable.

"No threesomes," he replied.

Relief made her sigh a plume of white smoke.

"I want you alone, T. But this woman lives in my building and is willing to go on a real date. I can't live on cybersex forever."

She snarled at the computer. Okay, she was a total goddess, but this was a seriously unfair handicap. Even the best cybersex in the world couldn't compete with mouth-on-flesh contact. "Does she have a disease? Or two? You should be careful."

There was a pause, and Theresa felt her heart quicken. If he was about to dump her, she had to dump him first. Desperate or not, she couldn't take being rejected by him.

But his reply came in before she could make her claws type a response. "You and I need to take our relationship to the next level or end it. Tomorrow night. Eleven o'clock. There's an upscale bar called NightGames. I'll be the only one there wearing a baseball cap. Red Sox."

She sat back on her haunches and stared at the screen, her soul aching with yearning. To meet Zeke in person. To go to a bar like a normal person. To be out in society. God, how she wanted that. She caught her lower lip in her fangs and typed a terse response. "I can't. Back off."

"Then it's over. I'll wait until midnight tomorrow night. Then I change my screen name and move on. Be there, T. Please."

And then he was gone.

She slammed the computer closed and dropped it on the couch next to her. Then she grabbed one of the cushions and held it to her mouth to muffle her scream of frustration.

Theresa was on her seventh pint of ice cream when Becca appeared in the apartment six hours later. She sat up on the couch and pointed her spoon at Becca. "Where have you been? I've been having a total crisis and I had no one to talk to!"

Becca threw off her leather jacket, revealing a slightly torn and dirty—and slutty—outfit. There was a long scratch down the side of her neck and she was bleeding from her left hip. "Do I look like I care?"

Theresa caught the metallic scent of Becca's blood and frowned. "What happened to you?"

"Misidentification of a potential soul. Thought he was human. He wasn't." She yanked open the door to the fridge and pulled out a bottled water. "It was a long night." She sank down onto a chair at the kitchen table and sighed. "I need a new job."

"You need a new job. I need a new life. We're twins!" Theresa bounded off the couch and plopped down next to Becca, making the kitchen chair creak in protest. Now, see? This is what she needed. Some serious girl bonding. "Want to hear about my night?"

Becca pressed the water bottle to her forehead. "I don't know how I didn't notice he wasn't human. How did I miss that?"

"Okay, fine. We can talk about you first." Theresa shoved the peppermint ice cream at Becca. "Here. So, what happened? Did you kill someone? Because if you did, you have to tell me all about it. It's been so long since I've killed someone I can't even remember what the high feels like anymore." She hooked the spike of her tail under the handle of the utensil drawer, yanked it open, and grabbed a spoon for Becca. "Eat. It'll make you feel better."

Becca ignored the spoon and rubbed her nose. "I *think* I killed him."

Theresa frowned at the weary Rivka. "How do you not know? I thought you were an expert killer. A stream of bodies in your wake and all that." At Becca's rueful look, she added, "But I'll still like you if you didn't kill him."

The Rivka scowled. "He vanished. Not sure if he was dead or not."

"Vanishing assailants? That sounds so interesting." Theresa sighed and rested her chin on her claws. "Don't even tell me he was also hot. Being a Rivka is seriously the best job ever."

Becca eyed her. "He tried to kill me."

"I know! And to think you get eye candy and slut outfits on top of it." She gestured at Becca's leather bustier. "You are *so* lucky."

Becca finally took the spoon and plunged it into the ice cream. "You have serious issues, Dragon."

"And you don't appreciate how awesome your life is. So, are you going to tell me or what? Was he hot? Bulging muscles? I need full visualization for my I-want-to-have-your-life fantasy."

"I was *working,* not lusting after men." Becca rolled her eyes and shoved a spoonful of ice cream into her mouth. "I was too busy trying to figure out *what* he was to notice if he was hot."

"Bo-ring." Theresa walked over to the freezer and picked out a pint of Muddy Moose Guava. "So? What was he?"

Becca shrugged. "No idea. I'm going to have to do a little research."

"Really?" Theresa slammed the freezer door shut and spun around. "I'll help you! I'm really good on the computer and I've spent billions of hours surfing the Net. I can be your assistant, doing all the legwork while you're out killing." She flopped down next to Becca. "You don't even have to pay me. It'll be awesome just to have something to do. But bring home juicy stories, okay? That's my only requirement."

"It's *my* job. *I* have to do it." Becca closed her eyes and seemed to sag in her chair. "I filled Quincy's kitchen with food. You can go back there now."

Theresa snorted. "As if! Justine never had sex or killed anyone if she could avoid it. Now that she's married? Forget it. Dullsville. I'm totally hanging out with you from now on. Your life will be so much more fun to live vicariously."

"Theresa! You can't hang out with me."

Theresa sat up at the serious look on Becca's face, gripping her pint of ice cream more tightly. "Really? You won't let me stay?"

"No."

"But, why not?" Quincy's empty house flashed through Theresa's mind, and she shivered. She couldn't go back there. Not tonight. Not ever. She was far too vital and passionate to die of loneliness and starvation in that miserable place. She deserved better.

"I don't hang out." Becca scooped up another spoonful of peppermint. "No offense, Theresa. It's not personal. With your addiction to violence, you're actually one of the least annoying people in my life. Except for the fact you want to toast my chef, of course. But you'll have to go back to Quin's house once it gets dark and you can fly again."

Well, that was it. Theresa had had enough of being excluded. Zeke threatening to cut her off, and now this? She threw down her spoon. "I want your life!"

Becca shuddered. "Trust me, you don't."

"What, I want my life? Not a chance." She folded her arms over her chest to ward off the desperation threatening to erupt into a violent, fiery explosion. "I *have* to change my life, Becca. I can't take it anymore."

The Rivka paused with the spoon halfway to her mouth. "What do you want from me?"

Theresa took a deep breath, her heart thudding so loudly she could feel her scales pulsing with its force. "I want you to introduce me to Satan."

Becca let out her breath and shook her head. "I changed my mind. A human fingernail isn't worth a deal with Satan." She started to take a bite of her ice cream, but Theresa snatched the spoon from her grasp.

"I don't want a fingernail. I want the whole shebang. Could he do it?" She held her breath and waited.

Becca gaped at her. "Of course he can, but—"

"No buts!" Theresa smacked her front claws down on the table. "Decision made." The cost simply didn't matter anymore. She had to get her life back or go completely insane. And if she had to agree to serve Satan, so much the better. Having Becca's job would rock.

But Becca, party-pooping Rivka, was shaking her head. "Derek would kill me if I let you give your soul to Satan."

"Oh, please. Can't you make a single decision without

thinking about your precious boss? It's not like he'll fire you."

A faint red flared in Becca's eyes as she sat back and folded her arms across her chest. "No."

Theresa contemplated threatening Becca with incineration, then had a better idea. Threaten the Rivka with what she'd fear most of all. Theresa grinned and fluttered her eyelashes (yeah, they were fake, so what? The fact that dragons didn't naturally have eyelashes didn't mean she had to go without, did it?) at Becca. "Fine, then. I'll just move in here with you, follow you around, and be your best friend. I'll always be here because I have no life and you'll have to do all my shopping for me since I can't go out in dragon form and I'll tell you all about my boring days and I'll sit here every night waiting for you to get home from soul harvesting so I can hear about every man you got to meet and—"

Horror flashed over Becca's face. "You win. You can meet with Satan, but I won't let you give him your soul."

"Really?" Theresa leaped to her feet, her claws trembling with nerves and excitement. *She was going to meet with Satan.* "Don't worry about me. I'll keep my soul *and* get my human form. I have a bargaining chip he won't be able to resist."

Becca grimaced. "He's *Satan.* As in, evil bastard who rules the Underworld. Any deal you make with him will have unbearable repercussions for you. It's the way he does business. You'll be tied to him for all eternity."

Theresa folded her arms across her scaly chest and met Becca's gaze. "I can handle him."

They stared at each other for a long moment, then Becca made a noise of disgust and got up from the table.

"Fine, it's your life." She threw the remainder of the peppermint ice cream into the freezer and slammed the door shut. "But don't complain to me when you get tired of being indebted to him."

"I will so owe you for this one." Theresa puckered up and gave her a few kissy noises. "I love you, Becca."

"Yeah, remember that after you have Satan pulling your chain." She stood up. "Ready to go?"

"Now?"

"Yes, now."

"Omigod." She clenched her claws and swallowed hard, trying to calm her nerves. Her scales were trembling and her tail was twitching so badly she couldn't stop it. "We have to drop Mona off at Quincy's office first. I don't want her anywhere near Satan." She uncurled her claws, picked up the espresso machine, and clutched her to her chest. "I might be desperate, but I'll never let that turn me into a bad Guardian."

"No problem. We can chew Quincy out for letting you starve when we stop by."

"Oh, great idea!" Theresa beamed at Becca. "You know, Rivka, I think my life is going to get way more interesting now that I'm hanging out with you."

Becca shot her a horrified look. "We're not hanging out, remember?"

"Give it up, Rivka. I'm yours, you're mine. Life is good."

"Oh, for God's sake. Are you ready or what?"

"To meet Satan?" A green puff of nervous smoke leaked out her left nostril, but she nodded. "Let's do it."

Four

"A massage parlor? I had no idea they had these in hell." Theresa paused outside the golden door, tracing her claw over the detailed carvings of naked women on the frame. "This art is amazing. It's not even tasteless."

Becca rolled her eyes. "Don't be fooled. Satan's as disgusting and crass as any other oversexed, egomaniacal male. Money buys nice furnishings, but Satan himself is a cretin."

Theresa arched her brow at Becca. "Give it up, Rivka. You aren't going to talk me out of making a deal with him." She checked the front of her white silk shirt for burn marks, frowning at the singed hem. She should know better than to wear white for important meetings. White didn't go well with dragons. "Dammit. Satan won't take me seriously if I'm burned."

"Satan never takes anyone seriously, but he's always in a good mood when women are fondling him. That's why we're visiting him here." Becca hit a gold-encrusted door with her hip and pushed it open, and Theresa sucked in her breath. *It was time.*

"Are you decent?" Becca called out.

"Never! I am Satan! There is nothing decent about me!"

She rolled her eyes at Theresa, then led the way inside. "Hey, Boss. Looking virile and masculine as usual."

Theresa grinned at Becca's sarcastic tone, then stumbled to a stop at the sight of a dark-haired man face-down on the massage table, completely naked. The muscles in his back were rippling under the efforts of three scantily clad women with breast implants. Even in a relaxed state, his biceps were popping, and he had the tightest little buns she could ever remember seeing. She couldn't see his face, but she could see enough of his pro-file to admire the strong lines of his jaw. Oh, yes. Satan was a man in every sense of the word.

The scent of coconut massage oil wafted into her nose, and she sat with a thump on the floor as her legs gave out.

"My favorite Rivka! Are you here to kiss my feet and worship my greatness?" His shoulders shook with the force of his bellow, his muscles flexing.

"I'd rather cut off your feet and worship your most hated enemy," Becca replied, eliciting a delighted chuckle from her boss. "Since when do your massage therapists wear clothes?"

Satan waved a hand, but didn't lift his head from the padded doughnut caressing his face. "Alas, I must adjust my personal habits if I am to have any hope of seducing former Guardian and woman of my fantasies Iris Bennett into an eternity of naked passion and lovemaking. I show her my devotion by eliminating all other breasts from my life. Monumental sacrifice."

"Well, if you hadn't screwed her over two hundred years ago by trying to steal Mona, you might be having better luck." Becca hooked her hand under Theresa's forearm and tugged her to her feet. "I brought someone who wants to make a deal with you."

"A deal? You mean a soul? I love souls." Satan immediately lifted his head, and fastened his gorgeous brown eyes on Theresa. "A dragon? I thought dragons were extinct."

Theresa narrowed her eyes at the reference to her ancestors' inability to survive. "Do I look extinct?"

Satan's mouth curved into a delectable smile. "Oh, a female dragon. One with spunk. I accept her soul. Put her in with the others. Good work, my favorite Rivka. And kill my dragon expert who told me they are extinct."

Theresa braced herself as one of the massage girls grabbed her arm and tried to tug her toward the door. "You can't have my soul, Satan."

Satan cocked his head, an interested gleam in his eye. "Do tell." At the jerk of his chin, the massage girl released Theresa and returned to Satan, where she slammed the point of her elbow into the back of his thigh. Satan yelped, then ordered her to dig harder, never taking his gaze off Theresa.

Theresa's heart started beating a little bit faster. What if Satan decided she couldn't leave? Would she be able to walk away? Becca couldn't disobey a direct order to lop off Theresa's head. Perhaps she should have thought this plan through more thoroughly. Aw, well. Nothing to be done about it now. It was time to play her trump card. "I'm the best friend of Justine Bennett, the Guardian of the Goblet of Eternal Youth, and—"

Satan erupted into a string of curses. "Rivka! You know I cannot freely torture the best friend of Justine Satanette

Bennett! Justine would complain to her mother, who is the lovely Iris Bennett, for whom I yearn so completely. A cruel joke you play! For that I tear off your arms and—"

"Shut up, Satan. Let her finish." Becca picked up a platinum rod with several gold massage balls on the end of it and rubbed it experimentally across her thigh. She nodded, then tucked it under her arm. "I'll keep this."

He immediately grinned. "My favorite Rivka, you make my day so much more interesting. No one else tells me to shut up, except Iris. I change my mind. You can keep your arms." He turned his gaze to Theresa. "You may speak, Dragon, and because of your friendship with Satanette, I promise I will refrain from most cruelly torturing you. Moderate torture only. Isn't that delightful?"

Right. Okay. She took a deep breath for courage, then launched into her speech. "When I drank from the Goblet of Eternal Youth—"

"What?" He propped himself up on his elbows, giving her a peek at a sculpted chest decorated with golden curls. "You drank from the Goblet? Oh, you are so fortunate. For centuries I have lusted after that Goblet. Only my burning passion for the former Guardian, Iris Bennett, has kept me from pursuing it and—"

"Yes, I know the story, and I know all about Iris. You don't need to keep explaining who she is. The point is that the Goblet turned me permanently into a dragon, and I want my human form back. I've tried everything, including donating to that televangelist Reverend Munsey, and nothing worked. Becca said you could do it."

"Turn you human?" Satan cocked his head and pursed his lips. "Yes, yes, that is well within the range of my many and sordid powers."

Her breath caught in her chest and she nearly staggered. *He could really turn her into a human.*

Satan swung his feet to the floor and stood up, rubbing his chin thoughtfully. "You give me your soul and I make you human. It is a deal. I commend your negotiating skills. I have much work for you to do."

Theresa averted her eyes, trying not to stare at the full-frontal view. Satan had obviously enjoyed his massage, and he wasn't afraid to show it. He was almost as well-endowed as she'd imagined Zeke to be. "I already told you that I'm keeping my soul. What else do you want?"

His perfectly manicured and flawless eyebrows drew together in a frown. "Your soul. I negotiate for nothing else."

"I can't give you my soul." She dug her back claws into the floor, trying not to panic. "Surely there is something else you want."

He yawned and stretched his arms over his head, making his proud parts pop up even more. "I have everything I want. I am Satan. Anything I want, I take. All I need to negotiate for are souls."

"There has to be *something*." With Satan's manly bits dangling in front of her eyes, her need to meet up with Zeke was nearly desperate. To be intimate. To be touched as a human, and a lover. To have a life. She *had* to find a way to become human again.

A delighted glitter flickered in Satan's eyes. "Negotiating error by the dragon. Did you notice it, Rivka?"

"Yeah." Becca sounded bored as she rifled through a box that apparently contained various massage items. She picked up one that had arms and a cord hanging from it and wiggled the forked extensions to see if they moved.

"She sounds desperate, you noticed, and now you're going to screw her because you realize she wants to be human so badly you can get her to do almost anything."

Uh-oh. Theresa pinched her nose shut, trying not to expel the green smoke of fear that was so telling for her species.

"Exactly!" Satan clapped his hands with delight. "This is so wonderful. I had no idea someone could be this desperate over a silly human form, but I accept."

Theresa's heart slammed to a stop and she stared at him. "You agree? To make me human?"

"Yes. I must think long and hard about what I will demand from you in return. Come back in three hundred years and I will have an answer for you."

Three hundred years? Her scales shriveled with dismay. "No." She took a deep breath and leveled a golden glare at him. "I need to be human by tonight."

"Oh?" Satan's grin grew bigger. "Why is that?"

"Because . . . I have a chance to have sex with a very hot man." *And it's my only chance not to lose the one person in my life who might actually care if I got run over by a bus.* Satan seemed like the kind of guy who'd relate to the sex opportunity, so she kept all her other reasons to herself, hoping she could get him to give her a little leeway through some we-love-sex bonding. He'd forget about taking advantage of her desperation, and she'd be human. "Great sex. Hot and sweaty. Multiple orgasms."

Satan's manly parts grew even more alert. "Excellent reason. I like you, Dragon. I agree to make you human, and you agree to give me whatever I ask when the time comes."

"Except my soul." Humanity was so close, she could

practically feel her teeth smoothing out and her breasts forming. It didn't matter what he asked for, as long as it wasn't her soul. A job working for Satan would be right up her alley, if Becca's life was any indication. She smoothed her features and tried to hide her eagerness.

"Agreed." Satan beamed at them both. "This is so excellent. My first nonsoul negotiation. I have much to contemplate. I will be in contact. Have excellent, multiple-partner sex tonight in my honor." He flicked a finger at her. "Human you be."

Raging heat burst over Theresa, and suddenly, everything glowed golden, so bright that it made her eyes ache. She threw her claws over her face, but the glow kept getting brighter until all she could see was a glittery light. "Becca? What's happening?"

Then her toes blistered with pain, and the searing agony crawled up her legs, a white-hot heat ripping through her defenses. She screamed and dropped to the floor, clawing at her legs. "Get it off me! Stop it!" It felt like her skin was being ripped off by some brutal force. She could hear Satan laughing, and she lashed out with her tail, even as tears poured from her eyes. "You bastard! We had a deal!" The scales on her stomach were screaming now and she doubled over, gasping for breath. She shrieked as the pain shot down her left arm, then her right, then tore into her face.

Oh, God. It was too much. She couldn't take it.

Then the pain vanished and she collapsed into a heap, moaning softly. The golden hue faded until she could see Becca and Satan standing there, watching her. They were tinged in gold, and Becca's brow was furrowed with what looked like concern. "Are you all right?"

"I think so." She moved one arm tentatively, then relaxed when there was no pain. The last hue of gold faded, and she glared at Satan, who was laughing so hard he'd sat down and was holding his sides. "You caused me pain on purpose."

"You should have seen your face! Big tough dragon, screaming like a sissy." He burst out into gales of laughter again.

Bastard. She started to slam her tail into him, but nothing happened. She jerked her head around and looked at her backside. No tail. Just two pale pink butt cheeks and a diamond stud that was embedded in the skin at the base of her spine. Elation rushed through her, and she jerked her hand up so she could see it. Fingers. Cuticles. Her throat tightened as she stared at them. "I have *hands,*" she whispered.

"And breasts. Very perky. I like pink nipples. Can I take a picture for my collection?"

Theresa looked down at her human body and it blurred as her eyes filled with tears. "Oh, God. Look at me!"

"I am looking," Satan announced. "I cannot take my eyes off those bouncing mounds of lusciousness."

"Shut up, you pervert." Becca shrugged off her thigh-length leather jacket and tossed it at Theresa. "Put this on. The clothes you wore here won't fit anymore."

Theresa didn't want to put it on. She wanted a mirror. Lots of mirrors. She pressed her palms to her face. Cheeks. Lips. She looked at Becca. "I can't believe it."

Satan shrieked suddenly and jumped up. "Holy terror of hell! Your face!" He screamed again and raced out of the room, yelling about salvation and demanding immediate medical care for his eyes.

Theresa jerked to her feet, clutching her face. "What's wrong with me?" She stumbled and nearly fell. "Oh, God, Becca! What did he do to me?"

Becca grabbed her shoulders. "Theresa! He's Satan. He lied! You're fine!"

Her mind began to clear. "What?"

"Satan makes a career out of torturing people. He lies, he manipulates, he cheats."

"He lied." She drew a deep, shuddering breath when Becca nodded. "So I'm okay?"

"Well, you're totally screwed because you just agreed to give Satan anything he wanted, but as soon as you get a makeover to update those eyebrows and the hair, you'll at least look decent when he destroys your life." Becca released her, picked her coat up from the floor, and handed it to Theresa.

Theresa shrugged the coat on, her hands still shaking too much to button it.

"Do you get what I'm saying, Dragon?" Becca impatiently fastened the buttons. "This is just a hint at the hell he's going to put you through. Are you sure you want to do this? I might be able to talk him out of it, since he hasn't even figured out what he wants from you."

Theresa looked at her hands, trembling, but human. Thought of Zeke at the bar, waiting for her. Of Quincy's lonely house. Then she shook her head and met Becca's gaze. "I'm a dragon. I can handle anything he throws at me."

Becca set her hands on her hips. "You're a fool." But there was a hint of sympathy in her green eyes.

"I can't go back to my life." She hugged the coat around her, feeling chilly as only someone in human form could. No dragon fat and scales to keep her warm. It was the best feeling ever. "I'm going to go get my hair done, and then I'm going to meet Zeke." Excitement warmed her and she grinned. "I have a real date tonight."

"What about Satan?"

Theresa shoved the jacket sleeves up to her elbows. "Bring him on."

After checking with Quin to make sure he was able to babysit Mona for another day, Theresa was ready to hit the city of New York for a day of modernization. She'd raided Becca's closet for a temporary clothing fix and she was armed with the Amex that she'd used only online until today.

But as she leaned against the wall of the elevator in Becca's condo building, her heart thudded with each floor the elevator dropped. Toward the street. Toward people. And daylight. And normalcy. Toward the world that had evaded her for so long.

The doors slid open, and for a moment Theresa simply stared through the lobby, out the glass doors of the building, watching a man in a suit rush by, his briefcase tucked under his arm.

Then a messenger screamed past on his bike, his wheels spinning in a blur.

Did she really belong in that world now? She felt as if it were a mirage, a fantasy that would implode the moment she tried to embrace it.

She wet her lips and clenched her fists. *It's real, Theresa. Get out there.*

The elevator doors started to close, and she jumped

through them before they could lock her in. There would be no closed doors for her anymore.

Steeling herself, she strode across the empty lobby, watched in awe as her human fingers curved around the door handle, then shoved it open and stepped outside in the sunlight.

She closed her eyes and sucked the warmth into her skin.

"Excuse me, please."

She jumped back as a dog walker hustled by with six dogs. All six furry heads snapped in her direction, tails went between their legs, and the German shepherd's hackles went up with a growl as the dogs sensed her true nature.

She froze, knowing she was exposed. A dragon roaming the streets of New York.

"Stop bothering the nice lady," the dog walker muttered, tugging on the dogs' leashes as he shot her an apologetic glance. "Sorry."

"Um, that's okay." She stared after them in disbelief as the little group hurried off, a growing sense of amazement spreading over her. She was human. She blended in with the world.

She grinned, then raised her arms to the sun, basking in the freedom. The freedom to be who she was, go where she wanted, and not have to hide. Never again. "I'm back!"

Then she threw her hand out to hail a cab. As it pulled up next to her obediently, she did a little jig of excitement.

First stop, Nordstrom's. To try on clothes. And bras. Skirts without a hole for the tail. How amazing was that?

She flopped back against the seat, fingering her hair. Second stop, Joacque LaFlaire to get her hair and makeup done.

Third stop, Zeke.

God, what a day.

At exactly eleven o'clock that evening, Theresa stopped outside NightGames and stared up at the softly lit windows of the bar. The tuxedoed doorman and heavy glass doors with beautiful etching suggested this wasn't any old bar. This place was classy, and she was so not going to fit in.

Then she lifted her chin and narrowed her eyes.

No.

She was in human form now.

She was Theresa Nichols, errant daughter of the richest dragon family in the Village of Uruloke.

Not only could she fit in, but she was a goddess slumming among ordinary humans who weren't worthy.

A satisfied smile curved her lips, and she marched up the steps, her new stilettos clicking on the cobblestones. "Good evening."

The doorman's gaze flickered to her breasts before he stepped back to open the door, and she almost hugged him. No more screams of horror! Just men trying to catch a glimpse.

God, it felt good.

She beamed and floated past him, unable to resist a hair flip. Hair! So much fun! She'd totally forgotten! Joacque LaFlaire had done wonders with her light brown tresses, which were now highlighted with all sorts of luscious blond tones that matched her newly shaped eyebrows. Artfully styled layers designed to look like sexy, tousled bedhead. Styling gel. Hairdryers. God, the world had evolved. She could never go back to being a bald dragon again. Ever.

Theresa stopped inside the mahogany foyer with its crystal chandelier, her heart racing at the sight of the maître d' hovering at the desk, waiting to greet her.

"Miss? May I be of service?"

She wet her lips and resisted the urge to check her cleavage for the fiftieth time. *It's still there, Theresa. Relax.* "Um, I'm meeting someone here. My name is Theresa Nichols." Her voice came out feminine and soft, not growling or snarling.

The man nodded. "Right this way." He gave her a serene smile and gestured for her to follow him into the lounge.

Her mouth suddenly dry, she clenched her freshly manicured nails around her new black handbag and forced her feet to move. Was she walking like a human? What if she accidentally tried to dump the entire contents of the bread basket down her throat? She blew into her hand to test her breath, but it was clean. Not a single shred of ash or smoke. She cleared her throat and hummed softly. Okay, she was good. *You can handle this, Theresa.*

She stopped suddenly as the maître d' disappeared around the corner of a gorgeous stone fireplace. What if Satan had made her human form temporary? What if the minute she saw Zeke, she turned into a dragon again? A cold sweat broke out between her shoulder blades and she took a desperate glance around the room to see if Satan was hiding in a corner, ready to enjoy another dragon humiliation, but she didn't see him anywhere. Could he change forms? Was he actually the cute old lady with blue hair? She bit her lower lip.

"Theresa?"

She jerked her gaze back to the fireplace in time to see a man step around in front of it. He was well over six feet tall, wearing a gorgeous pair of charcoal slacks and a button-down shirt with the sleeves rolled up to reveal strong wrists and a watch that screamed money and class. Dark hair, curling over his collar, a diamond earring, and the sexiest brown eyes she'd ever seen in her life.

He held up a Red Sox cap and raised his eyebrows in question.

She couldn't help the smile that broke over her face. "Zeke." His name came out as a breathy caress, and she felt her cheeks flame as a slow grin curved his lips.

"It's about damn time." He closed the distance between them in two long strides and bent down. She closed her eyes the instant before the soft heat from his lips brushed her cheek, basking in the subtlety of his delicious scent, in the nearness of his warmth.

Her body jerked with the shock of being touched by him.

In that instant, she knew she'd made the right decision, no matter what Satan asked of her.

Zeke pulled back from Theresa the instant his lips made contact with her skin. Heat flared through him and awareness crawled down his arms with a ferocity that made him blink.

Her gorgeous amber eyes widened. "What's wrong?"

"Nothing." The small shock he'd felt must have been from the raw lust that had slammed into him the minute he'd seen Theresa standing there next to the fireplace. Combine that with the tension still simmering through him from yesterday's missing dragon request, and it was no surprise he'd felt a little zing.

Her long black skirt was snug, showing every curve, and the silky camisole hugging her upper body was enough to make any man fall to his knees and beg for mercy. But it was the intricate tattoo on her collarbone that had really gotten him. Describing her tattoo had been her only capitulation to his requests that she tell him what she looked like. That tattoo symbolized the Theresa Nichols he'd gotten to know online for the last six months. No matter how classy and gorgeous she looked, that tattoo was the real Theresa, the one with no inhibitions, the one who said whatever was on her mind and never apologized for it.

He stepped back and gestured to his table. "Shall we?"

She gave him a worried look, but moved past him, her hips sliding easily beneath her skirt. He caught a faint whiff of her scent. An enticing aroma stirred a faint memory, something elusive that had him straightening up and searching the room for threats.

Theresa had stopped with one hand on the back of her chair, watching him carefully.

Zeke shrugged off the sensation and pulled out her chair. "I ordered your favorite wine."

"Wine is great. Thanks." She eased into the chair, her hand flicking behind her as if she needed to get coattails out of the way before sitting. She wasn't wearing a coat, however, and her cheeks turned red in a way that made him grin.

Yes, this was the Theresa he knew.

He slid into the chair opposite her, his foot accidentally bumping his briefcase. He frowned at the reminder. This wasn't a date, at least not until business was taken care of. "No haz-mat suit required?"

Her cheeks flared a deeper shade of red and she picked up her wine. "They found a cure earlier today."

"Convenient." He studied the curve of her nose, the line of her jaw, the angle of her eyes, and he knew she was the right Theresa Nichols. Her hair was different, but she definitely matched the black-and-white sketch his client had given him.

She lifted her chin and fastened her gaze on him. Her golden eyes were unyielding, daring him to challenge her story.

He shrugged and flashed her his palms in the universal sign for surrender. Until he came clean, he couldn't demand anything of her.

Tension eased from her shoulders, and she smiled. "You look different than I thought you would."

He grinned. "Better or worse?"

Her eyes drifted over him, and his body tightened. "Well, I like the earring and the hair, but the rest of you is a little more conservative than I expected." She tilted her head, fiddling with her dangling earrings, rubbing her thumb over her earlobe as if it were some hidden treasure she'd just discovered. "I thought you would be more of a bad boy." She gestured at their surroundings, awash with the murmur of dignified conversation and the soft candlelight. "I would have thought you were more of a smoky bar, loud music, and leather pants kind of guy."

Something shifted inside him, and he scowled. "Sorry if I'm too boring for you."

"I didn't say that." Theresa pursed her lips, a sparkle dancing in her eyes. "I know you've got that other side of you, even if you don't show it."

Zeke frowned and picked up his wine. "This is who I am. I don't go to loud bars, I don't get in knife fights in alleys, and I don't condone violence of any sort."

Some of the sparkle in her eyes faded. "Do you have a problem with violence? Gluttony? Destruction? That sort of vice?"

He couldn't help but raise his brows at the oddity of the question, but then he smiled. This was his Theresa, full of surprises and completely uninhibited. "I'm a vegetarian," he said firmly. "All living creatures should be treated with respect and honor. Violence is wrong, no matter what."

"Well." She set her glass down, her lips tight. "Well."

He cursed at himself for caring that she looked disappointed. They weren't here on a date. "Listen, T, I have a confession to make."

One gorgeous eyebrow curved up. "Didn't you just make one?"

"No." He grabbed his briefcase off the floor and set it on the table. "I am a missing persons expert, and I originally contacted you because I had a client who wanted me to find a woman named Theresa Nichols."

Wariness crept into her eyes. "What are you talking about?"

"It wasn't an accident that I met you in that chat room. I tracked you there." He grimaced at the increasing tension in her body, but plunged onward. "I needed to meet you in order to determine whether you were the right Theresa Nichols."

Theresa sat up, slowly, her muscles knotting in her

shoulders. "You . . . lied to me? All that talk, you were just trying to get to me for a *client*?"

"At first." Zeke quickly tugged a sheaf of papers from his briefcase. "But once I got to know you, you intrigued me on a personal level. But before we can get to that, I have to take care of business."

She said nothing, but her face was drawn, and her eyes were no longer quite the bright gold they had been. "So, when you told me that heart-wrenching story about how your dad was killed in a gang battle, it was a lie?"

He thought of the dragon that had felled his dad. "He did die. It did suck."

He could practically feel the trust between them disintegrating as she glared at him. "And when I confided in you when I was feeling lonely and depressed, when you spent hours trying to cheer me up . . ." She paused, taking a deep breath to try to contain her visible anger. "You were just trying to make me trust you for the sake of *your job*?"

He sat up, needing to convince her. "Yes, it was about the job, but it was also more than that, T."

"Don't call me T anymore," she snapped.

He grimaced. "I understand your anger, but—"

"Do you?" She leaned forward, her elbows slamming into the table. "How can you possibly understand how I feel right now? I was in that damned cell *forever*, and the *only* human contact I had was you, and now I find out that you were lying?" She reached across the table and shoved him in the chest with enough force to nearly knock him over. "Bastard."

He regained his balance and deflected her blow, bristling under her attack, even though he knew he deserved it. "*I'm* a liar? I know you haven't been in some FBI cell battling a contagious disease. You've been lying to me for months, too, so back off." When her face paled in acknowledgment of his accusation, he shoved the papers at her. "Listen to me for one second. You owe me that much, Miss FBI Research Project."

She folded her arms over her chest and leaned back in her chair, her fingers drumming restlessly against her forearm. "Fine. Talk."

For a second, he thought he saw a flicker of smoke drift out of her left nostril, but when he looked again, it was gone.

"Talk, Zeke, or I'm leaving."

He dropped the papers in front of her. "A distant relative of yours died and left you three million dollars."

She blinked. "What?"

He grinned. This was his favorite part of his job. "It's true. I checked it out. Raymond Vick lived in London, and he died six months ago, naming you as his only heir. Apparently, he was your mother's uncle's grandfather from an extramarital affair." He tapped the sheet. "Read it. It's all there. You're rich."

"But . . ." Theresa grabbed the papers and read, her eyes skimming the pages. "It's impossible. All my relatives are dead. All of them." She looked up, her forehead furrowed. "They've all been dead for a long time. A *really* long time."

"It's true, T. I do my research."

"No. It's wrong." She thrust the papers back at him. "You have the wrong Theresa Nichols." Her eyes glittered at him. "You courted the *wrong* woman for the last six months, Zeke."

"No." He fished the black-and-white sketch out of his wallet and handed it to her. "You match the sketch. That's why I had to meet you, to confirm you were the right Theresa Nichols."

She yanked the sketch out of his hand, took one look at it, then her face went white and she sucked in her breath. "Is Lyman Peressini your client?"

"Who? I don't know anyone named Lyman." He sat up, suddenly alert as fear rolled off her. "What's wrong? Why are you afraid?"

She jerked her gaze around the room as she jumped to her feet. "Because Lyman Peressini drew that sketch of me two days before he tried to murder me. He's the only one who would have the sketch, and the fact he's looking for me now means he's ready to do it right this time."

Zeke could smell the musky scent of her terror and anger, and he knew she believed her words. "T, calm down. I'm sure you're mistaken—"

But she was already gone.

Before he could decide whether to go after her, a loud crash from the front of the restaurant had him sprinting for the foyer.

Five

Zeke jumped over the upended dessert cart, sprinted out the front door of the bar, and vaulted down the steps to the sidewalk. Theresa was across the street, trying to hail a cab. "Theresa! Wait!"

A cab stopped, Theresa climbed in, and Zeke bolted across the street, slamming his hands down on the hood as it started to pull away. "Wait!"

The back door flew open and Theresa jumped out. "Get out of the way! I have to get out of here."

"Why?" He grabbed the door before she could close it, his fingers closing over her wrist. The shock that went through him at the contact didn't even startle him, not with this much adrenaline racing though him. "Talk to me."

She jerked her arm free with enough force to slam him against the side of the cab. Her mouth opened in horror. "Oh, crud. I'm sorry, Zeke. Are you hurt?"

"No." Confusion warred with old memories as he pulled himself back to his feet. "What's going on, T?"

"Later. He's probably here." Her gaze shot to the nearby roofs, and Zeke instinctively followed her glance.

"I don't see any snipers," he said. "I think you're safe for the moment." He rubbed his elbow where it had smashed into the car door. "I don't know about whoever drew that sketch of you, but it's not my client, I swear."

She hesitated, her gaze searching his. "How do you know?"

"Because I'm the best at what I do." He reached past her and grabbed her purse off the seat of the cab. "I have very strict standards about who I take for clients, and I make certain I know who I'm working for. Someone with a background in attempted murder would never slip through my safeguards."

She took a deep breath, and he could see the pulse in her throat hammering as she continued to search the street. "Did your client know you were meeting me tonight? Did you tell him where we were meeting?"

"No to both." He sighed at her continued restlessness. Gone was the day where a woman felt protected by him. "Get in the cab. I'll see you home."

Her gaze flicked to his. "I don't have a home right now."

"So, where are you staying?"

She grimaced, and he saw a flash of vulnerability in her gaze. Then her jaw tightened and her gaze glittered. "I can't go to Quincy's and endanger Mona," she muttered to herself. "I'll go to Becca's." She grabbed her purse from Zeke and climbed into the cab.

"Who's Mona? Who's Becca?" Zeke slipped in before she could slam the door on him. As long as he had a first name, he'd be able to find anyone, including "Becca." Theresa wouldn't be able to hide from him, not if he wanted to find her.

She glared at him. "You lied to me. Get out."

"You lied to me. I'd say we're even."

She scooted across the seat and got out on the other side. As soon as she started walking down the street, he groaned and jumped out of the cab. It drove away as soon as he got the door shut, he noted with satisfaction as he broke into an easy jog to catch up to Theresa. "Cab's gone."

She ignored him, keeping a steady pace while she continued to scan her environment.

Her tension began to affect him as he walked beside her, and a prickly awareness settled on the back of his neck, made his fingers twitch. He was going to need a full night of jazz and yoga to come down after this experience. At least three hours of meditation as well, to make a dent in the cold tension in his shoulders. "T, I swear I didn't endanger you. You really did inherit money. Can you please calm down? Your tension is really getting to me."

She shot him a venomous look. "Screw you, Zeke Siccardi."

"Fine." He stopped walking. "If that's the way you want it, I'm out of here. I don't need this crap in my life."

"Good." She didn't even look back.

Zeke watched her walk away with a surge of regret. "The money's still yours."

"Keep it," she shouted.

Zeke gritted his teeth and forced his fists to uncurl. *Easy, Zeke. Take it down a couple of levels.* This kind of stimulation was dangerous for him. Theresa Nichols needed to keep on walking out of his life.

But he couldn't force himself to return to the bar to retrieve his briefcase. Instead, he stood on the sidewalk and watched her until she was a speck in the distance. Then he sighed and started following her. He knew she was mistaken about his client, but he couldn't shake the tension vibrating through him. He'd never be able to decompress unless he'd assured himself she was safe, not after the genuine fear that she'd been emanating. He'd follow her to make sure she got home without incident and then walk away. For good.

His resolve lasted for six blocks, until he saw a dark figure grab Theresa around the neck and yank her out of sight. "Hey!" He bolted after her, violence spewing off him so thickly he could practically hear it hitting the ground behind him.

"Son of a bitch!" Theresa cradled her head as she was flung into a Dumpster, the pain of the collision vibrating down to her pedicure. She lurched to her feet as an annoying man in too much black circled her, waving a knife in her direction. "Idiot. Do you really think you can hurt me with that?"

He lifted his lip in a sneer and lunged at her.

She jerked to the left, shuddering as the blade glanced off her hip. Shit, she was out of practice. Slow, even for her human form. He snickered and circled around, blocking her exit from the alley.

She ought to change to a dragon and watch him scream in fear before she killed his sorry ass, but the mere thought of being in dragon form made her stomach lurch. "You will not make me become a dragon, you bastard."

He lunged for her again, and she dropped to the ground and slammed her foot into the side of his knee. His scream echoed through the air as he went down, his blade clattering uselessly by his feet.

Pain radiated up her arm and she rolled over, pulling her wrist out from under her butt. She flexed it and flinched. Sprained, or possibly broken.

She sighed. Some dragon she was. Couldn't even defend herself from a pathetic human without hurting herself. Justine would laugh her ass off if she knew Theresa had broken her own wrist by sitting on the damn thing. Gone were the days where she could take down a dragon slayer and—oomph. A thud hit her from behind, and her assailant rolled on top of her, grinding her face into the gritty ground. "Would you cut it out already?" She bucked to get him off her, but all he did was laugh and dig his knee into her back.

Could she get more pathetic?

His weight shifted and she saw his arm reach past her head. Theresa saw the glitter of the knife just beyond his fingertips and scowled. She'd never live it down if she let some street punk behead her with a five-inch blade. She was a dragon, for God's sake! A vicious killer! She flung her arm out to block him, then yelped as her injured wrist bent back. Dammit! Why couldn't it heal already? She was in a battle!

He laughed and his fingers closed over the knife. "He said you'd be a challenge. Either I'm really good, or you suck."

"I don't suck!" Rage ripped through her and she flung herself upward. He flew off her and collided with a trash bag, flipping over it and landing with a thud on his back. "Loser."

She ran over to him and had him pinned with her body before he could move. Her torn and bloody camisole brushed her arm, and she reared back in true dragon fury.

"Do you realize how long it's been since I've killed anyone? I'm going to enjoy this." Even as she spoke, her deepest dragon instincts were gathering strength, the fire bubbling in her chest. She closed her eyes for a moment, trying to control it long enough to get some answers. He twitched under her and she slammed her uninjured hand to his throat. "Don't piss me off."

His eyes widened, and she knew her eyes were probably going all dragon-on-a-rampage on him. Very difficult to explain golden eyes rimmed with flames to your average human. Yet another reason to kill him. She leaned down until her face was almost touching his, then blew a small puff of smoke into his mouth. "Tell me where Lyman Peressini is or you die an ugly and painful death."

The man's face paled. "Who? I don't know Lyman."

She frowned.

"Who's Lyman?" her assailant rasped.

"A bastard." Lyman had been her partner in crime when they were young dragons, causing trouble all through the Village of Uruloke. Her parents had believed that their daughter should experience the fun in life before shouldering the responsibilities of being the most socially elite and richest dragon family in the Village of Uruloke, so they'd been happy to buy her way out of any trouble, giving her license to play. And Lyman had been too far outside the fringes of acceptable society to care if he got in trouble.

The two of them together had been bad news, but in a lighthearted, harmless way. When she'd run into Lyman decades later, he'd become deadly. Evil. And when she'd realized it, he'd tried to kill her before she could expose him and his organized crime ring to Satan, whom he'd betrayed. "If it wasn't Lyman, then who hired you?"

He was trembling beneath her. "I don't know, I swear I don't."

Unfortunately, she believed him. He smelled too desperate and terrified to lie. "So, how'd you get the contract?"

"I got the envelope and cash earlier today, with a description of you," he answered immediately. "If you showed up at NightGames, I was supposed to kill you. That's all I know. I've had the ad in the paper for weeks and this was the first job I'd gotten. I wasn't going to turn it down. Will you let me go now? I've told you everything."

"Shut up. You're babbling." What kind of contract killer put an ad in the paper? And was it really Lyman's style to use someone so inadequate? Last time she'd been fighting for her life around him, he'd been surrounded by a bunch of badass henchmen who had easily overpowered her, even in dragon form. As an out-of-shape human, she'd be no match for Lyman's assassins today.

A cascade of tension sparks shot out of her nose and sizzled out on the cement, and she cursed at the slip. Didn't she have any control over herself anymore?

"Don't kill me," he rasped. "I swear I'll never come near you again."

"Damn right you won't. You'll be hanging out with Satan instead." She tried not to be swayed by his begging for mercy. As much as she liked killing, she had certain moral standards, one of which involved not killing someone who was cowering like a puppy. She needed another reason to kill him, since he wasn't an immediate threat to her anymore. "How many people have you killed in your life?"

"Dozens."

"Really? You're not very good at it."

He blanched. "Well, you were supposed to be my first one, actually."

Well, crapola. He hadn't even killed anyone and was practically prostrating himself for mercy. Bastard. How dare he ruin her night by not even being killable?

"T?"

She jerked her head up to see Zeke standing in the entrance to the alley. He was breathing heavily, and his face was strained.

"Lucky you," she whispered to her captive. "I can't kill you with witnesses. But if you ever take another contract, I'll burn you alive. Capiche?"

He nodded, and she stood up, mildly satisfied by the terror cascading off him. It was fun to be bad. He sprinted past Zeke, and Theresa faced Zeke, keeping to the shadows in case her eyes were still doing their dragon thing. God, she needed to burn something up, and if Zeke pissed her off right now, he might be her target. "What do you want?" The look of shock on his face was slightly alarming, making Theresa wonder how much he'd seen. "Zeke?"

"Are you . . ." His voice croaked and he had to clear it. "Are you a dragon?"

She froze at his question. That he knew enough to ask that question set all sorts of warnings off in her mind. Adrenaline racing, she did what she used to do best with men, and yanked up her camisole to reveal her already-healing stab wound and the underside of her breast. "He stabbed me and you're babbling about dragons? What's wrong with you? I'm *injured*."

He blinked, and he glanced at her stomach, as she knew he would. "What?"

She frowned at his failure to drop to his knees and declare himself her knight at the sight of her injured body. "I'm bleeding. Go call an ambulance."

He jerked his gaze back up to her face. "Are you a dragon?"

Tenacious little bugger, wasn't he? Not good. She let her shirt drop back down and tried again. "Are you insane? You're actually asking me if I'm a dragon?"

"Answer the question."

"No, I'm not." The panic induced by his question had curbed the worst of her dragon instincts, and she knew her eyes had returned to normal, so she stepped back into the light and walked over to him. She poked him in the chest and glared at him, trying an offensive tactic. "You do realize that wasn't a random attack, don't you? That man was sent by your client, Lyman Peressini. Thanks to you, there's now a contract out on me."

He blinked. "You think that was a hit by my client? It couldn't have been. I did my research."

"It was your client." She picked up her purse and scowled at him, glad that guilt had distracted him even if her body hadn't. "You lied to me and you exposed me to a man who wants me dead. You're a jerk and if you ever bother me again, I'm calling the cops." She scooped her purse off the ground, tucked it under her arm, and stalked past him, her heart thudding with his betrayal and the thought of Lyman out there, searching for her.

She flagged down a cab and turned to glare at him

before she got in. "All I can say is that I'm glad I'm out of my cell, because I don't need you for anything anymore. Get a life, Zeke."

Then she got into the cab and slammed the door.

Zeke didn't even move. He simply stood there and let her drive away.

Zeke caught up to Theresa's assailant three blocks from the site of the attack. The man was tense and agitated, and nearly wet himself when Zeke tapped his shoulder. "Excuse me."

The guy whirled around, his eyes wide. "What?"

Zeke took a deep breath, forcing away his desire to slam the man into the brick wall for touching Theresa. *That's not your thing anymore, remember?* Instead, he smiled pleasantly, the itch on the back of his neck growing stronger by the second. "I was just wondering about your altercation with that woman back there."

The man blanched. "I won't go near her again, I swear."

Zeke forced the muscles in his face to relax, ordered his hands to stay by his sides. "How did you pick her? That's all I want to know."

"This." The man dug into his pocket and thrust a piece of paper at Zeke. "Take it. I don't want it."

"What's this?" Zeke unfolded it, then clenched his jaw when he saw it was the same black-and-white sketch of Theresa that he'd been working from. God. He'd been a fool. He crushed the sketch in his fist. "Who are you working for?"

"I don't know. Like I told her, it was anonymous."

Zeke summoned up his favorite jazz song and let it run

through his head, swaying to the beat to try to stay calm. "Give me all the details. Now."

Less than forty-five minutes after the attempted assassination, Theresa was still shaking from the incident, from the realization that Lyman had found her. Her injured wrist was almost healed already, so she didn't bother with wrapping it. Instead, she'd raided Becca's closet for comfort clothes, and had just finished putting on a pair of pale blue sweats and a baby-soft T-shirt when someone pounded on Becca's front door. She yelped and dove behind an armchair, her heart thudding.

Someone pounded again, and she realized what she was doing. Dragons didn't hide, not even from other dragons who could kick their ass. Besides, it wasn't as if hiding behind a chair would save her from Lyman. Her only hope was to make him think she was more of an opponent than she was.

She forced herself to stand up, grabbed a nearby lamp, ripped the cord out of the wall, and held it over her head. He would kill her, but heaven help her, she was going to do her best to damage him before she went down.

Clenching the lamp, she eased toward the door, wishing Becca was back from harvesting souls. She could use a little fireball backup. She peeked through the spy hole, then the lamp fell from her fingers and she yanked the door open. "Zeke? What happened to you?"

He had a scratch on his left cheek and his beautiful shirt was torn and filthy. His hair was in total disarray, and he looked much more like the bad boy she'd imagined him to be. *Delicious.* He held up his hand for silence and leaned against the doorjamb. "First of all, I owe you an apology. You were right about my client. I don't know how it happened, but I screwed up."

At his confirmation, she had to grab the doorframe for balance as the room suddenly tilted. *Lyman really was after her.* He wanted to find her so badly that he'd hired Zeke.

But how could Lyman still be alive? When she'd gone back to find him after escaping his clutches, everyone said he'd perished in a fire that had destroyed half the town. A fire that had wiped out her family's holdings, the ones Lyman had usurped for himself.

How much worse had he become in the 180 years since she'd last seen him? She pressed her hand to her forehead and closed her eyes, trying to keep the nausea at bay.

"T? I apologized."

She dropped her hand, lifted her chin, and gratefully focused on being angry at Zeke, instead of afraid of Lyman. "And what about lying to me? Any apologies for that?"

He rubbed his temples and gave a soft groan. "Part of the job. It's what I do, but it's over now."

She scowled. "You don't get forgiven just like that."

A muscle ticked in his cheek. "Don't push me tonight, T. I'm on the edge."

"Oh, and I'm not? In case you didn't notice, someone tried to kill me tonight."

The muscle ticked more fiercely. "I noticed." He closed his eyes and took a deep breath. She could practically feel him willing himself to calm down. He opened his eyes and fastened his deep brown gaze on her. "Who *are* you?"

She shook her head and started to shut the door. "Leave me alone."

"No." He shoved his way inside, a show of masculine stubbornness that made her want to grab his belt and yank him against her. "I'm extremely expensive, and someone paid me a lot of money to find you. Why?"

"Why should I tell you? So you can betray me to someone else?" She stepped back as he paced the living room, a tightly strung energy rolling off him. Energy that seemed vaguely alarming, but familiar as well.

He came to a stop in front of her. "The betrayal was an accident, and I'm here to fix it. Tell me what's going on."

"Hah!" She tried to shove past him, but he caught her upper arms and held her in front of him. Heat flared in her from his touch, and she had a sudden yearning to throw herself into his arms and beg him to ravage her. She tensed and tried to clear her mind. "Let go of me."

He released her so quickly she stumbled, his face strained.

"For your information," she announced, "I don't make a habit of trusting my secrets to men who set me up to be killed. You lost your chance with me, Zeke, so leave me alone."

He studied her for a long moment. "I can't leave until I get the answer to one question."

"Fine. What's the question?"

"Are you a dragon?"

All her dragon senses flared into self-defense mode, and she eased back from him, her instincts suddenly reacting to him as a threat. "What's it to you?"

He met her gaze for a moment, then her nose was flooded with the most amazing scent of burning pine, of fresh woods, of earth, of melting chocolate. She had just enough time to panic, and then her legs gave out and she collapsed in a puddle of ecstasy.

Zeke caught Theresa before she hit the ground, cradling her, adrenaline spiking through him as her skin burned through his shirt.

"Oh, my God," she moaned as she wrapped her arms around him and nuzzled the crook of his neck. "You're a *dragon slayer.*"

"Ex-slayer." He staggered as she ran her fingers through his hair and showered frantic kisses on his throat. *Shit.* He hadn't meant to hit her that hard with his scent. All he'd wanted was to see if she reacted, since he knew she'd never tell him the truth.

"This explains a lot," she mumbled as she tried to unbutton his shirt. "I knew you couldn't have been good enough at cybersex to make me monogamous. God, you're an asshole." She got his shirt open and pressed her face to his chest, inhaling deeply. "You smell so amazing. You're going to kill me, aren't you? Ooh . . ."

"No." He made it to the couch and set her down. He tried to pull back, but she clutched at his shoulders, fighting to keep him near. Her eyes were closed, her body arching toward him. Old instincts swirled to the surface, and he had to look away from her exposed throat. "I'm an ex-slayer. Ex." *Remember, Zeke? Ex.*

"You can't be an *ex*-slayer. You are or you aren't." She tried to hit him, but she missed and nearly fell off the couch in a sluggish mound of female curves.

"Come on, T." He pulled her back up and held her upright on the couch. "I didn't release that much scent. Help me out here."

"Help you?" She blinked at him, her eyes glazed as she swayed toward him. "Help you kill me?"

"No." He stepped back, clutching his fists against the instincts pushing at him to do what he was born to do. "Help me resist."

"Resist? Hah. You slayers don't resist." She slid off the couch and rolled onto her back, her fingers reaching for him as she ground her hips into the carpet. "I can't believe this." She moaned with distress and desire. "I can't believe I want to have sex with you when I know you're about to kill me!"

Zeke closed his eyes against the need raging through him, the primal urge to follow his destiny, to destroy. *She's just a dragon, Slayer. They all deserve to die. Kill her now.* He cursed and shook his aching head. "I gotta go. I'll be in touch."

"Zeke!"

He sprinted for the door and slammed it shut behind him, his body pulsing with centuries-old needs that he'd kept at bay for so long.

Six

Still twitching with guilt and a raging need to slay after leaving Theresa in a gyrating pile on the floor, Zeke flung open the door to his apartment, kicked it shut behind him, and walked directly over to his CD player and turned on his favorite jazz piece. Then he sat down on the floor, turned his palms faceup, and tried to focus on peace. On the soft breeze off the ocean. On the sound of water rushing over the falls.

Theresa is a dragon.

He shook his head and shut that awareness out of his mind. The gentle blue of a cloudless sky.

I need to kill her.

Dammit!

He forced his muscles to relax, starting with his forehead. Ease the tension of his jaw. Let his tongue fall away from his teeth.

The dragon cannot be permitted to live. It is my destiny.

He grimaced but didn't open his eyes. The sky was fucking blue, the damn birds were chirping, and *I need to slay. It's been too long. I can't deny my heritage any longer.*

With a growl, he jerked his eyes open and rolled to his feet.

Forget meditation. It wasn't happening tonight.

Work, instead.

He stalked over to the computer and slammed his hand down on the mouse, opening his file on Ralph Greene, the attorney who'd hired him to find Theresa on behalf of some anonymous client.

He scowled at the screen as he scanned all the data from his background search on Greene, the one he'd done before he agreed to take the Theresa Nichols case. Everything seemed legit. He leaned back in his chair, clasped his hands behind his head, and stared out at the flashing lights of the city. So, Greene was either in the dark about the true nature of his client, or he knew exactly what he was doing and was great at covering up. Third possibility was that he didn't care either way.

Zeke drummed his fingers on his head and let his mind range over all his conversations with Greene. He finally ended up on their last talk. Something had happened to make Greene increase the pressure yesterday.

The question was, what was it?

He propped his feet up on his desk and hit the speaker on his landline. Dialed Greene's cell phone.

Greene answered on the second ring. "Greene, here."

"It's Siccardi."

Greene wasted no time on pleasantries. "Well? Did you locate Theresa Nichols?"

"I have a question for you first." He slid open his center desk drawer and pulled out a jeweled dagger, one he used for letter opening these days. The blade was inscribed with his name and the title of Dragon Slayer. His dad had given it to him during his Ascending Ceremony. It was the only weapon from his past he kept around.

"All I need is an answer," Greene said. "Did you find her, or not?"

"Have you ever put a contract out on someone?" Zeke traced the blade. Still as sharp as it had been the day he'd received it.

Greene hesitated for a split second. "You mean, a contract for someone to be killed?"

"Yep."

"Never. I'm extremely offended by the question, and I'm going to inform my client that I no longer recommend your services."

"The sketch you gave me of Theresa Nichols was in the pocket of a man who was paid to kill her tonight. He was sent the sketch and some money earlier today, and was told to watch out for a woman fitting Theresa's description at the place I was to meet her. Either you set up the hit, or your client did." He flipped the knife, caught it by the blade, then flung it across the room. It landed with a thud in the doorframe. "So, give me the name of your client, or I report you to the cops and to the Board of Bar Overseers. I have all your emails, the sketch you sent me, and the hit man's willingness to testify that you were the one who paid him."

"But I never—"

"Your choice. What's it going to be?" He spun around in his chair and studied the knife, wedged in the doorframe. It had felt good to throw it. Too good. Finally, he sighed and stood up.

"I can't divulge the name of my client. I would lose all credibility and—"

"Not nearly as much as you would if you wind up on trial for arranging a hit on someone." He picked up the phone handset and walked across the room, keeping his voice calm and nonconfrontational, with a hint of threat laced through it. He yanked the blade out of the wood, instinctively wiped the steel off on his pants, then shook his head. There was no blood on it. Just a bit of sawdust. "Give me his name, Greene." He fingered the dagger, studying the emeralds in the well-worn handle. It deserved better than being stuck in a drawer. Surely, he could handle seeing it on a regular basis, couldn't he?

"Give me a minute."

"Sure." He walked into his kitchen and pulled a paring knife out of his knife rack. Then he slid the dagger in its place and stood back to inspect. It was a good fit. Slicing tomatoes wasn't much of an improvement on opening mail, but at least it would be cutting open something that used to be alive. He took a package of deli turkey out of the fridge, set it on the cutting board, then shredded it with the dagger. He was grinning when he was less than halfway through.

"Okay," Ralph said.

He wiped the blade clean on his pants. "What's his name?"

"Edgar Vesuvius. He's a lawyer in London handling the estate."

"Spell it." Zeke carved the name into the cutting board. "Contact info?" He added a phone number, a street address, and then had to flip the board over to fit the email address on there. "How does he pay you?"

"He hasn't paid me yet. I haven't produced Theresa Nichols."

Zeke slammed the knifepoint into the board, then

flicked it to watch it vibrate. "Forward me all emails from him and mail me all written correspondence."

"That's taking it too far," Greene protested. "I'll get disbarred. Trust me, if he's a murderer, I want him exposed as well. I'll go through my files and if I find anything else that might help you, I'll send it on."

"Why don't I come by the office now and help you?"

"I'm not at work! It's almost midnight!"

Zeke grinned. "Sorry. Forgot." *I'll search your office alone, thanks for the invite.* His call-waiting beeped. "I gotta go. I want that info first thing in the morning, or I'm going to the cops."

"You promise you won't—"

Zeke hung up on Greene and clicked over. "T?"

"T?" a familiar voice bellowed. "Who the hell's T?"

Jesus. A voice from his past. Very distant past. Adrenaline rushed over Zeke at the sound of his best friend's voice. His former best friend and protégé, Alex Montageaux. Alex had been Zeke's right hand the day of the Dragon Cleansing, but their friendship hadn't been able to survive the slayer/ex-slayer rift. They hadn't spoken in ages. "Everything okay?"

"I need to call in the blood oath you owe me."

Zeke caught his breath and gripped the edge of the counter, letting his head drop forward. "That was almost 350 years ago, Alex. You were eight years old."

"You pulling out?"

"You know I'm not." This was one debt he couldn't walk away from, a debt that was greater than any desire he had to save his own soul. He closed his eyes, dread and anticipation racing through him. Last he'd heard, Alex had taken over the band of slayers Zeke had created. Slayers had one mission in life. One goal. There was only one thing Alex would need his help on. "What do you need?"

"Meet us at . . ." Alex's voice became muffled as he turned away from the phone. "What's the name of this joint?" he shouted.

Zeke closed his eyes and tried to think of blue sky and day lilies, but all he could see was the Village of Uruloke, burning to the ground as the bodies of dragons littered the earth. As the last of the European dragons were eliminated.

"We're at some dive called Poison II," Alex said.

"In New York." His voice sounded dead, but his body was pulsating with an energy he couldn't suppress.

"Hell, yes, in New York. You coming or what?"

"Yes." Zeke closed his eyes against a surge of need, not only for the slaying, but for the camaraderie and bond that he shared only with other slayers.

"Good. Make it fast." He hung up.

Zeke didn't move for five minutes. He leaned against the counter and made himself think about the little dragon he'd orphaned. The one that had made him walk away from his heritage for good. He recalled slaying its parents, then walking around the corner to find it cowering. He smelled the burning buildings, the metallic scent of blood. He heard the roars of dragons fighting for their lives. He breathed the smoke, felt it burning his lungs and stinging his eyes. He replayed the scene in his mind until it was so entrenched he knew he'd have nightmares for a week.

It was only then that he grabbed his dagger and walked out of his apartment.

Poison II was crowded and loud. The testosterone in the bar was crawling over Zeke's skin like a flirty woman in skimpy clothing. He stopped just inside the door, for the sole reason that he wanted to rush inside and let the dark energies consume him.

There was a reason he spent his evenings with his favorite jazz recording or a solo dinner at a five-star restaurant. Temptation.

He surveyed the mass of bodies, smelled the scents of sex, of perfume, of sweat, and clenched his fists to keep from plunging into the masses and absorbing every deviant sensation he could find.

His fists tightened when a heavily muscled man in jeans and steel-toed shitkickers walked toward him. Alex came to a stop in front of him, his shaved head reflecting the dim fluorescent lights of the bar. "Siccardi."

Zeke nodded. "Alex."

There was a tense silence, then Alex grinned and slammed his beefy hand down on Zeke's shoulder. "Damn, it's good to see you."

And just like that, Zeke's resistance vanished and the two men embraced. He thudded Alex on the back with his fists and felt the bruises forming on his back from Alex's greeting. Alex swung his arm around Zeke's shoulders and directed Zeke into the depths of the bar. "It's been so long, Siccardi. I thought you'd be old and fat by now."

"I'm only ten years older than you, and you're the one who looks like you've been stalking too many kitchens." He grinned and let the energies of the bar settle in his pores. It had been so long since he'd been with one of his kind, someone who understood him, who was connected to him through their heritage.

"Yeah, but I'm still faster than you."

"You were never faster."

"I'm faster and stronger."

Zeke grinned at the familiar argument, a feeling of peace settling in his limbs. "Slower and weaker, plus your ego makes you vulnerable."

Alex shot him a smug look. "Not anymore. I'd kick your ass any time."

Zeke raised his brow and saw the glint of true self-confidence in Alex's eyes. His friend had changed and become a leader. He nodded his acknowledgment, and Alex nodded back.

Alex set his hand on Zeke's shoulder and drew him to a stop in front of a corner table. Zeke inspected the two men seated there. One he knew, the other looked vaguely familiar. The one with short dark hair and black eyes jumped up and wrapped Zeke in a smothering hug and pounded his back. "Zeke, man! It's about time you came back! We missed your sorry ass!"

Zeke couldn't help but grin, and he thudded Marcus's back just as hard. "Missed you, too, Marcus. How's the woman?"

Marcus's dark face gleamed with happiness. "Kicking my ass every chance she gets, of course. She's withholding sex until I promise that if she has a son, I won't take him away and apprentice him to another slayer. I'm getting desperate enough to promise."

"Promise her. The old ways are wrong."

"Spoken like a man who understands my need for sex." Marcus laughed.

"Or a man who's still trying to pretend he's not one of us," the man still sitting in the booth said. His red hair was cut in a flattop, and he had a long scar where his left ear used to be.

"No way," Marcus said. "Zeke's our man. He wouldn't let us down." He looked at Zeke. "Right?"

Zeke pressed his lips together and felt his relaxation begin to ebb.

Marcus's laughter faded and his eyes took on a shadowed look. "Seriously? But you're here. I thought—"

"He's here because he owes me," Alex said. "I haven't told him what I need yet."

"He won't help," the third man said.

Marcus glanced between Zeke and the seated man. "But he will. He has to."

The third man stood up, leaned in toward Zeke, then slammed Zeke in the jaw with his fist.

Zeke staggered against the table, quelling the urge to strike back. "What the hell was that for?"

The redhead flashed missing teeth at Zeke. "So I could tell people I kicked Zeke Siccardi's ass and lived to tell about it. Look at you. You're not even thinking about hitting me back." He sat back down with a sneer of disgust. "He's useless. We should kill him."

Alex leaned over the man, with one hand on the table and the other on the seat behind the redhead. He said something quietly, and the redhead's gaze flicked to Zeke, then he nodded, and Alex stood up. "Rathe will behave. Have a seat, Zeke."

Zeke tested his jaw as he eased into a chair. "And you wonder why I don't hang with you guys anymore."

"You used to be the first one to lay out any newcomer," Alex said. "You've changed."

"Yep." Zeke ignored the pitcher of beer and empty glass in front of him and flagged a waitress to order a Perrier, ignoring the look of surprise on Marcus's face and the sneer on Rathe's. Alex simply looked resigned. "So, what's up?"

Alex grinned. "You look worried. You afraid I'm going to ask you to kill a dragon?"

Zeke shrugged, his knee bouncing restlessly under the table. "The thought had crossed my mind."

"I respect your decision to no longer slay." Alex held up his arm, showing the scar down his forearm from their blood oath. "I won't ask you to kill a dragon, brother."

Zeke met Alex's intense gaze, and a sudden yearning for the bond they used to share swept over him. "Thanks."

"I just need you to point one out for me, and I'll kill it. Put your missing persons skills to work for your brothers."

The faint twitch of alarm tingled at the back of Zeke's neck, but he kept his body and face relaxed. "What are you talking about?"

"We got wind of a dragon in the area. Female. Last we heard, she goes by the name Theresa Nichols, but that might not be current info."

No shit? What the hell was so special about Theresa that she had so many people trying to kill her? Zeke's fists tightened beneath the table, but he kept his expression neutral and leaned forward. "What's the deal with her? Why does your client want her?"

Alex shrugged. "Who knows? I just kill them."

Zeke pursed his lips, his mind racing. He and Theresa were going to have to have a little chat.

"Zeke? You in?" Alex asked.

He avoided the question by asking one of his own. "Is this a paying gig?" Back in the day, there was no such thing as being paid for slaying. It was simply what slayers did. Today, there were so few dragons around and so few slayers that the business had changed. It had become a specialty profession that paid very well. The few dragons that had survived the European Cleansing at the Village of Uruloke and the copycat cleansings on other continents were good at staying hidden.

Alex nodded. "We have a client with a deep pocket who wants the female. Usually, he finds the dragons himself and calls us in to take them out. They're almost always dominant, aggressive males. This is the first female he's asked us to kill, though." He gestured at the team. "Takes all three of us working together to take out the males he finds, but I'm thinking this female won't be too much trouble. We get a nice bonus if we get it done within the next seven days."

"Who's your client?" Zeke slapped at the back of his neck as the urge to slay suddenly flared up. "It wouldn't be a Lyman Peressini, would it?"

Alex raised his brows. "It's anonymous. Always is. It's how I like it. Humans get testy when they find dead people. I prefer not to have clients who can identify me when the bodies are found."

"We always kill them when they're in human form nowadays," Rathe explained, giving Zeke a condescending look. "Humans would never be able to handle dead dragons littering their naive little world."

Zeke shook out his arms as the twitch began to work its way down them. God, he wanted to do it. To sink his blade into the neck of a dragon, watching its lifeblood pour out . . . he cursed and wiped the sweat off his forehead. "I can't help you."

Alex leaned forward. "I'm calling in my marker on this one."

The scar on his forearm pulsed. Zeke rubbed his knuckles against it. "Why use the marker for this? Surely one dragon isn't worth it."

"The female is." Something flickered in Alex's eyes. Worry. Anger. Desperation.

Zeke looked around the table. Marcus looked curious, and Rathe looked sullen. Zeke was certain Marcus didn't know what was going on. He was too simple to put on a face. Rathe was an unknown entity. He let his gaze settle on Alex. "What's really going on?"

"Find the dragon."

Zeke's scar burned, and he knew he couldn't refuse Alex. But he couldn't be responsible for the death of another dragon. Especially not Theresa. He simply couldn't. Pointing a team of slayers toward a dragon was the same thing as wielding the blade himself.

He needed time to assess. He needed more information. He needed to get away from his kindred spirits before he grabbed his blade and led the way to Theresa's condo. He stood up and threw some cash on the table to cover his water, sweeping the bottle up in his hand. "I'm leaving."

Rathe looked disgusted, but Zeke ignored him and started to walk away.

"Zeke?" Alex called after him.

Zeke didn't turn around. He heard Rathe mutter, "I told you we should kill him."

Then Alex said, "Don't worry. He'll help. He just needs time to adjust."

He heard their beer steins clank together in victory, and a part of him wanted to go back and join the men who were once his life.

Instead, he clutched his Perrier and walked out of the bar, wishing he could have been lucky enough to have a blood brother who was a priest. Or a Boy Scout.

Hell, even an environmentalist would suffice.

Seven

Theresa awoke to the smell of leather and the stench of city streets. She pressed her hands to her throbbing head and groaned in protest at the sunlight burning her eyes. God, she felt awful.

Something firm nudged her cheek. "Wake up."

She frowned at the sound of Becca's voice and peeled her eyes open. The toe of Becca's black leather boot tapped Theresa's chin. "Time to rise and shine, Dragon."

"Your shoe smells horrible." She shut her eyes. "Go away. I need to die in peace."

"You can't die on my living room floor. I have nowhere to store your body."

"Your floor?" Theresa opened her eyes again and peered up. Becca was standing over her, her forehead furrowed with what could be mistaken for concern. She was wearing black leather pants, a metal-studded bustier, and way too much dark makeup. Obviously, she was just getting off Rivka nighttime duty. "Why am I on your floor?"

"That was going to be my question. After I asked you why you're wearing my clothes." Becca squatted next to her. "If you can revive yourself from your night of binge drinking, or whatever it is you've been doing, your new boss wants to have a word with you."

Theresa propped herself up on her elbow, blinking to adjust to the blinding morning sun. "What boss?"

"Satan."

"Crap." She rubbed her eyes and looked around the living room. Satan was on the couch, watching the television intently.

The sight of the couch brought back all the memories of last night with Zeke and his pheromones, and she jumped to her feet, then clutched Becca's arm as she swayed. "Am I alive?"

"Why wouldn't you be?"

She dug her fingers into Becca's arm. "Answer the question."

"Yes, you're alive."

She sighed with relief, then frowned as she assimilated the significance of the fact she was still in the mortal world. She'd never heard of a slayer leaving an incapacitated dragon alive. It simply didn't happen. Oh, God. *Zeke was a slayer.* She pressed her palm to her head against the sudden increase of pain.

"Dragon!" Satan snapped his fingers at the television. "This Reverend Munsey you mentioned, whom you sought help from. Is this him?"

"What?" As Becca ducked into the bedroom, Theresa glanced at the television, where a man with flyaway blond hair and white robes was gesticulating. "Yeah, why?"

"Interesting." He leaned forward, staring intently at the television. "Do you think he has Otherworld powers? Is that why you thought he could turn you into a human?"

"I don't know. I figured it was worth asking." She

wiggled her shoulders and tried to focus. Chills crawled down her arms and she rubbed her biceps, trying to generate some blood flow.

"Does Reverend Munsey get good ratings?"

She frowned at Satan. "I guess so. He was written up in the *Times* a few months ago."

"Hmm . . ." Satan stood up and faced her. "I came here to torture you for fun, but I have a new plan that is most impressive. You will arrange for me to be a guest on this ugly man's show. Many viewers. Most excellent for recruiting purposes. I have a new accountant soul, and he explained that my expenses are outpacing my recruiting."

Theresa blinked. "I don't know Reverend Munsey. I can't get you on the show."

"It is our agreement. You must." He beamed at her. "Sunday night at nine. My schedule is open. Iris will be most impressed if I am on a national television show endorsed by God, and I will also acquire more souls. Once again, I prove why I am Satan." Then he vanished in a poof of gold bubbles.

"Lucky dragon." Becca walked back into the room, now wearing a sharp black suit and demure makeup, in the fastest clothing and makeup change Theresa had ever seen. "I thought for sure he was going to cut off your arm or something. He spent the morning trying to get Iris to support his petition to have Satan Jr. released from Afterlife prison. She must have pelted him with over a hundred water balloons before he got too melted to continue. He was in such a rage when he got back to hell."

Theresa would have liked to have seen the water balloon attack. After seeing water melt Satan's son into a pile of goo, she could imagine how much fun it would be to melt Satan. Of course, Iris was the only one he'd allow to melt him. Anyone else would be dead by the time the first water balloon hit him in the head.

"I don't know which pissed him off more, the fact he'd failed with Satan Jr. or that Iris is once again immune to his charm," Becca continued as she walked to the fridge and pulled out a bottled water. "Lucky for you, he doesn't like to torture people unless they're conscious. By the time I was able to wake you up, he'd started watching that Reverend Munsey show." She whistled softly. "You should buy a lottery ticket today, Dragon."

"Yeah, lucky me." Being alive and untortured was sort of balanced by the fact that her childhood friend and mortal enemy Lyman Peressini had found her and her cyberlover was a slayer. "I don't really have time to be arranging Satan's media appearances."

"Be glad that's all you have to do. It could have been a lot worse."

"You mean, it could have been a lot better. If I'm going to spend time I don't have working for Satan, the least he could have done was have me go kill and torture some-one. Being his booking agent is almost as boring as baby-sitting Mona." Theresa frowned as she finally registered the significance of Becca's suit. "You're going to work?"

"I always go to work. I don't suppose I'll be lucky enough to have you gone by the time I get home?"

"Actually, you will." Since Zeke knew how to find her here, the chances that Lyman also did were too high. "I'm going to Quincy's, but don't tell if anyone asks."

Becca paused midsip of her coffee. "Are you in trouble?"

"Maybe."

"Really? What's up?"

She turned to the Rivka. "Really? You want to hear about it? I could really use some advice and—"

Becca cleared her throat and stood up. "Never mind. I just thought maybe there was someone you were going to kill, and I thought I could go along and nab his soul. If not, then I don't have time."

"Why are you so cold?"

Becca's eyes glittered. "Trust me, Dragon, you don't want to get close to me. It's for your own good."

"That's crap."

"I'm Satan's right hand, which means even if you and I were best friends, I'd have to kill you if he ordered me to." Dark red flashed in her eyes. "The mere fact we were friends might even be reason enough for him to give the order, depending on his mood."

Theresa cocked her head as she studied the Rivka's face. "Has he forced you to do that before?"

"I'm leaving." Becca slung her handbag over her shoulder and picked up her briefcase. "Keep in touch, okay? Derek asks about you every time he calls."

"Right. Derek." She didn't need Becca anyway. Or Zeke. She was human now, and it was time for her to find her own life. She picked up her outfit from last night and her new purse. "Have a good day. I'll see you around."

"Is that blood on your shirt?"

"Yes." Theresa shut the door on Becca's next question and walked out to start her new life.

On her way to Quincy's office to retrieve Mona, Theresa called the property manager who handled all the Guardians' safe houses. The Guardians' real estate assets were deeply hidden behind the veil of numerous fictional corporations, so as to keep the whereabouts of the Goblet untraceable.

As usual, he answered on the first ring. "Graham Winthrop, property manager. May I be of assistance?"

"Why do you always answer the phone so formally? You have my number in your speed dial and you know it's me." She loved teasing the proper gray-haired man who had no idea that the two women he'd been working for the last fifty years were actually the Guardians.

"Ah, Ms. Nichols. A pleasure, as always, to hear your lovely voice," Graham said in that warm voice Theresa loved, like Santa and your favorite grandpa rolled into one.

"Yes, as always. Listen, how are the repairs going on our condo?"

"They will be done in approximately four weeks. There was significant damage."

There was no curiosity at all in Graham's voice about what had caused all the damage. They paid him too much to be curious. "Well, do we have another location in New York City?"

She heard the typing of computer keys. "I'm sorry, but that is your only property within five hundred miles."

"Can you buy me a new one? I need a place within the hour, in the city, completely untraceable."

"It shall be done. Where shall I have the keys delivered?"

She paused to think for a moment. "To Quincy's office. I'll be there in about twenty minutes. I'll stay there until they arrive." Now that Quincy was the Interim Assistant Guardian, all his vitals were on record with Graham as well. "I need a couple of corporate credit cards, too. Justine took ours went she went on her honeymoon. Make sure my name isn't on any of the documentation for the credit cards or the condo."

"It never is, Ms. Nichols."

An excellent point. How had everyone been able to find her if she was untraceable? Would the new location even be safe? Not that she had a choice. She had to live somewhere. She'd just have to be careful until she could neutralize Lyman. Yeah, like that was going to be easy.

"Anything else, Ms. Nichols?"

"Nope, that's it. Thanks."

She hung up and hummed to herself as she leaned back in the cab. She sighed at the thought of never seeing her favorite slayer again, then chided herself. She was a human now. Independent. Self-sufficient. She was claiming her own life and didn't need Zeke anymore. Or Becca or anyone else. She'd find new friends and get a new life.

So there.

Theresa walked into Quincy's university office and found him sprawled back in his desk chair snoring. Mona was perched on the filing cabinet in the corner, and in front of her was a fresh cup of steaming espresso, and a thin man in a mismatched suit and glasses reaching for it.

"Hey!" she snapped. "Get away from that espresso machine!"

Quincy jerked upright, knocked his knee into the desk with a thud, and nearly fell over as he dove out of his chair toward Mona. "I told you my espresso machine was off-limits," he blurted as he scrambled toward the man in the corner. "Don't drink from her, Stuart, or I swear I'll have to kill you."

Stuart drew his shoulders up. "I've been grading exams for eleven consecutive hours. The coffeemaker in the lounge is broken, and I need caffeine. It's completely un-teamlike of you to be hoarding this for yourself."

Quincy stumbled to a stop in front of Stuart. "You poured some? Give it back."

Stuart hugged the cup to his chest. "No. It's mine."

Theresa folded her arms and leaned against the door-frame, waiting for the SOS from Quin. Because Quincy-the-math-geek would never be able to get Stuart or anyone else to do anything they didn't want to do.

"Did you drink any yet?" Quincy asked, showing a grasp of the situation that surprised Theresa. Usually he was too buried in his equations to waste brainpower on anything else.

Stuart's face turned red. "I had a drink earlier today. It's great espresso."

Theresa tensed. Stuart was now one-third immortal. What were they going to do with him? Kill him, of course, but if they murdered a professor on campus, someone was sure to notice. Damn Quin for being such a bad Guardian, and damn herself for actually trusting him to watch Mona.

"You *what?*" Quin slammed the flat of his palm into Stuart's elbow, sending espresso flying. It landed on Stuart's shirt, on piles of documents, and all over the floor. "You drank from her?"

"Quincy! Look what you did!" Stuart howled with dismay as the brown stains spread across his chest. "What is *wrong* with you?"

"You will take a nap now," Quincy ordered.

Stuart picked up a piece of paper and tried to wipe off his shirt, muttering about Quin's bizarre behavior of late.

"You will take a nap now," Quincy repeated. "You are very tired and need to sleep for three hours."

Theresa rolled her eyes as she realized Quincy was trying to use the power of suggestion to make Stuart fall asleep. Quincy, the mortal human, now fancied himself an Otherworld being with the power of suggestion? Two weeks ago, he was a disbeliever who refused to acknowledge dragons, Curses, or anything magical, and now he was deluding himself that he was actually one of them? It was sort of cute, actually, to see him finally accepting that the Otherworld was real.

Stuart balled up the piece of paper and tossed it at Quincy. "What are you talking about? I don't have time to sleep."

Quincy grabbed Stuart's shoulders and stared him down. "You will sleep now! I order you!"

Stuart shoved Quin off him. "Get a grip, man! You're losing it! I won't touch your damn coffee again, all right? Back off!" He spun toward the door and slammed to a stop when he saw Theresa. "Well, he-llo."

Quincy jerked around, his eyes widening. "Who are you?"

She raised a brow at Quincy. "I'm who's going to save your sorry Assistant Guardian behind, that's who I am."

His mouth dropped open. "Theresa?"

"Yep." She crooked her finger at Stuart while Quincy gaped at her. "Come here, Stuart."

Stuart straightened his tie and strutted over to her. "Are

you a student? Or a teaching assistant?" he asked hopefully. "Are you *my* teaching assistant?"

"I'm looking for a job, actually."

Quincy motioned for her to wait, and then ran to his desk and dialed his phone. Theresa levered herself off the door and assessed Stuart, trying to decide the least messy way to kill him.

"Don't hurt him yet," Quincy said. "Give me a second."

A lecherous gleam appeared in Stuart's eyes as he gave Theresa an appraising look. "You're going to hurt me?"

Before she could answer, Quin interrupted. "Stuart! Phone!"

She and Stuart both looked at Quincy, who was holding out the handset to his desk phone. "For me? I didn't hear it ring."

"For you." He gestured with the phone. "Just talk to him."

Stuart gave a self-important shrug and then walked to the desk and took the phone. "Hello?"

Theresa raised her eyebrows at Quin, and he winked at her.

Thirty seconds later, the phone clattered to the floor and Stuart collapsed in a pile. He was snoring before his head hit the ground. Quincy grinned at Theresa. "I called Xavier, your doorman. He told Stuart to sleep for six hours. How did you become human again? You look great, by the way."

Um, there would be no need to tell Quincy she'd made a deal with the devil. "I had no idea the power of suggestion worked over the phone." Theresa shut the office door and locked it, then walked over to Stuart and nudged him with her toe. He grunted and curled up into the fetal position and started to suck his thumb. "That's disgusting." She turned back to Quincy, who was trying to clean up the spilled espresso. "Since when do you have the power of suggestion?" Or not.

Quin grinned. "I've been hanging out with Xavier a lot lately, and he told me that a lot of humans actually have Otherworld genes somewhere in their heritage. He tried his power of suggestion on me, and I was actually somewhat resistant to it, unlike my wimpy brother. Xavier said that might indicate that I have the power, too, so he's training me." He straightened up. "I feel this weird tingling sometimes when I'm trying to suggest something, which I think is my power trying to burst free."

"Or it's your human brain about to implode on itself."

He gave her a disgusted sniff. "Doubt all you want, but I've run some equations on it, and I think the odds are quite high that I have some sort of Otherworld gift. It's just a matter of identifying it."

"And if your equations indicate it's true, then it has to be true."

"Math never lies."

Theresa snorted. "Whatever you say, Mr. Math Professor." She walked over to his chair and sat down, putting her feet up on the desk. "So, are you going to kill Stuart or can I?"

"We can't kill him." Quincy straightened his buttondown shirt, tucking it back into his khakis. "He's my colleague."

"Should've thought of that before you let him drink from Mona." She frowned. "Who else has drunk from her? Do you even know?"

"No one, I swear." He shot her a hostile look that she'd never seen from him before. "If you hadn't dumped her on me without any preparation, I wouldn't have been in this situation."

"Fine. *I'll* kill him." She sucked in some air and began to churn up some heat in her chest, ignoring Quincy's protests that there could be no killing. Tension eased from her body as the prickling flames burned her lungs and crept up her throat.

But before she could incinerate Stuart, there was a high-pitched ringing that had her groaning. She was still trying to swallow the flames when Iris Bennett, defrocked Guardian and the bane of Satan's love life, appeared in the middle of the desk. "Theresa Nichols, tell me you haven't made a deal with Satan!"

Theresa winced. Like she needed a lecture from Iris, her surrogate mother, right now.

"What?" Quin whirled toward Theresa. "You made a deal with Satan, and you dare get all over *me* for falling asleep at my desk? The Council will fry you for that!"

"Theresa!" Iris's usually pristine hair was bedraggled and soggy, and her expensive pants were dripping with water, no doubt from her rumored water fight with Satan. "I've been trying to find you for the last hour, ever since Satan showed up in purgatory, making some insane claim that you'd made a deal with him—" She stopped talking as she took in Theresa's appearance. "You're *human*. You *did* make a deal with him."

Theresa decided to clean up the spilled espresso. Not much point in denying the obvious.

She yanked a napkin out from under a croissant on Quincy's desk and started to mop up Mona, while Iris clasped her hands to her chest and made a noise of distress. "I'm *devastated.* I shall have to report you to the Council immediately. How can my daughter's best friend, whom I have nurtured and cared for like my own since she was thirteen years old, betray me and the Goblet like this?"

Theresa slapped the napkin at a textbook. "I didn't *betray* anyone. I have to get Satan on a television show. That's it. Mona is safe, everything is fine. I needed to be human in order to guard Mona appropriately."

"How do you even know what you need to do? All you do is have cybersex and burn people up." Iris shook her head in dismay. "I'm going to request that they make me Interim Guardian while Justine and Derek are out of town."

Theresa whirled toward Iris. "I'm sick and tired of having everyone think I'm worthless. I'm going to be Guardian and I can handle it." She jerked her chin at Quincy. "He's the one who let someone drink from Mona."

Iris squawked and shot a glare at Quincy. He drew his shoulders back. "I'll handle it. Theresa and I will kill him."

Theresa blinked at the conviction in his tone. Hadn't he just refused to kill anyone? What was up with the change of heart?

"I'm going to get both of you taken off Guardian duty," Iris said. "Don't you even know you don't have to kill him if he's had only one drink? It's the subparagraph of the third footnote on page 186 of the appendix to the *Treatise.*"

Appendix? There was an appendix? She looked at Quincy, and he shrugged once. "Don't you think it would have been *helpful* for someone to give us a copy of the appendix?"

Iris raised her brows. "You don't have one?"

"No. Never heard of it."

Iris shook her head. "I swear, it's like the Council wants the current Guardians to fail. Am I the only one who knows all the details of Guardianship?"

"Um, yeah?"

Iris nodded at the acknowledgment of her greatness. "I'll get you a copy of the appendix tonight." She eyed the suckling Stuart. "If he doesn't get another drink from Mona within seven days, he'll return to his ordinary self. Keep him imprisoned for a week and he'll be fine. It's only after two drinks that the effects become irreversible." The ringing began again. "I'll be back soon. In the meantime, try not to compromise the safety of Mona, okay?"

"Thanks—"

But Iris had already vanished, no doubt on her way to get them both removed from duty. So unfair. Just because she'd been forced to be a useless sidekick for the last two hundred years, no one gave her any credit for being able to accomplish anything. Like she was supposed to know the rules of an appendix no one had ever told her existed!

Screw that. She was going to prove she was capable. She stood up. "I'm taking Mona."

To her surprise, Quin didn't argue. "Keep her hidden for a week so Stuart can't find her—or anyone else who might have drunk from her." He looked at Theresa. "I screwed up. I'm sorry."

She couldn't stay mad at the genuine remorse on his face. "You're really apologizing to me?"

"Yes. Sorry about letting you starve, too." He ran his

hand through his hair, and she suddenly noticed that it was getting a little long. Not much, but enough to hint at even more changes in Quin's life since he'd met his first dragon. "It's just, well, this whole Otherworld thing has really thrown me for a loop."

"I understand." She touched his arm. "It's a little overwhelming."

His eyes glittered at her. "It is, but I'm not going to let Iris get me fired. I'm completely capable of handling this."

She grinned at his fire. "You're not nearly as much of a wuss as I originally thought you were, Quincy LaValle. Keep it up, and I might actually start thinking of you as hot."

His cheeks flushed a faint pink and he cleared his throat. "So, what now? You going back to my place?"

"Nope. I got a new safe house, so I'll be heading there."

He frowned. "What's wrong with my place?"

"Security breach. It'll be too easy for them to find since it's registered under your own name." Finding Quin's would be a no-brainer for Zeke, and even Lyman wouldn't be challenged.

"Them?"

"Yeah." She stood up and walked over to Mona. "Come on, girl. We're going for a ride."

"Them who?"

"No one I can't handle." She studied Mona. "Hey, if you can turn into something small and subtle, I'll take you around the city with me while I try to track down this asshole from my past."

The espresso machine didn't change.

"He tends to have lots of heavily muscled men working for him. It'll be a serious battle if they find me. Lots of violence and fun stuff like that. Way better than sitting around Quin's office reading the covers of math textbooks, unless you really want to stay behind all by yourself . . ."

The espresso machine flashed and in its place was a leather cord threaded through a crystal vial. The vial was filled with a blue-tinted liquid. Theresa picked it up and tied the cord around her neck, so the vial rested between her breasts.

Quincy frowned. "You think she'll be safe with you?"

"I'm an immortal dragon, Quin. I can handle anything."

Except maybe a particularly virile dragon slayer.

Eight

After spending a day trying to figure out how to deal with the reappearance of Lyman and the fact that her cyberlover was a slayer who'd nearly killed her, Theresa had decided her only option was to get tough.

It was time for some aromatherapy.

It was late morning when Theresa pulled her eighth chocolate cake out of the oven and set it on the counter in her new condo. She made sure the pillows were spread liberally over the kitchen floor, then she leaned over the cake, pulled the cotton wads out of her nostrils, and inhaled.

The aroma of freshly baked chocolate cascaded into her nose and her knees buckled.

She dropped to the floor, but clutched the counter, keeping her head above the cake. *I can handle this.* She inhaled again, concentrating on redirecting the luscious scent away from her receptors. The room started to get fuzzy, but she gripped the counter tighter and sucked in more cake odor. She scrunched her eyes shut as she visualized a door slamming shut and the scent drifting down a different hallway, away from her vulnerable core.

She took another breath, and another, and still she

didn't collapse. Her grip didn't slip from the counter and her brain stayed on the useful side of fuzzy. After a few more minutes, she opened her eyes.

Dizziness hit instantly as she lost her focus, so she shut them again, visualizing the door and the hallway. She grinned as the strength returned to her limbs.

Still breathing deeply, she climbed to her feet and pressed her nose against the cake as it began to cool and the intensity of the aroma faded.

Finally, she opened her eyes and smiled. "I am a goddess."

It was the first time she'd made it through the chocolate cake challenge without ending up on her back on the floor. Eight tries, but victory was still victory.

Maybe she'd been a sucky dragon her whole life, and maybe her parents weren't around to care, and yeah, it was a little late to be getting her act together, but she was going to do it or die trying.

Literally.

Plan for the day:

First, become immune to Zeke's pheromones.

Second, find that rat bastard Lyman and kill his sorry ass.

But God, if Lyman was alive, then that meant she wasn't the last dragon on the planet. She didn't want to kill one of her own kind, not when their race was all but extinct.

Lyman had told her that he was the only dragon who'd survived Uruloke, and when she'd learned he was dead, she'd thought she was the only dragon left. Sure, there'd been rumors of other dragon enclaves besides Uruloke, but dragons kept to themselves, so she'd never confirmed their existence when she was living in Uruloke, and she'd never found a hint of their existence in the centuries since.

But if Lyman was alive, there was at least one other dragon on the planet. He was an ass, but he was a dragon, and just knowing he was out there made her feel less alone.

Or it would until he killed her.

She sighed and flopped down on her new couch. For the first time in forever, she had a fragile woven textile for a couch covering. It would never stand up to a dragon's scales, but for a human, it was soft and delightful.

She surveyed the room, with its soft lighting and fragile furnishings, none of which were fireproof or tough enough to withstand the smack of an irritated tail. It was perfect, and it was hers. All hers. Only hers. She pursed her lips and realized it was a little weird to be officially living alone.

Which was great. Perfect. Because she was going to take that freedom and buy herself a new life, with new friends.

She picked up her laptop off the wicker coffee table and logged on so she could Google Lyman. But she hadn't even typed his name before an IM from Zeke popped up. "T. We need to talk."

She shivered with excitement, then immediately rolled her eyes. She couldn't even smell him and she was still useless. "Why didn't you kill me last night?"

"I'm an ex-slayer. I don't kill dragons anymore."

"No such thing as an ex-slayer."

"As I'm learning."

She frowned. "What does that mean?"

"It means next time we meet, you need to turn off your scent receptors."

The thought of meeting him again made goose bumps

pop up on her arms. Pathetic, she was. "You think? What a brilliant idea. Wish I'd thought of that myself."

"T, listen. I feel really bad about my client setting up a hit on you."

She sighed and shut down her desire to forgive him and ask him to come over and give her a full body massage. "What do you want, Zeke? I don't have time to be trading messages when I have to find the man who's after me."

"I needed to find you, so I went online."

Find her? She jerked upright and sniffed, but she didn't smell him. "Find me how?"

"I'm a missing persons expert. With enough information, I can find anyone."

A knock sounded at her door, and she jumped. "Is that you?" she typed.

The message appeared on her screen. "Yep."

Excitement mingled with fear as she stared at the door that separated them. "Can't you respect a girl's need for privacy?" she called out.

"Nope. Open up." Zeke's voice carried through the door. "I won't stun you, I promise."

"The last words a stupid dragon gets to hear." She set the computer on her coffee table and went to the door. She peeked through the spy hole and felt her heart tighten. Zeke had one hand on each side of the doorframe and he was leaning on it. His face was drawn, and there were circles under his eyes. He looked like hell.

Good. "Go away."

"If I was going to kill you, I could have done it last night."

"Not a chance. I was faking it. You're lucky you left when you did, because I was about to burn you up."

He lifted his head, an amused smile curving the corner of his mouth as he stared at the spy hole. "I'm tracing the London attorney managing your supposed inheritance. There's no record of him in London, but there are some leads locally. If you help me by telling me what you know about Lyman, I can put all the info together and find him. Shut him down before he gets you."

It was tempting. She didn't have the foggiest idea how to find Lyman. And it was sort of sweet that Zeke wanted to save her. "But I can't trust you."

His eyes glittered. "Listen, Theresa, here's the deal. I inadvertently endangered a dragon's life, and that's unacceptable. I'm going to guard you and keep you safe until we eliminate the threat, and that's the way it is."

She yanked the door open and glared at him. "So, the only reason you want to help me is that I'm a dragon? Is this part of your slayer ten-step recovery program?"

He blinked. "Yes."

"Jerk." She shoved him in the chest, but unlike last time when she knocked him into the taxi by accident, he didn't even budge. She frowned, and shoved harder. Like a wall. "I thought you were some weak excuse for a man."

He looked resigned. "Some of my slayer traits are returning. I figure that it's because I have unresolved issues."

"Such as?"

"Slayer issues. You wouldn't understand." He picked a duffel bag off the floor in the hall, then shouldered past her into the condo. He dropped his bag on the floor, walked to the window and peered out, muttering under his breath about the fire escape being right under the window.

"Hey, slayer boy. I don't want your help."

He turned around, leaned against the windowsill, and looked down at her. "I screwed up, T. I'm not walking away from it."

She stepped back from the energy pulsating off him. He was too dangerous. "Okay, here's the deal, Zeke. You lied to me, you set me up to be killed, and you're a slayer. I would be a fool to trust you."

Something flickered in his eyes, something that made her hackles rise. Zeke was hiding something.

"We've been instant-messaging for six months," he said. "You know you can trust me."

"What do I know about you? Everything was a setup." She narrowed her eyes. "Do you even *own* a model train set and play with it at night to alleviate stress?"

He looked embarrassed. "No, but—"

"Do you actually like to be tied down during sex?"

"It goes against my slayer instincts not to be in control," he admitted.

"I don't even know you, so how can I trust you?"

He raised his hand as if to touch her, then spun away and walked to the other side of the room. He leaned against the arm of the couch and folded his arms across his chest. "My favorite color is blue. I hate being a vegetarian and I love a good fight, even though I'm trying to change. I hate that I've killed hundreds of dragons, and the fact that I was the one who organized the Dragon Cleansing of 1788 still keeps me awake at night."

Her hands went to her stomach. "You were in charge of the Cleansing?" She grabbed the arm of the couch and sank into the cushions, unable to hide her horror. "My parents *died* in the Cleansing."

His lips tightened. "In the last twelve hours since I met

you, all the instincts I've suppressed for so long have come back with a vengeance. So I need to channel that into something productive. Not that I'm going to be violent while doing it. I'm just going to change my future by saving dragons. You, for example."

"So, I'm an example." Not quite what she'd had in mind last night when she'd headed to the bar to meet him, with visions of Zeke adoring her and worshipping her body. Zeke, the man who might have made her an orphan . . . her throat suddenly tightened up and she had to blink several times to clear the tears from her eyes. She didn't want Zeke to really be the enemy.

He touched her arm, and they both jumped at the jolt, but he didn't let go. "T, I'm struggling here. I need your help. Let me protect you." There was a desperation in his gaze that felt all too familiar. She knew what it was like to despise your life. "I have to do this," he said. "And you need my help. Without me, this guy will find you before you find him, but I can stop him if you'll let me. We can help each other."

Oh, that sounded so nice in theory, but Lyman wasn't a man who would be easily stopped. "And what if you kill me in a moment of accidental reversion to your slayer heritage?"

He winced. "If you act human around me, I should be all right. It's when you start doing dragon things that it gets tough."

"Like what?"

"Like letting smoke curl out of your nose. Growing a tail. Dropping at my feet in a gyrating pile when I release my pheromones."

Like she could control that. "I feel *so* much safer around you now."

He flinched, but he didn't stop pressuring her. "I'm the best at finding people."

She cocked her head, trying to think strategically instead of emotionally. "I admit, I could use your missing persons expertise."

"So, we work together?"

"On certain conditions." She paced away from him, her mind racing. "First condition: We team up from a distance. I don't trust you not to kill me, so you have to stay away from me."

He frowned. "I can't protect you if I'm not near you."

"You're not going to protect me! I'm a dragon! I can save myself from anyone except you. Yeesh. Men get so full of themselves sometimes." She spun toward him and jiggled up some energy in her chest, then sent a bolt of flame out of her mouth and set his hair on fire. "See?"

He slammed the flames out with his palms, his eyes suddenly going all dark and smoky. "You are *so* hot."

Her lower body suddenly tightened in response to his expression. "Oh, no, you don't, Slayer. Stay away from me."

He walked toward her, and she backed up. "Here's my first lesson as your new protector: Did you know that the attraction between slayers and dragons isn't one-sided?" His gaze caressed her body as he neared her. "It's supposed to give the dragons a chance. Even the odds."

She felt the wall against her back and she tensed as Zeke's hands landed on either side of her head. "No one ever told me that before." Or maybe she'd missed the lecture on it. Obviously, blowing off dragon education as a kid and then being yanked out of dragon society as a teenager had seriously impaired the development of her dragon skill-set and knowledge base.

"We try not to advertise our vulnerability." He leaned forward and pressed his nose against her throat and inhaled. "What my scent does to you? Your flames do that to us."

Oh, God. His breath against her skin felt so good. "Flames really work you over? But how come you guys don't go down when we try to fry you in the heat of battle?" She winced when her voice squeaked.

"Because we train to resist it." His lips brushed her neck, and she had to grip his waist to keep from falling down. "I'm a little out of practice. No dragon has shot fire at me in a really long time."

The heady excitement of power rushed through her. "So, I could render you defenseless if I were to do this . . ." She blew a small flame onto his shirt, and he groaned. "Or this . . ." She let a flickering torch simmer at the end of her tongue.

He slammed his hips into hers and dropped his head, taking the flames into his mouth just before his lips crushed hers. New heat flared out of her and flames burst from her mouth and into his. He groaned and his knees buckled. He landed with a thud between her feet, his arms wrapped around her waist. He pressed his face into her belly, making all sorts of noises of distress.

She clutched his head to her body, her hips pressing against him. He was putty in her hands, and the rush was incredible. Dragon instincts burst to the surface, and she stared down at the slayer between her legs. He was at her mercy. *I must destroy him before he kills me. It is time for the slayer to die.* She grabbed his hair, softly tugging until he was forced to tip his head back and look at her.

His eyes were glazed as he stared back up at her. "T . . ." The throaty groan was all he could manage, but the sound of her nickname on his lips reached deep, penetrating past the instincts that were demanding his death.

I don't want to kill this man.

But the flames surged in her chest, and she knew she couldn't stop. She had to kill him. It was her destiny. "Zeke . . ." She gasped as more flames shot out of her mouth. "Do something."

He groaned again and sagged against her, his hands gripping her butt so tightly she was sure he was going to leave bruises. She saw awareness flicker in his eyes, the realization that he was facing his own death. Her fingers tightened in his hair and she bent down, sparks dropping all over him as heat and an uncontrollable urge to fry him surged to her chest.

Oh, God. She was going to kill him. Now. "Zeke . . ."

Suddenly she was hit with his slayer scent and her legs buckled. He caught her as she dropped and she flung herself against him, desperate for his mouth on hers, for the feel of his flesh against hers. Flames burst out of her nose as he slammed his mouth onto hers, drinking in her fire as more of his scent filled her mind, took over her body.

She had to have him. Had to feel him. She yanked at his shirt, and he stripped it off, tearing her blouse as he fumbled for her body. The carpet caught fire and he rolled her on top of it, smothering the flames with her body as he pushed her skirt up and tore off her panties, his mouth everywhere, his fingers diving into her most intimate parts as she drank in his scent, sucked in through her pores.

"God, T, I can't wait."

"Don't wait. Please don't make me wait." She tried to get his pants unfastened as she twisted under his ministrations, but her fingers were too uncoordinated. She sent a stream of flame at his waist, and his belt disintegrated into a cloud of ash. His pants followed and she grabbed his hair, tugging him upward. "Do it now, Slayer. Now!"

She wrapped her legs around his hips as he plunged into her, screaming as the rush of sensation ripped through her body. He shouted her name and drove deeper as smoke rose up around them. She threw her head back and clutched his shoulders as flames burst from her, spewing upward past Zeke's face. His eyes rolled back in his head and his body convulsed against hers. A burst of his scent flooded her and fire exploded inside her, her body twisting and sizzling as release cascaded through her.

She screamed his name and he caught her shout with a kiss as the last tremors vibrated through both of them.

Zeke returned to consciousness slowly. His head was throbbing, his body ached, and something was digging into his back.

Then he realized he wasn't alone. A warm body was lying across him, and hair was tickling his chin.

He peeled his eyes open and lifted his head. Tousled blond curls were spread over his bare chest, and suddenly he remembered what had happened. *Oh, shit!* Had he killed her? Then he felt her ribs expand with a breath. *She was alive.* He curled his fingers into her hair and rubbed gently, inhaling her scent. Dragon, cinnamon, and smoke. His lower body twitched, but he ignored it. As long as she didn't flame him, he'd be all right. "T? You okay?"

She mumbled something and nuzzled her face into his chest.

He smiled and let his head drop back to the floor, still playing with her hair. "Theresa. Wake up, hon."

She groaned again and moved against him. Then he felt her body tense, and she lifted her head, ever so slowly, until she was looking at him. Her gold-flecked eyes blinked warily at him. "Zeke?"

He nodded. "How do you feel?"

"Like I went on a drinking binge."

"Me, too."

Her brow furrowed as memory came back to her, and he grinned when her cheeks flamed red as she recalled how the encounter had ended. "Oh, God." She rolled away from him, fumbling for the first clothes she could find, which ended up being his shirt. She sat up, her back toward him, while she tugged it on.

He grabbed the collar and pulled it up over her back as she tried to get it over her shoulders. "I didn't hurt you, did I?" Her hair caught in the collar and he lifted it free.

She shook her head. "I'm fine. You?" Her voice was brisk, cool.

"Alive."

She finished buttoning his shirt and turned to face him. "How come your face isn't burned? Didn't I blow flames on you?"

"I'm somewhat immune to fire." He propped himself up on his elbows and ran his mind through the muscles of his body. He felt weak, as if he'd been sick for months. "Natural selection for slayers."

She frowned. "So, how are dragons supposed to kill slayers?"

He raised his brow. "You really don't know?"

Her cheeks got red again, and she stood up, tugging her skirt down as she went. "Oh, sure, I know. I was just checking." She ran her fingers through her hair and stared down at him with a haughty look. "Just so you know, I'm an expert in dragon fighting techniques. No slayer has a chance against me. I graduated at the top of my class."

"Then how come you can't block my scent?" He stood up, and Theresa averted her eyes while he tugged his pants back up.

She stalked into the kitchen and he heard something crash. "For your information," she shouted. "I can block your scent. You just caught me unaware." Another loud bang and then something shattered.

He peered around the corner. Theresa had a mixing bowl in her hand, and there was broken pottery at her feet, along with a metal pot. She stopped when she saw him, her arm up as if she'd been about to hurl it to the floor.

"Is that how dragons let off their steam when they can't burn stuff up?"

She blinked. "What?"

He eased into the kitchen. "Well, you're pissed because you just lost control and had sex with a slayer. You're frustrated because you weren't able to block my scent. You can't burn me up because you need me to help you find the guy who's after you. So you have to do something." He shrugged. "Makes sense."

She stared at him. "You're not going to tell me to stop?"

"Why would I? You have to do what you need to do. I'd rather you break dishes than shoot me." He eyed the floor and felt a certain envy for her ability to embrace her heritage. "So, I'll just go wait in the other room until you're finished and we can talk." Good thing he had brought his iPod. He'd put on some jazz and meditate while Theresa did her thing. "Take your time."

He turned around and walked out, before he lost self-control and grabbed that bowl from her and hurled it against the wall.

He unzipped his bag and grabbed his iPod and his yoga mat. There was a place in the corner where the rug wasn't charred from their lovemaking—fresh heat surged through him at the thought—so he set up there, crossed his legs, and closed his eyes.

Thirty minutes later, Theresa stared at the mess she'd made of her kitchen and felt relaxed for the first time she could remember. Every new dish Graham had furnished the place with was broken, and the roll of paper towels was a pile of ash in the sink. So were the wooden spoons and a wooden salad bowl.

She picked up a handful of ash and let it sift through her fingers, drifting back down to the stainless steel.

How different it felt to let her inhibitions go, without worrying about Justine telling her to control herself. No censorship. Just a complete and unashamed embrace of who she was.

She clasped her hands over her head and stretched, relishing the energy pulsating through her body. Sure, it wasn't the same as actually killing someone, but she couldn't believe how good she felt.

Good enough to deal with the man in her living room.

Nine

Theresa peeked around the corner at Zeke, but his eyes were closed. His chest was naked and barely moving with his breath. He was completely at ease, sitting cross-legged on a red yoga mat, but his body was well-defined, and she half expected him to leap up with a sword at any second.

Involuntarily, she licked her lips, and it wasn't because the dragon in her wanted to eat him.

Get it together, Theresa.

She detoured into her new bedroom to put on underwear and some less-alluring clothes, then returned to the living room. She walked over to him and nudged him with her toe.

His eyes opened immediately and he shut off his iPod. "Finished?"

She nodded. "Let's talk."

He rolled to his feet with an easy grace that reminded her that he was a slayer, not an ordinary man with a perfect chest. "You're going to tell me about Lyman?"

She stopped him with a hand to his chest, jumping at the jolt that went between them, the jolt that she now knew was the slayer/dragon reaction. "First, though, we need to talk about the sex we had."

His eyes got dark and smoky, and her heart started thudding.

So she turned away and walked to the other side of the room. She sat down in her computer chair and tucked her feet up under her and waited for him to sit on the couch. He did, and she realized she should have brought him his shirt from the other room. It was too hard to concentrate with him half-naked.

No, it wasn't. She'd just destroyed an entire kitchen. Her dragon urges were under complete control. She lifted her chin and folded her arms across her chest. "That sex meant nothing. Even if I thought you were a freak, we still would have had sex because of the slayer/dragon thing." When he said nothing, she got a little nervous. "Right?"

Finally, he nodded. "Yes, I expect you're correct." He stretched his arms out along the back of the couch and rested his right ankle over his left knee. "I've never had sex with a dragon before, so I wouldn't know from personal experience." A faint flush of aggravation stained his cheeks. "No decent slayer would let himself succumb to the allure of flames."

She felt a tinge of empathy. "Well, I failed at being a good dragon, too, so I guess we're both out of practice."

He met her gaze and nodded. "We had no chance to stop ourselves."

"So it meant nothing?"

He shook his head. "It meant something."

She dug her toes into the seat, clinging to the fabric. "What did it mean?"

"It means we have to be careful around each other. You almost killed me, Theresa. And last night, when I hit you with my scent and you went down? I almost killed you."

He drummed his fingers on the back of the couch. "We're dangerous together. Our heritage demands we battle to the death." He lifted his hand. "Look at my fingers. See how they're curling? Every minute I'm with you, I'm thinking about how you're a dragon, and I get this twitch." He closed his eyes and let his head lean back. "I have to fight it constantly." Then he opened his eyes and looked at her, his eyes glittering. "And at the same time, I want to screw you until we're both too exhausted to move. And none of these emotions have anything to do with you or me personally."

She shivered at the intensity in his gaze. "You think the attraction we had online was the slayer/dragon stuff? That's what it's been from the beginning?"

"Yes." He sat up and leaned forward. "We can't trust any of the intense emotions between us, T. They aren't real."

She pursed her lips. He was right, and it was easier that way. She'd never felt intensely about any member of the opposite sex in her entire life, and she didn't intend to start now. Her first loyalty was to the Goblet—who would protect Mona if she was killed? Besides, Zeke had lied to her, set her up, and wanted to defend her honor only to exorcise the demons from his own past. "Just so you know, I still don't like you."

Something flickered in his eyes, but he shrugged. "That's your prerogative. So, tell me about this Lyman person who wants you dead."

She fingered the crystal vial at her neck and tried to think about how to tell the story without revealing Mona, or her Guardianship status. "Lyman Peressini is a dragon."

He waited.

She played with Mona.

"That's it? That's all you're going to tell me?"

She tried to decide which nugget about Lyman to share. "He's probably rich and involved in something illegal."

He raised his brow. "Was he your lover?"

She felt her face flush. "That's none of your business."

"Yes, it is. Personal vendettas are different from professional ones." He shifted forward on the couch, and his eyes became intense, focused. "Why does he want you dead, T?"

She cleared her throat. "There are several possibilities."

"*Several?* What did you do?"

She bit her lower lip, her mind racing. She'd never told anyone about her time with Lyman. There wasn't a person alive, either in the mortal world or in the Afterlife, who knew.

"T?" He was on the edge of the couch now. "You can trust me."

She met his gaze. "Can I?"

Before he could answer, her cell phone rang and she grabbed it, grateful for the respite while she gathered her thoughts. "Hello?"

"Theresa. It's Becca. I'm at NBC and I just finished a media interview for Vic's Pretzels. The assistant who helped us also works on Reverend Munsey's show. I traded a free pass good for one mortal sin in exchange for the Reverend's schedule. Reverend Munsey's doing a book signing at Between the Pages right now, and he'll be there for forty-five minutes. You're welcome, this isn't about friendship because you now owe me, and I'll collect." Then she hung up.

Theresa grinned as she hung up. *She loves me.* "I gotta go."

Zeke frowned. "We're not finished."

"I have to run an errand." She assessed her "I'm a killer dragon" outfit and decided it wasn't quite appropriate for winning over a televangelist. More cleavage and thigh needed. He might be a preacher, but men were men and they were no match for a woman on a mission. "Work on finding Lyman. I'll be back."

But when she emerged from her room five minutes later, Zeke was standing in the living room, waiting. He didn't even give her a chance to protest. "My job is to keep you alive, so I'm coming."

She tucked a pale blue handbag under her arm. "I don't want you following me around. I'm still not sure I trust you." Truthfully, she wasn't sure *she* trusted herself around *him.* Whether or not the attraction between them was personal, it was still hard as hell to resist.

He rubbed his jaw while he considered her request. "If something happens to you . . ." Anguish and guilt flashed in his eyes, and he shook his head. "No. I won't let it."

She shrugged off the surge of sympathy she felt for him. The man had slaughtered thousands of dragons, quite possibly her own parents! There could be no sympathy for the slayer. And how could she be *attracted* to him? *Call upon your ruthless dragon instincts, Theresa.* She set her hands on her hips and leveled a glare at him. "You need to leave me alone. Got it?"

He narrowed his eyes. "All clear."

"Good." She opened the door. "Let me know what you

find out about Lyman. You can work from my place if you want. Make sure no one breaks in while I'm gone."

He didn't move as she shut the door behind her.

Theresa kept it together until she got into the elevator. The minute the doors closed, her legs buckled and she started shaking.

God, Zeke made her nervous. She closed her eyes and leaned her head against the elevator wall. If he was the one who had orchestrated the Dragon Cleansing, then he was *the* slayer of legendary skill. The best there ever was. *She would have no chance against him.*

None.

Every minute in his presence, she was at his mercy. At the whim of his willpower.

How was she ever going to learn how to block his pheromones? She sighed as heat pooled in her lower body. Just the thought of his scent made her want to drop to the floor and beg him to take her. She didn't *want* to block it and that made her, truly, the worst dragon in the history of the world.

Theresa walked into Between the Pages, pausing just inside the door when she saw Reverend Munsey seated at his book-signing table. Instead of the white flowing robe he wore on television, he was wearing a red kimono that had what looked like fourteen-carat-gold designs woven into it. Hanging from the bottom were glittery tassels that made her blink when they caught the light. His nose was oversized, his skin a little mottled, and he had only four fingers on his right hand. She'd never noticed that on television.

He didn't look as grandiose as he did on the small

screen. He almost looked as if he was overcompensating in an attempt to win over the room. He looked sort of weak, not a man of power at all.

And to think she'd thought he could turn her back into a human. What an idiot she was.

He looked up from the book he was signing and handed what was apparently his last copy of *To Heaven with Love* to a little old lady wearing all green. She was beaming at him, and his long, flyaway gray hair seemed to actually vibrate with energy. "It was such a pleasure to meet you, Reverend," the lady said. "If you ever need a Manasa reading, I'll do it for free."

Theresa jerked to attention at the reference. Did Reverend Munsey know what a Manasa was?

The Reverend's eyes glittered, and in that instant, she knew he was more than he seemed. He clearly knew that Manasas could not only read minds but ferret the deepest secrets out of even an unwilling soul.

So, was his impotent appearance a farce? A trick? She studied him with renewed interest, fire bubbling in her chest in reaction to the identification of a potential threat.

The Manasa waddled off, and Reverend Munsey watched her leave, a thoughtful and calculating look on his face. He was so caught up in whatever he was planning that Theresa was able to walk right up to him unnoticed.

She slapped both hands down on the signing table. "Hello."

He jerked back, his pale blue eyes flicked to hers, then he jumped to his feet, leaped backward, and crashed into a display of *New York Times* best sellers. The stand tipped over and a cascade of paperbacks rained onto his head, but he didn't even notice. He was staring at Theresa with his mouth open, his eyes wide with shock.

Oh, God. Had she turned back into a dragon? She jumped away from him and glanced down at her body, ready to bolt. But her breasts were still there, and there were no scales to be seen. Then what was wrong with him?

She returned her gaze to him. "Reverend Munsey?"

He scrambled to his feet, stepped on a tassel, and went down again, his forehead clunking with a painful thud on the signing table. He landed in a full face-plant on the carpet and didn't move.

The Manasa was by his side instantly. "Call an ambulance," she shrieked. Then her eyes turned green and started flashing alternately like giant orbs as she tried to read the unconscious man's mind. "This woman attacked the Reverend and tried to kill him! Arrest her!"

Whoa. "I didn't touch him." Theresa backed up a step as people swarmed around the downed leader.

The Manasa leaped to her feet, her eyes pulsating in her head as she pointed at Theresa. "You shall pay, you . . . you . . ."

Theresa felt a weird tingling and realized the Manasa was trying to read her. Theresa wrapped her fist around Mona and bolted for the door. What was a Manasa's range? Ten feet? Twenty? It couldn't be more than that, could it? Another five feet and she'd be outside. She glanced back over her shoulder and saw the Manasa had pulled the Reverend's head onto her lap, and she was crooning at him, showering his staticky hair with kisses.

Suddenly, a heavy weight slammed into her from the side and she crashed into the security reader next to the front door. She landed on the floor and a man pounced on her, his stinky garlic breath making her nose wrinkle.

"I got her!" he shouted. "Reverend Munsey will not go unavenged!"

As if he could keep her down. She was a *dragon,* for heaven's sa—*oomph.* A middle-aged woman with a dog collar around her neck and a skull-and-crossbones tattoo covering the left side of her face flung her body across Theresa's pelvis. "I'll help!" she yelled. "Reverend Munsey will save my soul if I keep his attacker from escaping!"

Idiots. Two measly humans couldn't incapacitate a dragon. She rolled her eyes, then tensed to fling them off. *Off you go, loser humans—omigod.* Her breath whooshed out as a man who probably did sumo wrestling in his spare time dropped on her chest. "Count me in for the soul saving," he announced as he flattened her breasts with his enormous butt cheeks in the mammogram from hell.

She tried to shove him off her chest so she could catch a breath. What kind of rabid followers did this guy have, anyway?

A pair of teenage girls vaulted onto the sumo wrestler's lap, and she felt her ribs crack.

Can't.

Breathe.

"Me, too!" Someone landed on her left ankle, and she felt it wrench. Then pain shot through her right knee as someone else jumped on that, shouting about salvation.

Getting.

Dizzy.

Gray spots began to dance across her vision and the room began to darken.

No! No decent dragon ever fainted. Ever! She would *not* faint.

Would.

Not.

Fai—

"Theresa!" Zeke sprinted around from the front window he'd been watching through, slammed the doors open, and grabbed the first foreign ankle he could find, hauling a preppy college kid off the pile.

He realized where the guy had had his hand, so he flung him into the wall, grinning at the satisfying crash. The twin girls went tumbling more gently, the biker chick landed on top of them, and six more people found themselves sitting on the carpet instead of his dragon.

He ignored the screeching of the customers and faced off with the largest man he'd ever seen in his life. Theresa was almost completely hidden beneath the spread of his body. "Get the fuck off her, you bastard." He didn't even wince at the violence building inside him. He opened his senses, embracing it, drawing in the strength he knew he'd need.

The man folded his Stonehenge pillar arms across his chest. "My soul will be saved. You cannot remove me."

"I beg to differ." He wrapped his hands around the man's forearms and yanked. The man flew past Zeke and plowed into the crowd of onlookers, taking out at least a dozen. Limbs flailed, people shrieked, and Zeke bent over Theresa.

She wasn't breathing. Her lips were blue, and there

were tinges of gray around her eyes. Her legs were contorted and her hip looked as if it had been dislocated. "Jesus." He pressed his fingers to her throat, but he couldn't find a pulse. A sharp pain knifed through his gut and the edges of his mind began to blacken.

"Wake up, T," he ordered, his voice cracking. "You have no right to die while I'm trying to protect you." He laid his hand on her chest, willing her to revive, then dropped his head when he felt the shattered ribs collapse under his light touch.

He pressed his forehead against hers, leaving his hand resting on her sternum, between her breasts. "Oh, God, T, I'm so sorry. I promised I'd save you and I failed."

He heard yelling about Reverend Munsey and he closed his eyes to shut it out.

Then he felt her ribs shift again, and he turned his head to look. Was it his imagination, or was her chest no longer as concave as it had been? He jerked upright as he felt more shifting under his hand, not daring to hope for the impossible. But the bones were definitely moving. What was going on?

He glanced over his shoulder, but no one was paying attention to them. They were too busy trying to help the people he'd sent flying. He turned back to Theresa, and his breath caught when he saw that her lips weren't blue anymore, and her hip seemed normal again.

He had to be imagining it. Deluding himself. Dragons lived for about seven hundred years, but they weren't immortal and they didn't have special healing capacities.

Then he passed his hand over her face and felt her breath, watched her ribs rise. *Yes.* He leaned forward, cupping her face in his hands, his chest tight with hope. "T? Come on, hon. You can do it. For me."

She coughed, and then her eyes opened, her golden gaze flicking to him. "Zeke?"

Oh, God. He slumped forward, pressing his lips to her forehead. "Never scare me like that again, or I'll kill you." He smiled softly as he rubbed his thumb over her cheek. He felt as if he could touch her forever. He laid his hand on her ribs. "Are they cracked?"

She took a shuddering breath, then nodded. "Yeah, but they're all right. They'll be good in a couple of hours."

He frowned and helped her sit up. "So, want to tell me how a dragon can heal from broken ribs in a couple of hours? Not that I'm complaining. Just insanely curious."

Her cheeks turned bright red and she cursed under her breath. "I have to get out of here. There's a Manasa around here somewhere. A green one."

Zeke glanced around the store, but saw only regular humans. He peeked out the window and saw an old lady in green hovering over a stretcher as it was being loaded into an ambulance. She climbed in behind it, and then it roared off with the squeal of sirens. "She's gone."

"Thank God." Theresa leaned forward, letting her head rest between her knees. "I can't believe I was bested by a bunch of humans." She shot a sideways glance at Zeke. "Did you hurt anyone?"

"I merely asked people to get off you." He scowled at the memory of how good it felt to fling those people aside. "Don't try to distract me. I want to know how you healed."

"Go away."

"No." He cupped her elbow and their gazes met with

the shock that jumped between them. "Let's go before anyone notices you're still here."

"Right." She hauled herself to her feet, clearly trying not to lean on him for support. He released her, but kept his hands near in case she needed him. He'd never expect Theresa to ask for help on anything, or to admit she needed it.

A cop was suddenly blocking their path. No, two cops. "I'm afraid we need to ask the two of you some questions."

Theresa sighed. "Will this take long? I really need to get going."

"Not long at all."

Ten

A dragon too inept to avoid jail was an offense to all of dragonkind.

And the fact she was unable to escape on her own was even more of an offense to all dragonkind.

Theresa tugged on the bars, and wasn't able to bend them even a little. In the old days, it was impossible to keep dragons in jail. They'd simply break free, or all their dragon comrades would raid the jail and rescue their friend.

She leaned her forehead against the bars. She'd been in jail for six hours already, and there would be no dragon coming to her rescue. The only dragon she knew was Lyman, and he'd be more likely to kill her than rescue her . . . She jerked her head up and sucked in her breath. If he found out she was here, she'd be a sitting duck.

But there was no way out—she was surrounded by cement and iron bars. Three cops had been to visit her, and she'd told them again and again that she'd had nothing to do with the Reverend's tumble, but they hadn't let her go.

"T?"

She spun around to find Zeke heading down the hallway toward her, being escorted by a guard. "Zeke!"

He gave her a reassuring smile that made her feel better, then stood back while the guard unlocked the door. "You have fifteen minutes, Siccardi. That's all I can give you."

"Thanks." Then Zeke stepped inside and the guard locked the cell door behind him.

Theresa immediately flung herself into Zeke's arms. He cursed and released her instantly. "Every time I touch you, I want to kill you *and* have sex with you," he growled.

She pulled herself together with a shudder, forcing herself not to grab him again. "I feel the same way."

He walked to the other side of the cell and leaned against the bars. "Stay over there for the moment, okay?"

She sat down on the cot and hugged her knees to her chest. "Why am I still in here? Did you find out what's going on?"

"Reverend Munsey died." He looked grim.

"Seriously? All he did was hit his head."

"The Manasa is claiming that she saw you assault him."

"I don't get it. Why would she lie? And why are they listening to her?"

He scowled and pulled a worn dagger out of his pocket, absently fingering the emeralds on the handle. "Someone's putting the pressure on the department to keep you here. I can't figure out who's behind it, but I'm working on it." He looked up and met her gaze. "They're talking about charging you with homicide."

She gulped as a sudden thought occurred to her. "Do you think Lyman arranged it? What if he set it up so he could come get me?" She jumped to her feet and nervously scanned the cell. "I have to get out of here."

"He couldn't have set it up. How would he have known you were going to go see Reverend Munsey?"

She swallowed hard and tried to quell her rising paranoia. "You don't know Lyman. If he has set up shop in New York, he'll have tentacles everywhere." She shook the bars. "You have to get me out!"

"I'm working on it. I should have you out by this afternoon. They can't keep you here on no evidence, no matter who is pulling the strings." Zeke touched her arm, and the shock made her jerk around to face him. "The media are already reporting on Reverend Munsey's death. One station announced a woman named Theresa Nichols has been taken into custody, but no one has a picture of you yet."

She felt the blood drain from her face.

"I'll stay at the station the whole time, and my buddies are the ones assigned to watch your cell. You'll be safe until we can get you out."

She nodded, feeling his conviction. Slayer or not, he was going to keep her safe. "Thanks."

He managed a tight smile. "I have to tell you something, T. Lyman's not the only one searching for you. There's a team of—"

A dark, inky shape formed on the floor of the cell. Zeke eyed it, then took a step back as Becca rose from the floor. She was wearing her Vic's Pretzels attire, which consisted of a red suit, scarlet heels, and demure gold studs in her ears. "Theresa, Satan is *pissed*."

"Who the hell are you?" Zeke raised his dagger and moved between Becca and Theresa.

A fireball flared to life in Becca's hand. "Don't threaten me, boy. I'm not in the mood."

Theresa shouted, "Don't kill him! This is Zeke Siccardi."

"*Oh*. Different story." Becca extinguished the fireball. "You're the one who helped them track down Satan Jr., right?"

"Uh-huh." He eyed her hand. "Are you a Rivka?"

She narrowed her eyes. "I'm not *a* Rivka. I'm Satan's number one Rivka, thank you very much. Why are you here?"

He spread his hands in a show of innocence, his dagger in the flat of his palm. "Trying to get T sprung."

Before either of them could reply, the back wall of the jail cell turned gold and a bunch of bubbles burst from it, Satan in the midst of them. There was black smoke coming out of his head and his eyes were glowing like burning coals. "Dragon! You killed Reverend Munsey! How am I going to get on television now?" He flung a glowing finger toward her, and she dove to the floor as the cot she'd been on exploded in a ball of hellfire. Flames were nothing to a dragon, but she wasn't willing to test her resistance on Satan's hellfire.

"Satan. Chill out." But even Becca was staying out of range.

Satan stepped to where Theresa was lying, billows of black smoke swirling around his head. "Our deal was that you would get me on Reverend Munsey's show, and instead you killed him!"

"I didn't kill him!" She scrambled to her feet and ran to the far corner of the cell as another bolt of fire shot from Satan's finger and charred the urinal. "I'll do something else for you. Want me to go soul harvesting with Becca? I'd be really good at that."

"No! I want something that no one else has! Souls are boring!"

"There has to be something Theresa has that you want." Becca shoved Satan with her foot just as he was taking aim at Theresa, so he missed and blew a chunk out of the cement wall instead. "Think, Satan. This is a great opportunity."

His eyes glittered with sudden energy, and his glowing finger dropped to his side. "I want the Goblet."

Becca muttered, "Uh-oh."

"No!" Theresa clutched the crystal vial that hung around her neck, the one that she'd hidden from the cops when they'd booked her into jail. She stumbled away from Satan, tripping on the smoldering mattress.

Zeke caught her and she twisted away from him, trying to get as far from Satan as possible.

Satan's eyes dropped to the vial and they widened. "She is there?"

"She's at my condo." Theresa backed into the corner, her heart thudding. "She's an espresso machine, remember?"

He leaned forward, staring at her fist. "Give her to me."

"I can't."

"Then I take back the human form."

She stared at him. "No." The protest came out as only a whisper, and she was vaguely aware of Zeke sucking in his breath. "I can't go back."

Satan waved his hand dismissively. "It matters not. I do not actually give you that option. I want the Goblet. The contract demands you give it to me." The smoke around his head began to thin, and he held out his hand. "Now."

She tightened her grip against a sudden urge to hand it to him.

"You're totally hosed," Becca said. "The contract has power in itself. You'll be unable to resist, just as I can't resist a direct order."

Theresa tried to back up farther, but her body was already pressed against the bars. "I can't." There was no greater failure for a Guardian than to lose the Goblet to Satan, as Iris could attest to. Theresa would not only be fired, she'd get sent to the Chamber of Unspeakable Horrors for all eternity.

And worse than that would be having to live with the knowledge that she'd ended up being the failure everyone had always proclaimed her to be.

Her hand began to tug on the vial, trying to break the leather strap that held it around her neck, and she realized she wouldn't be able to stop herself from handing it to him.

Satan's eyes gleamed and a smile grew on his face.

Oh, God. She tore herself away from his stare and fell to her knees in front of Zeke. "Kill me."

Satan harrumphed in aggravation and Zeke's face tensed. *"What?"*

"I can't resist Satan's demand. A Guardian must choose death over giving the Goblet to Satan or suffer eternal torture at the hands of the Council, in the Chamber of Unspeakable Horrors." She stared up at him, desperate. "If you kill me, Zeke, it will save your soul forever."

She saw a darkness roll over his eyes. "You're the Guardian of the Goblet of Eternal Youth?"

"Interim Guardian." Her hand tried to creep toward the necklace again, so she tucked her hands under her legs to immobilize them. "You have to behead me. It's . . . the only way to kill me." Under other circumstances, she'd be concerned about telling a slayer exactly how to kill her, but at the moment, regret was a wasted emotion.

"But . . ."

"Do it, Zeke." She closed her eyes. "Do it for me, the way I did it for Iris. Save me from myself, Zeke."

"He won't kill you," Satan snorted. "He is too enraptured with your breasts to consider slicing off your head. You do not have the luck of the Iris." He snorted and slapped his leg. "I am so entertaining. Did you comprehend my pun?"

Theresa opened her eyes and looked at Zeke. He was staring down at her, a look of horror on his face. But there was a burning violence in his eyes, an instinct that was rising to the surface. He would take her life to save her soul. A puff of green smoke leaked from her nose, but she laid her head back to expose her neck. "Do it."

Zeke's gaze fastened on her throat, and he withdrew the dagger from his waist, his jaw grinding and his body nearly twitching. She could smell the violence and death emanating from him. "Kill me," she commanded. "I beg you, Slayer."

"Slayer!" Satan shrieked. "Completely unfair to seek assistance from a dragon slayer!" A bolt of flame shot past Theresa's head and slammed into Zeke's chest. His eyes widened and he clutched his chest, a pillar of smoke leaking between his fingers.

"Good God," he croaked. "That hurt like hell." But he blinked, and she saw him adjust his grip on the blade, and she recalled that he said a slayer had some built-in protection from flames, even from hellfire, apparently, though she doubted he'd be able to hold out for long against Satan. "Do it, Zeke," she whispered, laying her head back, further exposing her neck. "Now."

He drew the blade back and she closed her eyes, tensing for the blow.

"No!" Satan shrieked.

There was a whoosh of flames, and Theresa snapped her eyes open in time to see Zeke's chest catch fire again. He cursed and sat down next to her, wheezing. "Jesus, T. You accuse me of having secrets?"

She sat up, and a few billows of green smoke leaked out of her nose. "You okay?"

His eyes grew even darker and he brushed his hand through the smoke as if he was drinking it in through his skin. "Yeah, I'll kill you in a second. I just need a minute."

She saw the pain in his eyes and realized that despite her assurances, killing her would destroy him. How could she ask him to do that for her? She touched his cheek. "I'm so sorry."

"Damned slayer!" Satan grabbed Zeke and flung him aside. Zeke landed with a thud on top of Becca, and then Satan sat down next to Theresa, his gaze worried. "Guardian, you do not need to die. I do not intend to abuse the Goblet. I hear many rumors that there are people out to kill you. Assassin yesterday. Slayer team today. If you die, the Goblet will be unguarded. Very bad. Iris will be most angry if the Goblet falls into the wrong hands. I propose to hold the Goblet for safekeeping until you can protect her safely."

Slayer team? Oh, God. *Please let that be one of*

Satan's lies. She scooted away from him, clutching Mona in her fist again. "You're Satan. You lie."

Zeke groaned and rolled off Becca, who was bleeding from her forehead.

"Yes, I lie often and well. I am glad you noticed my talent. I would lie about this, as well." Satan sighed. "But you know about my burning need for Iris. If I abused the Goblet, would she ever have sex with me?"

"No way."

"Exactly. I cannot risk it." A soft yearning fell over his face. "If I hold the Goblet and do not use it, what greater test of my love is there? She will realize I am worthy, and she will stop fighting her need for me." He sighed with longing. "This is my opportunity to win her heart forever and ensure a flawless eternity for us both."

Zeke shook his head as if to clear it, and he looked at her. The torment in his gaze was apparent. How could she send him to an eternity of personal hell because of her own stupid bargain?

Besides, she knew Satan wasn't lying about his situation with Iris.

She took a deep breath and unclenched her fist to look at the crystal vial. She could have given Mona to Quin for safekeeping while she eluded various assassins, but it was too late for that now.

Please let this be the right thing to do.

She reached behind her neck and untied the leather thong, her fist tight around Mona. "I want one of your ironclad agreements that you will give Mona back to me when I have ended the threats to my life. Lyman and the . . . slayer team, most specifically." God knew, as a

Guardian, there could be threats against her life forever. She had to be specific.

He licked his lips. "Agreed. It is done."

Theresa looked at Becca. "Is he lying?"

The Rivka shook her head. "He added it to your previous agreement. You'll get her back when you're no longer in danger from them, but not before."

Theresa held Mona up. "Be safe, friend."

The blue liquid flashed silver, then Theresa dropped the vial into Satan's outstretched hand, her stomach churning with acid. "Iris will never forgive you if you use Mona," she reminded him.

Satan's eyes sparkled as he held up the vial. "She is so beautiful. So powerful. A legend. I am in awe of her."

Oh, God. What had she done? Theresa managed a tremulous smile, knowing Mona would appreciate being adored. "Feel free to take her to some cool museums. She'd like that." *Be positive.*

The vial flashed bright red, and Satan nodded. "I own the best pornography museum in existence. I will take her through that."

Theresa grimaced. "That's not exactly what I meant."

Satan stood up, then fastened Mona around his neck. "We shall have lots of fun." He sighed. "I wish Satan Jr. was unfrozen so he could enjoy this moment."

Theresa almost choked at the thought. Mona would not be safe with Satan's son. "Is he getting out any time soon?"

"Not yet, but once Iris sees I am a man worthy of her, she will sign my petition. The Council will not be able to turn down a request from a former Guardian." He stroked the vial. "Come, Goblet. I want to show you off."

"Um, Satan, if you show her off, someone might try to steal her." Or the Council might find out and come knocking.

"So? I am Satan. I am unmatched in my manliness."

"Or Iris might think you had the Goblet to be cool, and not because you wanted to keep her safe," she tried. Her heart was racing, and she felt sick watching Satan fondle Mona.

Satan frowned. "The dragon makes a fairly intelligent point. I shall contemplate it before taking action." He snapped his fingers. "Rivka. Come along."

"I'm right behind you," Becca said. She had wiped the blood off her forehead, but there was still a red smear.

"Excellent." Satan disappeared in an explosion of gold bubbles, still fondling Mona.

The golden hue faded, leaving the three of them alone in the charred and blackened cell. Zeke sat up with a groan, leaning on the smoking mattress. "So, I don't have to kill you?" His voice was strained.

"Not at the moment." She took in his sooty appearance, the violence still smoldering in his gaze. "I'm so sorry I dragged you into my mess."

He dismissed her with a flick of his wrist. "I need a minute." He crossed his legs, closed his eyes, and rested his hands, palms up, on his knees. A faint humming emanated from his lips.

Theresa dropped her face to her hands, a shudder raking through her.

"Dragon." Becca's voice was quiet, and Theresa lifted her head to find Becca extending a hand toward her.

Theresa grabbed it and let the Rivka pull her to her

feet, waiting for a smart-ass comment about how she'd warned Theresa.

But instead, Becca flicked some ash off Theresa's shoulder. "That was a good recovery, given the situation." She pulled a wet wipe out of her jacket pocket and handed it to Theresa. "He's not planning to use Mona, but he's Satan, and I doubt he'll be able to resist the allure indefinitely. You better get rid of your stalkers soon."

Theresa pressed the wipe over her face, basking in the cool wetness while she tried to think of a plan. "Does he have a cell phone?"

"Sure. Why?"

"Text me his number. I'll have Zeke continually text him reminders about Iris until I'm out of jail, and then I'll do it."

Becca grinned. "I like it. Guilt-tripping Satan has to be a first. I'll send him some, too." She saluted Theresa. "Good luck, Dragon. I'd hate to see you in the Chamber. I'd stay and chat, but I have a meeting to discuss our advertising plan for our new blueberry pretzel."

Oh . . . pretzels. It seemed like so long since her biggest problem had been when she was going to get her next pretzel fix. The thought of them made her stomach grumble. "Can you get me some samples?"

Becca nodded toward Zeke, who was still meditating. "That was one great coup, calling out a slayer to kill you. You nearly blew Satan's brains out from the shock. For that, I will get you some blueberry pretzels." Then she turned into an inky black puddle and dissipated into the floor.

Theresa sighed and sank back down, her legs a jellied

mess. She let her head drop to her knees as she hugged her legs to her chest.

"T?"

She lifted her head. "How are you feeling?"

His eyes were their normal shade of brown, and his face was calm again. "You made a deal with Satan to regain human form?"

She nodded. "Two hundred years ago, Iris Bennett was the Guardian of the Goblet. She was also the mom of my best friend, Justine, and she was my guardian, since my parents had been killed in the Cleansing."

Their eyes met, and she quickly continued. "She fell under Satan's spell and was going to give Mona to him, so she begged me to kill her. She was quite the badass, so I had to go into dragon form to kill her. I then had to drink from Mona so I could become the Backup Guardian." She managed a rueful smile. "I was in dragon form. I couldn't change back after I drank from her. Been stuck that way ever since, until a few days ago."

"Until you made a deal with Satan so you could meet with me?"

She shrugged and concentrated on cleaning the dirt off her hands with the wipe. "The point is that I'm the Guardian of the Goblet of Eternal Youth, and I just handed Mona off to Satan. Oy." She rubbed her temples and eyed him. "And I'm supposed to kill you now that you know."

He raised his brow. "Are you going to?"

"After you get me out of jail."

He smiled. "Thanks for the heads-up. I'll be sure to keep it in mind." He let his head rest against the cement wall, propped his knees up, and rested his forearms over his knees. "So, you think Lyman could be after you because of the Goblet?"

"No," she said with certainty. "He never knew about that part of my life."

"You sure? You might talk in your sleep."

She felt her cheeks flush again, and Zeke looked surprised at her embarrassment. "He *was* your lover."

"It was only for a week, and it was 180 years ago. Our short-lived affair has nothing to do with why he's after me today."

He searched her face. "Then what does? You might as well tell me. It can't possibly be a darker secret than the fact you made a deal with Satan and just handed him the Goblet."

She stuck her tongue out at him. "Was that necessary? I'm already freaking out about it. There's really no need for reminding."

"Sorry." True regret flashed in his eyes, making her feel a little better.

Her hand went to where Mona had been around her neck, and she frowned when she encountered nothing but skin. She didn't know whether to tell Zeke the rest of the story about Lyman, but she was so tired of being alone. Would it be so bad to have someone helping her out?

"T?"

Before she could answer, a sharp rap on the bars caught her attention. She and Zeke both jumped to their feet. The guard had returned, and with him was a tall, attractive man wearing an expensive suit and a pair of stylish glasses. The man was standing slightly back, and Theresa couldn't see him that clearly. The guard eyed the cell. "What happened here?"

Zeke answered before she could think of a plausible explanation. "Exploding gas main. Almost killed us. Right?"

The cop raised a skeptical brow. "Gas main? You'll owe me if I put that in my report, Siccardi."

"You got it."

The officer nodded, then looked at Theresa. "Your attorney is here. Siccardi, you can come out."

"I don't have an attorney." She let her nostrils flare, trying to catch a scent of the attorney. He smelled like cologne and ordinary human. She shot a glance at Zeke, and he gave an almost imperceptible nod. He hadn't scented anything dangerous about the guy, either. But why was he here? She hadn't even been charged.

The man stepped forward into the light. He had a strong jaw and broad shoulders, and his eyes were intelligent and strong. He met her inspection and didn't look away. "Theresa Nichols, I presume?"

She nodded.

"I'm Percy Adams. I'm a defense attorney and a Massachusetts senator. I'm here to offer you representation."

The guard unlocked the door. "Siccardi, if my boss catches you in there, I'll be screwed. Get out and let the attorney in."

Zeke hesitated, and Theresa waved him off. As long as Percy wasn't a slayer, she could kick his ass. Dragon versus human. Hmm . . . who got the over/under on that one? Dragon wins, all the time. "I'll be fine."

He frowned. "You sure?"

"Yes. Just go work your connections to get me out, okay?"

"No problem. I'll be back." He gave Percy a long look, then stepped past the man.

Percy walked into the cell with his briefcase, and Theresa flinched as the door clanged shut behind him. She suppressed the urge to call Zeke back. Instead, she folded her arms across her chest and declined to sit on the burned-out cot. "Why are you here?"

Percy waited until Zeke and the guard were out of sight, then he answered. "You're being charged with murdering one of the most renowned television personalities of the decade."

"But I didn't do it, they have no evidence, and the charges will be dropped."

He smiled, and she was startled by the warmth in it. His eyes crinkled up and he looked kind. "This is a really high-profile case, and you'll be in high demand from every criminal attorney in the state. Let me represent you and I'll get you off." He leaned forward and she saw his gaze flick to the tattoo on her collarbone. "For free. That's how much I want your case. The publicity will be great for my career."

"Well, as long as it's not because of any concern for my well-being." Seemed to be a habit with those around her. "Are you any good?"

"I'm the best. Ask around. You'll see."

She shook her head. "I don't need your help."

Something flickered in his eyes, but he smiled again. "Your friend won't be able to get you sprung. You need me."

Something tingled at the back of her neck and she studied him more closely. "And how, exactly, would you know he's not going to succeed?"

He gave a smug grin. "Because I'm connected. Too many careers can be made by solving the murder of such an esteemed citizen as Reverend Munsey. You will be a pawn, and I have the political connections to clear your name."

She tilted her head as she sniffed again. There was something about his scent. Something odd. But she wasn't practiced enough at sniffing people out to know what it was. But something was up with Percy. She'd keep him close until Zeke could check him out and figure out what it was. So she forced a grateful smile onto her face. "If you can get me out of jail today, you can represent me."

His teeth flashed in a big smile. "Wonderful. I'll take good care of you."

Yeah, she didn't doubt that.

As he stood up and beckoned to the guard to release him, she wondered briefly if she should have waited for Zeke to check him out, but what choice did she have?

God help her if this was as bad a deal as the one she'd made with Satan.

Eleven

That evening, Zeke scowled when Percy pushed open the front door of the police station and strolled into the reception area. The man was too suave to be trusted, though he'd checked out so far. Percy was indeed a senator, he had a successful law practice, and he'd even graduated from Yale Law School. His resume was flawless, but Zeke didn't buy it. He'd keep digging until he found out what Percy was hiding.

Theresa had told him about their conversation, and he'd agreed it was smart to keep stringing Percy along until they could figure out what was up. Maybe Percy was merely a crooked politician jumping on the chance for some press. And maybe he was more.

Percy noticed Zeke and arched an eyebrow in greeting. "Mr. Siccardi. How nice to see you again. Have you been waiting for Ms. Nichols all afternoon? I should have let you know what time she was getting released."

The pleasure's all yours. Zeke ground his teeth and attempted to be polite. "Thanks for getting Theresa out of jail." True to Percy's claim, Zeke had been unsuccessful in leveraging her release. Someone was leaning hard to keep her in jail, but Percy had managed to pull the right strings.

Zeke scanned the man's outfit. Impeccable suit and hair. A little too much cologne, but for the less-sensitive humans, it would probably be unnoticeable.

Percy nodded and slid into a chair on the opposite side of the room. "It's my job." He hesitated, then said, "Are you planning to take her away when she is released?"

"Yep."

"I need to meet with her again."

Zeke shrugged. "You'll have to work it out with her."

Percy shifted in his chair, and Zeke could practically smell the anxiety leaking off him. Zeke grinned to himself and went back to reading his newly accumulated file on Lyman Peressini. Yeah, Zeke was a peaceable man nowadays, but somehow he couldn't drum up any regret about making Percy quiver with fear. As long as Percy was afraid of Zeke, he'd be less likely to think he could get away with anything regarding Theresa.

"Siccardi!"

Zeke looked up to see one of his police buddies (he'd made lots of useful contacts in several centuries of missing persons work) stick his head into the reception area. "Your girlfriend will be out in a couple of minutes."

"Thanks."

He started to shut down his computer, then felt Percy staring at him. "What?"

"I didn't realize you and Ms. Nichols were romantically involved."

Zeke shrugged and didn't bother to clarify. He continued shutting down his computer. Then the back of his neck twitched, and he jerked his gaze to the door of the station just as Alex shoved the door open and stepped inside, trailed by his two slayer flunkies, Marcus and Rathe.

He eased his laptop shut as Alex walked over to the reception desk, oblivious to Zeke's presence in the corner.

"I'd like to visit with a detainee," Alex said.

The receptionist handed him a form and a clipboard. "Fill this out, sign it, and return it to me with two forms of identification. No guarantee your request will be granted, however."

Zeke set his laptop on the chair next to him as Alex scowled at the receptionist. "I don't have time for a form. This is critical. Her name is Theresa Nichols and—"

"Alex." Zeke stood up as Percy's gaze jerked away from his magazine and settled on Alex.

Alex spun around, his features tense. "Zeke."

He glanced over Alex's shoulder at the faces of his comrades. "Hey, Marcus. Rathe."

Rathe ignored him, but Marcus gave him a happy smile.

"You haven't returned my calls," Alex said. "Makes me think that you're not going to honor the life debt you owe me." His eyes darkened. "According to slayer code, that's a death sentence."

"I know." Zeke's heart stuttered as the door leading to the holding cells opened, but a young man walked through. Not Theresa. Zeke had to get the slayers out of there. "You said seven days. It's been less than twenty-four hours."

Alex's gaze narrowed. "So, you're saying you'll help me?"

Zeke heard Theresa's voice through the door, and his adrenaline spiked. "Yes, I'll help you." He shot another glance at Percy, but the lawyer had turned his back and was rifling through his briefcase. Zeke lowered his voice anyway. "Assuming the Theresa Nichols they have in custody is the person you're looking for, you can't kill her while she's in the police station. And if she learns you're after her, she'll disappear." He began to direct the slayers to the door. "Why do you think I'm here? I'm using my contacts, but if you hang around, you'll ruin it." He shoved the door open and held it, tensing as the holding cell door began to open. "I'll call you later and report. I promise."

Alex studied him, then clapped him on the shoulder. "Thanks, man."

The thanks was so heartfelt that Zeke was immediately suspicious. "What's really going on, Alex?"

"Nothing." Alex herded his men out the door. "We'll wait to hear from you. You let me down, and I *will* kill you." The door swung shut behind them, and Zeke frowned. Something was off.

"Zeke?"

He spun back around at Theresa's voice. Her face was drawn and her clothes were still charred from the bout with Satan, but her eyes were bright. "T!" He was across the room in three big strides and hauled her against him in a fierce hug. Electricity made them both jump, but he didn't let go, and after a moment, she relaxed against him.

He glanced at the front entrance again, but there was no sign of the slayers. He felt her sigh, and he hugged her tighter.

"Ms. Nichols?"

"What?" Theresa quickly released him, and Zeke scowled as Percy stepped up to them.

"We need to talk about our game plan for getting the

charges dropped," Percy explained. "I think a press conference is key."

"No!" Zeke and Theresa responded at the same time, and Percy looked startled.

"We need to keep my identity a secret," Theresa said. "Is that possible?"

Percy wrinkled his brow. "Of course not. The story will be top news tonight. Reverend Munsey was well-loved and admired. Many people will be devastated by his death."

"But can't we keep me out of it as much as possible? No cameras. I didn't even touch him, and after I get cleared, I don't want people pointing at me for the next six months." Her voice was getting a little high-strung, and Zeke touched her arm. The jolt made her jump, but it also gave her the strength to rein in her emotions. "You can be the media presence. Invent a reason why we have to keep me hidden. You can turn it into a big mystery. The media will love it." She focused her big, golden eyes on him. "Do you think you could arrange that?"

A faint tinge of red flushed Percy's cheeks, and he nodded vigorously. "Well, yes, I think I could do that for you."

She beamed at him, and aggravation rumbled through Zeke. "T, we really have to leave."

Percy put his hand on Theresa's shoulder, and Zeke briefly envisioned accidentally breaking the man's wrist. Percy's gaze flickered to Zeke's, and he quickly removed his hand.

Zeke smirked at him.

"Ms. Nichols, we need to talk."

She hooked her fingers through Zeke's belt loop, keeping him close. "Fine. We can go get some coffee or something now."

"Not a good time." Zeke glanced again at the door, half expecting Rathe to come charging back in at any moment. Or this Lyman fellow, who still didn't have a face. "We really need to go."

Theresa picked up on his urgency. "How about dinner tonight, instead?"

"Excellent. Where?"

"My place," Zeke said. "Come to my office."

Percy shook his head. "I need to have a private conversation with my client."

"No worries. I'll give you space." He shot a look at Percy, then on a whim, threw his arm over her shoulder, prepared for the jolt before it happened, so he didn't even react outwardly. "Come on, hon. Let's get you home."

She raised an eyebrow at him, and he winked at her.

"I'm not your hon." She flicked his arm off her shoulder. "Percy, I'll meet you at the Gas Griller at seven tonight." Then she shot an annoyed look at Zeke and walked out, leaving both men behind.

Percy grinned, watching the sway of her hips as she walked away. "A woman with spirit."

"Shut up."

Theresa hadn't even flagged down a cab by the time Zeke caught up to her.

"What was with the dismissal?" he asked, sounding grumpy.

Grumpy? He dared to be *grumpy* after he'd just jerked her around like that? She whirled toward him, her hands on her hips. "You hugged me! I actually thought you were worried about me, that you cared what happened to me!"

He frowned. "I do care—"

"But it was only to show off to Percy. To make him think you had me. There was so much male testosterone leaking out of you, I could have filled a bathtub." She poked his chest, completely ignoring the electricity that jumped between them. "You don't even care what happens to me, do you?"

He grabbed her fist and wrapped his hand around it. "I do care! I've been sitting in that reception area all day waiting for you to get out, calling in every favor I have to free you."

"Only because you think saving a dragon will save your soul." She yanked her fist free. "Percy wants to use me for media fame, you want to use me to save yourself, Satan wants to use me to get Iris. I could kill lots of people for Satan, but does he want that? Of course not! I'm sick and tired of everyone using me! Do you realize that I have value on my own? Do you?" She pushed him again, and a trickle of smoke puffed out of her nose. "God, I'm sick of this!" A cascade of sparks spilled free, and she spun away from him.

God, she was pathetic. Every time she got upset she started leaking dragon bits, for heaven's sake. Just because Zeke didn't care about her as a person didn't mean she should get upset and—

"Theresa!" Zeke grabbed her arm and spun her back toward him, and she caught her breath at the blackness of his eyes. Shit. She'd forgotten about tempting him with her sparks. He covered her mouth and nose with his hand and leaned forward, his face strained. "Theresa, there's a band of dragon slayers in town looking for you. They were in the lobby right before you came out, and they could still be out here, waiting. Get it together, get in the cab, and get the hell out of here."

She stared at him and felt the strength drain out of her body. "How many?" She might be able to kick the ass of any human, or even any Otherworld being, but a slayer? A *team* of slayers? A sliver of green fear smoke trickled out between his fingers.

They both stared at it for a moment, then he cursed and pinched her nose shut. "You have to get ahold of yourself." His voice was raspy and harsh. "Get out of here. I'll come by in a little bit."

"But what if they find me?" She winced at the tremble in her voice, but she couldn't help it.

"You'll be safe at your new place." He flagged a cab with his other hand and it pulled up beside them. He jerked open the cab door and shoved her inside. "Don't leave the house until I talk to you."

She nodded and yanked the door shut, twisting around to watch him as the cab drove away. The lines of his body were tense and rigid, and she could tell he was straining to keep his slayer instincts at bay. She sighed and flopped back against the seat when he disappeared from sight.

It was a good thing he wasn't taking the "keep Theresa alive" mission personally. She'd been an idiot to pin any hopes on that amazing hug in the police station. What kind of future could they have? It wasn't as if she could control her dragon persona and keep it hidden all the time, and it wouldn't exactly work to have a boyfriend who would kill her the first time she blew some smoke in the midst of a PMS rage.

Ironic that she'd wanted to be in human form for so long, and now that she was, it wasn't enough to solve her problems.

An hour later, Zeke still hadn't fully regained control after holding Theresa while she was spewing smoke. He'd hung around the station to make sure the slayers hadn't followed her and to wait for Percy, but he finally bailed before he lost control and barged into the station and assaulted the lawyer.

Finally arriving home, Zeke slammed his apartment door shut, violence and the need to destroy roiling through his body. Who was he kidding, thinking he could hang out with Theresa and guard her? He was a fool. A damn fool.

But he had to keep her safe. Lyman . . . Alex . . . the threats were real, and he'd brought both to her door.

He didn't even bother with the yoga mat. He simply walked over to a door that he hadn't opened in years, keyed in the alarm code, then stepped inside.

The interior room was pitch black and it smelled of mold and leather and metal.

The spores tickled his nose, and he sneezed as he caught the string hanging down in the middle of the room, right where he knew it would be. He tugged it and the single lightbulb came on.

In the corner were his trunks of weapons, accumulated over 150 years of slaying and 200 years of retirement. He picked up a bejeweled sword and blew the dust off the handle, and sneezed again. This was what he'd have to use to kill Theresa now that she was immortal.

Growling, he threw it aside and picked up the punching

bag that was propped in the corner. A cloud of dust blew into his lungs, and he coughed as he hung up the bag. Then he stepped back and studied it.

Walk away, Zeke. Meditate.

Screw that.

He dropped his shields, embraced the violence, and slammed his fist into the synthetic leather. Dust billowed in the air and choked him. He bent over and coughed, trying to rake oxygen into his chest.

"Bastard!" A heavy blow came down on his back and Zeke dropped to his knees, groaning from the pain.

"Alex?" He rolled to the right as a club came down onto the mat, right where he'd been. Mold and dust burst from the mat and Alex dropped the club as a cough racked his body.

Zeke jerked his shirt up over his nose to filter. "What are you doing here?"

Alex cleared his throat, then glared at Zeke. "I saw you with the female dragon outside the police station. That was her, wasn't it? You're trying to protect her from me, you bastard!" He grabbed the club and swung again. Zeke ducked, and the bat slammed into the punching bag.

Zeke's lungs convulsed as another cloud of moldy dust released into the air, and he grabbed a gun from the pile of weapons as Alex bent over, his hands on his knees as he sucked in a wheezing breath. The gun was empty but he aimed it at Alex anyway. "Truce?"

Alex held up a hand while he finished coughing. "Bastard," he rasped. "You die."

Zeke coughed again. "Who's got your balls in a vise?"

Panic flickered across Alex's face. "No one."

"Liar." Zeke cleared his throat. "You tell me, and I'll

tell you about the dragon. Then you try to take me out and I whip your ass. It'll be like old times." He pulled his shirt over his face again and inhaled shallowly. "We can't fight in here anyway or we'll both die." He saw the indecision on Alex's face and he pushed harder. "Alex. It's me. No lies."

Finally, Alex nodded and flipped the bat to the mat, then jerked his shirt over his nose as another cloud of spores puffed up. "This place should be condemned."

"Thanks." Zeke tossed the gun in the corner. "Come on."

Five minutes later, they were settled on Zeke's couch with a couple of frosty Heinekens, Tostitos, and salsa.

Zeke leaned back on the couch and set his feet up on his coffee table. "What's going on, Alex?"

Alex leaned forward, resting his forearms on his thighs as he spun the bottle in his hands. He stared at the table, not meeting Zeke's eyes. "There's a woman."

"Theresa Nichols?"

Alex shook his head and leaned back, his left leg jiggling. "The daughter of a slayer. Her name's Jasmine Swift." He stared at something on the wall across from him. "I love her."

Zeke sat up. "You do?" Slayers didn't fall in love. In accordance with their heritage, they mated, they enrolled their sons in slayer-training camp once they started walking, they abandoned their mate and daughters once they'd fathered a son, but they never, ever fell in love. "I don't understand."

Alex sighed, and a small smile curved his mouth. "A slayer on my team was killed in battle. I was badly injured and couldn't fight anymore, so I took his body back to his mate for burial." He shrugged, and Zeke was astounded by the soft look in his eyes. "His daughter Jasmine was the only one who was home at the time. She took care of me. I was in love before she finished cleaning the blood off my shoulder."

"Damn." Zeke leaned back and rested his arm on the back of the couch, the bottle swinging from his fingertips. "I don't know what to say."

Alex's eyes darkened. "She didn't want me to slay anymore. Said it was too dangerous, and since I'd just brought home her dad, she had a point."

Zeke grinned in smug satisfaction as he absorbed the meaning of Alex's words. "You're giving up slaying? Welcome to the club, man."

"I said I'd think about it, but I haven't told the team yet." He gave Zeke a resigned look. "She was very convincing."

Zeke thought of how tough Theresa was, and he smiled. "I can imagine."

Alex sighed and ran his hand over his shaved head. "A couple of weeks ago, my client, the one with deep pockets, gave me the Theresa Nichols assignment. Said he was in the process of locating her, and he hired me to kill her once she was found."

Zeke stopped swinging the bottle and listened intently.

"Jasmine wouldn't let me do it, so I said no. Said I was settling down." His eyes grew dark and weary. "He took Jasmine the next day."

Zeke cursed and sat up, trying not to think of the crazed rage he'd fly into if someone ever kidnapped Theresa.

"I have to kill Theresa Nichols in six days or Jasmine is dead." Alex hung his head. "I split up my team and have half of them looking for Jasmine. Marcus and Rathe are with me to make sure Theresa doesn't live."

"What about the client? Why not find him?"

Alex shook his head. "I've made sure that all our contacts are untraceable so he couldn't identify us. Ironic, huh? Even you wouldn't be able to find him." His gaze met Zeke's and his eyes were pleading. "I can't lose Jasmine, Zeke. For her, I'll do what she has forbidden me to do and kill Theresa Nichols." He snorted. "Ironic, isn't it?"

Zeke thought of how he'd almost beheaded Theresa in the jail cell. It wasn't quite the same thing, because he'd been under the influence of her smoke, but still. He set his hand on Alex's shoulder. "I'm with you."

Alex looked at him, desperate hope in his eyes. "Really? You'll hand Theresa Nichols over to me?"

Zeke ground his teeth. "We have a blood oath, my brother. If it comes to that . . ." He took a deep breath. "It won't come to that."

"But if it does?"

"It won't." If it did . . . it would be an impossible choice to make.

Twelve

Lyman Peressini inspected himself in the mirror and flexed his muscles. He admired the cords of his arms, his washboard stomach, and his well-defined quads. Yes, Theresa Nichols might have rejected him before, but when she saw what he looked like now, she would finally be his. *Finally.*

He licked his lips and felt his groin tighten.

And if she didn't succumb to him, she'd die.

God, he was good.

One of his cell phones rang, and he picked up. "Yeah."

"Vido here. There's a green Manasa named Sheila here to see you. Want to talk to her?"

Ah, the Manasa who had dedicated herself to Reverend Munsey. She liked to supplement her income by sharing secrets with Lyman. Sometimes she had items of interest, sometimes not, but often enough that talking to her was worthwhile. A Manasa without scruples was a precious find indeed. "Put her through."

"You want to meet her?"

"No, you ingrate. I never meet anyone in person. Put her on the phone." Vido was a relatively new employee, but he should have learned by now that no one ever saw Lyman's face.

There was a clicking sound, then a female voice came on the line. "Hello? Sir?"

"Yes?"

"I was there when Reverend Munsey died, and I picked up something I felt you should know."

He sighed with impatience and stroked his hand over his abs. "What is it?"

"The woman who killed him? Theresa Nichols? She was there on behalf of Satan. Apparently, Satan wanted to be on Reverend Munsey's show, and she was going to try to negotiate it."

Lyman sat down with a thud on his black leather sofa and cursed Reverend Munsey's death. Having Satan on the Reverend's show would have been the perfect opportunity to manipulate the leader of the Underworld. He slammed his foot through the wall. Plaster dust exploded all over the hand-woven carpet, making him stop and take a deep breath.

There was no need to get upset. His original plan was still proceeding nicely. He would get what he wanted, and he would take advantage of this opportunity to learn more about Satan. He sat down on the sofa and crossed his legs, setting his left hand on his thigh. "Are you certain she is working with Satan?"

"I read her mind. I never make errors."

He chuckled. Sheila was convinced Theresa had killed Reverend Munsey, but the green Manasa had been set up, and was too foolish to realize it. "Excellent. Thank you."

"I also got a vibe of something else, but I couldn't totally read it."

He admired his pedicure and envisioned Theresa sucking his toes. He groaned and fell back against the couch, moving his hips as he slid his hand over the front of his pants.

"I think Theresa has something to do with the Goblet of Eternal Youth."

Lyman's head snapped up. "*What?*" He stood up, clutching the phone to his ear. "Tell me now!"

"I . . . I . . . I . . ."

"Stop blubbering in fear! Tell me what you saw!" He paced the room, his mind racing as he waited for corroboration of the one piece of unconfirmed information his entire plan was built on.

"I don't know exactly, but she definitely has a connection to it. Maybe she knows where it is or guards it or something. I'm not sure, but I definitely saw the Goblet." She paused. "And the sensation was so familiar. I'm sure I've seen it before."

"Excellent work. Tell Vido to pay you ten thousand dollars for exclusive rights to this information." Exclusive rights meant she would forget the information and be unable to sell it anywhere else. "Any more information on Theresa Nichols, Satan, or the Goblet that you bring me will earn double, as long as it's true. If the information turns out to be false, then you will be tortured and killed, of course."

"Oh, I know, sir. I would never forget. You're so ruthless and—"

Lyman disconnected and let the phone dangle from his fingertips, his mind whirling.

Satan knew Theresa.

Theresa's connection to the Goblet was confirmed.

He grinned. After a lifetime of planning, everything was finally coming together. He walked over to the mirror and gazed at himself again, smiling at his booming erection. He didn't know which was more exciting, Theresa, the Goblet, or finally having Satan at his mercy. Once he took care of all three of them, he wouldn't have to hide from Satan anymore. He could finally come out of hiding and accept the glory due to him, Lyman Peressini.

He hit the walkie-talkie function on his phone. "Vido. Send in the redhead and two blonds. Blindfold them as usual."

"Excellent choices, sir. They will be right in."

Lyman threw down the phone and closed his eyes, envisioning Theresa in her naked glory, writhing under him as she screamed his name.

Soon.

Iris Bennett was sitting with Jerome, a pirate who was the only modern-thinking member of the Council. They were engaged in a heated debate about the proper wording for the amended section on Guardian chastity in the *Treatise on Guardianship* when an explosion of gold bubbles burst through the wall of her living room.

Jerome jumped up and whipped his sword out of its scabbard, and Iris felt the heat of embarrassment rise in her cheeks. A visit from Satan was *not* what she needed while trying to work herself back into the Council's good graces.

"Iris, my love!" Satan was wearing a casual pair of black slacks and a gold silk shirt with puffy sleeves. The shirt was open to his waist, revealing a tanned and buff torso.

She grimaced and dragged her eyes away from his body. "This is not a good time."

"Nonsense. It is always a good time to bask in my sexuality."

Jerome sheathed his sword and picked up the bottled water he'd been drinking. "You're not welcome here. Leave."

Completely ignoring Jerome, Satan dropped to his knees in front of Iris. "As I have freely admitted on many occasions, I am devastated by your refusal to open your heart and legs to me."

Jerome pressed the lip of his water bottle against Satan's left ear, and Iris glared at Satan. "Shut up, *now.*"

His fingers danced down her calves and sent shivers up her legs. "I know you have not forgiven me for using you to try to steal the Goblet, and you do not believe I have reformed myself, so I am bringing proof."

Jerome interrupted before she could kick Satan in the shin. "Let him talk. If he really has redeemed himself, this would be a good thing for the Council to know." But he tilted the bottle until a drop slipped out and hit Satan's ear.

Satan yelped and jumped sideways as a small hole melted through his earlobe. "Do that again and I will skewer you with a thousand acid-laced needles," he snapped. "Only because Iris is here do I not rip your intestines from your body and weave them into a new sweater for myself."

Jerome held the bottle higher. "Just try it."

"Hey, boys! Ease down!" She folded her arms over her chest. "Satan, talk already."

Satan beamed at her and slid his finger under the leather strap around his neck. He lifted it, and a crystal vial containing blue liquid winked at her. "See this? You admit I have this vial under my control, yes?"

She frowned. "Yes, so?"

"So!" He spread his arms and beamed at her. "It is the Goblet of Eternal Youth!"

Jerome sucked in his breath and she felt her heart stutter. "*What?*"

"Yes!" He leaped to his feet and bowed deeply. "I have been in sole possession of the Goblet for several hours, and all I have done is take her to my porn museum and gaze at her with respect and awe."

Iris stared at the sparkling crystal. "You lie," she whispered. "It has to be a lie. That's not Mona."

"No, it is not a lie!" He traced his fingers reverently over the vial. "Theresa Nichols, Interim Guardian, is being stalked by many bad people and may die at any moment. She gives me the Goblet for safekeeping until she knows she will stay alive." He laid his hand over his chest, pressing his palm against the bare skin. "She trusts me, and you should as well." He lifted Mona to his lips and kissed her.

"*Theresa gave Mona to you?*" Bile and horror curdled Iris's stomach and she lunged for the vial.

Satan spun out of her reach. "You know how badly I yearn for Mona, to use her for my own benefit and to increase the resources of hell, yes?"

"Yes," she croaked, not daring to look at Jerome, who was on his cell phone and calling for help. Realizing his bottle of water was inadequate for dealing with the situation, he was ordering machine guns loaded with purified water, and she saw Satan shoot a look of alarm in Jerome's direction.

Tap water would melt him, but he'd regain his form in moments. Purified water would put him down for months, possibly with permanent damage. "Satan," she said. "Give her back."

"No." He turned back to her. "It is only my love for you that is keeping Mona safe." He strode to the window and peeked out, no doubt looking for the Council's troops. He inspected Iris's yard, then dropped the curtain. "You shall see now that I am worthy of your love and your body. I am Satan. You are Iris. We will have an eternity of perfection together, no?" He dangled Mona between his fingertips, making her swing back and forth. "Please, feel free to openly admire my brilliance."

Oh, God.

She felt Jerome lean into her. "Get it back from him," he whispered. "*Now.*"

Iris held out her shaking hand. "Satan, you have proven yourself. I believe you, so you do not need to keep her anymore. Please, give her to me and . . ." She swallowed hard. "And I will go on a date with you tonight."

"No!" He jumped to his feet, clutching Mona in his fist. "I want an eternity! I do not forgo the political advantages of Mona for one date! Nothing less than forever will suffice!"

Jerome shouted and threw the bottle of water at Satan. The leader of hell screamed with rage, slammed Jerome against the wall with some invisible force, then whirled around and vanished in a funnel cloud of gold and black bubbles.

"Accept his offer, Iris," Jerome groaned. "Sacrifice yourself."

She stared after Satan. She'd never seen black bubbles

from him before. He was always gold. Pure gold. She swallowed hard. Black bubbles meant they were in really deep trouble.

Lyman was a badass dragon who would rip her apart without breaking a sweat. The slayers would down her with only their scent. Put them together, and Theresa knew it was time to start making a will.

Hah. As if she would admit defeat. She was a dragon, and dragons kicked ass, end of story. Okay, fine, maybe she wasn't as much of a lethal weapon as she needed to be, but that was something she could change.

It was time to learn how to fight and master the ability to block the slayer's scent.

And there was one man who could teach her both, as long as he didn't accidentally kill her.

She scowled and slammed the hammer onto a huge nail. The hammer slipped out of her sweaty hand and thudded onto her toe, sending pain shooting up her leg. "Crap!" She grabbed the hammer, wiped the perspiration off her brow, and glanced at the clock again. Zeke could be here any minute and she wasn't finished.

She grabbed her cell phone and called Becca.

The Rivka answered on the first ring. "What's up, Dragon?"

"I need your help. Can you come over?"

"I'm about to fire someone for trying to steal the recipe for our new blueberry pretzels. I've been looking forward to it all day. Can it wait?"

"No. Please?" She bit her lip and hoped the Rivka wouldn't turn her down. "I'll owe you."

"You already do."

"I'll owe you more."

Becca sighed. "Fine. I'll be right over."

Theresa sighed with relief and shut her phone as an inky black shape rose up from her floor and took the shape of Becca. "What's up?"

"Thank you so much for coming. You're the best!"

"It's for Derek. He'd want me to help you."

"Of course it is." She didn't have time to worry about the reasons. She held up a heavy iron ring. "I'm trying to attach these to the wall, but they keep coming out when I yank on them." She pointed to the one already hanging on the wall, about five feet above the ground. "Watch." She looped a few fingers through it, planted her left foot on the wall, then yanked as hard as she could. After the third tug, the ring came free and she flew backward and crashed into a floor lamp. The lightbulb shattered as it hit the floor, and Theresa jumped back up. "See?"

"You called me over here for home decorating?" Becca was frowning at her. "What do you need these for?"

"I need to immobilize someone who's really strong." She thought for a second. "It'll be kind of like torturing."

Becca's face relaxed into a smile. "Why didn't you say so? I'm an expert at torturing."

"That's why I called."

Becca set her hands on her hips and studied the wall. "See, your problem is that the walls aren't built for this kind of activity." She walked around the apartment, taking inventory and shaking her head. She even stuck her head into the bedroom. "You've got nothing here that'll do. We'd have to do some major reconstruction."

"No time. He could be here any second."

Becca pursed her lips and tapped her foot. "I'm sure I

could arrange for Satan's torture chamber to be available."

Theresa shook her head. "Transportation issues. I have no way to get myself or anyone else to hell."

"But I can."

Theresa raised her brow. "I thought you had to go fire someone."

Becca walked over to the couch, sat down, and crossed her legs. "For torture, I'm happy to stay." She sighed and rested her arms on the back of the couch. "Ironic, isn't it? I hate torture, but because I have Satan's life force keeping me alive, he orders me to embrace torture and even like it, so I have to." She rolled her eyes. "I disgust myself."

Theresa stared at the Rivka. It was the most Becca had ever revealed about herself, and it made Theresa want to grab a couple of wine coolers and kick back with her. "That sucks."

Becca shrugged. "Well, nothing I can do about it, right?" She sat up and seemed to shake off the melancholy. "Let's get on with it. What's the plan?"

"Remember, Iris will reject you forever if you use Mona." Theresa hit SEND on her phone and forwarded her eighth message to Satan in the last ten minutes, nervously whiling away the time while she waited for Zeke to show up. She hadn't seen him since the police station, and she was a little antsy, wondering when he'd appear and what state he'd be in when he showed up.

She and Becca were ready, though. Ready and nervous. Becca was hiding out in the bedroom, Theresa was positioned on the couch. Waiting.

She was typing her ninth text message to Satan when the door to her condo opened and Zeke walked in. The phone slipped out of her fingers as she drank in his scent. God, she'd missed him. Even if it was only a slayer/dragon attraction, it didn't matter. She simply felt better having him around.

He looked tired and strung out, but there was an energy rolling off him that she hadn't seen before.

It was a dark and violent energy, and it made her want to get down on her knees and crawl across the floor to him so she could rub up against him and absorb him into her body.

She hugged the tasseled throw pillow to her chest instead and bit her lower lip.

Zeke kicked the door shut with his foot and threw his leather jacket onto a chair. "You all right?"

She nodded, not quite trusting herself to speak.

"Good." He sat down on the armchair, set his elbows on his knees, and dropped his forehead to his palms.

After a moment of silence, Theresa frowned. "Are *you* all right?"

He finally lifted his head, and she saw intense weariness in his gaze. "No, I'm not."

She scooted toward him so she could stroke his shoulder. "What happened?"

He managed a half-smile, then took a deep breath as he leaned into her touch. The weariness left his gaze and his shoulders became stronger. "Okay, Theresa, here's the deal. The slayers in town? They're my old team. I trained them. They're the best."

She raised her eyebrow. "I feel much better now, thanks."

He grimaced. "I owe one of them a life debt, and he wants me to hand you over."

She peeked at the door. Unlocked.

"I was trying to avoid it," he continued. "But I just found out that if I don't help him kill you, the woman he loves will be murdered."

She walked over and locked the door. Then slid the dead bolt.

"She's already been kidnapped." His voice was strained. "I can't let him lose her."

Zeke's torment was so intense that she wanted to wrap her arms around him and hug his sadness away. Then she scowled at herself. *He's a slayer, remember? Have no mercy.* Her life was at stake, and she had to make that her priority.

She shoved aside her guilt and turned her back to him. Then she slipped the earplugs out of her pocket and shoved them up her nose. Tried to inhale through her nose. Impossible. *Perfect.*

"I have six days until you have to die, so I figure we have time to try to find his mate." Zeke slammed his fist into the couch. "We *have* to find her."

Theresa didn't turn around to face him. "What about Lyman? I thought you were going to help me find him." She flinched at the nasal twang in her voice, hoping he wouldn't notice.

He cursed and sounded so weary she almost abandoned her plan. "If you stay hidden here, you should be okay. This place is pretty untraceable, and it's as safe as we're going to find. We'll tackle Lyman next week."

"Hidden?" She stalked into the kitchen and yanked open the top drawer where she'd stashed the items she'd purchased on the way home from the police station. "I've been hiding forever and I'm sick of it." She slammed the drawer shut with her hip. "I don't have to protect Mona anymore, so I have no reason to hide out. I'm taking charge of my life, starting now. I'm not going to sit around waiting for Lyman or your friends to find me."

She turned around, then jumped when she realized Zeke was standing right behind her. He caught her arms. "T? Are you listening to me? The situation with my friend's mate is a major complication."

God, he looked so miserable that she almost changed her mind.

But she couldn't afford empathy. Not now. She touched his cheek, trailing her finger over his bristled jaw. "I'm so sorry, Zeke."

Then she opened her mouth and set his shirt on fire.

Wariness flickered over his face, and then his eyes went all smoky. "What are you doing?"

More flames came out of her mouth, and he clutched her arms. "T?"

Heat surged into her lower body, but she willed it away and blew flame rings past his right ear. His gaze followed them, and then he looked at her. The lust in his eyes was so intense that her knees almost buckled. "God, Theresa, you're so hot."

"I know." She blew more flame at his chest, and he groaned.

Then he grabbed her face and kissed her. His tongue thrust into her mouth and she nearly cried at the heat pouring through her body. "Oh, God, Zeke." She threw her arms around his neck and let her fire erupt into his mouth. It seared into his throat, and he deepened the kiss.

She sighed and pressed her body against him. *Need to breathe.* She broke the kiss so she could inhale through her mouth, and she saw Zeke's glazed eyes blink in surprise. "Why aren't you reacting?"

She realized then he must have released his pheromones, and a sense of pride burst through her. Sure, she'd needed earplugs in her nose, but still. Victory to the dragon! She held his face between her hands and blew more flames onto his face turning his skin red.

"T?" His knees gave way and he slumped to the floor at her feet, gazing up at her with such raw lust and despair on his face, that she was unable to resist.

She let him tug her to the floor, and he rolled on top of her, his lips frantically sucking at her neck, her throat, her collarbone. She clutched at his back, sliding her hands under his shirt as she sent more flames shooting past his head. It felt so good to let go.

His left hand cupped her breast, and she shuddered even as more fire poured from her nose. He ground his hips into her and pleasure pooled in her lower belly. She tugged him closer. *Have to have more. Need him closer.*

His mouth closed on her nipple through her shirt and her hips came off the ground with an involuntary yelp and an explosion of flames. "Oh, God, Zeke."

Then his body quivered, and he collapsed on top of her in a dead weight.

"Zeke?" She tapped his shoulder. "You there?" His face was pressed against her breasts, his body limp on top of her.

She sighed and let her head flop back on the floor as she wrapped her arms around his muscular back. *It worked.*

But what about her? Why had she responded with that much passion? She'd been protected from his pheromones, and yet she'd been as helpless to resist as she'd been when he hit her with them.

"Damn, Dragon. You weren't exaggerating," Becca said from the doorway. "Even Satan doesn't have that kind of power over the opposite sex."

There was the slightest hint of admiration in Becca's voice, and Theresa smiled. She couldn't remember the last time anyone had admired her for anything, and it felt brilliant. She twisted her head so she could look at the Rivka. "Want to help me with him?"

"I think I need a cold shower first."

Theresa grinned, and she tried to roll Zeke off her, but his dead weight was too much. Pathetic Dragon Disease strikes again. "Becca?"

"Oh, fine."

Together they got Zeke off Theresa, settling him gently on the kitchen floor. Becca grabbed the handcuffs, but Theresa shook her head. "We have to wrap towels around his wrists so he doesn't get bruised."

Becca raised her eyebrow. "Isn't he your mortal enemy?"

"Yes." Theresa tugged open her dish-towel drawer and removed the softest ones.

"Didn't I overhear him saying he was going to help his slayer team kill you, if necessary?"

Theresa winced at the reminder of his betrayal. "Maybe." She decided one towel wasn't thick enough, so she doubled them up before wrapping up his left wrist and tying it softly. She stuck her finger underneath to make sure he still had circulation, then started on his other wrist.

"So, why do you care if he gets bruised?"

Theresa carefully locked the handcuffs around the towels, then sat back on her heels to inspect her handiwork. Zeke looked so defenseless. The lines were gone from his face, and he looked younger than his 350 years. He looked as she'd imagined he would, stretched out on her bed after a night of passion.

"Dragon? Why do you care if his wrists get a little bruised?"

She shrugged and wiped some ash off his cheek. "I don't know, okay? Leave me alone."

Becca whistled softly. "The dragon has a soft spot for the slayer, huh?"

She glared at the Rivka. "Shut up and help me get him to hell before he wakes up, okay?"

Becca grinned, an amused glint in her eyes. "Anything for the badass dragon."

Thirteen

Zeke's head felt as if someone had clubbed him with a sledgehammer. He groaned and tried to rub his forehead, but he couldn't reach it. He snapped his eyes open and found himself staring at a cathedral ceiling covered in the most incredible swirls of color and paint, all of it gilded with gold. They were ancient scenes of . . . he narrowed his eyes and looked closer. A man was sprawled on his back, thousands of tiny daggers wedged in his body. Satan was standing over him, a delighted grin on his face . . . *Oh, shit.*

He jerked his arms with renewed force, wincing as pain wrenched through his shoulders. The heavy iron chains clanged, but he couldn't begin to break them. Sweat trickled down his back as he struggled harder. *Crap.* What had he done to warrant ending up *here*?

"Oh, good. You're awake."

"Theresa?" He lifted his head, searching desperately for her. When he saw her standing at the foot of the king-sized bed he was lying on, he nearly groaned in relief. "T! Get me out of here!"

"It's okay, Zeke. You're safe." She was wearing a pair of jeans that fit her curves just right, and a black T-shirt that showed off the tattoo on her collarbone. Her hair was swept up in a disheveled knot on top of her head, and her eyes were concerned. "Are you okay?" She crawled onto the bed and knelt next to him, checking his restraints.

"What's going on?" He stared at her while she shifted the padding on his wrists. "Did you bring me here?"

She sat back on her heels, her jaw clenched in determination. "I'm really sorry I had to kidnap you, but it was the only way."

"Tell me I'm not in Satan's torture chamber."

She grimaced. "Yeah, sorry. I didn't have anything set up at home, and Becca arranged for me to borrow this place."

He searched her face, trying to figure out what she was thinking. "So you could torture me?"

"No." She swung off the bed and walked over to a golden control panel on the wall. "For training."

"Training what?"

She hit a button and the top half of the bed began to rise, until he was sitting up. "Craftmatic bed," she said. "Comes in handy."

From this position, he could see the entire room. There were all sort of strange-looking devices adorned with leather straps and metal bits. But there were also several shelves of erotic massage oils and objects that looked Otherworld in origin. He shifted and felt a tug on his ankles. A quick glance told him he was shackled there as well, but again, Theresa had covered his skin with thick towels to protect him. He frowned and looked at her again. "Fill me in, T. What the hell's going on?"

She came to stand at the foot of the bed, shifting restlessly. It was then he saw the apprehension in her eyes.

The fear. He softened his voice, wishing he could reassure her with his touch. "T, what's wrong?"

"I need to learn how to protect myself from slayers."

He raised his brow. "But you didn't react in your apartment."

A faint pink flushed her cheeks. "Earplugs in my nose."

He grinned at her embarrassment. "Excellent idea."

She shook her head. "I don't want to walk around with a plugged nose for the rest of my life. I can be a good dragon. I know I can." She slammed her fist into her palm. "So this is what we're going to do. You're going to teach me to resist your pheromones."

He frowned. "You want me to hit you with them?"

"Yes." She gave him an apologetic pat on his shin that made him jump. "But I don't trust you not to kill me if I go too crazy, so I decided to incapacitate you."

His frown deepened and he tugged at his chains. "I can resist killing you."

"Maybe, but it's not a risk I want to take." She leaned on the brass footboard and leveled her gaze at him. "Tell me everything about the pheromones. Are they all the same or do they differ?"

He closed his eyes. Helping her was a great step in overcoming his past, but it was also a betrayal of his life debt to Alex, and could possibly endanger Alex's mate.

"Zeke?"

He opened his eyes to find her golden eyes fastened on him, begging for his assistance. The fear in the eyes of his indomitable dragon did him in. "I'll help."

A relieved smile lit up her face, and the ache in his gut eased. "Thank you."

He nodded and refused to think about Alex or his mate.

She threw her leg over the end of the bed and climbed up next to him. "So? Talk to me."

He cleared his throat and shifted as much as his chains would allow. "All slayer pheromones will rob you of your strength. They'll make you dizzy and relaxed. You won't care if you die or live because you'll be in this blissful state of euphoria. You'll see the slayer as the bringer of such pleasures that you'll adore him, beg him to come close to you. That's how the slayers can get close enough to stab the dragon in the underside of the neck."

She made a noise of disgust. "Slayers should be ashamed of themselves."

He eyed her. "It's instinct. It's nature. We didn't plan it."

"Still annoying." She pulled her knees up to her chest and rested her chin as she looked at him. "What about the . . . other stuff? You didn't mention that."

"The sexual attraction part?" At her nod, he continued. "Well, the way you react to me is unusual."

Her cheeks flushed. "How unusual?"

He finally said the words that had been bothering him all along. "I've never had it happen before."

She raised her eyebrows. "Really? Never?"

He shook his head. "I've killed hundreds of dragons, plenty of them female." A flicker of rancor ran through him at the thought of all the dead dragons, and he scowled. "It was never like this."

She scooted forward slightly, so her toes were brushing his hip. "It's not your fault you killed them."

"I don't want to talk about it."

"Then I'll talk." She probed him with her gaze. "I think it's admirable that you want to change your destiny."

He gritted his teeth and stared at the shelf of massage oil.

"I mean, I'm not saying that I necessarily think you're going to succeed, but it makes me hate you less for the fact you might have killed my parents."

He glanced at her, years of pain burning in his chest. "I am so sorry if I killed your family. If I could bring them back, I would. No matter what the cost to me."

She tilted her head and looked at him, sadness heavy in her eyes. "I believe you."

"But if I did kill them, could you forgive me?"

After a long moment, she shrugged, her fingers absently playing with the hair on his forearm. "Honestly, I don't know. It's sort of strange to think about forgiving a slayer for doing what they do. I mean—"

"Forget it."

They were both silent for a long moment, then Theresa cleared her throat. "So, um, the way you react to my flames—is that unusual, too?"

He met her gaze. "I don't know. You're the first dragon whose flames I've been unable to block."

A look of pride settled on her face and her eyes glimmered. "Really? Because I'm so powerful?"

"I thought it was because I was out of practice, but now I'm not sure." The second she'd hit him in her apartment, he'd thrown up his defenses, and it hadn't made a bit of difference. He knew his barriers had been secure, and she'd burst right through them. If he were in the slaying business, it would seriously concern him. As it was, it made him feel better, knowing she had a defense against him if he did lose control. Not that he planned to, but the more time he spent around her, the more his old slayer tendencies were resurfacing, and it was getting more and more difficult to deny who he was.

Theresa smiled. "I think it's because I'm a brilliant dragon. So maybe all your slayer friends will fall at my feet. They will all lust after my body and—"

"Let's practice your defenses so you don't have to use the flames," he interrupted.

She raised her brow. "Why are you so testy?"

"Because I'm chained up in Satan's torture chamber. Can we get to work so I can get out of here?"

"Fine." She scooted closer to him, and he caught a whiff of her scent. Not her dragon scent, but her aroma as a woman and a human. She smelled like vanilla and soap, and something soft and vulnerable that made him want to grab her and protect her.

Hah. As if she'd let him do that. Which made him want to do it even more.

"Zeke? What else do I need to know?"

He dragged his thought away from her softness and tried to focus. "Okay, so when we use our pheromones, we try to sneak up on the dragon and release them before the dragon knows we're there. If they see us coming and shut down their sensors, then we're screwed." She was listening so intently he felt uncomfortable. "Very few slayers can take down a fully functioning adult dragon."

"You can."

"What?"

"The slayer who orchestrated the Cleansing was said to be able to best any dragon." She met his gaze, but there was no accusation in her face. Just curiosity. "That's you, right?"

He grunted. "In the past. Not anymore."

She nodded. "It's good for me to learn from the best. Continue."

"First, you'll have to learn how to block my scent." He could feel her toes wiggling against his hip and he instinctively shifted his hips to be closer to her. "But then the tough part is learning recovery."

Her forehead furrowed. "What's that?"

"My team will sneak up on you and hit you with pheromones before you can block them." That battle strategy was a little embarrassing when he explained it like that. Felt like cheating. But it was the destiny of slayers, and they had no choice in the matter. "You need to learn how to recover once you've been hit."

She chewed her lower lip. "I practiced that with chocolate cake. Slayer scent is way tougher, but it's the same concept, right?"

"Same concept," he agreed. He smiled and wanted to touch her, give her comfort. He tugged on the chains and was able to move his wrist far enough to tap her ankle. "Don't look so worried. You'll be able to do it."

She lifted her chin. "Of course I will."

He grinned. "Okay, so, you ready?"

She met his eyes, and he saw the trust in them. Something swelled in his chest, and at the same time, he felt fear. Fear of letting her down.

"Give me a second." She closed her eyes, and her forehead furrowed in concentration. Her lips were pressed tightly together and the tendons in her neck bulged.

"T, relax."

"I can't."

"Yes, you can. Clear your mind." He gave her the same instructions he'd used when he taught young slayers to resist the flames of dragons. "A tense mind is jumbled and vulnerable. Focus only on blocking the scent. Know you can do it. Don't stress about failing. Nothing bad will happen to you."

The tension in her neck eased and her hands relaxed.

"I'm going to release some scent now, okay?"

Her neck became tense again and she nodded even as she scrunched her face up. "Do it."

"Relax, T. Envision your goal of immunity." He sent a minuscule amount of pheromone into the air, and Theresa sucked in her breath. "Soften your mind. Picture the scent drifting through your body, unable to latch on to anything." He kept focused on the feminine curve of her throat, taking his own advice and clearing his mind from the fact she was a dragon, his prey. "Send the scent out through your fingers and toes. Carry it through your body and release it untouched into the air."

He smiled as he saw her body relax and he increased the dosage. "It is harmless, a visiting chemical that you will acknowledge and then send on its way."

Her body was still, except for the rise and fall of her chest as she breathed.

His throat tightened with pride at her accomplishment, and he opened the dams, hitting her with the full force of his scent. "Let it roll through you, T, like a visitor passing through. You don't fear it, and it cannot touch you."

She inhaled deeply, her face relaxed and her body at ease.

He fell quiet and continued to bombard her with the pheromones, letting her work through it on her own.

After several minutes of success, he said quietly, "Brand the image of the scent leaving your body, then open your eyes. Keep your vision soft, focus on your inner eye."

She opened her eyes and he saw the blurry golden hues. "Release the chemical from your body, Theresa."

Her gaze flicked toward his face, and suddenly she sucked in her breath. "Zeke." His name was a throaty whisper and his groin tightened.

"Focus, T. Calm your mind."

"Oh, God." She shut her eyes again and her body relaxed again almost immediately. "I can't keep focused with my eyes open," she whispered.

"Yes, you can." He took a moment to clear his own mind. "Open your eyes, T."

She scrunched them shut, and he chuckled.

"You're laughing at me," she complained.

"I'm laughing with you."

Her eyes snapped open and she glared at him. The glare lasted less than a second as lust swept over her and she fell forward, her hands on his chest. "Oh, God, Zeke."

Jesus. Her lust slammed into him and his muscles clenched. "Theresa. Clear your mind. There is no lust. No fear. Simply your own power."

She straddled his hips and yanked his shirt out of his jeans. Her lips caressed his belly and he groaned. He couldn't stop his hips from thrusting against her. He leaned his head back against the pillow, willing the violence out of his body. "Theresa," he snapped. "Look at me."

She curved her neck to look at him, even as her hand slipped under the waistband of his jeans. "Shut them off, Zeke."

"No. You can do it. You can recover." *I can recover.* His breath was coming heavy now, his body straining against the front of his pants, the itch creeping down the back of his neck and down his arms. He tried to pull her head away when she licked her way up his stomach, but the chains tightened around his wrists. *Damn.* "Envision each cell in your body rejecting my scent." He swallowed hard as she pressed her pelvis against him. He wanted to throw her onto her back, grind his hips into hers, and— *No.* The violence lured him, yanked at his self-control, but he forced himself to relax even as he wanted Theresa to writhe on top of him.

You could kill her right now, Slayer.

"Theresa! Visualize yourself triumphing over it." He focused on doing the same. He would *not* succumb.

She groaned and his body tightened. Her eyes met his, and he could see the lust in her gaze, the hopelessness and despair. "Take me, Zeke."

Take her, then kill her. "No! You don't want me." *And I don't want to kill you.*

"Yes, I do." She crawled up him, her body pulsating with lust and fear and need.

She rubbed her breasts over his chest and he almost jerked at the chains to grab her, but he restrained himself, forcing his hands to lie quietly on the golden weave of the bedspread. "Theresa. Look at me." His voice was raspy and harsh, but it was still his, and he was still in control. Barely.

Her moan made his body clutch, and she looked at him, her body pressed against his. "Make it stop."

"You fail only because you think you can't succeed." He met her gaze, drove her with his willpower as his instincts grew more powerful, pulsating in every pore of his body, demanding that he finish the task he'd begun. *I will not kill the dragon.* "You are stronger than this, Theresa. I believe in you."

Her eyes widened, and a new defiance surged into them.

"Yes," he whispered. "You've got it." Unbidden, his body released more pheromones, and he knew he was beginning to lose the battle to keep her safe from him.

She kept her gaze focused on his face, but he could feel the strength returning to her body. She slipped her hand out of his pants and sat up, her nostrils flaring. "I'm doing it."

He clenched his fists. "Good job."

She rolled off him and jumped off the bed. "I'm doing it!" She clasped her hands over her head and did a little hip shake that had him groaning. "I rock!" She jumped onto the bed next to him and did a drum roll on his belly, grinning hugely. "Release more, release more!"

"You're already getting all I've got." His instincts recognized that she was no longer a helpless victim, and his slaying needs began to slacken, replaced by the self-awareness that the dragon was a full-strength threat and it was time to retreat. *Thank God.*

"And you didn't even try to kill me." She looked delighted by that realization, and he groaned to himself at her unawareness of his internal struggle. "Thank you so much for helping me. I'm so pumped!" She leaned over and gave him a quick kiss on the cheek and the jolt jumped between them.

She pulled back and rolled off the bed.

Zeke exhaled in relief and regret. Even as his slayer instincts to throttle her faded, his body had responded to her lustful attentions, and those feelings were still pulsing through his veins.

But she hadn't used any flames on him, so he couldn't blame that. Either it had been part of his destructive slayer instincts reacting to her defenselessness, or he'd responded to Theresa, pure and simple.

If it was the first, then he was angry with himself for being unable to control his instincts.

If it was the second, then it scared the hell out of him. How could he possibly be attracted to a woman who made him into exactly what he didn't want to be? A slayer.

No. It could never work.

This was business only, and it was time to remember that.

Fourteen

Later that day, Theresa let herself into her apartment. Becca had picked her and Zeke up in hell and dropped them off at Vic's. Zeke had gone to his office to check messages and follow up on his friend's mate, after making Theresa promise she wouldn't go to meet Percy until he came back to escort her.

She flung open her door and kicked it shut. On the one hand, it was kind of cute that he wanted to protect her, but on the other, it was really annoying. Protect one day, turn her over to a band of slayers the next. It was enough to drive a dragon insane.

"Theresa."

Theresa jumped and spun toward the kitchen to find Iris standing in the doorway, her arms crossed and her eyes flickering with anger. "Iris! What are you doing here?"

"Where's Mona?"

"Uh . . ."

Iris's face paled. "Tell me she isn't with Satan. Tell me he was lying to me."

"Well . . ."

"Sweet mother Mary, Theresa!" Iris flung up her hands. "I knew I should have gotten you replaced!"

"No, it's fine. See, he's just keeping her safe because I have all these assailants after me . . ."

"That's no excuse for handing the Goblet over to Satan." Iris stalked past her, her black silk pants swishing as she walked. "Okay, here's what we have to do." She reached the middle of the room and turned to face Theresa. "Jerome was present when Satan showed us his vial and claimed it was Mona—"

Theresa stumbled, her hand going to her throat. "The Council knows?" she whispered. "Are they coming for me?"

"Jerome sent me here to find out the truth. As soon as it's confirmed, you'll be confined to the Chamber of Unspeakable Horrors forever, and probably Justine will as well, since she's the official Guardian." Iris took a deep breath and spread her hands, trying to maintain her composure. "I'm not going to let you drag my daughter down with you."

"Hey." Theresa had had enough of Iris making her feel inadequate. "I did the best I could in the situation. I will get Mona back and everything will be fine."

Iris glared at her. "God help all of us if you're wrong."

"Hey! Don't give me that look! You forced this life on me. I'm doing the best I can, and you're all over my case all the time. For God's sake, you've never even thanked me for killing you!" She shot a burst of flames through Iris for emphasis. "I made a deal with Satan that had nothing to do with Mona, and then he ordered me to hand him Mona and I couldn't disobey, so I told Zeke to kill me instead!"

Iris's eyebrows shot up. "You did?"

"Yes! He's a slayer, so I even blew flames on him so he wouldn't be able to resist killing me."

Iris stood up straighter, an odd look on her face. "Really?"

"Yes, really! It would have destroyed Zeke to kill me, but I was going to sacrifice both of us to save Mona. Then Satan pointed out that if he abused Mona, he'd lose you forever, and that's when I knew he really didn't intend to use her. So I agreed, and I put extra safeguards in the contract to save her, confirmed by his Rivka, Becca. Mona's safe, and I'm doing everything in my power to end the threats to me so he has to give her back. So leave me alone!" She blinked suddenly, realizing Iris had disappeared behind a thick cloud of dragon smoke.

Iris waved her hand through the smoke, trying to clear it, a proud smile on her lips. "It's about time."

"About time what?" Theresa frowned at the delighted look on Iris's face.

"It's about time you grew up." She smiled at Theresa again, then settled herself among the cushions on the couch. She patted the pillow. "Come sit."

Theresa folded her arms over her chest. "Why do you look so happy? You never look this happy when you're talking to me."

Iris looked at Theresa with obvious affection. "When you came to live with Justine and me after your parents were killed, you were irresponsible and flighty. I worried about you all the time, but I had no idea how to help you find your balance."

Theresa frowned. "My parents had encouraged me to embrace life."

"Yes, I know." Iris shifted on the couch and studied

Theresa. "When you showed the strength of character to kill me and then took the Oath as Justine's successor, I hoped that you would rise to meet the demands of the position, but you didn't. You simply sat around, spending all your time worrying about being stuck in dragon form and engaging in cybersex."

Theresa's shoulders drooped and she sat down on her new armchair. A few faint sparks sagged out of her nose. "Was I really that bad?" Iris had raised Theresa since she was thirteen, and she'd thought of Iris as her surrogate mom. To know Iris had had such a low opinion . . .

"But I can see the difference in you today." Iris leaned forward, her gaze intense. "I can tell you're taking responsibility for your actions, and I'm impressed."

Theresa lifted her head slightly. "Really?"

Iris nodded. "For that reason, I'll stall the Council. I'll tell them I haven't been able to locate you. My portal is linked to the work and home locations for you and Quincy, and I'll fiddle with the settings so it can't link to you directly. That way, as long as you're not in any of your known locations, we won't be able to find you."

Theresa cocked her head. "Can you do that?"

Iris's cheeks turned pink. "Satan taught me how to adjust my portal so I could have more freedom to travel. Of course, I greatly disapprove of breaking the rules, but to save you and Justine, I'll do it." She stood up. "I doubt I can get you more than a day or two. Once the Council confirms you gave up Mona, they'll put you in the Chamber and you won't have a chance to get her back." Her eyes were soft and warm as they settled on Theresa. "Make me proud, Theresa. I know you can."

Theresa lifted her chin. "I'm going to make myself proud."

A high-pitched ringing filled the apartment. "I have to go. Good luck, sweetie." Iris faded from sight as she was blowing Theresa a kiss.

Theresa leaned back in her chair to absorb the discussion. Even though she'd handed Mona over to Satan, Iris *believed* in her. What an amazing feeling. She sat up and clenched her fists. She would make this work out. She *would*.

"Theresa Nichols at last."

"Crap!" She leaped to her feet and whirled around at the sound of a long-forgotten male voice.

Lyman Peressini was lounging in her bedroom doorway, leaning against the frame, his arms folded loosely over his chest.

"Oh, God." She ran for the door and he broke stance and sprinted, slamming his body in front of it a split second before she reached it.

"You're not getting away from me this time, Theresa." He flashed perfect white teeth at her and turned the dead bolt on the door.

She backed away slowly, her mind frantically whirring. He was so much bigger than he used to be. Taller, more muscular, tougher. His dark hair was short, his suit expensive, his watch a Rolex. "Did my parents' money buy that watch?"

"This?" He held up his wrist and started walking toward her. "I spent your family's money centuries ago, before I set the fire to fake my death. This is mine."

She bumped into the end table, then grabbed the lamp and brandished it like a weapon. Why didn't she have a stash of guns like Justine? She couldn't burn up another dragon. The flames would just bounce off him.

Lyman grinned. "A lamp, Theresa? Surely you can do better."

"Why'd you send that hit man to kill me?"

He snorted. "Oh, please. I never thought that human would have any chance of killing you. I wanted to let you know I was around. Tease you a bit."

"Great bit of fun it was," she said, backing toward the window and the fire escape. "Thanks for the laugh."

"Ixnay on the fire escape." He waggled his finger in the direction of the window. "I'm much faster than you are. You'll never make it." He gestured to the couch. "Have a seat. There's so much to discuss."

She tightened her grip on the lamp. "I'll stand, thanks."

"Suit yourself." He settled on the couch, crossed his legs, and rested his arms over the back of it. He looked relaxed, and she knew he was messing with her, giving her the ol' "I'm so physically superior to you that I can practically fall asleep and still kick your ass if you try to escape" routine.

Bastard. Why had she spent the last two hundred years screwing around instead of honing her combat skills? Pheromone-resisting skills weren't going to help against another dragon.

"So, I have three options for you." His voice was pleasant and friendly.

"Lay 'em on me."

"First option: Become my mate."

She blinked. "What?"

"Mate. Sex. That kind of thing." Lyman's eyes gleamed and his fingers began to drum on the back of the couch.

Her belly churned. "What're my other options?"

"Give me the Goblet of Eternal Youth."

She became distracted by a sudden rattling noise. "The what?"

"The Goblet. I know you're the Guardian. The Manasa read you." The gleam in his eyes became even more vibrant. "In fact, I want both. I want the Goblet and I want your body."

That damn Manasa. They should all be shot. Reading without permission. Totally unethical. And how the hell did he know the Manasa had read her? The green bitch had probably tattled to him. The rattling noise grew louder, and she glanced at the window. No one was there. "Third option?"

"Die."

She swallowed and suddenly realized the rattling was the lamp, vibrating because her hands were trembling so badly.

Lyman's gaze followed hers to the lamp, and he gave her a smug smile.

Ugh. She *hated* that smile. She threw the lamp at his head and he barely ducked in time. It smashed against the wall and fell to the floor in a bunch of pieces. Good. She hadn't liked the lamp anyway. "I'll give *you* two choices."

He arched an eyebrow. "Yes?"

"Leave me alone."

"Or?"

"Die." Hmm . . . it had sounded much more believable when he said it. Damn. She narrowed her eyes and let a puff of smoke out to accentuate her badassness.

He grinned. "I don't know which I like more, your

spirit or your body. Last time I ravaged you, we were both in dragon form. Your human form is even lovelier."

"You're disgusting. You don't have permission to fantasize about my body."

"All the more reason to do it."

"Cretin."

"Slut."

As if that insult could upset her! She'd worked hard to be promiscuous when she was younger. It had been her only outlet when Justine and Iris hadn't let her incinerate anything. "You're just jealous because I had way more, way better sex than you did when we were growing up."

His face darkened and he stood up. "I have all the sex I want nowadays."

"Then you don't need me."

"You're right, Theresa." He walked toward her, and she forced herself not to back up. He came to a stop in front of her and looked down at her.

She lifted her chin and met his gaze.

"I don't need you," he agreed. "I *want* you." He reached out and traced his finger down the side of her face. *Ugh.* "Come with me. Be my mate. I'm very rich now and I'm gaining power. All I need is the Goblet, and soon I will be able to dethrone even Satan." He rubbed his thumb over her lip. *Gross.* "I will be God, Theresa, and you will be by my side."

God? Was that what this was all about? She studied him, trying to piece everything together. "You've really raised the bar for yourself. Last I heard, you wanted to rule the Village of Uruloke. Now you want to be God?"

"Uruloke was practice." He leaned forward and closed his eyes, inhaling deeply. "You smell so good, Theresa. I will be so sad if you choose death over being my mate. It would be such a waste of a good fuck—"

"Enough!" She slammed her knee into his crotch. He gasped and crumpled. She grabbed his head and smashed her knee up into his face. Then she jumped back as he fell to the ground.

"You bitch!" His beautiful nose was gushing blood all over her new floor. She started to run for the door, then skidded to a stop as she caught the scent of unfamiliar men on the other side. Of course he wouldn't go anywhere without his flunkies.

She spun around and sprinted for the window. For the first time in two hundred years, she was glad she was a dragon. She lifted her arms to shield her face, then flung herself through the window. The moment she was free of the building and sailing through the air, she whispered her trigger word to turn herself into winged dragon form. "Floghdraki."

Nothing happened.

"Floghdraki." She quickly said it out loud, watching the cement rush up toward her with alarming speed.

Still human.

Shit!

"Floghdraki!"

Nothing.

"Crap!" She curled into a ball just before smashing into the pavement.

As Zeke approached Theresa's apartment, he heard a crash come from within. Two heavily armed men were guarding her door, and he broke into a sprint when he heard someone moaning on the other side of it.

For the first time in decades, he didn't try to suppress his slayer instincts.

One of the men jumped in front of him, and Zeke dispatched him with a kick to the head and took out the other with a nicely aimed chop to the throat. He crashed through the door, splinters flying as the doorframe shattered. What was she doing with such a weak doorframe? He'd have to upgrade that.

He skidded to a stop in the living room. A man was trying to crawl to the door, blood gushing from his nose. Theresa was nowhere. "T? Are you okay?" He sniffed, but her scent was faint. She wasn't there anymore.

The man coughed, and Zeke put his foot on the man's shoulder to stop him. "Who are you?"

"She jumped out the window."

Thank God she'd gotten away. Zeke grasped the front of the man's shirt, pulled him up to his knees, and had to stop himself from flinging the man across the room by accident. *Calm down, Zeke.* He put him back down.

There was a stirring from the downed men in the hall, and Zeke frowned. "Who are you?" he repeated.

"I'm her boyfriend," the man said, his voice raspy from the blood and the broken nose.

Zeke narrowed his eyes and studied him more closely. "Lyman Peressini?"

The brief twitch under the man's right eye confirmed his suspicions, and Zeke grinned. "I've been wanting to meet you." He patted Lyman's head condescendingly. "I'm a slayer, and I don't like you."

Lyman's eyes widened, and then his gaze flicked toward the door. "You can't take us all," he said.

"I only want you." Zeke grabbed Lyman by his lapels,

pulled him to his feet, then threw him on the couch. "Alex Montageaux's mate, Jasmine. Where is she?"

"I have no idea what you're talking about." Lyman's right eye twitched again in confirmation of Zeke's suspicion.

Rage roared through Zeke. Dragon or not, the man would pay for threatening the only two people Zeke cared about. Suddenly glad he'd started carrying his slaying knife with him, he pulled it from the sheath under his arm and flicked the tip. "Oh, Lyman, you make this far too easy. Did you know I have access to Satan's torture chamber? Want to go on a field trip? I bet you'll be excited to talk, and as a slayer, I imagine I'll get a certain pleasure out of convincing you . . ."

Lyman paled, and Zeke gradually became aware of shouting outside the window, coming from the alley. He hesitated for a moment, listening to the shouts. Horror. Disgust. Grief. He cocked his head, his grip tightening on the weapon. "You kill anyone down there?"

"I told you, Theresa went out that window."

"*Shit.*" He bolted to the window and looked down. There were people standing in a circle around . . . something. He was on the fifth floor and it was dark, so even his slayer eyes couldn't see clearly what they were looking at. He leaned out and inhaled. Blood. *Theresa.*

Horror ripped through him, but he shoved it off as he stared at the carnage, trying to figure out what was going on. It couldn't be Theresa down there. She would have changed to dragon form and flown off. And if she caught a wing and had a hard landing, she'd be fine because of her immortality.

He glanced over his shoulder and saw Lyman crawling

toward the door, where his men where climbing to their feet.

Then he looked back into the alley and sniffed again. Dammit. He could definitely smell Theresa. "Theresa!"

No answer.

He looked back into the room, and saw Lyman's men had pulled him to his feet and were heading out the door. Getting away with information about Alex's mate. The man who'd lied to him and put two contracts out on Theresa. He could not be allowed to walk away.

Zeke turned to go after Lyman, then spun back to the window, jumped through the opening and started racing down the fire escape.

Fifteen

Theresa awoke feeling as if she'd just been run over by a cluster of stampeding teenage dragons. She moaned and pulled her pillow over her head. "Ow." Even that hurt.

The bed shifted as someone landed on it. "T? Are you awake?"

She lifted one end of the pillow to find the slayer of her fantasies peering at her, his forehead furrowed in concern. His face was drawn, his whiskers long, and his eyes looked weary. "Zeke? What's wrong?"

"You." He gently tugged the pillow out of her hand and cupped his fingers under her chin, a soft jolt of energy sparking between them. "You had me worried, T. Never do that again."

Before she had time to digest what he was about to do, he leaned down and brushed his lips over hers. His touch was soft, gentle, his lips warm against hers, filling her with a sense of rightness and warmth.

She sighed as he broke the kiss, and he smiled down at her, stroking her hair. "I think that's the first time we've kissed when neither of us was under the influence of the slayer/dragon aphrodisiacs."

"It didn't suck."

He raised his eyebrows. "Didn't suck? Do you realize that you could totally destroy my male ego by saying that after I kiss you?"

She wiggled deeper under the covers and sighed. Her bed had never felt this comfortable before. It was cupping her aching body and easing the pain out of her muscles. "It wasn't a kiss. It was more like a nuzzle."

"Nuzzle?" Challenge flashed in his eyes and he laid his hands on either side of her face. "I'm completely insulted." This time when he bent his head, his lips caught hers in a kiss that had her toes curling. His breath was minty and delicious, and when he slipped his tongue between her teeth, she felt as if she was going to melt into the bed.

His fingers were in her hair, his mouth deep on hers, and it was the most amazing kiss she'd ever had in her life. When he broke the kiss, he eyed her. "Well?"

She realized her hands were in his hair, holding him to her. She probably ought to let go. In a minute. "It was amazing."

He grinned and kissed the tip of her nose, then sat up, rolling out of her reach.

"Wait. Where are you going? That's it? You're going to tease me with that kiss and walk away?"

He raised his brow. "Doesn't your body hurt?"

"Yes . . ." She frowned as the full extent of her aching body sank into her consciousness. Every inch of her was throbbing with pain. "What did you do to me?"

"What did you do to yourself? Two days ago, you jumped out of your apartment window and apparently decided turning into a winged dragon that could fly off to safety was a bad idea." He frowned at her. "What were you thinking? I know you're immortal, but your body was nothing more than a pile of Jell-O by the time I got to you. I had to knock out six bystanders, because they wouldn't let me take you. They wanted the ambulance to take you to the hospital. I figured that would raise too many questions, so I brought you to my place."

"Your place?" She finally glanced around the room. Navy walls, a couple of paintings of nature scenes. The furniture was wooden and functional, but not interesting. Typical bachelor pad. She looked down at the red plaid sheets and smiled. She was in Zeke's bed.

"T? What happened with the window? Why didn't you change?"

"Um . . ." She frowned as she tried to recall what happened.

"Did Lyman push you out?"

"Lyman?" She sat up suddenly, yelping as pain shot through her body. "Omigod. He was at my apartment!"

Zeke carefully wedged a pillow behind her back. "I know. I met him."

"You did? You were there?" She leaned against the pillow as the memories came rolling back. "He knows about Satan and the Goblet and he threatened to kill me so I kneed him in the . . ." She stopped as she suddenly recalled her trip through the window. "I couldn't turn into a dragon. That's why I crashed. I couldn't turn into a dragon!" She held out her arms. "Floghdraki."

Zeke jumped off the bed. "I don't think you should be turning into a dragon in front of me."

"I can't! Look!" She waved her hand at him. "Floghdraki! Floghdraki! Floghdraki! I'm not changing." Oh, God. Oh, God. "I can't turn into a dragon!"

Zeke sat back down next to her. "T. Calm down!"

She clutched the comforter, her chest tightening until she couldn't breathe. Black spots started dancing in front of her eyes and she kicked at the blankets, struggling to get free. To run. "I can't turn into a dragon!"

"Theresa!" He grasped her shoulders and turned her toward him.

She struggled against him, trying to wrench out of his grip. "What did Satan do to me? I can't be a dragon anymore? It's who I am! I can't deal with—" His pheromones smacked her in the nose and she scrunched her eyes shut, immediately focusing the way he'd taught her in the torture chamber.

When she opened her eyes a few minutes later, Zeke was looking at her with an expectant expression on his face. "You ready to talk rationally now?"

"Talk? You tried to kill me!"

He raised his brow.

"Okay, fine, you didn't," she conceded. She scowled at him. "But it was a low blow to hit me with the pheromones when I was already freaking out."

"Not at all. You need to learn how to get over it when you're distracted." He looked pleased with himself. "You did great."

She grinned suddenly. "I did, didn't I? I'm a brilliant student."

"Or you have a great teacher."

"Nope," she said. "It's definitely the student. Haven't I told you what a great dragon I am?"

"Many times." He pulled a chair next to the bed and sat

down, and she instantly missed his presence on the bed. "Okay, T, I talked to Lyman. I'm pretty sure he's the one who has my friend's mate."

"Talked?" She frowned. "You didn't kill him? He's a dragon, you know. You could have tortured him for information and then killed him to save me." She narrowed her eyes. "Did you actually let him go?"

His eyes flickered. "I won't slay him."

"Oh, right, the Slayeraholics Anonymous probably wouldn't give you your next chip if you do." She sighed at the hurt look on his face. "Listen, it's not that I don't respect your desire not to slay anymore, because I do. For God's sake, I'm a dragon. Trust me, I support it. But don't you think the situation called for it? I mean, Lyman's a horrible person and he's killed so many people." She sighed as she replayed her words. "I meant, I *used* to be a dragon."

"You spent two hundred years trying to get out of dragon form," Zeke said. "Why do you care if you can't take a dragon form again?"

"Because it's who I am! You deny your heritage, but I embrace who I am. The reason I needed to be human again was that in this society, being permanently in dragon form is unbearable. If I were still in my village with hundreds of other dragons, it wouldn't be a big deal. But I want both. I need both. I love being human, but I'm also a dragon and I'm proud of it."

He leaned back and stared at her, as if the concept of embracing heritage was completely foreign to him. "Really?"

"Yes." She touched the tattoo on her collarbone. "See this?"

"Of course."

"It's the mark of my family. All the dragons in my father's lineage have the mark. My mom developed one after she married him. I'm proud of this mark, and I will never hide it."

He ran his finger over it, his touch sending tingles down her spine. "I haven't seen this on other dragons. I had no idea it was a dragon mark."

She tensed at the unreadable expression in his eyes. "Does it make you want to kill me?"

He met her gaze. "No."

"Glad to hear it." She sighed and leaned back on the pillow, letting her arms flop above her head. "In the dragon world, my mark makes me extremely desirable. It's a sign of power and wealth and longevity." She frowned. "Expectations are extremely high if you sport that tattoo, and I hated that as a kid. I did everything in my power not to meet any expectations whatsoever."

Zeke leaned forward, his forearms resting on the mattress. "Did you know Lyman from back then?"

She nodded. "He was at the other end of the spectrum. His family lived in a run-down house on the outskirts of the village. His dad believed that stealing and being drunk all the time was his mission in life, and that's all he did. Everyone in the family was a total loser, but I liked Lyman. He was smart and he was determined to do better than his heritage. He hated it when people looked down on him for being a Peressini, and he used to talk about how someday he would rule them all and they would be forced to bow to him." She frowned. "He called himself God when he came to my apartment, actually." What had he meant by that? It hadn't sounded like a random brag. "I think he's trying to become his version of God."

Zeke frowned. "What would that mean, to him?"

"Ruling everyone. Humans and all Otherworld beings, I suppose." She pursed her lips and tried to think of what Lyman would be up to.

After a few moments of silence, Zeke asked, "So, when did you guys become lovers?"

She slanted a glance at Zeke. "Why does that matter?"

"Helps me figure him out." He shifted in his seat. "I chose to go after you instead of following Lyman, so I don't know where he is. I need as much information as I can get."

"And knowing about his sex life will help?"

"Yes."

She narrowed her eyes, but she saw no jealousy in his expression. Just determined curiosity. Not that she wanted Zeke to be jealous, but, well, okay, fine. She wanted him to be jealous, and that was just silly. "After I'd been the backup Guardian for twenty years, Justine, the Guardian, fired me as her successor."

Zeke raised his brow, but didn't interrupt.

"So, I went back to Uruloke. I hadn't been there since the Cleansing, and I wanted to see if my family's house was still standing. It was, and Lyman was living in it, spending my family's money." She frowned, recalling that visit. "At first I was excited to see him, because I thought I was the only dragon who had survived the Cleansing. He admitted he'd always had a crush on me, and, well . . ." She snuck a glance at Zeke, starting to feel uncomfortable. "We sort of got together."

Zeke's eyes darkened ever so slightly. "Did you love him?"

"No, but I was pretty lonely, having been cast off as a Guardian and stuck in dragon form." She felt her cheeks heat up. "Since he was a dragon, he was the only one I could . . . well . . . you know."

"So he's never seen you naked in human form?"

"No." She grabbed one of the pillows and hugged it to her chest. "So, anyway, after I'd been there a few days, I realized there was something weird going on in the town. I did a little investigating, and discovered Lyman was ruling the town through violence, crime, and blackmail. He was like a little dragon mafia boss, terrorizing the village of humans. He'd also made a deal with Satan, but he was cheating him."

Zeke whistled softly. "Cheating Satan? How?"

"Satan had an Otherworld Detector that he used to expose Otherworld beings who were hiding out as humans. It helped Satan handpick the souls that he wanted to recruit for hell, since Otherworld souls bring more to the table." Needing comfort in the face of the memories of Lyman, she instinctively reached for Zeke.

He cupped her left hand between his palms. "Let me guess. Lyman wanted the Otherworld Detector so he could identify Otherworld beings who didn't want the world to know they weren't human. Instant blackmail."

"Exactly. Satan had leased it to Lyman, demanding 95 percent of the profits from its use."

Zeke made a noise of understanding. "Lyman lied about the profits."

"Big-time. And I found out." She picked a piece of lint out of Zeke's whiskers and rubbed it between her thumb and forefinger. "So, I told him to move out of my parents' house and leave the town, or I'd tell Satan that he was cheating him. We both knew that Satan would not only take Lyman's toy back, but also torture Lyman big-time."

Zeke grinned. "I like your style, T."

She returned the smile. "Justine thinks I'm too extreme."

"Never." He jerked his chin. "Continue."

Her smile faded. "He and his henchmen tackled me. Even immortal, I had no chance against them. They tossed me into one of the rooms in the basement, which had been turned into a dungeon."

Zeke's eyes narrowed and his hands slid to her thigh, his fingers digging in ever so slightly. "And?"

"And there was a slayer in there."

His jaw flexed. "A slayer?"

"Uh-huh. They'd tortured him until he was crazy with rage. They locked us in and left us there to battle to the death." She shuddered at the memory of the pheromones flooding that little room, and Zeke's hands rubbed her thighs.

"What happened then?" His voice was tight.

"The slayer pretty much beat the hell out of me, and he couldn't understand why I wouldn't die. Why I kept reviving." She managed a smile. "I guess I forgot to tell him he had to behead me in order to kill me."

Zeke let go of her thigh to grab her hands, his grip so tight it almost hurt.

She didn't ask him to let go. "Anyway, the last time, he was sure he'd killed me, and he collapsed in exhaustion and passed out. We were in the side of the cellar where my dad had put in an emergency tunnel, in case of an attack by the slayers, so as soon as he went down, I took off." She frowned. "I still don't understand why my family didn't use the tunnels to escape the Cleansing."

Zeke rubbed the back of her hand with his thumb. "So you got away?"

"Yep. I think the slayer followed me, but he was too far behind to catch me." She shrugged. "So, I went back to Justine to tell her what happened, but when I arrived, she was in the middle of killing the man she'd appointed Assistant Guardian—he was trying to steal Mona. As soon as she killed him, we took Mona to the Amazon to hide. I didn't get a chance to go back to Uruloke for ten years, and when I did, Lyman was gone and my house had been burned down. Rumor was that he'd died in the fire." She sighed and studied their intertwined hands. "I figured justice had been served, so I left." She met his gaze. "Guess I figured wrong, huh?"

"Guess so." He released her hands and shoved his chair back. He walked over to the window, leaned on the window frame and stared outside.

"Zeke?"

He didn't turn around. "Never in my life have I wanted to kill a dragon more than I do right now."

The anguish was heavy in his voice and she felt his conflicted emotions. He hadn't been willing to kill Lyman at her apartment to get his friend's mate back, but after hearing her story, he wanted to.

The knowledge warmed her, and she kicked back the covers, frowning when she realized she was wearing clothes that weren't hers. Oversized sweats and a baggy T-shirt, both of which smelled like Zeke. Had he changed her clothes for her? Seen her naked? She wasn't wearing a bra anymore. She smiled and walked over to him. He tensed at the jolt when she slid her arms around his waist, but she ignored it and laid her cheek against his back. "You don't have to kill him," she whispered. "I'll kill him."

He didn't relax, but he didn't pull away, either. "You weren't strong enough before."

"Yes, but I've spent the last 180 years honing my skills while he's obviously sat on his butt eating pretzels," she teased.

Zeke snorted. "He looked fit to me."

"Yeah, he did." She shuddered at the memory of how quick he'd been, how big. "He looks like he's put on about two hundred pounds of muscle." She buried her face in Zeke's back and tried not to think about the fact she wasn't even close to the physical condition she'd been in before she'd gone soft on pretzels and house arrest. "Just out of curiosity, when you slay dragons without using your pheromones, how do you do it? Gun?"

"A gun doesn't work unless it's really high caliber and I shoot the dragon about twenty times in the same place."

"So, how do you kill them?"

"Dagger in the underside of the neck." He turned around in her embrace and set his hands on her shoulders. His eyes were so dark they were almost black, and his neck muscles were so tight they looked like steel cords. "I can't have this discussion with you right now, T. I want to slay so badly I don't know if I can stop myself." His hands slid to her neck, his thumbs tracing circles on her throat.

She swallowed. "Do you want me to flame you?"

His eyes narrowed. "I don't know how long that will keep working. I think maybe I've been letting it work because I wanted you to stop me." He slid his right hand lower and cupped her tattoo. "But if you tried to stop me right now, it might have the opposite effect. It might fuel the rage instead of changing it to lust." He let go of her so suddenly that she almost fell over. His eyes were black, very black.

She reached out to touch him, and the instant her fingers brushed against his skin, he jumped away and spun toward her. "Don't touch me right now." His eyes glittered. "I'm going back to your apartment now. I'm going to see if I can track Lyman through scent."

"And if you find him?"

"He dies."

She saw the anguish flash in his eyes even as he said it, and her chest tightened. "Zeke, don't go now. If you kill him, you might never forgive yourself."

"If you or Jasmine die, I'll never forgive myself either." Then he slammed the bedroom door shut behind him and was gone.

Theresa stared after him as she heard the front door open and shut. Should she follow him?

No. He wouldn't find Lyman. The dragon was too smart to leave a trail for a slayer to find.

She rolled her shoulders, grimacing at the ache. While he was running around, she'd do her own sleuthing. It was time to find Lyman and face him down, but not before she took care of some business of her own. She felt in her pocket for her cell phone, then frowned. It was still at her condo.

There was no phone in the bedroom, so she walked out to the living room and saw a phone on the sofa table. She walked over, rubbing her back as she walked. She'd fallen five stories onto cement. How could her body have recovered already? It should take at least a day or two . . . or had it? How long had Zeke said it had been?

She eased to the couch and dialed Zeke's cell phone.

"What?" he snapped.

"How long was I unconscious?"

"Just over two days."

Two days? Iris said she'd be able to hold off the Council for a day or two. By now, did they all know? Was she out of time? "Zeke, will you do me a favor and grab my cell phone and a bunch of my clothes? I can't go back there for a while."

She heard his heavy breathing and the rapid thud of his feet, as if he was sprinting. "Because of Lyman?"

"No, I'd like to stay there in hopes Lyman showed up again so I could kick his ass. It's Goblet of Eternal Youth issues. And if a pirate, a businessman, and an old man are at my place looking for me, don't hurt them, and don't give them your name or any way to find me, okay?"

His footsteps stopped. "Are you in trouble?"

"Yeah, you could say that."

"How can I help?"

She smiled at the concern in his voice. "Just get my stuff for me, okay?"

"Sure." He hesitated. "T? Be careful, okay?"

"I'll do my best not to get killed, if that's what you mean."

He growled. "I meant, don't go out and do anything stupid. Remember, the team of slayers is still in town . . . *shit.*"

She sat up at the sudden tension in his voice. "What?"

"Alex knows where I live and can get into my place.

You're not safe there. If he finds you, he'll kill you. You need to get out."

She jumped to her feet, then groaned and bent over as the pain shot through her. Two days was not enough time to recover from a five-story skydive. She straightened gingerly, her hands on her lower back. God, she felt older than 232. "So I'll meet you at Becca's, okay?" She set her hands on her hips to hold her pelvis together and waddled toward his bedroom. "Did you salvage my sneakers?"

"I had to toss them. They smelled like your blood and it was a little distracting."

Ah, the difficulties of slayer/dragon intimacies. "Guess it'll be barefoot then. Unless you'll be back soon with my stuff?"

He grunted. "Get out of there as soon as you can."

"Yeah, you're right." She pulled open his closet and studied his shoes. A pair of Teevas, some loafers, and three pairs of running shoes. They all looked too big. Surely he had some really old pair in the back, from an old girlfriend or something? "I'll see you in a bit." She hung up and eased down to her knees and crawled into the closet, feeling around in the back. When her hand hit a large box, she tugged it out.

She opened it, then jerked her hands back when she realized what was inside. Heavy boots with steel toes. Black pants with thousands of metal rivets, welded to thick, tough leather that would stand up against dragon teeth and claws. It was his slaying armor.

She stared at it for a long moment, then cautiously rubbed the leather. She could feel the energy of all the dragon blood pounded into its depths, and she quickly dropped it.

There were answers in that leather. He'd been in Uru-loke for the Cleansing. He might have killed her parents. Did she really want to know the truth? What if she got an answer she didn't want?

She had to know, for her sake and Zeke's. She closed her eyes, picked up the pants, and pressed the leather to her dragon mark.

No reaction. Not even a faint tingling.

She pressed a different part of the leather to her mark. Still nothing.

She systematically went through the entire fabric of both pant legs, and then his boots, and her mark remained quiet.

She stared at the stiff leather, her mind racing. A slayer received his armor when he made the rank of slayer, and he wore it for all slayings from then on, because it was supposedly imbued with magic protection. Her mark hadn't reacted, which meant her family's blood wasn't on his slaying armor.

Zeke hadn't killed her family.

She hugged his pants to her chest, unable to stop the trembling in her body as she scrunched her eyes shut. At that moment, she realized she wouldn't have been able to forgive him if he'd killed them.

But he hadn't.

Sixteen

Zeke's phone rang suddenly, and Theresa jumped, then groaned as her body protested. She grabbed the handset. "Zeke?"

"Theresa? Is that you?"

She frowned at the unfamiliar voice. "Who is this?"

"Percy. Percy Adams. Are you all right?"

Her attorney. She'd forgotten all about him. "I'm fine. Why?" She packed Zeke's things back into his slaying box and shoved it back into the bowels of the closet.

"You didn't show up for our dinner the other night. I've been calling your cell phone. I was getting concerned."

"Just got busy. How did you know where I was?" She grabbed Zeke's Teevas and strapped them on, pulling the straps as tight as they'd go. About three sizes too big, but they'd have to suffice.

"I didn't. I finally tracked down this number when I couldn't reach you. I have to report to the judge tomorrow. Can we get together?"

She grabbed the door handle and pulled herself gingerly to her feet. As much as she didn't want to deal with Percy, he was a lead they hadn't checked out yet. "Fine. What time is it?"

"A little after ten."

She glanced at the bright sunshine. Ten in the morning, apparently. "How about lunch, then?"

"Dinner would be better. I have to be in court today."

"Fine. How about seven? We'll try the Gas Griller again?" She shut the closet door and leaned against it for a moment, feeling the strength beginning to return to her body.

"Excellent. Shall I pick you up?" She heard the rustle of papers. "I have Mr. Siccardi's address right here."

"No, I won't be here anymore."

"Trouble in paradise?"

"Something like that. I'll see you then." Zeke's phone beeped. "Gotta go. Later." She clicked over. "Zeke?"

"Theresa!"

She grinned at the sound of her best friend's voice. "Justine! How'd you find me here?"

"Oh, my God! You gave Mona to Satan?"

Theresa's smile faded. "How did you find out?"

"Everyone knows, Theresa! *Everyone!* The Council showed up in the middle of our honeymoon and took me and Derek into custody. They're holding us responsible for your actions. We're in the foyer of the Chamber of Unspeakable Horrors!"

"Oh, God." Oh, God. Oh, God. *Oh, God.* Bile churned in her belly and she sank to the floor, clutching the phone to her ear. "I'm so sorry, Justine. I didn't think anyone would find out and I didn't mean to and . . ."

"I can hear the screams of the people being tortured, Theresa! I can feel their pain. The sound of their terror is so horrific I can't stop shaking! And I'm only in the *foyer*! If we don't get Mona back, they're going to throw

Derek and me into the Chamber. Did you hear me? The *Chamber*!"

Theresa's body began to shake. "I'm coming. I'll turn myself in and—"

"No! Don't you dare! If you do they'll put you in here, too. You have to stay out of the Council's reach until you get Mona back."

"I'll find her, I promise. I'm so sorry."

Justine took a deep breath, and seemed to regain some of her control. "Don't be sorry. Just retrieve her. Fast. Before Satan uses her. Mom's working on Satan from her end, but she and the Council are in disagreement about how to handle him. They want him dead, she wants to negotiate with him. So, it's up to you."

She clenched her fists. "I won't let you down."

"If you do, I will kick your ass from here to hell." Then she hung up.

Theresa leaned her head against the closet door, clutching the phone to her chest as she tried to regroup. What had she done? Endangering her best friend? Just so she could be a human? She groaned and pressed the heels of her hands to her forehead.

She had to calm down. Justine wasn't in the Chamber yet. It was just another move by the Council to pressure Theresa into making a strategic error.

She could fix this. She *would* fix it.

First things first. She had to take out Lyman. But how was she going to manage that as an injured human? He'd change to dragon form and bite her head right off. And the slayers would kill her, too. And none of that would matter if Justine was in the Chamber being tortured for all eternity.

She sighed. She had to talk to Satan. Every time she talked to him, things got more screwed up, but she had no choice. Frowning, she dialed Becca's cell phone, almost hoping the Rivka wouldn't pick up.

Becca answered immediately. "Becca Gibbs, Vic's Pretzels."

"It's Theresa. I need to meet with Satan."

"Sorry, Dragon, but he's in a meeting all day starting in ten minutes. Do not disturb, or he'll rip off your head and serve it for afternoon tea and all that jazz."

"So we have ten minutes. I'll be fast. Please? It's really important."

Becca sighed. "You're becoming extremely demanding."

"I know. I owe you. Isn't it nice to know I'm going to be forced to be your humble servant for the next ten years to make up for all your favors?"

The Rivka gave a moan of capitulation. "Fine. I'll come pick you up. Where are you?"

"Zeke's. You're the best. I'll love you forever."

"Now that's a terrifying thought. I'll be there in a couple of minutes."

"Great. Thanks." She touched her mark and frantically tried to come up with a plan that might actually work.

Zeke opened Theresa's top dresser drawer and jumped back at the sight of more lace than he'd ever imagined existed, let alone had bonded together in one place. He stared at the contents for a minute, then inched toward the bureau. She'd asked him to pack up a bunch of her clothes and that probably included undergarments.

But handling her lingerie was so *personal,* and he was

doing everything in his power not to make this personal. There was too much at stake to make this personal.

He took a deep breath and peered into the drawer, keeping his hands clasped behind his back. Lots of black and red. Some emerald green and blue. Gold to match her eyes. A set of pearly black buttons caught his eye and he tentatively reached inside and tugged a lacy top free.

He held it up, the thin shoulder straps dangling awkwardly from his scarred fingers, then he grinned. Theresa had bought this top less than a month ago. He still recalled when she'd described it to him, telling him she'd bought it just for him. But with the whole Satan Jr. fiasco and now this, they'd never had time to cybersex with it. He fingered the tag. Still unworn. She'd saved it for him.

He grinned and tossed it in a Vic's Pretzels duffel bag he'd found under the bed, along with the rest of the clothes he'd grabbed for her.

Feeling much more comfortable, he rifled through her lingerie drawer, picking all the items that she'd described to him at some point. After six months of cybersex, there were a lot he recognized. He held up one zebra-print thong and chuckled at the memories.

"So, you're a pervert now."

Zeke jumped, threw the thong back in the drawer, and slammed it shut. Then he spun around to face his friend and enemy, Alex. "What are you doing here?"

Alex was leaning against the doorframe, his arms folded across his chest, an amused grin curving his mouth. "I was tracking a dragon to kill her. Instead, I discover my former mentor is obsessed with the female dragon's underwear. Are you planning to wear it or just put it under your pillow to foster erotic fantasies?"

Zeke felt his cheeks burn, and he yanked open the drawer again. "Shut up. I'm packing a bag for her."

"So, you're having sex with her instead of killing her?" Alex's tone hardened. "Is that how it is?"

"It's complicated." Zeke grabbed another handful of lingerie and shut the drawer. That would have to be enough. He threw them in the bag and started to zip it, frowning when a thong got stuck in the zipper. He grabbed the red lace and tugged as he heard Alex shift behind him.

He'd just wrapped his hand around the fabric to give it a good tug when he felt the cold metal of a gun against his temple.

He froze.

"Refusal to honor a life debt is payable by death."

Zeke turned his head slightly so he could look at Alex. "Wouldn't Jasmine be happier if you could rescue her without killing a dragon?"

"I don't care." He tossed an envelope at Zeke. "I got this today at my hotel room."

Zeke caught it, then quickly untangled the red lace from his hand. He shook the contents of the envelope into his hand. It was a picture of an attractive woman with blond hair. Her hair was tangled and there was dirt on her face. She looked furious and was giving the camera the finger.

Zeke couldn't help but grin at the fire in her eyes as he imagined it directed toward his friend. A well-muscled man in a tight T-shirt, jeans, and copious amounts of hardware stood off to her right, slightly behind her, watching her with careful scrutiny. "Is this Jasmine?"

"Yeah." Alex leaned over his shoulder to peer at the photo. "She's a tyrant." Affection made his voice soft.

"No wonder you gave up slaying for her. She looks like she's more than a match for you." He studied the photo for a long minute, then tapped the photo. "I've met that guy."

Alex grabbed his shoulders and shook him. "What? Where? When? Who is he?"

"He was here earlier today. I broke his nuts." Zeke shrugged out of Alex's grasp, got the zipper closed, and slung the bag over his shoulder.

Alex aimed the gun at Zeke again. "So, where's he keeping Jasmine?"

Zeke cleared his throat. "Well, I got distracted before I could torture him for information."

Alex growled and released the safety. "You let him go? You disgust me."

Zeke didn't back down from the metal barrel. "After I took out his boss, I was about to interview all of them in a dignified way when I discovered Theresa had fallen five stories out the window in her escape from them."

Alex pulled the gun back and peered at Zeke. "You rescued the dragon instead of going after the man who'd attacked her and stolen my mate?"

"Yeah."

Alex rested the gun barrel on his shoulder. "Shit, man. You have a real thing for the dragon."

"Never." He shoved past Alex and walked to the front door of Theresa's condo. "It's part of my attempt to overcome my slaying history. Save the dragon and all that."

"This really complicates things," Alex muttered. "How could you be so stupid as to fall in love with a dragon? At least I fell in love with a woman who was the daughter of a slayer. I mean, she doesn't want me to slay, but at least I don't have to worry about accidentally killing her if she leaks a little smoke in the heat of passion."

Zeke slanted him a look. "I'm *not* in love with Theresa."

"Good. Then killing her shouldn't be a problem."

"I'm an *ex*-slayer, remember? Slaying any dragon is a problem for me."

"You're not going to *slay* her. You're going to kill her to save my woman. That's not slaying. It's honoring a debt. I'd ask you to do it even if you weren't a slayer."

Zeke grimaced. "Let's find Jasmine and then it won't be an issue."

"Whatever you say, lover boy."

"Shut up." He opened the door, stepped out into the hallway, then closed his eyes and inhaled. "I figured I could track them from here."

Alex came to stand beside him and breathed in. "Which is the leader?"

"The one that smells like dragon."

"They all smell like dragon."

Really? Zeke frowned and breathed in again, but he was unsure what he was scenting. It had been a long time since he'd tracked dragons. The only dragon scent he could think of was Theresa's, and Lyman's scent was mixed with hers. Probably got it on him when he was trying to hurt her. Anger roiled through him, but he forced his voice to remain steady. "You might be right. Smell the one that's high-pitched?"

Alex gave him a wary look, but didn't comment on the

tension in his voice. "The one that smells like anabolic steroids?"

"Yeah. That's him." Zeke started walking down the hall, following the medicinal scent. He hadn't realized that's what Lyman smelled like, but now that Alex pointed it out, he realized his friend was right. No wonder Lyman was a big guy.

They said nothing as they rode down in the elevator, but Zeke felt Alex studying him thoughtfully.

Zeke ignored him.

They got outside and stood for a moment, sniffing.

"Steroid guy got in a car," Alex said.

"His name's Lyman Peressini."

"Lyman, huh?" Alex rolled the name over on his tongue. "I get to kill him when we find him."

"We'll both take him out." He sniffed again. "One of his flunkies got in the car with him, but the other headed down the street."

"To the right."

"Then let's go."

Zeke slung the duffel over his shoulder and started walking down the street. Hunting dragons with Alex. It felt so wrong, but at the same time, it felt more right than anything he'd done in a long time.

God, he was losing his mind.

Seventeen

Three minutes later, Theresa and Becca arrived in the lobby of what appeared to be a twenty-four-carat-gold porn museum. Arched marble ceiling, huge pillars, marble floors, and more obscene scenes than even a cybersex addict could possibly imagine. Theresa stared at the ceiling mural. "Are those supposed to be humans? Because I don't think humans can actually do that."

"Don't even ask. Satan can expound for days on the stuff in here." Becca headed toward a set of double doors at the back of the room, each of which had a set of golden breasts positioned at head height on the door. Becca lifted up a pair of golden hands and brought them down so they cupped the breasts. She whacked them firmly together several times.

A loud catcall sounded from the other side of the door, and Becca took a deep breath. "Every moment in his presence is a risk. You realize that, don't you?"

"Unfortunately, I do." She touched the Rivka's shoulder. "Thanks."

"You so owe me." Then Becca shoved her hip into the fifteen-foot-high gilded door and it swung open. "Hi, honey, I'm home."

Theresa followed Becca into the room, and stopped short. There wasn't a single gold item in the room. No sexual objects, not even a hint of anything inappropriate. It was the epitome of a Fortune 500 CEO's office. Beautiful wooden furniture, maroon leather couch, tasteful paintings . . . "Is that a Picasso?"

"Yes, it is. He signed it to me personally." The wall folded out and Satan stepped through a hidden door. He was wearing an expensive charcoal gray business suit, polished black loafers, and a Rolex with a black leather band and a diamond face. "Dragon. Are you here to offer your soul? I am most pleased, but do not have time to talk." He frowned at Becca. "I have a most important meeting in several minutes and I need time to prepare myself. I have great opportunity for world domination."

Theresa frowned. World domination? Sounded a little too familiar. "Who are you meeting with?"

He flicked his finger toward her, and suddenly she couldn't breathe. She grabbed her throat and fell to her knees. *Help? Anyone?*

Becca gave her a worried glance. "Satan? Can you let her go? She just has a quick question."

"She intruded in my business." He walked over to his desk and studied the plush chair for a moment before easing into it. "Do I look regal and domineering? Intimidating and in possession of a brilliant and analytical business mind? Shrewd and ruthless?" He pulled a leather-bound photo album out from under his desk. "Should I put the album of my best tortures out, do you think? Would that impress or seem arrogant?" He tugged at his tie. "Does my tie match?"

Omigod. Her lungs were *burning*. Head spinning.

"Satan, you look great." Becca tilted her head. "Are you actually nervous about this meeting?"

"Never. I was trying to make you feel valued by asking questions. It is practice for making Iris think I value her for more than the luscious curves of her pearly-white body."

"Ah."

Theresa whacked Becca on the leg as her lungs seized.

Becca glanced down. "Oh, right. Hey, Satan, if you kill Theresa, Iris will be pissed."

"Excellent point, Rivka. This is why I endure your failure to grovel at my feet." He flicked another finger at Theresa and the pressure on her throat vanished.

She sucked in air. *Oh, thank God.*

Satan sighed with a bored air. "Well, Dragon? What do you want?"

She dragged in another load of oxygen and staggered to her feet. "When you turned me into human form, I think you forgot to leave me the ability to change back into a dragon."

He flashed his pearly whites at her. "Nonsense. I forget nothing."

She frowned. "You did it on purpose?"

"Of course I did. You didn't specify, so I took advantage. Dismissed." He reached into his drawer and put on headphones and closed his eyes.

Becca gave her a resigned look. "I told you making a deal with Satan was a bad idea. Ready?"

"No, I have to follow up." Her heart was thudding so loudly she wouldn't have been surprised if Satan started dancing to its rhythm, just to mock her.

Becca raised a brow. "You're sure you want to risk it?"

She thought of Justine and Derek in the foyer of the Chamber and nodded. "Definitely."

"Fine." Becca tapped the desk in front of Satan.

He lifted the headphones off one ear. "What?"

"Hey, Sex God, the dragon's not finished. Can you give her another few minutes?"

"Why should I?"

"Because Iris is my surrogate mom," Theresa said. "She cares what happens to me." God, it felt good to say that and know it was true.

Satan grunted his annoyance, but removed his headphones. "You have thirty seconds. Go."

She didn't waste time. "I need to be able to change into dragon form. Will you fix it?"

"No."

"Can we make another deal to include that option?" She ignored Becca rolling her eyes at her.

"No."

"Is there anything I can do to get the dragon form back?"

"I like to watch stupid people suffer when they make bad deals. No dragon form. Suffer and make me happy."

She lifted her chin, suppressing her rising panic. "I'm not suffering. I like being human. It's just that I need to be able to get into dragon form to get Mona back."

"Hah! Hah!" Satan shoved back the chair, beaming with delight. "I am so glad you need her back! Excellent bonus! I can feel your desperation! Brilliant! Brilliant!"

"That worked well," Becca muttered from behind her. "You couldn't have thought of a better approach?"

"Shut up."

Satan was laughing so hard she could barely concentrate.

She had to come up with *something*. "Iris is very upset with you."

The laughter stopped instantly and Satan stared at her. "Iris came to you? She's in love with me, is she not? The Goblet put her over the crest, no?"

"I think it would help if she didn't have to worry about the Council throwing me and Justine in the Chamber."

"What? Satanette in the Chamber?" He jumped to his feet in outrage, a little funnel cloud of smoke rising from the top of his head. "Why would that happen? I would never endanger the fruit of my loins!"

"Justine has been detained by the Council. If I don't get Mona back from you, they'll put Justine and me in the Chamber. Iris is very upset about that."

Satan slumped in his chair, his hands clasped in his lap. "How is it possible that my brilliant plan backfired? I am so confused."

"How about you give Mona back to me? Then Iris will be happy and Justine will be safe." It wouldn't give her back her dragon form, but at this point, she didn't care.

Satan straightened his back and his eyes blackened with steely resolve. "No. I will not admit failure. I will resolve this situation in my favor. I have the Goblet until you eliminate the threats against you, and I shall make the best use of this time." A knock sounded at the door and he jumped.

Theresa and Becca exchanged glances as Satan tugged at his tie again and ran his fingers through his hair. "Time to go, Dragon," Becca said.

"Wait a sec." Theresa moved forward. "Satan, if you give me back Mona, I'll give you the identity of a man who cheated you." Screw Lyman. If she couldn't kill him herself, she'd let Satan do it.

"Many try to cheat me. They all end up here when they die and then I have them at my mercy for all eternity." Satan brushed her off and stood up. "Begone, peons. It is time for a power summit."

"Lyman Peressini cheated you. He lied to you about how much money he made from the Otherworld Detector. He didn't die, and he's probably still using it and making tons of money from it."

"I know that already." Satan rolled his eyes. "Lyman Peressini will die soon enough and I will torture him forever. It is too much effort to track him down. He will do more bad things and have such a black soul that he will be very useful to me. Now, leave or I shall rip out your intestines and pour burning acid down your throat."

Becca grabbed her arm. "Trust me, Theresa, leaving while you still have all your body parts is the smart thing."

"Fine." She followed Becca to the door. Why stay? Iris and Lyman had been her trump cards, and she'd played them and failed. Now she had nothing more to leverage Satan with. Dammit! There had to be another way!

Becca opened the heavy door and stepped back to admit the person who'd knocked.

A large, well-muscled man in a double-breasted suit, a black trench coat, dark sunglasses, and the most enormous nose she'd ever seen walked into the room. He turned his head toward them, then his step faltered. "Theresa?"

Theresa tensed. Did she know this man? Did she want to? He looked like a mafia stereotype, right down to the two armed men in dark glasses walking in behind him. "Who are you?"

He stared at her, or at least he looked as if he was. She couldn't see his eyes past the glasses. His face and body weren't at all familiar, so she carefully opened her scent receptors and sniffed. He smelled faintly reminiscent of . . . she wasn't sure. Had she scented him before? Any decent dragon had a photographic memory for scents, but she'd already demonstrated exactly how well her nose worked.

Satan was suddenly standing next to them. "Do not bother my esteemed guest, peons. Be on your way to do my bidding and harvest souls." He giggled nervously at their guest. "These two are my servants. Lovely breasts, no?"

"And on that note, we're leaving." Theresa skittered past Satan and his guest and stalked into the lobby, Becca right behind her.

The Rivka pulled the door shut behind them. "So, what now? Since that worked so—"

Theresa slapped her hand over the Rivka's mouth as she caught the echo of the conversation between Satan and his guest. Had his guest just mentioned an Otherworld Detector? "Shh!"

Becca knocked Theresa's hand away. "Touch me like that again and I'll fireball you."

"Be quiet." Theresa moved next to the door and pressed her ear against it. The thick wood muffled the conversation, so human ears wouldn't hear it, but she wasn't human, was she?

"He has surveillance cameras and motion detectors to

protect his privacy. He'll kill you for eavesdropping." Becca stepped back, distancing herself from Theresa.

"Just give me a sec." She closed her eyes and reached out with her senses, trying to hear.

"How did you get my Otherworld Detector?" Satan asked.

"I killed Lyman Peressini and took it."

Theresa frowned. Was Lyman really dead? If so, she'd take this dude out to dinner for sure.

Satan barked with laughter. "Oh, I love lies. If you had killed Lyman, he would be in hell. Stupid humans do not do their research. Do you think you can lie to Satan? I am not the leader of the Underworld for nothing. Tell me why you are really here or I shall cut up your body in little bits and feed them to my oversized Japanese goldfish."

The man cleared his throat, but the wood was too thick for Theresa to scent for fear. "I *do* have the Otherworld Detector."

"So?"

"So, I want to offer a trade."

"Trade? I do not make trades."

"The Goblet of Eternal Youth in exchange for the Otherworld Detector."

Satan burst out into roars of laughter. "As if the Otherworld Detector is worth the Goblet! You make a good joke, or you are very stupid and are not worthy of a meeting with me. Besides, it is already mine. I do not need to trade for it. If you have it, you must return it."

Theresa moved over as Becca cozied up next to her. "He must not have armed the door," the Rivka whispered as she pressed her ear against the door.

Theresa grinned at the Rivka. "If I was a lesbian, I think I could fall in love with you. Killing, harvesting souls, breaking the rules at work . . ."

"Shut up. I can't hear."

Theresa's smile widened. When all this was over, she and Becca were so going to have to hang out.

". . . I want the Goblet," the man said.

"That is most excellent to know. I will enjoy knowing you are yearning for something you cannot have."

"Then, how about if I triple your take on the souls of Otherworld beings in return for the Goblet?"

There was a long silence, then Satan finally spoke, the amusement gone from his voice. "A most interesting offer. How is it that you have such an appealing thing to offer me?"

"I am the leader of the Otherworld mafia. I control the Otherworld, and if I can get the Goblet, I will own all of the beings in the Mortal world. You control the Afterlife. Together, we can rule over all."

"I do not share power," Satan said.

"Neither do I, but if we both more than double our current territories then we're both better off."

"Perhaps."

Theresa flattened her palms on the wood. "If Satan agrees to give up Mona, I'm going in."

"Shh."

"Alas," Satan said. "No matter how tempting the offer is, I cannot give up the Goblet. She is mine only temporarily, and then I must return her to the dragon."

Good boy, Satan.

"Theresa Nichols will not be a problem." The man's voice was strained and something familiar pinged in

Theresa's memory. She was certain she knew him, and he certainly seemed to think he knew her. She glanced at Becca, who shrugged.

"If you agree to the deal," the man said, "I will accept the terms of your deal with the dragon. She will not interfere with my plans."

Men. So arrogant. So annoying.

"No, I reject your offer. I need to use the Goblet to seduce the woman of my dreams. That is more important."

"Are you sure about that?" The man sounded a little too calculating for her comfort.

"Certainly. Yes." There was a thud as if Satan had slammed his fist into the table. "Yes. Yes!"

A beep sounded and Becca jerked Theresa back from the door. "The sensors just came on."

"Someone is listening!" Satan shrieked and a loud crash came from inside.

"Time to go." Becca grabbed her arm and Theresa let the Rivka drag her through the floor into an inky black puddle.

Eighteen

Zeke and Alex halted when they reached the exterior doors to an office building. They'd tracked Lyman's flunkie to the door, and the man had apparently gone inside.

Alex stared up at the modest redbrick building. "You think Lyman has his offices here?"

Tension gripped Zeke. "I think I have *my* offices here."

Alex looked at him. "He came here for you."

"Apparently." Zeke shifted the duffel bag and wished he'd brought a gun, then chastised himself. He didn't carry guns anymore. "Let's see if he's waiting for me."

They rode the elevator up in silence, the scent of their prey heavy in the small enclosed area. The familiar twitch started at the back of Zeke's neck and crept down his arms, and he didn't even try to suppress it. He could only hope they didn't run into Theresa, or any other innocent, for that matter.

He followed the scent right to his office door, then inspected the air. "He's not here anymore."

"Well, let's go inside and see what gifts he left you."

Zeke opened the door, which was already unlocked, and they stepped inside. Nothing looked disturbed, but the scent of their prey was everywhere. Without speaking, they split up, Alex taking the reception area and Zeke inspecting his office.

He walked carefully around the room, touching nothing, but couldn't find anything amiss.

Finally, he reached the trash can and peered inside. Nothing in there except trash. He was about to set it down when a photo caught his eye. The dragon that Twitchy Guy and Bony Guy had tried to hire him to find. He fished the photo out and studied it.

It wasn't Lyman, and the name on the back of the photo was Zeus. What were the chances he had nothing to do with Lyman? Slim to none, Zeke would bet. Too many dragons springing up to be a coincidence. He found the business card at the bottom of the trash. No name or address. Just a phone number.

He grabbed his office phone and punched in the number. It was an automated voice-mail box, so Zeke said, "Zeke Siccardi here. I'm considering taking the Zeus assignment, but I need to meet with you and get some more information. Please call me as soon as possible." He left his cell phone number then hung up, rubbing his fingers over the corner of the card.

Alex came into the office. "I can't find anything that he touched."

"Me either."

Zeke tucked the photo and business card into his back pocket. "Let me just get my computer and some other stuff, and then we'll see if we can pick up his scent outside again." He dropped the duffel bag on the floor, then walked around his desk and sat down.

He leaned back in his chair and something clicked in

the seat cushion. It was so quiet that human ears wouldn't have heard it, but Alex jerked his gaze to Zeke's. "What was that?"

Zeke froze. "Booby trap?"

"Well, get up."

"What if that triggers it?"

"What if you already did and you have one second to move before your balls get blown off? How are you going to satisfy your dragon?" Alex was already next to him, peering under the chair. "Ooo . . ."

"Ooo . . . *what?*"

Alex sat up. "Bad news, man."

"*What?*"

"You have a piece-of-shit chair and your out-of-shape ass broke one of the springs." He held it up and grinned.

"Bite me." Zeke grabbed his computer and shoved the chair back as he jumped to his feet.

"No thanks. Save that for your dragon. If a dragon nibbles on you during sex, does it hurt as much as when they bite you in battle?"

Zeke ground his teeth. "I wouldn't know." He didn't count the sex they'd had as real sex. It had been pheromone-induced. Nothing more.

Alex caught his arm and spun him toward him. "Wait a sec. You're this hung up on this chick and you haven't even slept with her?" He looked delighted at the idea. "She too smart to succumb to your charms?"

"She's a dragon. I'm a slayer. It's not a good match."

The amusement in Alex's eyes glimmered. "It took Jasmine kicking my ass for me to become a one-woman man." He slammed his hand down on Zeke's shoulder. "Welcome to the club, man."

Zeke glared at him. "How can you rib me about this and then tell me I have to hand her over to you in the same breath?"

Alex sobered. "You're right. Jasmine would accuse me of being callous." Then he shrugged. "I can't help it. I enjoy the thought of killing a dragon, even if it's your woman."

"You're a bastard." Zeke grabbed the doorknob to his office door, and the explosion threw him back into Alex and hurled them both into the opposite wall.

Zeke awoke a few seconds later. He was sprawled across Alex, his head ringing and his body blistered from the heat. But his laptop was still clutched against his chest. Damn, he was good.

Beneath him, Alex groaned.

Zeke rolled to his side and realized that the front of his office was full of flames. He sat up and elbowed Alex. "Get up."

"Son of a bitch." Alex groaned. "It was a setup. We were supposed to follow his scent here."

"No kidding." He'd been an idiot to think Lyman would have been dumb enough to let his man accidentally leave a trail for them to follow. After Theresa's story, he should have realized Lyman was a formidable opponent. "You okay?"

"No. I'm pissed."

"Not as pissed as I am." Lyman had destroyed his office. Invaded his personal space. Manhandled his dragon . . . er . . . a dragon that was under his protection. It was personal now. Zeke stood up, then grabbed Alex's arm and hauled his friend to his feet. "At least he's too egotistical to bother learning that fire isn't the best way to kill slayers."

He shoved the computer under his shirt and ran through the flames, Alex on his heels.

As soon as they floated up through the floor of Becca's apartment, Theresa turned to the Rivka. "I need you to teach me how to fight."

The Rivka raised a brow. "Why?"

"My old boyfriend wants to kill me, and if I can't turn into a dragon, I have no chance against him." There was no time for a pity party about the fact she would never get to fly again. Oh, wow. She sat down heavily on the couch. She was never going to be able to fly again. Or knock out someone with her tail. Or incinerate someone. Then she lifted her chin and shoved the thoughts aside. She had bigger concerns. "I need to learn how to kick his ass in human form."

Becca glanced at her watch, then shook her head. "I can't. I have so much to do at Vic's, then I have to hit the streets tonight. I still haven't found that guy who tried to kill me after pretending he was human. Satan wants to know what he is, and until I find him again, I'm risking Satan's wrath, and I really hate that."

Theresa frowned. "I want to go with you."

"Don't you have enough going on in your life right now? Plenty of people who need killing, a very hot guy who worships your body, and the upper hand in your dealings with Satan."

Theresa brightened. "You think Zeke wants to worship my body?" She immediately chastised herself for even thinking it. "He's a slayer. He wants to kill me."

Becca took a sip of her water. "Just because you have to kill someone doesn't mean you don't wish you didn't have to." Her face darkened. "Hell, you can kill someone you love. It doesn't lessen your love. It just makes you hate yourself and hate your job."

Theresa tilted her head at the Rivka, watching the anger cloud her features. "True."

"Damn true." She slammed down the bottle. "I have to go." Then she vanished through the floor.

Well, okay then.

When this was over, she and the Rivka were so going to need to have some girl talk. That girl had issues that definitely needed chocolate and wine coolers to resolve.

Ten minutes later, Theresa was wearing a pair of Becca's black spandex shorts and a red sports bra. She studied the woman on the DVD and tried to mimic her stance. Balance on left foot. Right knee up.

She frowned as Cameron Diaz jumped up in the air and did a triple kick into a guy's head before doing two somersaults and landing on top of a two-story building. Something that would be much easier to do in *dragon* form.

Nothing like the special effects of *Charlie's Angels* to make a woman feel inadequate.

She lifted her chin as the three Angels advanced on the Thin Man. "I can so do this. They're underfed, overglammed movie stars, and I am so much tougher."

She slammed her foot into Becca's dining room chair, then karate-chopped it, and pain shot up her hand and wrist. She yelped, then smashed her heel into the padded seat. "I will kill you, you bastard!"

"Maybe you should try recovering from your five-story

swan dive before attacking household furnishings," Zeke said from the door.

Her heart leaping, Theresa spun around. Her smile faded as she took in his dirty face, the burns on his neck, and his blackened jeans. "Omigod. What happened to you?" She ran over to him and touched his injured neck, and he jerked under her touch. "Sorry." She sniffed him, but didn't smell any blood. "Are you all right?"

He dropped her duffel bag on the floor and cupped her face in his hands. "Are you okay? Did Lyman come after you again? Or one of his henchmen? Any threats?"

She shook her head. "I'm fine. But you're not. What happened?"

He sighed and let his forehead drop until it rested against hers. He closed his eyes and didn't say anything.

After a minute, she gently tapped his stomach. "Zeke? Talk to me."

He lifted his head and met her gaze, his face mere inches from hers. "Don't let that bastard get to you, okay?"

She nodded, aware of his warm breath on her lips. "I wasn't planning on it. Will you teach me how to fight in human form?"

"Yes."

She blinked. "Yes? You aren't afraid of accidentally killing me?"

He grimaced, then let go of her. "You need to be able to protect yourself. He's more of a threat than I thought, and you need to be prepared. I'll handle my instincts."

She frowned as he released her and turned away. "What happened?"

"Where's the bathroom?"

"Guest bathroom is down the hall to the right. That's the one I use."

He turned and headed toward it.

Her worry about him began to morph into annoyance as she watched his back disappear into the bathroom. When he slammed the door, that was it.

She marched over and knocked on the door. "Zeke. Aren't you going to tell me what happened? Did you find Lyman?"

The shower turned on. "No."

She waited, but she heard only the thud of his jeans hitting the floor. "Well, what happened to you?"

"Alex was at your apartment. He found out where you lived."

"He tried to burn you up?" She grinned. "Did you tell him you wouldn't help him kill me, so he tried to take you out?"

"No."

Oh. "So you told him you'd help him kill me?" She glanced at the front door. Unlocked. "Is he coming over?"

The shower curtain slid and she knew he was in the shower. He cursed as the warm water hit his burns.

"Zeke!"

"It's under control."

Argh! Very annoying me-male-protector-you-weak-female attitude. She stalked over to the front door and yanked it open. Clouds of steam billowed into the hall, and she stepped inside and slammed the door shut behind her.

She heard Zeke jerk in surprise and then a clunk as he knocked an elbow or some other bone into the wall.

She walked over to the shower curtain and flung it open.

He jumped, spun around, and had her in a headlock against his chest before she had time to react. They both stood there for a long moment as she watched a trail of soap trickle down his corded thigh, over his knee, and down his shin to his cute little toes. When water began dripping off her breasts, she finally said, "It's me."

"I know that *now*. Don't sneak up on me. I'm not in a good state right now."

"Are you going to keep me in a headlock against your naked body indefinitely?" She assumed he was naked. The angle of the headlock was keeping her from seeing any really interesting parts.

"I'm thinking about it."

She grinned. "Becca says you worship my body. Is that what this is all about?"

He cursed and released her, but didn't push her out of the shower. So she slowly stood up and faced him, blinking against the water blasting her in the face. His hair was flat against his head, his chest delightfully furry, sparkling with droplets. Perfect abs . . . she trailed her glance downward and smiled. "You were wasting time with cybersex, Zeke. You're definitely worthy of in-person sex." During their pheromone-induced sex, she hadn't had the opportunity to appreciate his attributes. Her loss, apparently.

He growled. "I'm trying to take a shower."

She dragged her gaze off his manly regions and looked at his face. His eyes were dark and stormy, like those of a man who had suddenly realized that a sexual siren was standing in his shower wearing nothing but spandex shorts and a sports bra. "No, Zeke, you're trying to avoid me by taking a shower. I don't like being manipulated, so I'll just stand here while you shower, so I can ask questions."

His gaze flickered with something dark. "I'm having a tough day."

"Me, too." She folded her arms and glared at him, trying not to flutter her eyelashes as they were pounded by the shower. "I found out Satan intentionally took away my ability to change into a dragon and I'll never get it back on my own. The Council knows I gave Mona to Satan, and they have Justine in custody, and if they catch me before I get Mona back I'll be in the Chamber of Unspeakable Horrors for all eternity. And Satan met with a man who proclaimed himself head of the Otherworld mafia, and he wants to make a deal for the Goblet, so if I don't get this situation taken care of quickly, I could be in so much trouble. And then my self-appointed protector comes home covered in burns and he won't tell me what happened." She grabbed a bar of soap and handed it to him. "Don't let me stop you. I like watching you massage your own body. It's like cybersex with a Netcam."

His face darkened and his eyes flicked over her body. Was she wet and shiny? Totally delectable? Probably. She smiled and wiped some water off her breastbone, grinning when his eyes followed her hands. Men. Such putty when it came to the opposite sex. "Zeke. How'd you get burned?" She didn't even need to woo him with flames. Wet workout clothes were more than enough.

He took a deep breath, then closed his eyes and began rubbing the soap gingerly over his chest. "I followed the scent of Lyman's man to my office. He'd set a bomb for me."

Her chest tightened. "A bomb?" she echoed, her voice slightly faint.

"Yeah, but he forgot that flames don't kill slayers."

Thank God. She sat down on the edge of the tub, belatedly realizing that put her face right at the same height as a certain perky body part. Um, *hello.* "For you to get burned, it must have been pretty intense."

"Yeah, I guess."

She closed her eyes for a moment, trying to ease the ache in her chest. After a bit, she opened her eyes. "So, he wants you dead, too? But why?"

"I don't know." He turned to rinse his chest, putting a set of very tight buns so close she could practically lick them. "I brought a photo I want you to look at. It's in the back pocket of my jeans, if it didn't melt in the fire."

But I don't want to go get your pants right now. She liked where she was. "So, what about Alex?"

"He understands I don't want to kill you or help him." Zeke began to soap his back. She watched his hands run the soap over his lower back and over his butt and down the backs of his legs, and she began to feel slightly warm. "But he loves Jasmine, and her safety trumps." He threw the soap in the corner, and it hit with a thud. "Unfortunately, my life debt trumps all as well."

She thought of what Becca had said. "Well, at least you don't sound happy about contributing to my death. That makes me feel slightly better."

He turned around to rinse his back, his gaze hot on her face. "God, T, you're making me crazy."

The ache in her chest suddenly turned into something silky and hot. "I am? What did I do?"

He reached with one hand and pushed her wet hair back off her face, his fingers trailing through the tangles. "You need to get out of my shower."

She didn't move. "It's Becca's shower."

"Lyman tried to kill me tonight."

"He tried to kill me 180 years ago. Now you and I are practically twins."

His fingers tightened in her hair, and she gripped the edge of the tub, all too aware of his nakedness and the fact her face was at hip level. He sighed. "What am I going to do with you?"

"Ravage my body?"

He stared down at her.

"Or you can teach me how to defend myself and we can kick Lyman's ass and retrieve Jasmine. Then I'll be safe, you'll be safe, the Goblet will be safe, and we can revert to our cybersex relationship." Her heart was pounding as she gazed up at him. She managed a casual shrug as she watched the water cascade over his chest, down his belly, over his . . . "Whatever works for you."

He thumbed her dragon mark, his touch a caress that made her want to rub up against him. "Nothing about you works for me," he finally said. "You and I. We don't work."

She stood up finally, her breasts brushing against his chest through the drenched sports bra. "Don't worry about killing me. I can handle you."

He cupped the back of her neck. "How do I choose between you and my life debt, T? How?"

"Don't let it come to that," she whispered.

His gaze drove into her eyes, the pain in their brown depths palpable. "How do I take you, knowing I took everything away from you? Your family, your world, your village?"

She licked some water off her upper lip. "I found your slayer armor."

He tensed.

"Did you wear it for every slaying you did?"

He dropped his hand from the back of her neck, shut off the shower, and got out. "I don't want to discuss that." He grabbed a towel and scoured his hair with it, ignoring the water all over the rest of his body.

She stayed in the shower, her heart thudding. "I need to know. Did you wear that for every slaying you did?"

He brushed the towel once over his chest, then wrapped it around his waist. "I want you to look at the picture I brought back with me." He picked up his burned pants and fished around in the back pockets.

"Did you wear it for every slaying?"

He shoved a photo at her, holding it in front of her face. "Do you recognize him?"

She didn't even look at it. "My parents' blood wasn't on your slaying armor. You didn't kill them while you were wearing it."

A look of disbelief swept over his features and he let the photo drop to his side. "What?"

She stepped out of the shower and walked over to him. "You didn't kill them while you were wearing your armor. I ask again, did you wear that for every slaying you did?"

He stared past her, looking at the wall behind her with

a distant look on his face, as if he was immersed in memories he couldn't share.

"Zeke?"

"Yes."

"Yes, what?"

He looked down at her. "I wore that for every slaying. In accordance with the custom of slayers, the blood of every dragon I ever killed is on that leather. Even if I had to go back later to get it, I did as my kind requires, and I spilled their blood." The pain in his face was so heavy, she couldn't help but lay her hands on his cheeks. He stared at her. "I didn't kill your parents?"

"You didn't kill any dragon I was related to. My mark would have felt it." She tried to lighten the moment. "Does this mean we have a seriously screwed-up relationship? Since we actually have to discuss whether you slayed my family?"

"Screwed-up doesn't begin to describe it."

"In a good way, right?"

He sighed and leaned against the sink, pulling her up against him. She nestled between his legs, letting her hips press against his towel-clad nether regions. He held up the photo. "Do you know him?"

"You want to talk about photos when you've just been liberated from your past? Shouldn't you be showing your exhilaration by ripping off your towel and throwing me to the ground and violating my body in more ways than any dragon has ever heard of?"

"Now you sound like the Theresa Nichols I knew online." He managed a grin, but she could still see the strain on his face.

Darn it. She wanted to take that pain away. Light sexual

banter wasn't doing it. So, what else was she supposed to do? No one had ever accused her of being particularly adept at sensitive commiseration. She sighed. "Okay. Show me the photo."

Hating one's heritage was unfamiliar territory for her, so she wasn't exactly sure how to help him. After all, he had killed lots of dragons, and he still wanted to. As Becca said, it didn't make him bad. Hmm . . . maybe she should get him and Becca together for some "we hate what we are compelled to do" bonding.

He held up the picture and she glanced at it briefly. Then she grabbed it. "Omigod. I totally know him."

Nineteen

Zeke watched the shock come over Theresa's features, and a part of him wanted to reach out and wrap her up against him. Not to comfort her. To comfort him. To know that she forgave him for who he was.

But he couldn't ask, because he didn't want to know if she didn't forgive him. And if she did, it wouldn't matter anyway. He would still kill her if his blood oath gave him no choice, and that pretty much ended the topic right there.

She frowned at the picture, running her finger over it. "I mean, I don't *know* him, but I saw him today." She looked up. "He was the one talking to Satan. He's the one who wants Mona." Her eyes narrowed. "I'm positive he knows Lyman. I think they're working together."

"Really?" A break like this could be the connection he needed to piece everything together. "His name is Zeus."

"Zeus? Stupid name."

"He's a dragon."

"A dragon?" She sat down on the toilet, leaning against Zeke's thigh as she tapped the picture on her chin. "New York City is becoming dragon central." She looked up. "So, how do we find him?"

"I was hired to find Zeus so a couple of guys could kill him." He reached over and gathered Theresa's hair, squeezing the water from its ends. It dribbled with a musical trickle onto the tile floor. "I told them I wouldn't do it. You know, my whole I-don't-kill-or-endanger-dragons-anymore shtick."

"I'm familiar with that philosophy." She followed his movements with her gaze as he grabbed another towel and draped it over her hair, patting the water out of it, but she didn't move away, or move to help him. She simply sat still and let him do what he felt like doing. "So, if we can find him, we can torture him until he admits where Lyman is."

"I don't torture dragons." He rubbed the towel over her back, wiping away the droplets from her smooth shoulders.

"Dragons don't have such qualms. I'll do it." She turned slightly so he could access her entire back. "So, how do we find him?"

He skimmed the cloth over her lower back. "I have a call in to the men who hired me. I said I was thinking of taking the case, and I needed more information."

"Tell them I'm your sidekick. You hired me to do the dirty work you don't have the stomach for anymore."

He ran out of skin to dry, so he tossed the towel into the sink, and Theresa turned back to face him. "I'd rather not have any dirty work done," he said.

Theresa smiled and stood up. "I know, darling, but the world's an ugly place. I'll protect you as much as I can, okay? You find the bad men, and I'll take care of them." She leaned in and gave him a quick kiss on his mouth, then bounced away before he could decide whether to grab her and haul her against him or order her never to touch him again. "You just need to help me hone my battle skills, and I'll be ready to take them on for you."

He stared after her as she flounced out of the bathroom. She turned just as she reached the door, a big grin on her face. "You do realize that's one of the best ideas I've ever had, don't you? I'll satisfy my dragon urges by doing lots of violent stuff, and you can pretend that the world is a peaceful place. We might be the perfect team, Slayer." Then she winked and pulled the door shut behind her.

Satan fiddled with the vial, cocking his head in time to the swooshing of the liquid within as he tossed it back and forth. Iris nearly had a heart attack each time it went airborne across her living room. "Give her back to me, Satan."

He looked at her and spun the leather cord around his little finger. "So, I presume you have an answer for me? This is why you contacted me?"

She'd gotten the Council's consent to track him down and attempt a negotiation, and he'd responded to her summons almost immediately. She leaned forward, giving him a clear view of her cleavage. To her surprise, he didn't even try to sneak a peek. He just kept fiddling with the vial restlessly.

She spoke the words the Council had ordered her to say, based on their theory that negotiating with people who stole Mona would encourage copycat behavior. "I can't marry you and move to hell. I'm sorry, but that's too major a commitment at this time." She hesitated, realizing that if she delivered the rest of the Council's message, Satan would walk.

So she ad-libbed her own idea. "If you return Mona, I will go on a date with you, and we can see how it goes." It was the most she could offer. The Council would notice if she packed up and moved to hell, but a date was innocent enough to fall below their radar, especially if she was able to retrieve Mona.

"No." He stood up. "You are saying that only to get me to turn over the Goblet." He leaned down and pressed his face against hers. "You have no intention of marrying me, do you?"

"I said I'd start with a date, and I will." She noticed his lack of endearments and flirty comments, and frowned. "Do you even want me? Why aren't you trying to seduce me?"

"Because I have a grand offer." He hung Mona over his left ear and swayed his head back and forth, letting her tap softly against the side of his head. "I choose you over world domination, but if you will not admit your love for me, then world domination will do much to fill my lonely nights. I can wither away in yearning for your love for only so long. I had Dragon at my mercy and I used my wish on you, and it did not pay off." His eyes were glittering. "I am Satan. I do not waste opportunities, so I do not waste this one. You spurn my show of devotion. I accept your spurn. I move on."

She frowned. "You're moving on? You're giving up on me?"

"Yes."

"I don't want you to give up on me!" She stood up as gold bubbles began to fill the room. "I just need time."

"Take the time. You come grovel to me when you decide your love for me is too powerful to deny. Satan is done groveling." He jerked his head and sent Mona flying up into the air, then caught her behind his back. He grinned. "I am Satan. I have an important phone call to make." Then he vanished in an explosion of gold bubbles just as Iris lunged for him.

"Wait!"

But he was gone. With the Goblet.

Theresa's duffel bag rang just as she shut Zeke in the bathroom with his burned jeans. It wasn't her phone. His? She ran across the room and dug her hand into an outside pocket of the bag, grabbing the ringing phone. She hit SEND. "Hello?"

Silence.

"This is Zeke Siccardi's phone. May I help you?"

A man finally answered. "I am returning his phone call."

"Excellent. You're calling about Zeus, right?"

Silence, but she heard the rhythm of his breathing change. Oh, he was calling about Zeus, definitely.

Theresa carried the phone over to the couch and sat down, curling her feet under her. "I'm Zeke's new enforcer. I do the dirty work so he can continue to live in his la-la land. I liked the money you offered—" Had they offered money? They must have. "So I told him we needed to follow up. We need more information on Zeus to be able to find him."

More silence.

"Yes, well, anyway, I have dinner plans at the Gas Griller tonight. I assume they have a bar? Maybe we could all meet there after dinner? Would nine work for you?"

More silence, but she could hear him breathing.

"I know, you're probably wondering if I'm some freak who stole Zeke's phone. I'm not. He's in the shower. You want Zeus found, you know Zeke's your man. We're in high demand and have a number of pressing cases at the moment, so if we're going to fit this in our schedule, we need to move fast. Be there at nine and bring all the information you have. And bring the payment as well. We don't work for free."

Finally he spoke. "I am glad to hear Mr. Siccardi has changed his mind. We will be there."

"Excellent." She hung up just as Zeke walked out of the bathroom. Sadly enough, he had pulled his jeans back on, but he had been considerate enough to leave the top button undone, and his shirt was apparently still in the bathroom.

She settled back on the couch and inspected him. "You know, for someone who is all into peace and eschewing violence, you've kept yourself pretty fit."

Heat flickered in his eyes, and her belly answered immediately with a dance of its own. "Who was on my phone?"

"The Zeus guys. We're meeting with them at nine at the Gas Griller, after we meet with Percy."

He flicked a strand of wet hair off his forehead. "Percy?"

"My attorney. Remember the whole 'arrested for attempted murder' thing?"

"Forgot about that."

"I know." She tossed her phone onto the couch. "So many things to keep track of. I think I need a secretary. You think Becca would help?"

His gaze trailed over her. "You're getting the couch wet."

She sat up at his odd tone. "So?"

"So, it's not your couch." He wiped a drip of water off his forehead and shoved his wet hair out of his eyes.

"Again, so?"

He raised his brows.

"Oh, fine." She slammed her feet to the floor and stood up. "Happy?"

"You're dripping on her floor."

"I'm wet. These things happen."

He shook his head. "It's rude."

She frowned. "What's your problem, Siccardi?"

His face was inscrutable. "You. You're tracking water all over your friend's house."

"She's not my friend, she's—"

"If you were really polite, you'd take off those wet clothes and put them in the dryer so they didn't ruin her house."

A sudden heat raced through her and she drew her shoulders back. "Is that so?" she asked slowly.

"Mmm-hmm . . ." He walked toward her, his gaze fastened on her face. Not even a single peek at her body, but she still tingled as he approached.

He stopped in front of her, not touching, but the heat from his body was pressing against hers.

She tilted her head so she could look up at him. "You look like a man with sex on the brain."

The corner of his mouth curved up. "Am I offending your delicate sensibilities?"

"Not at all, but I'm just wondering what changed. Wasn't it like five seconds ago that you were all high and mighty about how you might kill me?" She reached up and traced her finger over the thick stubble on his jaw. "I mean, not that I'm opposed to it, but I have a firm rule when it comes to sex: Both partners must always have a clear understanding of what it means. Saves trouble later."

He growled, and excitement whistled through her. "You make me think about it, and I'm going to decide it's not a good idea."

"We can still have sex even if it's a bad idea." She flattened her hand on his chest and was pleased to see him suck in his breath. She knew it wasn't from the jolt, because they were both so used to it, they barely noticed it anymore. "But here's the thing. I need to know what you're thinking. If this is raw animal need to channel your suppressed slaying needs, that's one thing." She looked up at him and swallowed hard. "If it's because you've decided that you can't live without me as your nearest and dearest, that's something else entirely. I need to know." She leaned forward and kissed his left nipple and then his right one, giving each a farewell swipe with her tongue. She smiled when Zeke groaned softly, and looked up at him. "Well? What's the deal, lover boy?"

"I don't know."

She sighed with disappointment, then immediately chastised herself. What was her problem? Disappointed about what? It wasn't as if she wanted a commitment from him. Wasn't this whole "seize the human form" thing about becoming independent, even from him?

Right. She forgot. Good to remember. She forced herself to shrug. "No sex until you know what it is. I don't like mix-ups in the bedroom."

He frowned and traced her nose with his finger. It was

all she could do not to tip her head up and let his finger slide into her mouth. "You sound like a woman with a plan."

"I am." How, exactly, was she supposed to talk rationally while his finger was tracing her collarbone? She folded her arms across her chest. "Before I became stuck in dragon form, I had a lot of sex, and I learned quickly that not having rules could create a big problem."

He rubbed her dragon mark. "Did you ever love Lyman?"

"No."

His fingers drifted lower, skimming the edge of her bra. "Not even when you were a kid?"

"No, but he had a crush on me. He was a skinny kid and totally geeky when we were teenagers. Not nearly manly enough for me." She closed her eyes as he dropped his head and trailed his lips down the side of her neck.

"You like manly men?"

"Of course." She swallowed when he kissed her throat. "Only manly men can keep up with me."

"Am I manly?"

"You're a *vegetarian*. I need a man who rips the meat from the bones, not one who uses scissors to open his package of frozen soy burgers."

He gently bit her shoulder, and her knees began to tremble. "Would something like *that* satisfy your needs for a manly man?"

"Maybe." Her fingers itched to grab him but she wouldn't do it. She wouldn't make the first move, only to have him pull back with some lame excuse about accidentally slaying her. She clasped her hands behind her back and kept her eyes closed.

His teeth grazed her shoulder again. "What time is dinner with the lawyer?"

"Seven. Eight. I can't remember. Seven."

He grabbed her wrist and turned it so her fingers brushed against bare flesh that wasn't hers. "Your watch says it's almost four." He brought her hand up to his mouth and kissed her palm. "We have time."

"Time for what?" Oy! Her voice had totally sounded way too breathless there. She was the sex goddess. She was the one who took control in the bedroom. But by not taking control here, she was taking control. Making him decide.

She already knew what she wanted.

He took his time answering, and she felt his energy draw back in a concerted effort before he answered. He stopped licking her body. "Time to do some B&E."

"B&E?" *B is for breasts, E is for erotic?*

"Yep. Want to come?"

She opened her eyes. That was way too crass for Zeke to have meant it as she'd taken it. He wasn't crass. He was a delicious cyberlover who used romantic and wonderful language. "What are you talking about?"

"I found a local address for Edgar Vesuvius. It's not too far away."

She blinked. "Edgar Ves—who?"

"Edgar is the London attorney who hired Ralph Greene, who paid me to find you. I haven't been able to link Lyman to Ralph Greene, so I'm hoping I can do that through Edgar."

"Oh." She tried to shake off the hormones still bubbling inside her belly, but dragon needs raged in protest. They'd been stirred up and would not go to sleep so easily. "You want to go search his house? *Now?*"

"Yeah. I doubt Edgar Vesuvius was his real name. I'm thinking it might be an alias for Lyman, so I want to check the house out and see if Lyman lives there. Or at least see if we can find any info there that leads us to Lyman." His eyes were still dark, his thumb caressing her palm where his lips had been.

Dammit. She felt like slamming her tail into a wall. Or two. She'd been so certain he'd been ready to capitulate to his need for her. What was his problem? She scowled at him. "I seriously thought you were about to seduce me."

"I was, but you talked so much I had time to think about it. Decided it wasn't a good idea."

Argh! "Seriously, Zeke, as a dragon, I have needs."

He raised his brow.

"Violence, food, sex. Burning things up." She shoved him off her and stalked away. "It's part of who I am, and I embrace it, unlike you. But it means I need outlets." She paced across the room. "I can't burn stuff up very well now that I'm in human form. Kicking Lyman in the nuts was good, but it really wasn't enough. Pheromone-induced sex was great, but I was so out of it, I don't really remember it." She spun toward him. "And then you get all wet in the shower and then come out here and fondle me, and get me all worked up, and then you shut me down! You don't want me to torture anyone, you won't have sex with me, and now that I'm permanently in human form, six pizzas for lunch is going to have major repercussions for my svelte figure." She slammed her hands on her hips and glared at him. "I'm a dragon, dammit, and you've just put me over the top!"

He stared at her, and she knew any hope of anything between them was so over. She was everything he couldn't abide about himself, so how could he accept those traits in a woman? "I can't take being around you anymore. You're so calm, you deny all your instincts. Well, I can't and I won't!" She whirled around, her skin crawling with the need to turn into a dragon and go on a rampage. A scream of need echoed inside her, but she clenched her teeth. *I will not fall apart in front of anyone.* "I need to get out of here." She spun around, grabbed Becca's spare key from the coffee table, and turned toward the door, then stopped abruptly.

Zeke was standing in her way, feet spread, fists clenched, violence rolling off him in thick, black waves. His eyes were so black she couldn't see his pupils and the tendons in his neck were flexed.

She felt her body tremble in response to his energies. "Zeke?"

"I can feel your needs. They're echoing through my body." His voice was strained, his jaw clenched. "Your need to destroy something is taking over me."

"You hate it, don't you?" She tossed the keys onto the couch and circled him. If she'd had a tail, it would be twitching with anticipation. "I love it. I love who I am, but I'm sorry if I make you into someone you hate."

He moved toward her with a sudden lurch, and she jumped over a chair to get out of his way. "You're everything I don't want in my life," he said.

"I know." She flexed her fingers, watching his body for clues to which way he was going to go. She could feel the violence rolling off him, but it wasn't deadly. It was simmering with the thrill of battle, the adrenaline of a good fight, and her own need for action flared in response. "So sorry."

"You're not sorry."

"I know." She jumped at him, kicked at him with her left foot. He caught her ankle, flipped her onto the couch and lunged for her.

She rolled off the couch, landed on her hands and knees, then jumped to her feet and scrambled out of his reach as he sprang to his feet. Her heart was thumping, energy racing through her. "I've never battled with a half-naked man before."

Dark energy smoldered in his gaze as he circled the couch. "You need to practice fighting. Self-defense."

"Is that what this is?" She caught a hitch in his gait and she dove to the left to avoid him. "I was hoping it was foreplay."

To her surprise, he lunged in the same direction she was going, and his shoulder hit her in the belly, knocking her onto the floor. She kicked his left foot out from under him and rolled away as he dropped to the ground.

But his hand closed around her calf. Adrenaline raced through her and she slammed her bare foot into his head. But he'd already moved and her heel thudded into the muscle of his biceps instead. He sucked in his breath and hauled her toward him.

Her body raked over the carpet as she slid toward him, and she flung up her arm to block him as he dropped over her, his elbow pointed at her neck.

He stopped with the tip of his elbow pressed against her throat, his body pinning her to the ground. There were beads of sweat on his brow, and his body was hot against hers. His eyes were dark, but there was a level of positive energy in there that hadn't been there before. Amusement and an undercurrent of sexual energy.

Twenty

Theresa swallowed and felt his elbow press harder against her neck. "Are you going to take me out?"

He moved over her, so he was looking down at her, his eyes smoldering. "You need a lot of practice. I beat you and I wasn't even trying."

"Me either." She shifted suddenly and tried to slam her knee into his stomach. Excitement rushed over her when he blocked her and trapped her leg between his thighs. *Yes. This was the kind of man a dragon needed. One she couldn't hurt. Did it get any hotter than this?* "I was afraid I'd hurt you and I didn't want my slayer to start blubbering."

He replaced his elbow with his hand, wrapping his long fingers all the way around her throat. "Seriously, T, you really do suck at hand to hand."

"But it's only in human form. In dragon form, I'd kick your ass." They both knew she probably wouldn't, but who cared?

"I'm terrified." He sounded amused.

Her body quivered with the adrenaline of the tussle. "Let's go again. This is exactly what I need."

He pressed harder against her, and her belly tightened. "I don't want to hurt you, T. What if I lose control?"

"You won't. Do you feel violent toward me right now?"

He frowned and she watched the confusion come across his face. "But how—"

"It's your heritage, Zeke. You have to have an outlet for your needs. If you won't slay a dragon or do anything violent, it builds inside you until it explodes. I know. It happens to me all the time." She tugged her hand out from under his hip, well aware that he allowed her to free herself. He was stronger than she was, end of story. She laid her hand on his chest. She could feel his heart racing under her touch. "By sparring with me, by letting out your needs in a safe way, you satisfied your instincts enough that you can control them."

The muscles in his jaw were working and his forehead was furrowed. "When I used my punching bag, it only made things worse."

"Maybe your needs are directly related to a dragon. A punching bag doesn't cut it." She shrugged. "Any kind of excess eases my twitches, but you need a dragon in your life." She immediately bit her lip. Why had she just said that? If he suddenly came begging to her, she wouldn't know whether he wanted her for who she was, or because she could take away that part of himself he hated the most.

He shook his head. "I don't buy it."

Or maybe she had nothing to worry about. "You're a slayer. Accept it and deal with it. Stop denying it or you'll—"

He put his hand over her mouth, and she bit him. He jerked his hand away, his eyes blazing. "You bit me."

"I know. It felt great. Will you bite me?"

She could feel the struggle within him. "No. I can't bite a dragon."

"Yes, you can." She touched her fingers to his lips. "It's all about channeling your instincts in a socially acceptable direction. Or morally acceptable, in your case." She tapped her finger against his teeth. "Ravage a dragon, Zeke. See how it feels."

"I can't." But he lightly grazed her finger with his teeth.

She nodded, suddenly breathless. "Do it again. Bite the dragon, Slayer."

He frowned and suddenly levered himself off her. He sat back on his heels, his face wary. "Stop it."

"Stop what? Stop forcing you to admit all those needs and feelings churning inside you?" She propped herself up on her elbows and felt a rumble in her chest. Shit. Now was not the time for flames. She wanted him in his sane mind, not groveling at her feet in a chemically induced hormone puddle. "You're a slayer. You slay. You slay. *You slay.*"

His face darkened, and it killed her to see the pain in his eyes. "Not anymore."

"You'll always need to slay. Admit it and channel it." She fixed her gaze on his. "I need this outlet. You need this outlet. Embrace it. Maybe we'll be good together."

A growl emanated from deep in his chest, and her heart fluttered. She rolled to her belly, then scooted over in front of him. He was still sitting on his heels, so she licked his stomach.

He jerked and she lightly ran her teeth over his abs.

His fingers sank into her hair, pressed against her

scalp, pressing her *against him*. She came to her knees so she was level with him. "I want to eat you."

He sucked in his breath, then grabbed her around the waist and tossed her onto the couch. She landed with a thud and grinned as he loomed over her. "Ravage the dragon, Slayer."

He dropped onto the couch, a knee on either side of her hips, his eyes burning with emotion. Not violence, not anger, not even simply lust. It was need. Stark, burning need for her.

She reached out for his face, and he caught her hand and pressed his lips into her palm, his gaze never leaving hers.

He released her hand just as suddenly and dropped his hands on either side of her head and loomed over her. His biceps were corded, his chest flexed, his face dark with emotion. "If I start to hurt you, kill me."

Her heart clenched for him and she laid her hand on the side of his face. "I'm not going to have to kill you, Zeke. If anything, I'm the one who might hurt you—"

"Promise me. If I start to turn on you, promise me you'll kill me. There's a gun in my duffel bag. It's loaded."

She frowned. "I hate guns."

He bent his arms and lowered himself several inches, then brushed his lips across her mouth. "Promise me, T, or I'll walk away. I can't take the chance of hurting you."

"You have serious issues, you know that?" At the warning look in his eyes, she slid her arms around his neck and tugged him toward her. "Fine. I'll shoot you in the heart, okay?"

He groaned and dropped his body onto hers. Heat flickered in her lungs as his bare chest pressed against her skin, as his lips enveloped hers, as his energy soared through their skin and into her body. Sparks rumbled through her and she tangled her fingers into his hair, trying to kiss him back deeper and deeper. "I need more," she whispered.

"What do you want?" The words slipped from his lips into her mouth as he wrapped his hands around her stomach, his fingers tracing her ribs, singeing the skin on her belly.

"Teeth," she whispered.

"You're a naughty dragon."

"Can't help it." She groaned as she felt his teeth scrape across her left nipple, through the wet sports bra. Her body burned as if he'd left a searing mark in his path. "I haven't burned up anything in too long. I'm trading vices."

His fingers caught the edge of her bra, and he tugged it upward, catching her nipple between his teeth before it was even fully free. His breath was warm, his bite sent chills shuddering through her body. She twisted under him, trying to get more of his body against hers. His skin was hot, his body hard, his muscles curving under her touch. "This is nothing like cybersex," she mumbled as she dropped her head back to let him work his way up her body.

"I would hope not." He nibbled on her throat while his hands roamed the curves of her body. "I've always been a physical person, not a word guy."

"Your words kept me going just fine for the last six months." She let her hands slide down his back, marveling at the dip of his spine between his shoulders, the curve of his lower back. He was all man. He was real. And he was with her. It had been so long. Too long. The pheromone sex had been a chemically driven blur, but this was real. Intense. Overpowering.

She slipped her hands under the waistband of his jeans and over his tight ass, feeling the muscles clench under her touch. She grinned and bit his shoulder. His body spasmed, and he jerked his head up to look at her. "You like to take risks?"

The heated look in his eyes sent chills rushing through her. "I'm a dragon. I have to."

He growled, then grabbed her wrists and held them over her head. "Don't keep reminding me you're a dragon." He caught her mouth in a kiss that drove all thought from her brain. All she cared about was his taste, his energy, his spirit, and she clawed at his kiss with her mouth, trying to draw him in.

She tugged at her wrists, desperate to feel his body against hers, but his grip tightened as his kiss increased in intensity. She writhed under him then tugged again, intentionally forcing him to tighten his grip. For the first time ever, she was sleeping with a man who was tougher than she was. The fact that he didn't want to acknowledge his hard edge and his toughness made her crave him even more.

Lyman had been stronger, but he'd tried to kill her. Zeke was stronger, tougher, and wanted nothing more than to be a gentle softie, even as his true self fought to erupt. *So hot.*

He slid down her body and caught her left breast between his teeth again, and she groaned. "Leave a mark, Zeke. Mark me."

"I can't." The strain in his voice, the burning need,

threw her own answering need into a rage, and she yanked her hands free with an unexpected strength, then grabbed his shoulders and flung him off the couch. He landed with a thud on his back and caught her as she dropped on top of him. He yanked her bra over her head, sliding it down her arms. But when he got to her wrists, his eyes flashed with something that made her belly shiver with excitement.

He glanced at her face, then twisted the straps around her wrists, locking her arms together. Then he cursed and started to undo it.

She pulled her hands out of his grasp. "No. I trust you."

"I don't." His voice was throaty even as his hands cupped her breasts, his thumbs flicking the tips.

"Never argue with a woman who is half-naked and sitting on your pelvis." She scooted backward, letting her bound hands trail over his chest. She curled her fingers around the waistband of his jeans, then bent and swirled her tongue around his nipple.

He cursed and caught his fingers in her hair, his stomach flexing until she could see every muscle in his flat belly. She scooted her butt toward his feet, letting her tongue trail over his skin even as she fiddled with his zipper. A little difficult with the bra handcuffs, but with a growl of success she yanked it down, then slipped her hand inside. She'd just cupped the silky hardness in her hands when Zeke grabbed her wrists and pulled her hands out.

Before she knew what he intended, he flipped her on her back, stretched her arms over her head. "You sure you trust me?"

She stared into the black depths of his eyes and shivered. There was so much emotion bubbling in there, pain, death, and something else. Something tender that made her nod. "I trust you."

He lifted the corner of the coffee table and slid her hands under the leg. "You can get free easily if you need to."

"Then it's no fun."

He dropped his head and caught her mouth in a kiss that had her body vibrating and her skin twitching. "It's as fun as I'm going to get."

"I think it'll suffice," she managed as he traced a path down her belly, licking and nipping at every inch of her body.

When he reached her spandex shorts, her whole body clenched in anticipation, yet the moment she felt the wet material slide over her hips, she was hit with such a powerful slam of emotional intensity that she gasped.

Zeke stopped instantly, his face level with hers. "What happened? What's wrong?" His brow was furrowed, his eyes worried.

She sucked in her breath, even as her body shifted under him, reaching for him. "I'm fine."

His scowl didn't lessen. "Are you sure?"

She lifted her head and kissed him, unable to keep herself from touching him. "It's just been so long that I wasn't prepared for how I'd react. This is nothing like the pheromone sex we had."

A smile of pure masculine smugness curved his lips, and he disappeared from view. Then there was a whisper of a tickle on her inner thigh, and her shorts slid over her feet and vanished. His hands wrapped around her legs, and then his mouth met with her inner core. The resulting bolt of electricity brought her hips off the floor, and she heard him groan as it struck him.

In the back of her mind, a part of her brain wondered what the jolt meant, then his mouth and hands were everywhere and she forgot about everything but him, his touch, his soul, his being. He shifted, and she was vaguely aware of the thud of his jeans hitting a vase and a crash as it hit the floor, then he was moving up her body, nipping and licking as his skin slid over hers in a tease of heat and electricity.

She tugged at her wrists, desperate to grab him, and the coffee table flew over their heads. He covered her with his body as it crashed into the wall, then he grinned down at her, a flicker of lusty amusement in his face.

She'd never seen him look like that, so at peace, and she wrapped her legs around his hips and pulled him against her. "I need you, Zeke."

The amusement vanished and he shifted his weight and suddenly drove into her. Her body lurched with the influx of heated energy, and she grabbed for him, desperate to crawl inside his skin and cuddle against the heat burning inside him. He would make her warm, so warm. She knew it, if only she could get inside him. She lifted her hips, trying to bring him deeper inside her, closer to her heart, inside her soul. It's where he needed to be, she knew it. For both of their sakes.

The intensity of emotion building inside her continued to grow until she felt it would burst out through her skin and consume them both. It was heat, it was fire, it was smoke, it was everything she was and everything he was and it was fusing into one.

The orgasm came with such unexpected force that she grabbed his shoulders, hanging on in a futile attempt to keep her body from coming apart. She was vaguely aware of him shouting her name, his arms like steel pipes as he kept himself from crushing her with his own explosion. She felt his heat shoot through her body, curl around her belly, wrap itself around her lungs, and squeeze her heart until she was nothing but him.

Zeke buried his face in Theresa's hair and inhaled deeply, using his legs and arms to tuck her into the curve of his body. She was hot to the touch, and little jolts of electricity shot into his skin everywhere they touched. He smiled and tugged her closer, embracing the tremors nipping at their bodies.

He hadn't killed her.

He hadn't even been tempted.

And he couldn't remember the last time he'd felt this at peace. The constant itch at the back of his neck was gone.

She wiggled against him. "Zeke?"

"Yeah?" He kissed her earlobe.

"How do you feel?"

"Excellent. You?"

"I'm not sure."

A tremor in her voice caught his attention, and he lifted his head to look at her. She looked worried, and her mouth was tense, an expression he wasn't sure he'd ever seen on her face. "What's wrong?"

"Did you feel it? All those shocks and the electricity?"

He traced the furrows in her brow with his thumb. "Yeah."

"What do they mean? Why does that happen between us?"

He propped himself up on his elbow to get a better

look at her. Her eyes were wide and she was chewing her lower lip. "I don't know. Why does it matter?"

She hugged her arms to her belly, her golden gaze searching his. "I just, well, for a moment there, I felt like I couldn't live without you. Like our souls were one." She frowned at him, still chewing her lower lip. "I didn't like that feeling."

He idly rubbed his palm over her belly. "I felt it, too."

"It was just because of the shocky things, don't you think?"

She sounded on the edge of panic, so he nodded. "Probably."

"Probably?" She rolled away from him and stood up, fisting her hands on her hips and staring down at him.

That's when he noticed the marks on her body. Breasts, belly, thighs. Lots of little bite marks. But instead of panic or violence surging through him, a sense of rightness settled in his gut. His marks were on her, and he liked it.

She immediately frowned. "What's that smug, male look for?"

He nodded at her and she looked down. Then she smiled. "Well, see? You didn't kill me." She trailed her finger over a mark on her breast and he felt his body hardening again. When she looked at him, he could see the heat smoldering in her own eyes, which elevated his even more.

"You liked that I bit you."

"Of course I did. I'm a dragon." She sighed and dropped her hand. "A dragon without a tail. Two hundred years trying to get out of dragon form, only to start the full-court press to get back there. All I want is two forms. That's my heritage. Is it too much to ask for?" She whirled away, grabbed her duffel bag, and started walking back to the bedroom.

That's when he noticed the gold piercing at the base of her spine. A simple diamond stud, but it had him on his feet in a heartbeat, a low growl emanating from his chest.

She spun around to face him just as he slid his arms around her waist. For an instant, she leaned into him, but then pulled back. "We need to go search that guy's house. No time for another roll in the hay."

He let her slide out of his grasp and followed as she walked into the bedroom and tossed the bag on the bed. "What's wrong?"

She shrugged and rifled through the bag, her cheeks slowly turning red. "Every piece of lingerie in here was one we had cybersex with."

"I know." He sat down next to the bag and held up an emerald green lace bra. "Try this one."

She snatched it from his hand. "I'm not using any edible oil right now. We have to go."

"Fine." He leaned against the headboard, crossed his ankles, and clasped his hands behind his head. It just felt so right to sit there and watch her dress. He loved the soft curves of her body, the way she flipped her hair up to get it out of the way. "You going to talk to me?"

"About what?" She grabbed a black thong and slid it up over her hips.

"Whatever's bugging you. If it's not the marks, what is it?"

She paused with her black jeans on, but unzipped. "I've always prided myself on being an independent girl, Zeke. Since my parents died, I've been taking care of myself." She sighed and pulled on the zipper, but it was apparently stuck. "But when Justine left, I realized I'd become dependent on her, leaving me with nothing once I lost my place in her life. No one. And I realized I had to do something about that. Get a life. Become independent so I don't rely on anyone the way I relied on Justine." She yanked at it again, then made a noise of frustration.

He rolled off the bed and landed on his knees in front of her, tugging her hands off her pants. "There's some material stuck."

She set her hands on her head and stared at the wall while he worked on her zipper. "But when we were . . . when I felt . . ."

He freed the zipper and it slid up with an accommodating burl. "When you felt like you were crawling inside my skin and I was inside yours and it felt like we had to be together forever or we would both die?"

She stared at him.

He stood up and fastened the top button of her jeans, worried by the look on her face. "It's not a big deal. Just something about the slayer/dragon connection." He was certain it wasn't, but he wasn't about to let her know that. Not yet. Not until he figured out his own response to it.

She started chewing her lower lip again. "You think?"

"I'm sure." He pulled a black camisole out of her bag. "Here. We have stalking to do."

She glanced down, then started to laugh. "I can't wear a black camisole with a green bra. The straps will show."

"So?" He was relieved by her smile. "I like the green bra. If I see the straps, it'll make me think of hot oil and sensual massage." He fingered the bra straps. They were silky and soft and slid under his fingers like her soft skin.

Her smile widened. "Fine."

He watched her settle the camisole over her body, then studied how it hugged her curves and showed her dragon birthmark. He held up a sweatshirt. "And now you have to cover the whole thing up so no other man can ogle you."

She laughed then and threw the sweatshirt back at him. "Since when are you jealous and possessive?"

He caught the sweatshirt with a frown. "I'm not." He threw the sweatshirt on the bed even though he wanted nothing more than to pick it up and wrap her up in it.

"You have to get dressed." She tossed him a pair of boxers that he'd stashed in the bag, having stopped at his place before arriving at hers. "I prefer you in a leopard-print thong, but since you don't have one, these will have to suffice."

He tugged the underwear on. "So, now you're jealous and possessive? Is that why you want me dressed?"

"Never. I don't care if other women rip off your clothes."

"You sure?"

Annoyance flickered in her eyes. "I don't care if a thousand other women crawl inside your skin."

He yanked on the clean jeans she fished out. "Well, I'd care if anyone else crawled inside your skin." The minute the words were out and he saw her stiffen, he regretted saying them. Hell, he didn't even know why he had. Did he really care?

He watched her stalk out of the room and knew he did.

Twenty-one

A half-hour later, Theresa and Zeke were in the sub-
urbs about to engage in some illicit behavior, which
would make her day full of dragon delights: great sex, a
stop for take-out junk food, and some criminal activity. So
much better than sitting at home under Justine's lockdown.

She refused to think about what had happened during
the great sex. Everything was fine. Normal. *Nothing had
changed between them.* And just to prove it, she rested her
hands on Zeke's shoulders as she peered around him.
"See anyone?"

"Nope." After knocking on the front door and getting
no response, they'd scaled the brick wall at the back garden and were peeking around a statue of a naked woman.

She sniffed the air and scented nothing of concern.
"Seems good to me."

"Agreed." He led the way around a garden of expensive-
looking flowers and jumped over a pond of exotic fish.

They reached the back door of the quaint house, and
Zeke tested it. Locked.

"No problem." Theresa grabbed the door handle and
yanked. Her hand flew off it and the door stayed shut.
"Dammit. I'm a total wuss in human form."

Zeke pulled out a lock-picking kit. "Violence is over-rated."

"You're a pain in the ass."

The door clicked and he opened it up. "But I'm effective."

She hesitated in the doorway. Incinerating people was one thing. Breaking in was entirely different. It wasn't an activity that typically satisfied dragon urges.

"T?"

"Coming." She walked inside, sniffing scents, checking to see if someone was hiding. No one was there at the moment, but the smells were familiar. "I know who lives here. I've met him."

Zeke scented the air as well, and he frowned but didn't say anything.

She followed Zeke farther into the house, stepping around expensive antiques with fancy carvings and gold etchings. They were in a sitting room, with high-backed chairs covered in plush velvet upholstery and a huge crystal chandelier hanging from the ceiling. There was a twelve-by-twelve mural over the couch, a painting of a scenic village. Theresa took a closer look, then her belly lurched. "Oh, my God."

"What?" Zeke was rifling around in a desk.

"Look at the mural."

She heard him shift; then he sucked in his breath. "It's the Village of Uruloke. Before the Cleansing."

Her eyes raced over the mural, her heart jumping with each house she recognized. "Look! That's my house."

Zeke moved beside her. "The huge one in the middle of the town?"

"Yes." She climbed up on the couch, trailing her fingers over the building that used to be her home. "See those white curtains in that window? That was my room."

Zeke hopped up next to her. "Did you used to climb down that tree to sneak out?"

"Of course." She peered closer, then gasped. "That's my mom. Look! There she is!" Her eyes blurred, and she blinked quickly to clear her vision. "She's . . ." She blinked again. "She's kissing Lyman's dad. Where's *my* dad?"

"The guy in the expensive clothes is Lyman's dad?"

"Yes." She frowned and studied the painting more closely. "Lyman's dad never wore clothes like that. His clothes were always torn and filthy. He was too busy drinking and stealing to bother with his appearance."

Zeke peered closer. "Is that you?"

"Where?"

He tapped his finger on the image of a young woman wearing a beautiful gown, the kind her mom wouldn't let her wear because she always tore them and got them dirty.

She narrowed her eyes. "Yes, it is. My hair was brown back then, and I used to wear it like that."

"Is that Lyman you're with?" He sounded a little disgruntled. "I thought you never dated him."

"I didn't." But a guy who looked more like the suave Lyman of today than the skinny Lyman of their past had his arm around her. She was clutching his arm, gazing up at him with a look of total adoration. "I look fat."

Zeke shook his head. "Not fat. Pregnant."

"*What?*" Her hand went to her own stomach, trying to suppress the bile rolling around inside. But Zeke was right. In the painting, her other hand was on her swollen belly, and Lyman's hand was on top of hers, a look of smug male pride on his face. They both had wedding rings on, and looked happy. "Oh, my *God*. That's *disgusting*."

Zeke flicked at the image with his finger, then walked to the other end of the painting while Theresa dropped down on the couch and stared up at the ceiling. "I think I'm going to vomit."

"It was signed by the artist in 1945, after your interlude with Lyman."

She groaned and flopped her arms over her face. "I am so grossed out by this. I have a stalker."

"We have a bigger issue than that. This painting had to have been commissioned by Lyman. So what's it doing in Edgar Vesuvius's house?"

She frowned. "Well, maybe Edgar is Lyman's attorney."

"This is the kind of painting you have in your own home, T. Somewhere you can look at it every day. Either Lyman lives here now, or he used to live here."

"Here?" She scented again. The familiar scent could belong to Lyman, if he'd been wearing some cologne or something else to mask his scent. "You smell him?"

Zeke shrugged. "I thought I got a whiff of him when we first arrived. I don't smell it anymore, but it could have been him. Especially if he hasn't been here in a while."

She had sudden visions of Lyman lying on the sofa, staring up at her image while he . . . *Oh, gross.* She rolled off the couch and landed on her feet and felt the familiar heat building in her chest. "I need to incinerate this painting."

Zeke was at the other end of town, studying the painting intensely.

"Zeke? You better move. I don't want to burn you up."

He finally tapped the painting. "Who lived here?"

"Who cares? This is a stalker painting. It must be destroyed immediately."

He turned to her, and she was shocked to see the pain on his face. "Zeke? What's wrong?"

"That's the house. That's where it happened."

Before she had time to think about what she was doing, she was on the couch next to him, her hand on his arm. "Where what happened?"

He turned to the painting and touched one of the dirt roads in the middle of town. "I killed the dragons in this house, and then this one. Then Alex and the team took over the middle of the town and I went down here. We knew it was the bad section and figured the toughest kills would be in this area, so I took it." His voice grew hard and she could feel him will away the emotion.

He tapped a little shack that she recognized instantly. "I killed two dragons, then I walked into the other room and found a skinny boy there. He was trying to get away, but his leg was broken and he couldn't. He was too scared to change into dragon form. He just looked at me and waited for his death." He closed his eyes. "That's when I realized I was a monster. I walked away from that kid and left that life forever."

Zeke felt the pain in his chest with an intensity he hadn't felt in decades. Seeing the house brought it all back. "Who lived there, Theresa? Tell me his name." Sudden hope rushed through him as he stared at the little shack that had been so vivid in his memories. He'd find that dragon or his progeny, and he'd make amends. It was the only way to close the wound. "T? Who is it?"

She didn't answer. Her face was white and her eyes wide. A sick sense of dread settled in his stomach as he drew back from her. "What's wrong? Are you disgusted by me? You knew what my past was." His voice was harsher than he intended and he felt a twinge of guilt when she winced.

"No, it's not you." She swallowed hard and met his gaze. "I think it's best if you let go of the past. Nothing will be solved by hanging on to it. Save my life and the life of Alex's mate and you'll be even."

He grabbed her arm as she started to turn away, realizing that she was trying to hide the truth from him. "It was your family, wasn't it? A brother? A cousin?" His fingers dug into her arms. "Tell me!"

"You don't want to know!"

"I have to know. Dammit, T, tell me!"

"Fine! It was Lyman!"

He let go of her and sucked his breath in. *"What?"*

She nodded. "I was the one who broke his leg. He made a pass at me and I threw him off a roof. That's why I wasn't there for the Cleansing. My parents sent me off to live with Justine and Iris while my dad was running for mayor so I couldn't screw up his election. After the Cleansing, Iris kept me."

He sat down heavily on the arm of the couch. "Lyman?"

"Lyman." She kneeled between his legs and leaned on his thighs. "The fact his parents died isn't the reason he has turned into a freak, Zeke."

He lifted his head. "How did you know I was thinking that?"

"Because I know you." Her hands rubbed his legs. "You did him a favor by killing them. They were horrible people, and by freeing him from them, you gave him a chance. Of course, he completely screwed up and became an insane killer, but hey, not everyone can be me."

"No. I orphaned him." He ran his hands through his hair. "He's the one who has been haunting my dreams all this time. He's the one I have to save."

She tightened her grip on his thighs. "You can't save him, Zeke. It's *Lyman*. He wants to impregnate me and then kill me. He kidnapped Alex's mate. He cheated you and tried to murder you twice. He's not worth your regret."

He spun away from her, his head throbbing. He cursed and slammed his foot into an armchair. It flew across the room and slammed into the wall with a thud.

Theresa grinned. "Let it out, Slayer. Let's trash his house and burn it down."

"No!" He stalked over to the desk and yanked open a drawer. "There has to be another way."

Theresa slammed her hands on the desk. "Zeke! Lyman is not an innocent! He's a mass murderer!"

He met her gaze. "I've dreamed about that kid since that day. I cannot kill him. I can't do it."

She pressed her lips together and dug her fingertips into the desk, her jaw flexing in her attempt to contain her emotions. Finally, she grabbed a letter opener off the desk, walked over to the painting, then stabbed it through Lyman's face.

The anger rolling off her made the back of his neck twitch, but he didn't try to stop her.

She sawed her image out of the painting, then her mom's. Then she ripped out Lyman's house. Then she stalked back over to the desk, threw the pieces into the trash can, and set them on fire with a puff of flame that made Zeke's groin tighten. "Lyman will not control my life or yours anymore."

Then she turned around and stalked out of the room.

Zeke reached for the pieces of painting, to salvage what he knew would be dear to Lyman's heart, but they were already engulfed in flames. All he could do was watch them burn.

Now he owed Lyman twice.

Theresa walked into the bedroom and saw an enormous portrait of herself hanging over the bed. She was wearing a slinky white nightgown that she remembered all too clearly from her brief interlude with Lyman. Her stomach rolled at the memories it brought back.

She set the painting on fire, then sat on the floor and lifted the dust ruffle to peer under the bed. Lyman had always believed under the bed was the best place for putting anything important. There were a bunch of pillows there and an old rug. She pushed the rug to the side and grinned at the box hidden behind it. "Ah, Lyman, you never change."

She pulled the lockbox out and checked it. Locked. "Zeke!"

"What?"

She jumped when his voice was right in her ear. "You scared the crap out of me. What are you doing here?" She glanced up at his face, and instantly felt bad. His cheeks were hollow and his eyes heavy. "Had to get a look at my ass while I dove under the bed, huh?"

He managed a small grin, but a muscle in his cheek was ticking. "The house is pretty clean. I don't think anyone actually lives here. It's probably more of an auxiliary location. Since I couldn't find anything of interest in the rest of the house, I decided to check on your progress, but your ass is a bonus."

Oh, he was *so* tense. "Want to have sex to relieve your stress?" She regretted the words as soon as they came out of her mouth. She wasn't ready to be intimate with Zeke again.

His gaze flicked to the burning portrait over the bed. "Probably not the best time, but I appreciate the offer."

"No problem," she said quickly. "Open this."

She sat on the bed next to him as he took the box from her. Zeke jimmied the lock open and lifted out a date book.

She leaned over his shoulder and looked at it. "It's from last year."

They flipped through the pages. Each day was blocked off with meetings. Some of them were listed under the name Reverend Munsey and some under the name Zeus. "He knows Reverend Munsey, too?" She tapped her fingers on her chin. "You know, Reverend Munsey totally freaked when he saw me. I didn't know why, but if he was buddies with Lyman, that would explain it. He must have known about me."

Zeke made a small sound of triumph, and she peered at the page he was reading. "Percy Adams? He has Percy's meetings listed in here, too?" She looked at Zeke. "We are so going to torture Percy at dinner to find out what he knows." He gave her a look and she shrugged. "What? He's not a dragon. Totally torturable."

"You're incorrigible."

"I'm a dragon and I'm insatiable. You know you love it."

He raised his brow at her, and suddenly the room felt

way too small as she recalled the intimate feelings she'd had during their love fest. "I meant, you like my body. That's it." She jumped up and away from him. "Let's go find Percy."

"No torturing."

She ran out of the room. "Make me!"

She grinned at his snort of aggravation.

Satan sat on his heart-shaped bed with its fourteen-carat-gold quilt and stared at the three objects in front of him.

On the left was a picture of Iris on a beach, laughing at the camera.

On the right was Zeus's business card, on the back of which was scrawled the number of souls he would provide Satan.

In between the two of these was Mona.

A knock sounded at his door. "Satan. It's Becca. What do you need?"

"Enter, Rivka."

The heavy golden doors opened and she walked inside. He saw her take in the display on the bed, but her face revealed nothing.

He let his gaze flick back and forth between the objects. "World domination or another few centuries of rejection by the woman of my fantasies?"

She sighed and checked her watch. "I have a meeting in five minutes. Make a decision or let me come back later."

He frowned. "Are you still working at that pretzel establishment? That assignment is over. You should be devoting all your resources to spreading my power and influence far and wide."

She dropped her wrist, her face studiously bland. "I have a meeting with an informant about the being who tried to kill me."

"Most excellent. I hope it is someone worthy." He gestured at the display. "Tell me what to do."

"Give Mona back to Theresa and keep working on Iris. She's worth it."

"No."

She sighed. "So, go into business with Zeus."

"No."

He could hear her teeth grinding and he beamed at her. "I much enjoy making you wait. You are so impatient. Snap decisions for you. Indecision is torture, no?"

She shrugged. "Fine. If my mysterious assailant kills me next time, you'll be the one deprived of my services." She walked over to a chair shaped like his favorite female body part and sat down. "I'll skip the meeting."

He waggled a finger at her. "You try to manipulate me so well. You are a most excellent challenge. I make decision now." He studied the display.

Iris was no doubt what he wanted most, but she was not succumbing to his charms. Made the decision much more complicated.

He finally lifted his finger, let it glow red, pointed it at the business card, then at the photograph, then did it again. "Eenie meenie miney mo. Catch a woman by the toe. If she hollers, throw her in a pit of acid. Eenie meenie miney mo. You. Shall. Die." His finger ended up pointing at Iris, and he nodded with satisfaction. He had very admirable decision-making skills. He looked up at Becca. "Arrange meeting with Zeus. Tell him I will give him Mona."

"You ditched your chance at true love based on eenie meenie miney mo?" She looked incredulous. "Is this how you make all your major decisions?"

"Yes. Most excellent choice, no?"

She stood up, her face slightly pink. "Excellent," she snapped. "I'll go set it up." She vanished through the floor before he could think of more reasons to torture her.

So he sighed and stretched back on the bed. World domination would be most impressive. Surely Iris would be unable to resist a man of limitless authority. World domination *and* Iris. He would have it all.

Twenty-two

Zeke and Theresa showed up at the Gas Griller a fashionable six and a half minutes late after stopping at Becca's so Theresa could raid her closet and Zeke could grab some fresh clothes. Zeke looked hot in a pair of jeans, black boots, and a loose-fitting dress shirt that hid his heavily muscled upper body. She was wearing a new pair of black jeans, a pale blue camisole top and a cute, short jacket that showed just enough to be promising, but not enough to be slutty.

Percy was both a man and her attorney, so she needed to appeal to both sides of him.

Dressed in a sharp suit, he was waiting for her at a table in the corner, champagne on the white linen tablecloth, a red rose lying across the empty place across from him while he studied the menu.

"Doesn't look like a lawyer dinner," Zeke grumbled in her ear. His hand was on her back, and there was a humming of electricity jumping between them. "Looks like he's trying to seduce you."

She grinned at the edge in Zeke's voice. "Yes, it does. It will make it all the easier to get him to fall into my clutches and reveal all." She stopped and faced Zeke. "You need to disappear."

"What?" He shook his head. "No."

She could feel the tension rolling off him, so she tugged him out of sight of Percy, then wrapped her arms around his neck and gently bit his chin. He groaned softly and slipped his arms around her waist. "Cut it out."

"No." She kissed him, and he responded instantly, pressing her against the wall and burying her with a kiss that made energy sizzle through her body. When he finally broke the kiss with a nip on her neck, it was only his arms that were keeping her vertical.

There was a look of surprise on his face. "I feel better now."

"I don't." She gripped his forearms and tested her legs. "You're killing me here, Slayer." She rolled her eyes as his smile faded. "I meant because you're so sexually potent you rob me of the ability to walk."

"Oh." He gave a little head twitch that was all about testosterone, and she had to laugh.

She pushed him away. "Go hide in the corner and let me work my magic on Percy."

"I'll be here if you need me."

"I won't need you. I don't need anyone. I'm letting you stay only because I worry about you on your own out in this big, violent city." She flipped her hair at him, then swung away before her face could betray her. She might not *need* him, but she liked knowing he was backing her up. She liked it way too much, actually, and it worried her almost as much as the impact of their love fest did.

She shook her head to clear it. Now was not the time to think about Zeke. She smoothed her shirt, lifted her chin, and strutted around the corner. Percy saw her immediately, a warm smile lighting up his face. She immediately felt bad for all her thoughts about torturing him. Who could torture a man who had eyes that kind?

"Ms. Nichols, I'm so glad to see you." His voice was a little more nasal than she recalled, but he stood as she arrived, caught her hand, and kissed the back of it, then pulled out her chair. "I was worried when I didn't hear from you."

She allowed him to assist her seating, then gestured at the rose. "A lovely touch. Thank you."

He sat opposite her, and gazed at her. "You look gorgeous tonight."

She cleared her throat and felt a wave of hostility come from the corner where she'd left Zeke. "Yes, thank you. So, can you get the police to drop the charges?"

"Oh, let's not talk business yet." He lifted the bottle of champagne and filled her glass. "A toast to you."

She shifted in her chair and scratched her ear. "Cheers." She took a quick sip then set it back down. "So—"

"You do not like the champagne? I will send it back."

She tilted her head and studied him. "It's perfect. Relax. This isn't a date. You don't need to impress me."

Something dark flickered in his eyes, but was gone almost immediately as he lifted his glass to take a sip.

Theresa leaned forward, letting her cleavage distract him. "How well do you know Lyman Peressini?"

His face blanched and he coughed, spitting his champagne all over the table. "Who?"

"And Zeus?"

His face became even whiter, and he looked around the restaurant. "Keep your voice down," he hissed.

"And Reverend Munsey? It wasn't an accident that you showed up to represent me after his death, was it? How do you four fit together?" Boy, this was fun, watching him panic. It was almost as good as incinerating someone.

He grabbed her wrist and leaned forward. "Shut up."

"Shut up?" She felt a wave of anger riding in from Zeke and she pulled it in, absorbing it into her body. She leaned close to Percy until her nose brushed against his.

He yelped and jerked back, holding his nose. "Watch it."

She narrowed her eyes. "I barely touched you."

"Dragon strength."

Her breath sucked in. "You know I'm a dragon?"

He cursed, and she felt fire beginning to roll around in her chest. She grabbed his tie and pulled him toward her. "Who the hell are you?"

His fingers closed around her wrist. "Let go of me," he said quietly. "People are staring."

"You think I care?"

"If you do not release me, I will call assault and leave you to hang."

She snorted. "As I said, you think I care?"

His face darkened. "If you release me in a way that does not draw attention to this table and affect my professional reputation, I will tell you what you wish to know."

She stared him down, suddenly aware that Zeke had moved closer. She released Percy and tried to calm down. "Talk." She dropped her hand to her hip and then waved in Zeke's direction, willing him to back off. "Make it fast."

Percy straightened his tie, took a quick glance around

the room, then looked back at her. "One of my platforms as a senator is environmental issues, as I'm sure you're aware."

"I ignore politics."

Annoyance flickered over his features. "I have been arranging the purchase of several large tracts of land in the western part of the state. Preservation of forests." He leaned forward, his eyes glittering. "But in actuality, I'm creating a haven for dragons."

Her heart lurched, even as she reminded herself not to trust him. "For all three of us?" What a party she could have with Zeus and Lyman. Rah, rah, rah.

He shook his head. "There are more than twenty living there now. Mostly females and smaller males. I'm going to regenerate the dragon population."

She sat back and drummed her fingers on the table, trying not to reveal her excitement at the thought of more dragons. Of a place where she could fly. Oh, right. She couldn't fly anymore. "So where does Lyman come in?"

"Lyman is my primary investor. He finds the dragons and brings them to the reserve. No dominant males so he can avoid territorial battles."

"You mean, so he can rule over all of them. Makes sense." She pursed her lips. "And Zeus?"

Percy scowled. "Zeus takes a percentage of the funds for himself."

"Why?"

"He has an Otherworld Detector and threatened to expose me."

"Really?" Well, that was a twist she hadn't expected. "What are you?"

"A dragon."

"Really?" Another dragon? She scented him again, then shook her head. "You don't smell like a dragon."

"I hide my scent."

She lifted a brow. "Impossible."

"I have resources at my disposal."

"Like what?"

He shook his head. "Professional secrets."

Okay, fine. She'd deal with that secret later. She had more important things to uncover first. "So, where does Reverend Munsey come into this?"

"A friend, is all."

She pursed her lips. "If he's a friend, why are you defending me for killing him?"

"He would want justice, and I think you are innocent."

She raised her brows. "Try again."

He studied her for a moment, then gave a slight inclination of his head. "I arranged for you to be held on trumped-up charges so I would have the opportunity to discuss the reserve with you."

"You mean, so you could blackmail me into doing what you want, by using the threat of incarceration to pressure me." She sat back in her chair and folded her arms over her chest. "What do you want from me?"

"I want you to join me at the reserve." He gave her a flattering smile, resting his hand on the table. "Be with me, Theresa. I can give you everything you've wanted. Dragons, a place to live, a man worthy of you."

Zeke's power crashed against her so hard she had to grab her chair. Percy sat up and looked around, scanning the restaurant.

She hastened to distract him. "What makes you worthy?"

He looked at her again, but she could sense his restlessness. "I have money and power. I am strong. I am attractive. I am a great lover. I am a dragon. Everything you want, I am." He reached across the table and grabbed her hand. "You and I, Theresa, we will rule the dragons, side by side."

She studied him. "That sounds like something Lyman would say. Have you discussed this little plan with him?"

"I will protect you from Lyman." He rubbed his thumb on the back of her hand. "Lyman will never bother you again. You like that, don't you? A man who will keep you safe?" He studied her intently. "Unless it is Lyman you yearn for. If so, I will step aside. Do you want Lyman? Is he your true love?"

It was far more than a casual question. Was he Lyman's pawn? Did this reserve even exist, or had Lyman created a fantasy, knowing it was the one thing that would lure her? Or was she missing something? She tightened her grip on his hand and lifted his hand to her face. She pressed her nose up against his wrist. She managed a partial inhalation before he yanked his wrist away.

But it wasn't soon enough. He smelled like Zeus. They both carried a strong masking scent that hid their true odor. It was the same phenomenon she'd noticed in the house of Edgar Vesuvius.

She studied him, watched the wariness in his features. "Get the charges against me dismissed and I'll visit the reserve with you."

He immediately took his phone out of his jacket, hit speed dial and spoke into the phone. "Drop the charges against Theresa Nichols, effective immediately." Then he snapped his phone shut. "See? With me, you will want for nothing. Without me, you will suffer. I'll take you to the reserve now."

She felt Zeke's warning, and she shook her head. "No, tomorrow. I have a meeting with some folks about Zeus later tonight. And I want to wait until I know the charges are dropped."

His neck flexed. "I don't trust you, Theresa Nichols. We go now, or you lose the opportunity forever." He nodded at her collarbone. "Some dragons at the reserve have that mark," he said casually.

Her hand went to the tattoo. "Are you certain?" She was unable to keep the excited hope out of her voice.

"Yes." An eyebrow arched. "Family, perhaps?"

She froze. Only Zeke knew about her mark. Zeke and Lyman.

Going with Percy would be walking into Lyman's lair, she was certain.

But what if he had her family? What if there were really other dragons? People she knew? Friends? She would never be alone again. She would *belong*.

"It is a short helicopter ride away," Percy murmured. "You can see your family. Run with dragons. Have your dreams."

A wave of tension came from Zeke.

I know, Zeke. It was a trap, the best one she'd ever seen or even heard of. But she wasn't the flighty dragon she'd been when she'd known Lyman. Not anymore. She ground her teeth and stood up, clenching her fists. "I'm not interested."

His eyes widened and he jumped to his feet. "You lie."

So true. "Good night, Percy." She spun on her heel and walked away from the table.

He grabbed her arm, his fingers digging in. "You belong to me."

She jerked her arm free, her heart racing. "I belong to no one."

"I shall permit you to walk away only if you choose Lyman instead of me. Any other choice is the wrong one."

Zeke was suddenly standing on her other side. He said nothing. He didn't try to interfere. Didn't try to do a manly "I shall rescue the fair maiden" thing. He simply *was*.

It was the perfect response.

"I choose to be alone," she snapped at Percy. "Lyman can go to hell and so can you."

His gaze flicked to Zeke. "Is this who you choose?" Disgust dripped from his voice.

Zeke said nothing, but suddenly a trickle of his pheromone wafted in her nose. She slammed her shields in place and snapped her gaze to Percy's face.

His eyes narrowed. "Zeus doesn't like people interfering in his pet projects."

"So, now you're going to sic Zeus on us?" she asked. The fact he'd noticed Zeke's scent indicated he was indeed a dragon. So how come he didn't smell like one?

"Zeus does his own thing. I have nothing to do with him." His gaze swept them again, then he spun past them. He stalked out of the restaurant, and they saw him through the window as he beckoned to a limo that was waiting down the street.

"Should we follow him?" She stared after him, unable to stop the creepies crawling up her spine.

"Yes. We have time before our next meeting." Zeke brushed his hand over her lower back, and she jumped at the intensity of the shock ricocheting through her body. There was so much energy emanating from both of them she was surprised they hadn't both started slaughtering everyone in the place. "You all right?"

She lifted her chin. "I'm fine. Let's go."

She could tell by the look on his face that he knew she was lying, but he didn't argue. He just tightened his grip on her and let her lean into him as they walked out.

If a woman leans on a man for support but nobody comments on it, does it really count as needing him?

She hoped not. God, she really hoped not.

Zeke scowled at the way Theresa sat apart from him once they got into the cab. He'd felt her reach out for him in the restaurant, but now she was on the other side of the back-seat, her body erect. He was tense, she was agitated, and the energies rumbling around the cab were making his skin itch. "It's okay to rely on someone else, T."

She frowned. "What are you talking about?"

He slid over and rested his arm across the back of the seat. "Percy freaked you out. So what? He bothered me, too."

She turned her head so she could look at him fully. "He did?"

"Sure." Zeke picked up her hand and fiddled with her fingers. "I wanted to slay him. I hate that."

A smile curved her lips and she tightened her grip on his hand. "I wanted to run away, but at the same time, I wanted to get down on my knees and beg him to take me to that reserve."

He rubbed his thumb over her hand. "You miss being around other dragons, huh?"

"Of course." She sighed. "I suppose you don't miss other slayers."

"Actually, I do, but being around them doesn't work for me."

She raised her brow and studied him. "So, you're alone and it sucks."

"It's fine." He cleared his throat. "Listen, I can find that reserve if it exists. We can go visit it on our own."

Her eyes suddenly filled with moisture. "You can?"

"Of course. You don't need Percy or Lyman for that." He grinned and wiped a thumb over her glistening cheek. "You might have to handcuff me to a bed, though. I'm not sure I'd be able to take being around a bunch of dragons."

She laughed then. "Oh, I think you're doing pretty well. I would have liked you to slay Percy, but you're way too controlled. It's not in me to do harm to other dragons, but if I were a slayer, I wouldn't have resisted." Her face darkened suddenly. "What did he smell like to you? Did he smell like dragon?"

"No. I should have realized it when I met him in the jail cell. He intentionally smells like nothing identifiable." He paused, hesitating to voice the thought that had been gnawing at him.

"That's what Zeus smelled like, too."

"Really?" He rubbed his chin, trying to make sense of it.

She studied him. "What are you thinking?"

"Did Percy or Zeus smell like Lyman to you? At all?"

"No, why?"

"Can any dragons take more than one human form?"

She stared at him. "Not that I've heard. Why? You think Lyman is Percy? Or Zeus?"

"Percy said too many things that sounded like Lyman. And the scent being off. And his sensitivity with his nose after you cracked Lyman's the other day."

She sat up, and he could see her pulse throbbing in her neck. "But dragons can't do that."

"Slayers can't have sex with dragons and not kill them, either. Things happen that aren't supposed to."

She lifted her brows. "Was that a necessary comparison?"

He shrugged. "Your camisole slipped down. It's the analogy that sprang to mind."

They both glanced down to where the curve of her breast was peeking out. She grinned and left it where it was and leaned back against his arm, which had somehow slipped off the back of the seat and was now around her shoulders. "So, you think Lyman, Zeus, and Percy are the same person?"

"It's quite possible." He drummed his fingers on her thigh. "Lyman uses the Zeus persona to rough up the Otherworld community and do his dirty work. He uses the Percy persona to get power over the human world. Hell, he could be Reverend Munsey, too, for all we know, using him to get more access to people, and get more money."

"But Reverend Munsey died. Lyman's not dead."

Zeke held up his finger, then pulled out his phone and dialed a number from memory. "Siccardi here," he said. "When's Reverend Munsey's funeral?" He listened, then winked at Theresa. "Okay, thanks. Let me know if they find his body."

She gaped at him. "His body is missing?"

He snapped his phone shut. "After he was pronounced dead, the ambulance was hijacked and his body stolen."

"Shit." She leaned back, pressing her fingers to her forehead. "How is this possible? Dragons can't do that."

"Dragons can't jump out of five-story windows and crash to the ground and walk away."

"I'm not pure dragon anymore."

"So maybe he isn't either." He absently rubbed her thigh while he tried to think of how Lyman could be changing bodies. She didn't pull away, and he smiled to himself. She might think she wanted to withdraw from him, but her instincts were driving her in the opposite direction.

He knew she needed to be independent, and he'd let her. As long as she didn't go too far away.

And he wasn't kidding himself that it was just because he wanted to keep her safe. It was something else entirely.

Theresa played with his watch, her fingers restless. "You know, Lyman may be hiding under these other identities because he's afraid Satan will find him and punish him for cheating. Maybe he wants me so he can keep me from exposing him to Satan. Then, when I'm under control, he can drop the identities and be himself publicly." She pursed her lips in thought. "I'll bet Lyman would want nothing more than to be recognized for all his money and power. It must be driving him nuts that he has to hide."

Zeke turned the idea over in his mind. "That makes sense. In order to go public, he has to kill either you or Satan."

"But I already told Satan."

Zeke met her gaze. "You know he doesn't want you only because of Satan, Theresa. He's obsessed with you."

She wrinkled her nose. "I know. It's disgusting."

He laughed at her expression and hugged her against him as the cab rolled to a stop. "The limo pulled up to the curb ahead," the cabdriver said. "What do you want me to do?"

Zeke sat up and peered out the window to see what was going on. The limo door opened and out got a man. Not Percy.

"It's Zeus!" Theresa bounced on the seat next to him. "Do you think Percy changed into him when he got into the car? I can't believe it. It doesn't make sense."

"Let's go see if Percy's still in the limo." He opened his door and hopped out, and Theresa scooted out after him. Something slammed into his back and he crashed into the side of the cab, then he spun around to see Alex with Theresa in a headlock, a knife at her throat. "Jesus, Alex. Let her go. We don't have time for this right now."

"No." Alex's eyes were bloodshot, he was unshaven, and his eyes had bags under them. "My client just went into that building."

"Zeus? Damn, man, why didn't you tell me?" Zeke didn't dare look at Theresa's face right now, or he knew he'd lose control. "We're onto him."

"Too late. I just got a call from him that I had until midnight tonight to kill Theresa, or Jasmine dies. He said you were following him, asked me where I was, and led you to me." His hand was shaking with anger, his eyes black with rage. "Forgive me, brother, but I have to kill the woman you love, and I'm doing it right now."

Twenty-three

Theresa bristled with outrage. How dare this son of a bitch threaten to kill her? And with a knife. A knife! It would take ten swipes to cut off her head with that measly weapon.

Alex's pheromones slammed her hard and dizziness whirled around her. She growled and slammed up her shields. Less than a minute and her head cleared. Damn, she was good!

Then she caught a glimpse of Zeke's face and nearly lost her concentration. He looked so angry and so worried that her belly went all warm inside. She recalled suddenly that Alex had called her the woman Zeke loved, and Zeke hadn't contradicted him. And right now, there was nothing in his face that indicated he was going to let his life-debt-brother kill her. He was terrified for her safety, and it was so cute she wanted to kiss him. Instead, she gently kicked him in the shin, and his gaze flickered to her face.

She stuck her tongue out at him.

He looked startled for a moment, then she saw the tension ease out of him as he recalled her special immortal status, of which Alex was not aware.

Of course, it would still hurt like hell if he jabbed her in the gut with the knife, so it would be best to avoid that.

"You know, Zeke," she said, "I'll bet they're holding Jasmine at the reserve."

"Where? You know where they're keeping her?" Alex's hold tightened on her throat, and she crossed her eyes at Zeke as he started getting concerned again.

"Probably." His voice was impressively calm as he regarded his friend. "Alex, we think Zeus is Lyman Peressini, the same guy who tried to kill me, who is trying to negotiate with Satan for world domination."

"So?"

"So, if you kill Theresa here, he's more likely to rid the world of one more slayer than to let you go. Who will rescue Jasmine once you're dead?"

She felt Alex's grip tighten even further, and she sank her teeth into his arm. He jerked his arm away from her. "You bit me!"

"I'm a dragon." She dodged out of his reach and rubbed her neck. "You were cutting off my air. What else would I do? It's not like flames would hurt you."

Zeke grabbed her and shoved her behind him.

"Listen to me, Alex," Zeke said. "The only way to save Jasmine is to keep Theresa alive."

Alex's gaze flickered between them, his dagger clutched in his hand. "I'll do whatever it takes." His voice was desperate.

"As you should. But if you kill Theresa, Zeus will kill you, as he's already tried to kill me. It's up to us now, Alex." He held out his hand. "Trust me."

Alex groaned and ran his hand over his shaved head. "What if you're wrong?"

"Have I ever been wrong when it comes to warfare?"

Zeke's voice was laced with a controlled danger Theresa had never heard before, and she knew she was seeing the emergence of the legendary slayer of yore. This was the bad boy she'd sensed inside him, and it made her insides want to crawl under his skin and make him hers forever.

She caught herself immediately. *There would be no skin-crawling between them.*

Alex met Zeke's gaze for a long moment, then shook his head. "You've never been wrong, but you're out of practice."

"I'm right."

Be still her beating heart. Men who oozed self-confidence were *so* hot. She causally laid her hand on his shoulder and nearly jumped from the energy that leaped off him, straight to her belly. His muscles were rock hard, and his skin was burning.

Alex finally nodded and slipped the dagger into his waistband. "Let's do it."

Zeke held out his hand and they did some weird hand-shake thing, then they both turned and started walking toward the limo, as if they'd psychically made battle plans. She jogged a couple of steps until she caught up with them. "So, do I no longer need to kick Alex's ass?"

Alex snorted and Zeke grinned at her. "I think he'll behave, right, Alex?"

"No dragon is ever safe from me. I'm a slayer."

She smiled at the bluff and wedged between them. "So what now?"

"First, questions to be answered." They reached the car and Zeke tried the door. Locked.

He nodded at Theresa. "Would you like the honors?"

"Totally." She looked around for a weapon, then Alex sighed and handed her a gun.

"Try not to break it."

"No promises." She grabbed the gun and slammed it into the window. It shattered on the second blow. She beamed at Zeke. "That was so fun."

He grinned back. "You need therapy."

"That's what Iris says, too."

Alex already had the door open. "Three women in here. No one else."

Theresa stuck her head inside. Three shapely women were lolling in the back of the limo, watching them with bored interest. They didn't seem particularly concerned that their window had been broken. "Where's Lyman?"

One of the women held out her wrists. "Kill me by slicing my wrists. It'll mess up his car with all the blood."

She grinned. "If you insist . . ."

Zeke immediately hauled her back and leaned in. "We're not here to kill you. We just need to find Lyman. And Percy. Did Percy turn into Zeus?"

The women stared at him in silent resistance. The one nearest Theresa was tapping her foot, and the action caught Theresa's attention. She glanced down in time to see the woman's foot transform from a slim and dainty size six to a lumberjack's booted size fifteen, and then back again.

Holy shit! She pinched Zeke's arm. "They're Mablevi!"

"*What?*" He stared at her. "But Mablevi don't really exist."

The woman who had changed the form of her foot was

glaring at the other two women, as if one of them had spilled their secret.

"Of course they don't." Omigod. This was so cool. It was like discovering an unknown species. "They can change into any human form. How would anyone catch them? It's the ultimate cover." She scooted in next to the foot-changing woman. "And of course, they have kept their existence a secret, or the world would get totally freaked that no one is what they seem. So, what can you guys do? Can you change sizes? Weight? Stuff like that? Is all that true?"

Alex opened the driver's door and pressed his dagger to the driver's throat. "Just in case," he said.

"My name is Veronica," the Mablevi said. "You free us from Lyman and we will tell you everything. Deal?"

"Total deal. What does he have over you?"

"Our children."

"Bastard!" She glanced at Zeke, who still had his battle face on. So hot. "Did you guys change Lyman's appearance for him?"

Veronica nodded. "He worked with us for decades, certain that there must be a way we could use our powers to change him. It only worked after he gave himself a transfusion of our blood. And even so, it takes all three of us touching his skin simultaneously to take effect. It lasts only two hours and six minutes. Lyman can become Zeus or Percy or Reverend Munsey."

Hot damn! They'd been right!

Alex interrupted. "I don't give a shit how he does it. Where's he keeping Jasmine?"

"The reserve." Zeke wasn't asking. He was stating.

The women nodded. "That's where our children are as well. It's heavily guarded."

Alex tapped the driver on the nose with his dagger. "You know how to get there?"

"Yes, sir."

"Good." Alex tossed the man into the passenger seat and got behind the wheel. "Get in, Zeke. We're going to go kick some ass."

Theresa scooted over to make room for Zeke. "So what's Lyman doing? Is he going to notice the car missing soon? We need to take him out as soon as we get back."

The Mablevi shook her head as Zeke sat down. "He's meeting with Satan to trade for the Goblet of Eternal Youth. Once he gets it, he's going to kill Satan. He'll be a while."

Theresa immediately bolted over Zeke toward the open door. He grabbed her arm as her feet landed on the pavement. "T! You can't go after him by yourself."

"I can't let the Goblet go. I'll be so screwed, and so will Justine!" She tried to wrench her arm free, but she had no chance against his grip. Big strong man wasn't so appealing right now. Annoying was a better word. "Let me go."

"I'm coming with you."

"No!" Veronica grabbed his arm. "One man will have no chance to free our children. Both of you must come."

Alex revved the engine. "Life debt, Zeke. Get in the damn car. We're going *now*."

Theresa couldn't stand the look of fury in Zeke's gaze, so she decided to make the decision easy for him. "I won't do anything until you get back, okay? I'll call Becca and get her to stall Satan." She pulled out her phone and saw six missed calls on it. All from Becca. Crap! She must not have been able to hear the ringer in the restaurant.

She dialed Becca, who answered immediately.

"Dragon! Where have you been? Satan is about to make a deal with Zeus to hand over the Goblet! Zeus is already in Satan's reception area, waiting for Satan."

"Shit! Can you stall him?"

"How? He's Satan! The instant he knows I'm trying to stall the meeting, he'll rush in there as fast as he can."

"Iris. Tell him Iris heard about it and she is coming to see him. I'll go get her."

"Fine. But you better be here within five minutes. He's really excited about world domination."

"I will." She hung up and looked at Zeke. "I have to go get Iris."

"Come on, Zeke," Alex snapped. "We have to go!"

He ground his teeth. "You swear you won't go near Lyman?"

"Are you kidding? He'd kick my ass. I'm not going near him." She was already dialing Quincy's office number. "Iris will talk Satan out of it and the meeting won't happen. We'll deal with Lyman when you get back."

"Promise?"

She nodded. "I'm not an idiot."

He growled then grabbed her and hauled her against him, slamming her with the force of his kiss. She embraced the electricity humming between them and sucked it into her body, desperate for the reassurance it gave her, which of course made her completely pathetic, but who the hell cared? If it gave her the courage to go deal with Lyman, she wasn't turning away from it.

He broke the kiss and stared down at her. "You get yourself killed and I'll be really pissed."

She grinned. "Just don't slay any dragons. If I have to spend the next two hundred years dragging you out of a pit of despair, I'm the one who'll be pissed."

"Two hundred years? Is that how long you're willing to hang around me?"

He looked too thoughtful for comfort, so she pulled out of his arms. "Go save a girl, will you?"

"Keep your phone on and keep me apprised."

She held it up.

He kissed her again, then released her with a reluctance that made her want to cling to him. So she let go instead.

He got into the car, but before he shut the door he reached out and squeezed her hand. "I'll look for dragons with your mark, okay?"

She blinked as moisture suddenly filled her eyes. That was the sweetest thing anyone had ever said to her. "Don't do anything stupid, okay? Any worthwhile dragon will kill a slayer first and ask questions later."

"I'm coming back for you, don't worry." Then he slammed the door shut and Alex took off.

The smell of burnt rubber scratched her nose, but she easily shut it out. It was about damn time she got a handle on her skills. She hit SEND to call Quincy, and prayed she wasn't going to have to face down Lyman by herself.

Twenty-four

Quincy's phone was picked up on the first ring. "Quincy LaValle's office."

"Iris?"

"Theresa? Is that you? Thank heaven! When I told you to disappear I didn't mean so I couldn't find you in the event of an emergency!"

"You heard about Satan?"

"Satan? I'm talking about Quin. When the Council couldn't find you, they took him instead. Now Justine, Quin, and Derek are all under house arrest, and they are going to start tossing them into the Chamber one by one at midnight tonight if you don't get back here. I'm sorry, Theresa, but you need to turn yourself in. The Council is at Quincy's house, waiting for you to call him there. Just go to Quin's and—"

No way! She wasn't giving up when she was this close. "Satan has a meeting with the head of the Otherworld mafia in five minutes to turn over the Goblet. He has given up on you, so he feels he has nothing to lose. I need you to come with me right now to stop him."

Iris made a sound of distress. "Satan really gave up on me?"

"What do you expect? You rejected him for two hundred years."

"So now you're on his side?"

"I need you to talk him into giving the Goblet back, and the only way that's going to happen is if you convince him he has a chance with you."

"But the Council has forbidden me to negotiate with him!"

"Here's your chance to save your daughter without hanging me out to dry. Make a decision, Iris. If you won't come with me, I'm going on my own." She sensed Iris's resistance building and had a sudden idea. "Satan has been celibate for a long time, and I know he likes my body. I'll offer him my body for all eternity if he'll give me back the Goblet. You know my reputation. I'm almost as famous for great sex as he is."

"You will *not* have sex with Satan!"

"It's the only way, Iris. I totally understand that you can't go against the Council. I'll do it. He's pretty hot. I'm sure it would be fun. Is he as good in bed as I've heard?"

Iris made a strangling sound and Theresa heard a crash, as if she'd hurled something against the wall. "I am the former Guardian," Iris snapped. "It is my responsibility to protect the Goblet when the current Guardians are failing."

Theresa grinned at the jealousy knifing through Iris's tone. "You're sure? I wouldn't want you to do anything you regretted."

"I can't have you mucking it up with some floozy offer for sex. It will have to be me. I will do it. The Council will not care about the method if I retrieve the Goblet."

Theresa gave herself a mental high five. So much for

Iris being totally over Satan. "You're at Quin's office? No Council?"

"No Council. Get over here now and take me to Satan."

"Will do. Becca and I will be there in a minute to transport you to hell." Theresa hung up the phone and dialed Becca.

Less than two minutes later, Becca, Iris, and Theresa melted up from the floor of Satan's office. He was pacing the room but whirled around when he saw the blackness on the floor.

Theresa held her breath as she watched Satan take in Iris. His face was impassive, his eyes cold. *Shit.*

Iris strode forward and stood before him. "Satan, I have changed my mind. If you give Theresa the Goblet, I will have sex with you."

Oh, that was romantic.

Satan snorted and sat down in his office chair. He slung his feet on the desk and clasped his hands behind his head. "Too late, Iris. I have moved on."

Iris's jaw jutted out. "You lie."

He gave her a bored look. "I lie often, but I do not lie now. A man can take only so much abuse. Zeus admires me greatly, and I realize how badly you beat me down. I accept it no more. I move on."

"I will not beg," Iris said haughtily, though Theresa could hear the hurt in her voice. "You have my offer."

"I know you throw your body at me only because you value the Goblet. I will not accept your body under false pretenses."

"But you want my body! That's all you've ever wanted!"

"No, it is all I ever asked for. I want your soul as well."

He rolled his eyes. "Not your soul as in your *soul,* but your soul as in your emotional commitment. Yes, I am Satan, and I deserve more than empty sex. I deserve more than merely being a tool for you to save the Goblet and recover your vaunted position as fabulous Guardian." He folded his arms over his chest and glared at Iris. "I reject your offer."

"You're an ass."

"Thank you. I work most hard at my more unsavory characteristics."

Dammit! Too much pride in the room for effective resolution.

Becca elbowed Theresa and nodded toward Theresa's breasts.

Theresa raised her brow in question and Becca grabbed her own breasts and wiggled them, mouthing, "*Make Iris jealous.*"

Theresa shook her head and whispered, "It'll work only if she thinks Satan wants me."

Becca just winked at her and fluffed her breasts again.

"Fine, but I think you're giving Satan too much credit," she whispered.

Then she shrugged off her cute jacket, slipped the straps of her camisole off her shoulders, and tugged down her top until it barely covered her breasts. She was standing behind Iris, so she waved to get Satan's attention.

His gaze flicked to her and then to her almost-exposed chest, then back up to her face.

Theresa pointed to Iris, then back to her own breasts.

Satan's eyes narrowed, then a wicked smile curved up. Then he turned back to Iris. "Please leave. There is nothing that can tempt me to stray from my plan of trading the Goblet for world domination."

Theresa took a deep breath to calm her racing heart, then stepped up beside Iris. She cupped her breasts, giving herself even more cleavage. "What about these?"

Iris glanced at her, then gasped as she looked at Theresa's cascading breasts. "What are you doing?"

Theresa walked around the desk and leaned forward, so her breasts were mere inches from Satan's face. "I know you like them."

He raised a brow, then leaned forward and smashed his face in them, rolling around for a long moment and making all sorts of moaning noises. Theresa had to turn her head and cough to keep from laughing at Iris's gasp of shock.

Finally he lifted his head, his hair all messed up. "Real. Very nice."

"I am well known for my sexual skills," she said. "I will become your love slave for eternity if you return the Goblet to the custody of a Guardian."

Satan raised a brow, and Theresa grinned at him, knowing Iris couldn't see her face.

Iris snorted. "He has plenty of women. He'll never take you." But there was a note of alarm in her voice that made Satan's eyes gleam.

He immediately grabbed Theresa around the waist and pulled her hips toward him. She threw her leg over his lap and straddled him. "What do you say? Do we have a deal?"

He grabbed her ass so Iris could see. "I have heard rumors of your sexual prowess. Plus you are quite a naughty dragon. I think we could have great fun torturing people while we were naked and writhing in orgasmic pleasure, no?"

She stroked his face, trying not to laugh at the mutterings coming from behind her. "I love torture."

He shot a lascivious grin at her. "A perfect match. Why did I not see it before? Sex and violence. We will have most delightful time. It is a worthy trade. I accept. The Goblet is yours."

"No!" Iris grabbed Theresa by the arm and yanked her off Satan's lap. Theresa hit the floor and rolled to her feet in time to see Iris shove Satan back from the desk and grab him by the tie. "I am the Guardian. It is up to me to save the Goblet. It is I whom you must have sex with, not Theresa!"

"My most beloved mortal! You really do want me! It has nothing to do with the Goblet! I am yours!" Satan beamed, wrapped his hand around Iris's wrist, and pulled her onto his lap. She went easily, wrapped her arms around him as she fell against him, her lips finding his as he pulled her close. Her fingers were in his hair, his hands frantic over her body, little noises coming from both of them.

Theresa grinned at Becca. "Excellent plan, Rivka."

Becca bowed. "I'm brilliant. Glad you recognize it."

There was a crash and they turned to see Satan clear his desk with a sweep of his arm and throw Iris on top. He had started to climb on top of her when Becca jumped between them with an impressive disregard for her own safety, given the look of sexual need on Satan's face. "Uh-uh-uh, Satan. Before you can consummate, you need to give back the Goblet."

"I can't." He shoved Becca out of his way and started to unbutton Iris's shirt as her fingers yanked his tie loose. "I already gave it to Zeus."

Theresa's stomach dropped with a thud. *"What?"*

"Yes. It will return to you when you satisfy the contract you made with me. Until then, Zeus will amuse himself with it."

"No!" Theresa grabbed him by the hair and hauled him off Iris. He whirled around, grabbed her by the throat, and reared back to throw her across the room.

"Stop!" Iris shouted.

He immediately dropped Theresa with a thud and turned to Iris, whose shirt was open, revealing a black bra. He started back toward her and she held up a hand. "Release Theresa from the contract so she can retrieve the Goblet from Zeus."

Theresa coughed and rolled to her knees, trying to catch her breath.

Satan gave a gracious sweep of his arm. "For you, my love, it shall be done. The contract can be nullified if both parties agree." He flicked a finger toward Theresa. "Do you agree to nullify it, Dragon?"

"God, yes."

"Wait!" Becca grabbed Theresa's arm. "If he nullifies it, you both go back to status quo."

"Great. Do it. We have to get Zeus!"

"No, Theresa, that means you go back to your prior state. You'll be stuck a dragon again."

Theresa jerked her gaze to Satan, who nodded. "It is the only way, Dragon. I do not make the laws of hell. Well, I do, actually, and this is one of them."

"No." Becca stepped between them. "Theresa, you can't retrieve the Goblet because of the contract, but I can. I'll kick his ass, take his soul, and hold on to Mona until you've satisfied the terms of the contract and can take her back."

Satan laughed out loud before Theresa even had time to drop to the ground in relief. "Rivka, since when do you consider yourself at liberty to assassinate one of my business partners? Even Satan must have some business ethics, and killing off people I make deals with as soon as I do the deal would make it most difficult to get people to bargain with me. And since souls must be freely given, I cannot threaten them." He waggled his finger at Becca. "Bad, bad Rivka. We must have some refresher training, I think."

Her eyes glowed red, and her hands went to her hips.

Satan giggled with delight. "Rivka, I order you not to interfere in any way with Zeus. Do not hurt him. Do not distract him. Do not do anything other than return him to the Mortal world when he requests it. And I order you to tell me now if I have left a loophole that allows you to interfere."

Her gaze flashed with rage. "Since when did you get that smart?"

"Lawyer souls. Very handy. Loopholes?"

She ground her teeth, but shook her head.

"Excellent." He turned to Theresa. "It is up to you. Tell me what you wish, and I shall do it, but decide quickly because my body craves my true love and I cannot wait much longer."

Panic raced through Theresa. Surely there was another way? If she became a dragon forever again, she would lose everything: her newly found freedom, her independence, and Zeke. But she couldn't let her friends be thrown into the Chamber. She couldn't fail at being a Guardian. Dammit! There had to be a way.

Zeke would help her. Together they could do it. "Give me a sec." She turned away and dialed Zeke's number. "Zeke? Where are you?"

"I'm coming back. Alex picked up the rest of the slayers, so they're going to the reserve. What's going on?"

Her legs trembled with relief and she clutched the phone. "Lyman has the Goblet. I need your help." She never thought she'd ask for help from anyone, but there it was. And it felt damn good to have someone willing to help her.

He cursed. "Don't go after him. We'll find a way to get it back. You can't retake it, but I can. I'll get it for you."

She heard the conviction in his voice and suddenly realized he planned to kill Lyman. His anguish over his decision cascaded over the airwaves, and her belly lurched.

She couldn't let him do it. "Zeke, don't come. It'll be over before you get here."

"Dammit, Theresa! Don't do it! I'm on my way! Send Becca up to get me right now!"

"I can't let you sacrifice yourself for me." She closed her eyes. "I love you, Zeke." Then she turned off her phone and tossed it on the floor. She squared her shoulders and faced Satan. "Do it."

There was a flash, then blinding pain, and Theresa fell to the ground as shards of pain blew through her body. She closed her eyes and shuddered as her body convulsed with agony. When it finally settled, she lifted her head and felt the long curve of her dragon neck. She glared at Satan. "Was the pain necessary?"

"Not at all. But it was fun, no?" He didn't wait for an

answer, but turned and swept up Iris in his arms. "Come along, my love. We have much to do."

Iris peeked at Theresa as Satan carried her toward the wall. "Get that Goblet back."

"I *know.*" Theresa rolled to her feet and stalked toward the door as Iris and Satan disappeared in an explosion of gold bubbles. "Where is he, Becca?"

"He still has to be in the reception area. He can't leave hell unless I escort him. A handy safeguard to keep people from running out on Satan."

"Well, let's go."

Resentment flashed in Becca's eyes. "I can't help you. If I go in there, and he asks me to take him back to the Mortal world, I'll have to. I'll stay in here, so he can't leave."

"Good call. I'll be fine." She took a deep breath, smacked her tail against Satan's desk to pump herself up, then pulled his door open and marched into the reception area.

Zeus was sitting in one of the plush leather couches, swinging Mona around on his finger. Zeus snapped his fist closed around the Goblet and sat up. "Becca? I'm ready to—" He saw Theresa and jumped to his feet. "Who are you?"

"Give it up, Lyman. I know it's you." She lashed out with her tail and he flew across the room and smashed into a statue of a naked woman.

He somersaulted to his feet and shoved Mona into his pocket. "I have no idea what you're talking about."

"No?" She slammed him with her tail again and flung him into the wall. "Give me back my Goblet." She tried to get him before he recovered, but he vaulted to his feet and over her tail, so all she did was clip his foot and make him fall on his face. Bastard. "Veronica talked. We know your shtick, Lyman. Zeus. Percy. Reverend Munsey."

Zeus ran behind a pillar. "Fine. I admit it. I am all of those men."

She smacked her tail into the pillar and it shattered. "Give me back the Goblet, Lyman." She swung again, knowing she had to take him out before he turned into a dragon. If they were both dragons, she had no chance. She clubbed him in the side of the head as he dove behind the couch, then she vaulted over the couch and landed on him, pinning him to the floor. She bared her teeth at him, letting her saliva drip on his chest. "I would have left you alone, Lyman. I didn't care what you did or who you cheated. But you sent assassins after me. Idiot."

He gave her a calm look. "So tell me, Theresa, does knowing how powerful I am make you want me?"

"Never." He twisted under her, and she dug her claws into his extremities. "You don't get to rule the world, Lyman. Not today. And you don't get to have the girl."

His face darkened. "I could have made you my queen."

"I already rule my own little world. Why would I want to share leadership with you?" A puff of smoke leaked out of her nose. "You tried to kill me the first time. Then you tried to kill me again. Quite frankly, I'm getting sick of it." She wound her tail up his leg, the spike aimed for a cruel blow. She let it hover over his crotch, waiting for panic to creep into his eyes. There was none. Yet. "You didn't give Satan the real Otherworld Detector back, did you? You cheated him again, only this time, I'm not going to let you get away with it."

A smug expression filtered into his eyes. "Let him test it. Then he'll know if it's real."

She stared at him for a long moment, then panic hit her. She jerked her head up. "Becca!"

The Rivka stuck her head in the door. "What?"

"The Otherworld Detector is a trap. If Satan uses it, it'll kill him. You have to stop him."

Becca hesitated. "So what if he dies? I don't have orders to save him."

"If he dies, so do you, remember?"

Becca pressed her lips together for a long moment. "If I die, I'll finally be released from him."

"Dammit!" She threw Lyman into the wall and galloped over to Becca. She grabbed the Rivka's shoulders. "You're the only person bitchy enough to put up with me. I'm going to be stuck in dragon form again and you'll be all I have! You are not allowed to die! Do you hear me?"

Becca frowned. "You'll have Zeke. You don't need me."

Theresa's heart burned with pain. "I'm a dragon again. You think the slayer will be able to handle that? Besides, boys are boys, and they can't replace girlfriends. I need a girlfriend and you're it!"

Becca stared at her, a look of startled surprise coming over her face. "Shit, girl, you're really desperate if I'm your best hope at a friend."

"Hell, yes, I'm desperate! Save your bastard boss already!"

"Fine. But you'll owe me for this."

"Add it to the list—" But Becca had already vanished through the floor.

Theresa spun back around and froze. An enormous silver dragon was standing in the middle of the reception area. His five-spiked tail was flicking restlessly, his sixteen-inch claws had already dug holes in the floor, and his wings were brushing against the top of the three-story cathedral ceiling.

Twenty-five

Lyman was even bigger than he'd been 180 years ago. At least four times her size, and his muscles were bulging under his scales. He was huge, and he was fit, and she was neither.

Her heart thudded and a billow of green smoke blew out of her nose.

His silver lips pulled back in a sneer when he saw the fear smoke. "Care to change your mind, Theresa? I might be willing to spare your life if you beg me and promise me enough."

"Never." She frantically glanced around the room for his discarded pants. She saw one cuff peeking out from behind another pillar. *Mona.*

Lyman followed her eyes and snickered. "You can't have her, Theresa. Not only do you have to retrieve her, but then you have to get out of here. You need Becca, and you just sent her off to rescue Satan. You chose your friend over keeping me pinned down." His enormous head shook back and forth. "Silly girl. What does it matter if Becca's alive if you're dead?" He whipped his tail suddenly and it slammed into her side and flung her into the wall.

She crashed into it and thudded to the floor, blood rushing down her side from the spikes. She ignored the pain and jumped to her feet. A few puncture wounds were not going to kill her. Not anymore.

Lyman bared his teeth at her again. "I know you're immortal, Theresa." He let his tail droop over his shoulder and ran a claw along his longest spike. "This will work very nicely for slicing your head off. Oopsie, no more immortality for you, huh?" He slammed his tail toward her, and she flew up into the air as it whipped harmlessly by.

Before she had a chance to congratulate herself, he lurched into the air and sank his teeth into her wing. "Bastard! That's my favorite wing!" She tucked her head and wings as she tumbled back to the ground.

She hit with a thud and jumped to her feet, adrenaline numbing the wing even as it drooped sadly beside her.

Lyman landed smoothly on the other side of the hall. "You don't get to reject me, Theresa. Your family was too good for me my whole life, and now I'm too good for you. I was willing to let you join my party, but you do *not* get to reject me." A burst of flames exploded from his mouth and set the couch on fire. "Do you understand? I am worthy! I am better than everyone! I will rule all dimensions! I will be known as the man who took Satan's kingdom while his own heir was trapped in a freezer!"

She circled to the left, watching for his next move. "So that's why you had to move now. Because you were afraid Satan Jr. would screw up your chance to huddle up with Satan."

"Satan Jr. is nothing. I will destroy him as well." He lunged for her and grazed her foot as she jumped over the wall of flames that used to be the sofa.

She scanned the room, searching for an option. She grabbed a piece of a destroyed statue and hurled it at him. It clunked him in the head, and he roared with rage and charged her.

She immediately dropped to her back and used her hind feet to launch him over her head as he dove on top of her. He crashed through the wall and she jumped up and spun around as he wiggled free, his tail whipping fiercely.

Flames were pouring out of his nose, black smoke obscured her view of him, and his tail smashed into the huge wooden doors and ripped one off its hinge. He lunged for her and his teeth sank into her leg and he flung her across the room, where she smashed into another statue and thudded to the floor, her body screaming in pain. "You die now, bitch."

A black image suddenly rose from the floor between them. "Calling a slayer's girlfriend nasty names is never a good idea."

Her mouth dropped open in horror. "Zeke?"

The image took the shape of Zeke, and he was facing Lyman. Becca shimmered briefly, then disappeared back through the floor. Zeke glanced back at Theresa, his eyes widening with shock. "T?"

She waved a claw, steeling herself for his rejection. "I'm a dragon again. For good."

He gave her a careful inspection. "You look good as a dragon. I like the bluish-green scales. Tail ring. Very sexy."

A slow warmth spread over her. "But I'm a dragon."

"I noticed."

Lyman roared with rage and zapped Zeke with a fireball.

"Zeke!" She dove into the flames to rescue him, sliding on the marble floor right past where he'd been standing. She scrabbled to her feet. "Where are you?"

"Over here, Lyman."

She turned her head to see Zeke standing on the other side of the room, leaning casually against a pillar. His body was relaxed, but his eyes were gleaming with deadly intent. This was the slayer that all dragons had feared, and she shivered.

Lyman snorted and danced around the room, circling toward Zeke. "Your pheromones won't work on me, Slayer."

Zeke didn't move. "Haven't you heard the legends about me?" His eyes tracked Lyman's every step, assessing. "I don't use pheromones."

Lyman hesitated for a fraction of a second, but Theresa saw it. "Lies. No way you could have killed all those dragons without pheromones."

Zeke smiled, a predatory smile that made her scales curl in instinctive fear. "See? That's why you dragons are so easy to kill. You underestimate me, and it makes my job so much easier."

Despite his smile, the violence was rolling off Zeke in thick waves. He was embracing it, but she could tell it was all directed at Lyman. He was doing what she'd told him: embracing it and channeling it. She was safe, but Lyman wasn't.

And Zeke wasn't.

She sidled next to him. "I can't let you do this, Zeke. I could never live with myself if you killed him. Let me do it."

He didn't take his eyes off Lyman, who was sneaking up toward them. "You said you loved me. Did you mean it?"

She sank her teeth into her lower lip. "If I say no, will you leave?"

He grinned. "Nope. I love you, so I need to save your life from the big bad bully."

"Dammit, Zeke! It's not worth it for you to lose your soul."

"See? You do love me. If you didn't, you'd tell me to kill Lyman and you wouldn't be worried about me. Duck."

They both ducked a fraction of a second before Lyman whipped his tail at them. It crashed through the air where their heads had been and three of the spikes got wedged deeply into the pillar.

Zeke took her claw and tugged her across the room as she glanced over her shoulder at Lyman trying to get his tail free. "How did you know he was going to do that?"

"Every dragon has tales." He shoved her onto the burning couch. "Sit."

She sat, staring at him. "But you knew before he moved."

Zeke glanced at Lyman, who was trying to chew his way through the pillar to free his tail. "Some people say I'm a little bit psychic when it comes to dragon warfare. I tend to agree." He pulled out a dagger. "Stay here."

"What? No!" She jumped up as he walked over to Lyman.

He ducked suddenly and Lyman's back claw caught Theresa in the gut and ripped open her belly and flung her across the room. She landed with a crash in the corner.

Zeke spun toward her, worry creasing his forehead. "Is your head still attached?"

"Yes, but my stomach hurts like a mother."

"Hang in there for a minute." She could see him shake off the concern and go back into battle mode as he swung back toward Lyman. He jumped out of the way as Lyman tried to bite him, then dove in the same direction Lyman swung his head and plunged his dagger up into Lyman's exposed neck.

Theresa clutched her own neck as Lyman gagged, recalling what had happened to her when the chef had shot her in the neck. Necks were dragons' Achilles' heel, and Zeke had just gotten a clear shot.

He yanked the dagger free and slammed it home again, blood pouring down his arm.

"Stop it!" she screamed. His anguish was smashing into her, driving her to her feet even through her own pain. "Zeke Siccardi, you stop stabbing him right now or I will never have sex with you again!"

He yanked the dagger free and turned toward her, his face tight. "We can't have sex. You're a dragon."

"I can still have cybersex," she snapped as she slithered her way across the floor toward him, holding her arm over her bleeding belly. "I can't let you kill him." She held out her hand for the dagger. "You'll never survive it."

Zeke raised his brow, ignoring Lyman's coughing behind him. "You're going to kill him? I'm the slayer. I can't let my woman do my dirty work. I'd never live it down." His eyes were still dark from the battle, violence still consuming him.

She wrapped her tail around Zeke's waist. "I'm not

going to let you kill him." She kept her grip loose, ready to tighten if he fought her.

Zeke glanced down at her tail and ran his hand over it. "This diamond stud is extremely sexy when you're in human form."

Heat rushed through her at his touch. "Stop trying to distract me."

"Stop acting like you can actually keep me from slaying him." Zeke took a glance over his shoulder to assure himself that Lyman was still stuck to the pillar. The dragon was pressing a piece of broken statue to his neck, trying unsuccessfully to stanch the flow of blood. "It won't work, Lyman. You'll die stuck to that pillar in Satan's reception area."

"No." Lyman threw the statue, but Theresa smacked it away with her claw.

She fastened her best dragon glare on Zeke. "Listen, slayer boy, I like you, and I don't want to see you torture yourself for another two hundred years. Lyman isn't going to die tonight." She knew that if she killed Lyman, it would still haunt Zeke as much as if he'd done it himself. For Zeke's sake, neither of them could kill Lyman, no matter how badly he deserved it.

"But you will, bitch."

Zeke whipped around and flung his dagger at Lyman. It sank into the dragon's neck, evoking a yowl of pain from Lyman.

Theresa tightened her tail around Zeke. "Zeke. Cut it out! I'm going to get Becca in here and have her take you home."

He glared at her. "As if I'm going to let Lyman live.

He'll keep coming after you, and I can't allow it. He has to die."

She realized suddenly that there was no haze of violence on his eyes. They were clear and brown. She sat down heavily on her haunches, but didn't release him. "You'd kill him for me? You'd sacrifice your soul for me?"

"Saving your life isn't a sacrifice. It's an honor." He rubbed the scales on her cheek.

She laid her claw over his hand and sighed. "That's the sweetest thing anyone has ever done for me."

"I secured world domination for you!" Lyman shouted. "I am the real man here."

Zeke took her claw and kissed it. "T, I realized something while I was kicking Lyman's butt. The cold-blooded slaying of a dragon is wrong, but killing someone to defend the woman I love is an honor. If he happens to be a dragon, then that's the way it is."

"But what about the fact you killed his parents?"

"That's why I had the hit out on him," Lyman crooned. "I knew that all along. I was going to use him to find you, and then kill him when I was through with him. Hah! The joke is on you, Slayer!"

Zeke didn't look away from Theresa. "I slayed his parents, and I will have to live with that. Your acceptance of your heritage is helping me accept my own past. Lyman deserves to die. Killing him saves you, and saving your gorgeous dragon hide is going to be my redemption."

She beamed at him and threw her forearms around him.

"Easy, T," he gasped. "You weigh about twenty times more than I do right now."

She immediately let go of him, and he grabbed her face and pulled it down until she was at eye level with him. "Theresa Nichols, you saved my soul and I will love you forever. Even if we can't ever have real sex again, I'll hang out with you and watch cable all night. If the reserve really exists, I'll take you out there and hang out while you do your dragon thing. We'll figure out a way to make this work."

She blinked again, but this time, she couldn't keep the trickle of dragon tears from inching down her scaly face. "But I'm a dragon."

"And I love you." He kissed the tip of her nose. "We might have to have lots of intense virtual sex to channel my slaying tendencies, though. Is that okay?"

She sighed like a total girl. "Oh, Zeke, you completely rock."

"Does that mean you love me?"

"Totally!"

He grinned. "So, then, are you going to let me kill Lyman so we can get on with our lives? If we let him live, it's just a matter of time until we both die by his hand."

"Well, that would suck." She couldn't stop grinning. "I'm so excited that my man has finally acknowledged the thrill of killing someone. I knew you had it in you!"

"Killing is justified only in self-defense or defense of those you love." He gently poked her in the neck. "You still need therapy, you bloodthirsty dragon."

She rubbed up against him, trailed her tail spike over his back. "Oh, tame me, slayer boy," she purred. "Please."

"Hey!" Lyman shouted. "I'll make a deal with you."

Zeke turned toward Lyman, caressing Theresa's tail.

"It's too late for that, Lyman. My mate agreed to let me kill you."

Her heart thudded to a stop. "Your mate? You want me to be your mate?"

He grinned at her. "Of course I do. Didn't I make that clear?"

"I can make Theresa human again," Lyman shouted, his voice squeaky with desperation.

Theresa's gut dropped as she and Zeke looked at Lyman. "What did you say?" Zeke asked, his voice completely calm, even as his fingers dug into Theresa's tail.

Lyman lay quivering, his head flat on the floor, his tail still wedged in the pillar. "I've been coveting the Goblet ever since I found out Theresa was the Guardian 180 years ago and—"

"How did you know back then? I didn't tell you!"

"You talk in your sleep."

"Oh." She felt her cheeks heat up and gave Zeke a sheepish smile.

He simply rolled his eyes and turned back to Lyman, his hands continuing to caress her tail. A man who wasn't threatened by an affair almost two centuries ago was a man who was secure in his masculinity. God, he was hot. "So?"

"So, while I was trying to track her down and raking in money as Reverend Munsey and extorting money using the Otherworld Detector as Zeus, I had a team working on the problem Theresa encountered when she drank from the Goblet. I didn't move on the Goblet until I had a solution." His eyes burned with desperation. "I'll tell you how to override the Goblet so she can switch back and forth between forms if you let me go. I'll promise never to bother the two of you again, and you do the same. I'll trade my knowledge for my life, and then we have a cease-fire. Agreed?"

Theresa's heart was thudding and she leaned close to Zeke. "Do you think he's telling the truth?"

He turned toward her, his eyes masking his thoughts. "It's up to you, T. It's your life and your revenge. Either way, I'm not leaving you."

She met his gaze. "You really mean that, don't you?"

He took the tip of her tail in his hand and kissed her diamond tail ring. "It's your call, T."

She glanced at Lyman sniveling next to the post. "He deserves to die."

"Yes, he does."

She looked at Zeke. "But we deserve each other more."

He shook his head. "We'll still have each other."

"Okay, let me clarify. We deserve a great sex life more than he deserves to die."

Zeke grinned. "That's a lot of sex, because he really deserves to die."

She grinned back. "What can I say? You're really good in bed."

His grin turned into a lecherous leer. "You've only seen me on the floor of the living room. You won't believe what I've got in the bedroom."

Heat washed over her and she felt her tail tighten around him involuntarily. She was still staring into Zeke's eyes when she spoke. "Lyman, you have a deal."

Twenty-six

Accompanied by Zeke, with Iris, Becca, and Satan waiting outside, Theresa flung open the door to Jerome-the-pirate's bedroom. After careful discussion, they'd decided he was the Council member to approach, and they decided to do it when he was at his most vulnerable so he couldn't call in the Council enforcers to cart her off.

Her crew was ready to fend off anyone who tried to throw her into the Chamber, and it was the most amazing feeling. Not only wasn't she alone anymore, but she had a team behind her. And it felt great.

"Jerome!" She flicked on the overhead light. "Wake up."

There was a howl of holy terror, then Jerome leaped from the bed, landed on his feet, and grabbed a sword from next to his bed. He had it aimed at Theresa's throat a fraction of a second after Zeke had his dagger pressed to Jerome's jugular.

Zeke winked at her, and she grinned. He was so hot now that he wasn't totally suppressing all his slayer talents. And he was so much happier. "Say uncle, Jerome."

Jerome gagged and dropped his sword, his eyes flashing with rage. He was wearing only a pair of plaid boxers, and Theresa was surprised to realize that he was actually very fit. Didn't look half-bad.

"Stop gawking," Zeke ordered. "You're taken."

She blew him a kiss and didn't deny his claim. "Okay, Jerome, here's the scoop." She held up the crystal vial. "We got Mona back."

"Oh, thank God." Jerome sat down on his bed with a thump. Zeke had to jerk the dagger away to keep from impaling Jerome as he dropped. "Has anyone used her?"

"Nope. And we didn't even damage the tentative political truce with hell. Have the Council call off the bounty hunters searching for me and the assassins searching for Satan." She dangled Mona in front of him. "And then you'll free Justine, Derek, and Quincy, and I'll give Mona back to them."

He held out his hand. "Give her to me."

Theresa tightened her grip around Mona. "You know I can't give her to anyone except a Guardian. I'm not making that mistake again."

Jerome managed a smile. "Good to see you can learn."

Zeke jiggled the dagger next to Jerome's ear. "Don't insult my woman."

Theresa grinned. "So, Jerome? Deal?"

He rubbed his chin. "I can't speak for the Council."

"Why not?"

"Because I am but a member. I am not the final decision maker."

"It's a time of peril." She held Mona up. "I will hand her over to Satan if you don't give me what I want."

His face tightened. "That's blackmail."

"Is anything else going to keep me out of the Chamber?"

"Well, no."

"Then, yeah, I'm blackmailing you."

Jerome's mouth twitched in amusement. "As a pirate, I respect that approach. As a Council member, I have to officially protest." He finally grinned at her. "Oh, hell, what can I say? I admire blackmail. It reminds me of the good old days."

She dropped her hand. "So?"

"So, it's a deal. I think the Council is too uptight, and I'll enjoy going against what I know they would want me to do." He smacked his palms on his thighs and stood up. "I'll tell them you coerced me in an ugly battle of wills and I managed to negotiate an excellent deal." He cocked his head. "How about, I fired you from Guardianship even though you begged me repeatedly not to take away the one thing in life you cared about?"

She waited for the rush of failure, but it didn't come. Zeke raised his brows at her, and she shrugged. "I'm okay with that, I guess."

Zeke nodded. "You don't need that job anyway. Too much interesting stuff going on."

She nodded slowly. He was right. She didn't need the Council's approval or the Guardianship anymore. She was good enough on her own. She grinned at the sense of freedom. "And you'll free Justine, Derek, and Quin?"

Jerome nodded. "Of course. We were just using them as pawns to trap you. That was my idea, actually. I did that once when one of my enemies made off with my ship. Killed the bastard in cold blood when he came crawling back to try to rescue his friends." He sighed with longing. "That was a good day."

Zeke sheathed his dagger and sat next to him. "How'd you get on the Council with that kind of background?"

Jerome shrugged. "They needed an enforcer, since they're too pristine to get their hands dirty. Not that they let me do much. Not like the old days." He shook off the melancholy and looked up. "So, we're good, then? I'll file the paperwork and Justine or Derek will come by to pick up Mona, if you can manage to restrain yourself from handing it back to Satan?"

"For you, anything." She tied Mona around her neck again, fingering the vial with a bit of melancholy. She wouldn't miss the restrictions on a Guardian's life, but she'd miss Mona and her shape-shifting, and she had a feeling Mona would miss her as well. The Goblet's life was even more boring than Theresa's had been, and Justine would never take her on field trips as Theresa had. She held her up. "I promise I'll come visit."

Mona flashed bright white once, and Theresa smiled and tucked Mona inside her shirt. "Ready to go, Zeke?"

He stood up. "You got it." He eyed Jerome. "Word of advice?"

The pirate raised his brows. "Sure."

"Sounds like you need to go back to pirating." He grinned at Theresa. "Denying your heritage is the path to misery."

Jerome shot Zeke an appraising glance. "Who says I don't have my own agenda right now, in perfect alignment with my heritage?"

They both looked at him in surprise, and he gave Zeke a shove. "Get your girlfriend out of my bedroom, Slayer, before I change my mind."

"We're going." Zeke offered her his hand, and she took

it, holding tightly as he led the way away from the Council and her old life.

Theresa stretched, relishing the feel of Zeke's naked body wrapped around hers.

He didn't lift his head from her breasts. "Sometime, we'll have to make it to the bedroom. I'm really good in there."

She glanced up at the underside of his kitchen table. "I don't know, Zeke. You're awfully good in the kitchen. It takes a real man to admit he's great in the kitchen."

"I'm great in the kitchen."

She grinned and ran her hands through his hair, enjoying its softness. "We should probably go."

"Probably."

"I think you ruined my dress when you tore it off me."

"Dragons should get married naked anyway. Clothes are for wimps."

She grinned. "I'm up for it, if you think all your handsome slayer friends won't mind seeing me naked."

He sat up and grabbed the blue-green silk dress from the floor. "They're a little uptight. You should be dressed."

She grinned as he grabbed her hand and pulled her to her feet, holding out the dress for her. It was the exact color of her scales, and she loved it. White wedding dresses were for wimps, and certainly not for dragons who had Satan and his ex-Guardian lover standing in as the parents of the bride.

Zeke leaned against the counter and watched her while she got dressed. She loved his fascination with her body, especially since she was equally enraptured with his.

"So, T, I have to ask you something."

"Go ahead."

"Now that you've been fired from Guardianship, I thought you might be looking for a job."

She stepped into the off-the-shoulder dress and gave him her back, running her fingers over the blue-green pearls while he buttoned her into her dress. "I was excited at being liberated from that confining lifestyle because I thought you were going to support me in the lap of luxury. Since those men had to pay up for your finding Zeus, you're loaded." She chuckled at the thought of Lyman trying to escape Twitchy Guy and Bony Guy. Seemed they had some problems with how the leader of the Otherworld mafia had done business, and silly Lyman had forgotten to add that to his negotiation for freedom.

"I was loaded before. Now I'm more loaded. But your long-lost relatives from the reserve are already demanding I give them freebies to find the rest of their clan." He finished the buttons and let his fingers drift over her shoulders. "They're going to drain me dry, and since they're your relatives, you owe me."

She turned to face him, wrapping her arms around his neck. "Fine, Slayer. What do you want?"

He kissed the tip of her nose. "Be my enforcer. Even though Alex is now my partner, Jasmine won't let him slay anything, not just dragons. You're the only bloodthirsty crew member, and since I know you need an outlet, I wondered if you'd be interested."

Excitement rippled through her. "You mean it? You're not going to be like everyone except Becca and tell me I have to be good?"

"You are good, but you're also a dragon and you have some rather violent needs that require satisfying." He grinned at her. "It's the least I can do as a worthy mate to provide an outlet for them so you don't burn down our place."

She beamed at him. "I'm the luckiest dragon ever. I have a man who can save me, who loves my body and loves me exactly the way I am."

"Does that mean you'll take the job? Be my partner?"

A sense of true completeness settled through her and she nodded. "Someone has to kick some ass around here. It might as well be me."

He grinned. "Well said, my love. Just remember, I'm here to back you up if you need me."

She smiled. "Oh, I need you, Zeke Siccardi."

"I never thought I'd see the day when you freely admitted you needed anyone."

She shrugged. "What can I say? You tamed the wild dragon."

"Not even close, T. Not even close." He pulled her against him. "And I wouldn't have it any other way."

About the Author

G olden Heart winner Stephanie Rowe wrote her first
novel when she was ten and sold her first book
twenty-three years later. After a brief stint as an attorney,
Stephanie decided wearing suits wasn't her style and
opted for a more fulfilling career. Stephanie now spends
her days immersed in magical worlds creating quirky stories about smart, scrappy women who find true love while
braving the insanity of the modern world and Other-
worldly challenges. When she's not glued to the computer
or avoiding housework, Stephanie spends her time reading, playing tennis, and hanging out with her own fantasy
man and their two Labradors. You can reach Stephanie on
the Web at www.stephanierowe.com.

More
Stephanie Rowe!

Turn the page for a preview
of her new novel,

He Loves Me, He Loves Me Hot

Available in mass market.

Chapter One

Nick Rawlings checked the deadbolt on the inside of the steel door to make sure it was locked, then he walked across the polished oak floor, his heavy boots thudding on the perfect varnish. He took a disinterested glance at the stacks of food and beverages in the corner that were supposed to sustain him for the next few weeks he was on guard duty.

He reached the white, horizontal freezer, broke the padlock off with a flick of his wrist, then leveraged the heavy lid up, letting it slam against the wall with a crash that left a nice dent. A three foot by five foot block of ice stared back up at him, swirled with a mixture of blurred colors: pink, blue, and a large amount of gold. It was almost as if someone had tie-dyed the ice cube. "So, you're the big, bad heir to the throne of hell, huh?"

The ice cube trembled, and Nick grinned. "I hear you were stupid enough to get yourself melted and then frozen before you could reform. True?"

The frozen block vibrated even more fiercely, and Nick heard the faint whisper of a particularly creative epithet he hadn't heard since he'd lived in hell. Literally. "Watch it, little man. I might hate your daddy as much as you do, but talking to me like that won't get you released on my watch, no matter who comes after you."

Jerome, one of the members of the Otherworld Council, which was the self-appointed governing body of all non-human beings, had hired Nick to guard Satan Jr. after getting wind that someone was going to try to spring him.

Seeing as how Nick was the baddest badass in the entire Otherworld and Satan Jr. was one sick sociopath with a hell of a lot of power, Jerome had figured hiring Nick to keep Satan Jr. in his icy prison was a worthwhile expenditure of Council funds.

Nick had been bored and figured fending off a major Otherworld assault on behalf of Jerome might be interesting. Especially since Jerome was doing it against Council orders.

Anything that could piss the Council off was high on Nick's list of worthy activities.

He heard a key turn the dead bolt, and he slammed the freezer lid shut, then spun around to face the door, his body tense. *Play time.*

He leaned against the freezer and rested his palms on the lid, on either side of his hips. He drummed his fingers on the metal. Waiting.

The steel door flew open like it was made of paper.

Ah, a challenge. Nice.

Then a man stepped inside, and Nick immediately rose to his feet as an intense sensation of belonging swept over him. There was no mistaking the wavering air around the man's body, like the heat rising off a sidewalk on a hot summer day. This man was like him.

But that was impossible.

Nick was supposed to be the only Markku left.

The man stopped suddenly and stared at the air above Nick's head, his eyes widening in surprise. He was just over six feet and solid, but not nearly as big as Nick. His black pants, black sweater, and black boots made him look like he was trying too hard, as did the military buzz cut. The man's gaze flicked down to Nick's face. "Who are you?"

"Nick Rawlings. You?"

The man cocked his head. "Don't recognize the name. You're not with us."

"Us, being . . . ?" Were there more Markku? Nick's heart accelerated for the first time he could remember.

But instead of dropping to his knees to honor the sole descendant of the former leader of the Markku, the man dropped only his shoulder and charged.

Shit! Nick barely jumped out of the way in time, totally unprepared for another being to be almost as fast as he was. The man slammed into the side of the cooler, his head smashing all the way through the metal. He roared and reared back, dragging the cooler across the floor as he tried to get his head free. Nick grabbed his gun, leveling it at the back of the man's head.

No. You must protect your men.

Nick hesitated at the command in his head. His men? He had no men. He was alone and he liked it that way.

This is your man.

"No. It's not." He gritted his teeth against the almost overwhelming urge not to shoot, covered his right eye with his left hand to protect against ricochets, and then forced himself to pull the trigger. He unloaded the clip against the back of the Markku's head. The bullets bounced off the man's skull, ricocheting all over the room, embedding themselves in the wall, the ceiling, shattering the water cooler that was supposed to keep Nick hydrated for the next three weeks, whizzing through the weapons closet in the corner and setting off a cascade of fireworks, and one bullet even bounced off Nick's shin. The man shouted in protest and twisted so his feet and palms were flat against the cooler. He shoved hard, trying to yank his head free as his body shuddered with pain.

Nick emptied his clip, grabbed his second gun and kept firing, slamming bullet after bullet against the Markku's skull as the Poland Spring water sloshed around his feet, ruining the perfect floor. He didn't bother to enjoy the fact that the Council would have to spring to get the floor refinished, jumping back as the man finally yanked his head free, sending metal remnants flying.

One piece whizzed past Nick's shoulder and sliced through the wall, disappearing from sight with the force of the Markku's thrust.

The Markku whirled around and slammed his foot into the side of Nick's knee.

Pain shot through Nick as he dropped to the floor, cursing his slowness, his failure to react to an opponent as fast as he was. The Markku pulled out a knife with a golden blade and Nick swore under his breath. What the hell was he doing with that kind of weapon?

The Markku drove the blade down toward Nick's right eye, and Nick jerked his head hard to the right. The blade scraped Nick's cheek and slammed into the wooden floor, barely missing its target. Fire scorched his skin from the brush of gold and he sucked the fire into his system, using the heat to fuel himself. Fresh energy flared in his body and he threw the Markku into the wall. Nick was on his feet and over the guy before the man had stopped sliding down the wall, leaving a big dent in the plaster.

The man hurled the knife and the blade plunged into the front of Nick's right shoulder. Nick dropped to his knees, gritting his teeth against the raging pain, against the poisonous fire spreading through his body. *Use the heat, Nick.* He pulled the golden fire into his body, charging himself with the flames, using the pain to fuel his body even as that same heat drained him, sucked away his life force.

The Markku jumped to his feet and lunged for the knife, but Nick grabbed it first. He yanked it out of his shoulder with a roar of anguish then slammed it into the Markku's right eye. The man exploded in a cascade of gold dust, his death scream his only legacy as it bounced off the steel door and echoed in Nick's ears.

Nick clutched the blade, and shook the gold dust off his eyelashes, watching it float down, mixing with the Poland Spring water to create a river of sparkling mud.

The door flew open and Nick reared back to throw the knife, diverting his aim at the last second when he realized who it was.

Jerome yelped and ducked as the blade sang past his ear and embedded itself in the steel door behind him. "It's me!"

"No kidding." Nick pressed his left hand to his stab wound, trying to stem the flow of blood. The more he could mitigate the damage now, the less trouble he'd be in later.

"Right. Because you'd have killed me if I'd been anyone else." Jerome straightened up, his scabbard swinging by his side. In honor of his mortal life pillaging on the high seas, he was sporting full pirate regalia today, including an eye patch, even though both his eyes were fine. Jerome only wore the eye patch when the seas were rough, so to speak. Having a Markku break into Satan Jr.'s freezer deep inside Council headquarters would qualify.

Nick kicked a piece of the water cooler out of his way, then stumbled with sudden weakness. *Shit.* He had to get out of there. He had less than a half-hour before he was dead to the world for at least a couple of days. How was he going to get out without explaining why to Jerome? As far as Jerome knew, Nick hadn't inherited the post-battle-weakness from his dad, and since no one else knew Nick was a Markku, no one knew about his vulnerability. He intended to keep it this way. So he folded his arms over his chest and glared at Jerome, mustering up all his energy to appear enraged and powerful. "Why didn't you tell me it was a Markku that had been hired to steal Satan Jr.?"

Jerome paled and he tugged the eye patch up so he could look at Nick with both eyes. "No shit? He was a Markku?"

Nick waved at the gold dust, and Jerome scanned the room, his gaze coming to a stop on the ice chest. A big hole gaped in the side, and the sound of dripping water was coming from the inside of the chest. "He's thawing!"

"Your problem. Not mine." Nick turned his back on Jerome to hide a shudder of fatigue, then he grabbed his stash of weapons and turned to head out, only to find a pesky pirate in his way. "What now?"

"You can't leave. What if they send more? No one can beat a Markku except you. You know that."

"I kept Satan Jr. safe. Now I'm gone."

Jerome drew his shoulders back and set his hands on his hips. "They'll keep coming. I'll keep paying. I need you."

Nick ground his teeth, trying to come up with an excuse to leave that wouldn't reveal too much. "Jerome—"

An old, bearded man in a white robe strode into the room, followed by a businessman in an Armani suit. Paul and Otis, the rest of the Council. Nick cursed under his breath, then locked his jaw against the crash of anger as he faced the two men who'd betrayed and killed his father, and wiped out his race.

In due time, he promised himself. In due time, the Council would pay for what they'd done to his legacy.

"Jerome! What's going on here?" Paul asked, his hands hiding inside the flowing folds of his white robe. Nick figured he kept his white hair dye in there. No way was Paul old enough for a white beard. Probably dyed it to give himself more clout in the Otherworld political arena.

"Jerome! Is that Satan Jr.'s ice chest?" The businessman, known as Otis to those lucky enough to get on a first-name basis with him, whipped out a BlackBerry and his manicured fingers started flying over the keys as he typed out an email. "We need backup refrigeration immediately."

Paul eyed Nick. "Who are you, and what are you doing here?"

Jerome shot a wary glance toward Nick, and Nick suddenly realized what Jerome was thinking. Unlike most people, who didn't bother to notice the heat-blurred air around his body, the Council might, and they'd know what it meant. And they'd have him killed. Time to go. "I was just delivering Jerome's dry cleaning. Gotta take care of those puffy silk things he calls shirts." Nick hoisted his machine gun over his shoulder, shoved his handguns into his shoulder holsters, and walked out, ignoring the protests of Paul and the curious stare of Otis.

"Wait!" Jerome grabbed his arm. "If you leave, who will protect Satan Jr.?"

"From what?" Paul demanded, his toupee glittering as the gold dust began to settle. "What's this dust from? What's been going on here?" He stopped suddenly and held out his hand, letting the glittering remains of the dead Markku settle on his palm. "Is this what I think it is?"

Nick had no idea how much Jerome was going to tell Paul and Otis, seeing as how Jerome was trying to effect a modern-day mutiny against them, and the trembling in Nick's legs told him he didn't have time to find out. "Fine. You're worried about Satan Jr.?" He walked over to the block of ice, pulled out a gun and peppered the corner of the block until a six-inch piece fell off, ignoring the shouted protests of all three Council members, who didn't quite dare approach him while the bullets were flying.

He holstered his gun and Paul lunged for the small block of ice. Nick swept out of his reach, walked over to the portable fridge that Jerome had set up for him.

He dumped out the contents, shoved the chunk of Satan Jr. inside, then tucked the fridge under his arm. "If anyone tries to re-form Satan Jr. without this piece, he'll be missing something important. Probably not worth the risk."

"You can't take that!" Paul threw himself in front of the door. "Otis. Call for backup."

"Already am." Otis was fumbling with his headset, trying to get it into his ear.

Nick looked at Jerome, who gave the slightest nod. So Nick picked up Paul, tossed him aside, and walked out.

He shuddered with weakness again, and broke into an uneven jog, forcing his failing body to hurry and willing his way through the pain in his damaged knee. Had to get out of here before he collapsed. No way did he have the thirty minutes he'd initially thought. The gold blade had taken more out of him than he'd anticipated. *Need to hurry.* Twenty feet to Jerome's office, where he'd anchored his black market portal. He preferred to travel using his motorcycle, but he'd figured that if Jerome was right about the threat to Satan Jr. and Nick got attacked, he might not have time to get back to his safe house by ordinary means, and he was glad he'd had the foresight.

He shoved open the door, kicked it shut, then strode to the middle of the room, to the faint circle outlined on the floor. The portal opened as soon as it sensed his presence and he closed his eyes against the faint humming that vibrated in his body. A couple more minutes. That's all he had.

The humming stopped and he opened his eyes to find himself surrounded by four walls of steel, deep underground. All that was in there was a bed, a fridge, and a bathroom. His body trembled and he dropped the ice box.

He grabbed the chunk of ice, his muscles aching with the effort, staggered over to the freezer, and threw it inside. Then he made it the three feet to the bed and collapsed, letting the weakness overtake him, like a black cloud.

He had a minute, maybe two, left of consciousness, and he relaxed. He was safe now.

Then his phone rang. He sighed with relief at the sound of Toby Keith, the ring his little sister had programmed into his phone for her calls. He hadn't heard from her in over a week, and he'd been starting to worry.

Groaning, he yanked his phone out of his pocket and flipped it open, letting it rest against the side of his head. "Where've you been?" He closed his eyes and let his hand flop to the mattress.

"Nick! You have to help me!"

The franticness in his sister's voice caught him and he battled against the wave of pending unconsciousness. "What's wrong?" His tongue felt thick and heavy.

"They're going to kill me if you don't do what they want!"

Her voice became distant and fuzzy and he cursed, struggling to stay conscious. *Not now.* "Who?"

Another voice came on the phone. "Kill the leader of hell by Sunday or your sister dies."

You've got to be fucking kidding.

And then the world went black.

"I can't believe you want your life force to be a goldfish."

"It's better than having my life force be Satan." Her heart thudding, Becca Gibbs, Satan's favorite Rivka and personal slave, carefully set the Tupperware container holding Ellie the fish in the middle of the spot she'd cleared in New York's Central Park. Three large flashlights were set up around them, illuminating the isolated clearing.

"Maybe. How do you know she isn't some evil life

force just waiting for a chance to force her soggy will on the world?" Theresa Nichols-Siccardi switched her tail in typical aggravated-dragon fashion, upending a small tree and crushing a drinking fountain. "Maybe she's Satan's worst nightmare and once you give her your body to act through, the world as we know it will be destroyed."

Becca slanted a glance at the testy dragon as she wiped her sweaty hands on her jeans. "She's a *goldfish*. There's no way she's harboring some evil soul."

"And everyone thinks Mona is only an espresso machine, but she's actually the Goblet of Eternal Youth, chock full of enough power to disrupt the natural order of hell and the mortal world. Looks can be deceiving." Theresa blew a puff of ash out her nose.

Becca tensed at a crackle in the dark woods, staring into the black night for a long moment. Waiting.

"Yo Rivka, what if you turn into a fish, huh?" Theresa wrinkled her blue-green-scaled nose. "You want me to eat you and put you out of your misery? I'm generally not into eating friends, but if it's that important to you, I suppose I could be persuaded."

There was no other noise in the woods, so Becca turned back to the circle she was creating, trying not to wince at each gust of wind. She knew Satan would figure out what she was doing. Her only hope was to get it done before he showed up. "First of all, we're not friends. Second, if you even think about eating me, I'll turn you into a pile of ash." She hadn't spent three centuries thwarting Satan only to have a prima donna dragon have her for a late-night snack. "Third, I'm not going to turn into a fish. I'm only going to connect to her life force."

The dragon snorted. "But you're nothing but a figment

of Satan's imagination, kept alive by his life force and his personality, so if you switch your life support machine over to Ellie's then won't you have the personality of the fish? Is a goldfish really better than Satan?" She flashed an apologetic smile at the fish. "No offense intended."

"If I link to a weaker spirit, then my personality will trump and I'll be able to be myself." *And then I'll truly be free.* Becca paused again to listen to the night. There were crickets chirping, an owl hooting off to her left, and frogs were croaking down at the nearby pond. Normal night sounds that indicated the leader of hell wasn't out in the darkness, sipping wine and waiting for her to cross that line.

She took a deep breath, then walked a circle around herself and Ellie, pouring purified water in an unbroken line.

The dragon burned a mosquito out of the air. "Don't you think it's wishful thinking that you actually have your own scintillating personality buried under there some-where?"

"No." Sweat dripped down her back, even though it was a cool night for summer. What if she *didn't* have her own personality? What if everything she was was Satan, and when she linked her life force to a goldfish, she no longer existed? She faltered in her steps and had to clamp her hand over the top of the gold vase to keep the purified water from spilling. No. She'd done her research. She was certain this would work.

"I seriously doubt he bothered to give you an identity when he created you."

"Would you please *shut up*? You're driving me

insane!" She clamped her fingers around the vase of purified water so she didn't drop it by accident.

"Sorry." Theresa sat back on her haunches and folded her wings. "So, where did you say you found this spell?"

"It's not a spell. It's a process. And I came up with it myself after three centuries of research." She finished pouring the circle, set the vase in the middle of it, and then took off her black boots and set them aside, wiggling her toes in the grass and the earth. Dirt was pure. Elemental. Real. Everything Satan wasn't.

The dragon snapped a stick as she shifted position, making Becca jump. "Why don't you find a spell that allows you to generate your own life force instead of merely transferring your lifeline from one being to another?"

She shot the dragon a disbelieving look. "You seriously think I'd be out here with a goldfish if there was a way for me to generate my own life force? I'm not hardwired that way."

"Well, that sucks."

"Gee, you think?"

Theresa was thankfully silent while Becca set up eight shot glasses at evenly spaced intervals around the inside of the circle, dropped a twenty-four-carat-gold ball inside each one, then filled each of them to the top with purified water.

"So, if you succeed and then some owl swoops down here and eats that fish, you're dead, right? It dies, you die?"

"I can protect a goldfish long enough to get her back to the Goblet of Eternal Youth to make her immortal."

Theresa sucked in her breath. "She can't drink from

Mona! That's so illegal! The Council would kick all our asses from here to hell!"

Becca looked up and met the dragon's gaze across the eerie shadows from the flashlights. "How many favors do you owe me, Dragon?"

Theresa whistled softly. "Damn, girl, you drive a harder bargain than Satan."

Becca managed a grim smile as she laid one of Satan's custom dress shirts in the center of the circle, and then poured a spoonful of Ellie's water in the center of it. "So, you'll help?"

Theresa held her claw over her heart. "I love you, girlfriend. I'll do anything you need."

Becca tensed and shot the dragon a red-eyed glare. "How many times have I told you that we're not friends? It's too dangerous for you."

The dragon snorted and flicked her tail in irritation. "Shut up, already. You can't scare me. I'm an immortal dragon who survived making a deal with Satan. Do your spell and let's get you and Ellie to Mona already, okay?"

She piled a stash of cedar sticks on top of the shirt, then sat back on her heels. "We are *not* friends."

Theresa put her claws over her ears and started humming the theme from *The Brady Bunch*.

"Oh, for God's sake." Becca gave up on the dragon, then took a deep breath and closed her eyes. Once she began the spell, Satan would feel it, and her only chance to survive would be to get it done and vanish before he arrived. She hugged herself and whispered a prayer to the heavens that she wasn't allowed to acknowledge. *It was time.*

Becca held out both hands and a fireball popped up on

each hand, heat and flame whirling in the dark night. She blew a kiss to Ellie, swimming happily in her little bowl. "Don't let me down, girl," she whispered.

Her heart was racing so fast all the heartbeats had blurred into one, and her breath was harsh in her chest. She fixed her gaze on Satan's shirt, and then whispered the words she'd spent so long working out. As soon as they were out of her mouth, she crossed her wrists and shot the pile of sticks with both fireballs. The shirt exploded in an array of golden sparks, her voice rising above the din as she shouted the next words.

"Shit!" Theresa shouted. "You melted the Tupperware container! Save Ellie!"

Becca felt her concentration slip, but she yanked it back. *I have to finish.*

She grabbed the northern-most shot glass and threw the contents down her throat.

The pain was instant, blinding. *Jesus.* She felt like her insides were being bled with acid.

"Becca? Are you all right?"

Bitterness sliced through her throat, blades ripped through her gut, searing agony tore apart her chest. This was wrong. Something was terribly wrong. Couldn't breathe. Couldn't think. It hurt like a mother-f—

"Rivka! You betray me! I am much chagrined!"

She flinched at the sound of a familiar male voice. Satan had found her too soon. Dammit!

"Rivka! You must look at me while I skewer the life from you! It is so much more pleasurable when I can bask in your fear."

She hunched over as thousands of invisible knives stabbed at her flesh, tasting blood as she bit her lip to keep herself from screaming. She was *not* going to give him the satisfaction. *Never.*

"Hey, asshole," Theresa said.

Becca struggled to find her voice, but the pain was too extreme. If she opened her mouth, she'd start screaming or sobbing or something equally unworthy of being Satan's best Rivka

"Theresa!" Satan exclaimed. "It is so lovely to see the comrade of the fruit-of-my-loins. You are wonderful with fire. Would you care to replace my best Rivka after I kill her? The benefits of working for me are quite extensive. I can send you a copy of my employee handbook, if you like."

"Let her go," Theresa said.

"Go where? She is dying, cannot you see that?"

Becca dropped to her knees, clutching her throat, trying to yank out the unseen daggers slicing at her skin. She'd never felt pain like this. She couldn't . . . think . . .

"Why is she dying?" Theresa's voice was blurry and distant, nearly crouched over by the pain shredding her body.

"Because she tried to cut my lifeline to her. So I poison the lifeline, then I throw it back in her face, and now she dies. It is delightfully ironic, is it not? She gets what she wants and then she dies for it? I love irony. Look at me now, Rivka."

Becca groaned and cracked her eyes open a slit and squinted up at her boss. Satan was dressed in an impeccable Italian suit, and he was wearing a boutonniere. He had a new haircut, and a fresh shave and looked debonair enough to be welcomed into any palace.

Bastard.

He beamed at her. "Even in death, you cannot disobey

me. Such is the fate of a Rivka. It will take you several thousand years to die. The pain will increase exponentially every six hours and your body will eat itself from the inside out. Does it not sound delightful? One of my new scientist souls just figured out how to do that to my Rivkas, and this is my first chance to try it." He peered more closely at her. "Does it hurt very much, Rivka?"

Several thousand years of this? Impossible. She gazed up into his beautiful blue eyes and knew he'd won. "Reestablish the link." Her voice was harsh, the words mottled with agony, but she knew he understood.

His smile became broader. "Hmm . . . you do not wish to suffer pain that is so extreme it would drive you insane if I were not present to ensure you stayed conscious and aware through the entire process?"

She gave him a snarky look that answered his question. How she managed a snarky expression through all the pain, she had no idea. Must be her naturally resilient attitude. More likely it was her Satan genes. It was his life force that gave her the strength to survive his torture. She was nothing without him. *Nothing.*

Her stomach lurched and she turned her head toward his feet. If she lost it, the least she could do was ruin his polished shoes.

"You are my best Rivka. I gain much benefit from having your services. Perhaps I should spare you despite your ultimate betrayal." Satan rubbed his chin and studied her thoughtfully. "So, what shall I demand in return for sparing you? Hmm . . . so many choices."

A groan leaked out of her and she crumbled the rest of the way to the ground, no longer able to will herself to stay on her knees. Satan chuckled. *God help me.*

"How can she owe you anything?" Theresa asked. "Doesn't she have to do everything you tell her anyway?"

"Yes, yes, just about," Satan said.

Just about? What didn't she have to obey? She gave a raspy hack as she rolled to her side in the grass, crunched in a ball.

"I shall have to consult my experts on how best to use this situation to benefit me and torture you," Satan said. "But I will collect. We agree to agree. Agreed?"

She knew it would be a mistake, but she had no choice. Like all of her life, she had no choice. Resentment churned inside her as she managed a nod. She grimaced when Satan clapped his hands together with glee. "This is a monumental event. I have outsmarted my best Rivka for the first time. This is quite fun. No wonder you do this to me all the time. I shall have to develop this skill more completely and I can torture you more often."

Please . . . No.

He leaned down and patted her head. "I release you from the pain, Rivka. You will live and I will be back to tell you what you owe me. Have a lovely evening." He smiled at Theresa. "I will still hire you as my second-best Rivka, if you like." And with that, he vanished in an explosion of gold bubbles, and the pain vanished abruptly from Becca's body.

She sagged against the ground, her face mashed in the cool dirt as her body gasped for air.

Theresa scooped Ellie up with the vase and sat next to Becca with a thump. "Wow. Are you okay?"

"Peachy." Becca closed her eyes as tremors began to rack her body. She was so cold. So weak. Couldn't move. Just wanted to lie there.

"Cold?" Theresa leaned closer, let out a growl, and then set Becca on fire.

Yes. Becca arched under the heat, absorbing it into her body, pulling it in to all the damaged cells as the tremors began to fade.

"So, he crushed you like a gnat, huh?"

Becca took a shuddering breath. "I'm not a gnat."

"You look sort of like one."

"Feel like one." Was she drooling? Probably. Too much effort to swallow. She'd just lie here for the next decade or so until she got her strength back.

She felt Theresa shift beside her. "Well, Ellie survived though. That's good news."

"I'm so glad to hear that." One less thing to feel guilty about. The night was looking up.

"So, are we going to try your spell again?"

"Not tonight." Such a bummer. Three hundred years of planning and anticipation shot to hell. Literally. God, she felt like crying. Like sobbing. Like lying on her stomach and throwing a full-fledged temper tantrum. "Thanks for saving me."

"That's what friends do."

Becca managed to peel her eyes open, then jerked back to find Theresa's golden eyes less than an inch from her face. "Theresa, we aren't friends. We can't be." She had to say it. Had to make the dragon understand. It was so important.

Theresa rolled her eyes. "Sometimes you're a bitch."

Becca couldn't keep from grinning, even though it hurt to move her face. She felt like her body was melting into the restoring earth. Not one single bit of strength in any area of her body.

"So, you going to stay there all night?" Theresa asked.

"No. Let's go." She mentally ordered herself home.

Nothing happened. She didn't turn into an inky black cloud and melt through the ground only to pop up through the floor of her condo. She was still in human form, and still in the park. Damn. She'd never been too weak to shimmer.

Theresa sighed. "Seeing as how I still owe you for about a zillion favors, I guess that means I'll have to fly you home." She tucked Ellie's vase inside Becca's shirt, then slid her claws under Becca's body. "Don't worry, Rivka, it's not because I like you."

"Good. Smart dragon." *Home.* Her bed sounded so good right now. Especially since she'd figured out how to ward it against Satan. Her condo was the one place Satan couldn't reach her.

Oy. She owed Satan. Something above and beyond soul harvesting, playing assassin, genuflecting to his greatness, enduring his attempts to amuse himself with other people's pain, most commonly her own, and other such Rivka obligations.

That was so very, very not something to look forward to.

THE DISH

Where authors give you the inside scoop!

♥ ♥ ♥ ♥ ♥ ♥ ♥ ♥ ♥ ♥ ♥ ♥ ♥ ♥ ♥ ♥

From the desk of Stephanie Rowe

Five reasons why fiery sexpot dragons and oh-so-hot ex–dragon slayers like the characters in MUST LOVE DRAGONS (on sale now) should never date:

1. *There's no such thing as an "ex" dragon slayer.* If he's got slayer genes, he's going to have the all-consuming need to kill any dragon he meets . . . even if it's his beloved cyberlover whom he needs to protect from an assassin that he accidentally sent after her. Protect the dragon, kill the dragon—it's all so confusing for a man. And the harder he tries to deny his heritage, well, it's like trying to hold back floodwaters with a paper towel. The pressure's going to keep building, and eventually . . . let's just say the dragon better be up-to-date on her slayer self-defense techniques.

2. *Slayer pheromones.* Talk about a ladykiller! All a slayer has to do is release a wee little bit of his pheromones, and bam! Instant dragon aphrodisiac. Makes it really, really difficult for a girl to say no. Pheromone-induced sex is definitely something to write home about . . . if you survive it.

3. *Flames take on a whole new meaning.* On the plus side, dragons aren't defenseless against those sexy slayers. Dragon flames will bring a slayer to his knees . . . and suddenly he's at the dragon's mercy. Which can be

fun. Heh, heh, heh. And if you mix some flames with some pheromones . . . watch out!

4. *His pesky friends*. Ex–dragon slayers attract other dragon slayers, who aren't trying to deny their heritage. Nothing like having a team of slayers on her tail to ruin a dragon's day. Especially when her ex-slayer protector has a life debt to the slayers that requires him to turn the dragon over to them. Life debt vs. love of his life. How does a slayer decide?

5. *That slayer/dragon attraction*. It's that whole "I need to kill you, but first I must make love to you until both of us are unconscious" thing. Literally. How is a dragon supposed to tell whether the sparks flying between them are the result of centuries-old instincts or old-fashioned true love?

Sincerely,

Stephanie

www.stephanierowe.com

♥ ♥ ♥ ♥ ♥ ♥ ♥ ♥ ♥ ♥ ♥ ♥ ♥ ♥ ♥

From the desk of Elizabeth Hoyt

Gentle Reader,

I have noticed over the years that there seem to be unwritten rules for the Romance Hero. Rules that all romance heroes appear to know and follow unconsciously. All romance heroes, that is, save my own, Edward de Raaf, the Earl of Swartingham and the hero of THE RAVEN PRINCE (on sale now). Sadly, Edward apparently never received the Romance Hero Rule Book, possibly due to the unreliability of the postal system in Georgian England. Below, I have listed a few of the rules and, ahem, Edward's own response.

1. Heroes are always handsome.
Edward: (snort) Well, that one is just plain ludicrous. Who wants to read about pretty boys and macaronis, I ask you? A scar here and there lends a certain gravitas to a gentleman's countenance.

2. Heroes should never fall off their horse.
Edward: Libel, sirrah! I have never, ever fallen off my horse, and I will meet in the field of honor anyone who dares say so. It is true that, upon occasion, I have been unseated, but that could happen to any gentleman and is an entirely different matter.

3. And if they do fall off their horse, they do not swear.
Edward: I was not swearing. I merely called the beast a revolting lump of maggot-eaten hide, and—follow my reasoning closely here—the horse did not know what I was saying.

4. Heroes do not start brawls in brothels.
Edward: I did not actually start the brawl. Besides, what would you have me do when attacked by four men? Note: I did end the brawl.

5. Heroes do not have trouble keeping their secretaries.
Edward: I am not sure what you are getting at . . .

6. Heroes always keep their temper.
Edward: I do not have a temper and anyone who says so—(censored)

7. Heroes should not fantasize about the breasts of their female secretaries.
Edward: What kind of namby-pamby novels are we talking about here? I should think—

8. Heroes should be romantic.
Edward: Ha! HA! I have you there! I will have you know that Anna found absolutely no fault with my lovemaking. In fact—

9. Heroes do not confuse romance with lovemaking.
Edward: (censored)

10. Heroes should be transported by true love.
Edward: With that I have no argument.

Yours Most Sincerely,

Elizabeth Hoyt

www.elizabethhoyt.com

Can't get enough of
vampires and dragons and witches?

Bitten & Smitten
by Michelle Rowen
"A charming, hilarious book!
I'm insanely jealous I didn't write it."
—MaryJanice Davidson, author of *Undead and Unwed*

Doppelganger
by Marie Brennan
"I can't wait for her next book!"
—Rachel Caine, author of *Windfall*

Kitty and The Midnight Hour
by Carrie Vaughn
"I enjoyed this book from start to finish."
—Charlaine Harris, author of *Dead as a Doornail*

Out of the Night
by Robin T. Popp
"A stellar job of combining intriguing characterization
with gritty suspense, adding up to a major thrill ride!"
—*Romantic Times BOOKclub Magazine*

Working with the Devil
by Lilith Saintcrow
"A unique and engaging mélange."
—Jacqueline Carey, author of *Kushiel's Avatar*

Want to know more about romances at Grand Central Publishing and Forever? Get the scoop online!

GRAND CENTRAL PUBLISHING'S ROMANCE HOMEPAGE

Visit us at www.hachettebookgroupusa.com/romance for all the latest news, reviews, and chapter excerpts!

NEW AND UPCOMING TITLES

Each month we feature our new titles and reader favorites.

CONTESTS AND GIVEAWAYS

We give away galleys, autographed copies, and all kinds of fun stuff.

AUTHOR INFO

You'll find bios, articles, and links to personal websites for all your favorite authors—and so much more!

THE BUZZ

Sign up for our monthly romance newsletter, and be the first to read all about it!